Da Game Ain't Fair

JERZ TOSTON

Da Game Ain't Fair

By: Jerz Toston

Cover Art Created by KREATIVEGRAFIKS.COM

Logo Designs by Andre M. Saunders and Jess Zimmerman

Editor: Anelda L. Attaway

Co-editor: Jerz Toston

© 2020 Jerz Toston

ISBN 978-1-7349014-2-9

Library of Congress Control Number: 2020908258

ACKNOWLEDGMENTS

First, I'd like to thank Allah (SWT) wit out Him this would not be possible.

Next, I would like to tell my kids Kai, Meesh, Jerz, Deivyan, Riya, and Ceer this is all for y'all; neva let anyone defer you or tell you that you can't do what ever you want.

All my niggaz from tha 8 Chulo Hammer, Hov, Shafee, and Killer.

My BF's Sissy and Deb.

My sister's Felisha and Nika LOVE Y'ALL.

My Lil' Bro Lbs.

My mother who always push me to be tha best I can be.

My other half, BF, and soulmate Tambra aka Mrs. Toston 2 U thanks for always having my back no matter right or wrong.

Ery body on lock down, Big Marv, John, Dac Dae, Matim, and C-how I'mma hold y'all down til y'all touch this side free from tha jails.

To Lil' Bro Cool Shoes Inc., keep doin' what you doin' for tha youth.

My barber Skills tha nigga that keep a nigga fly weekly.

To ery side of town holding it down.

Gotta say REZ Mom Betty, Moe, Ma5e, H, and my Big Sis Ericka keep watching over me and I'mma keep droppin' classics.

Finally, my publisher Jazzy Kitty, love ya.

Jus remember wit out loyalty there's no trust & trust is ery thing so always SSSSH hold yours. Y'all got to stop feeding these RATS cheese and embracing them knowing they ain't official Black & White don't lie.

DEDICATION

This book is dedicated to my niece Jannie Smallwood, u was taken to soon jus kno ur deeply missed & loved.

Rez Baby Girl.

TABLE OF CONTENTS

TABLE OF CONTENTS

INTRODUCTION

Nazir who at tha tender age of 11 was sentenced to juvenile life for tha murder of his abusive step-father grew up in tha system. His mother died when he was 14, leaving him to depend on his Nana and trust no one. He was released to tha mean streetz of Philly at tha age of 18.

He tried to find a job but had no luck finding a job outside of McDonald's or other fast-food joints which wasn't good enough. That's when he met up wit a local big-time drug dealer named Doe who quickly turned his life around.

Now wit Doe by his side he would become unstoppable surpassing his mentor which only created a problem. So take a ride wit me thru tha streetz of Philly as we bring you **Da Game Ain't Fair.**

CHAPTER 1

Tha Juvenile Life

"Get off of me, don't you ever touch me again. I want you out of my house." (SMACK)

"Bitch you better sit ya ass down before I smack you again." I jumped out of my bed and ran into my mother's bedroom.

"Nazir go back to bed Sweetie," my mom said holding her hand over her now swollen eye.

I charged James, "I hate you! I hate you!" I yelled throwing a bunch of wild punches.

He just shoved me back into tha dresser causing me to fall. I jumped to my feet and charged at him again. This time he met me wit a right jab to tha nose.

My mom leaped up, "No you didn't hit my baby, I want you out of my house wit ya AIDS Infected Ass!"

"Yeah, well you got it too!"

"That's because you gave it to me!" my mother screamed at tha top of her lungs.

At tha time I had no idea what AIDS was, I would find out 3 years later after my mother died from it.

"Now get out!"

He raised his hand to hit my mom again, I ran back into my bedroom, reached under my bed for tha shoebox. When I found it, I quickly took tha top off, reached in, and grabbed tha .380 I had took from my cousin earlier that day. As I ran back into my mom's room, I was just in time to stop James from hitting her again.

"Get tha Fuck away from her!" I yelled pointing tha gun directly at him.

"Put that thing down Boy before you hurt ya self!"

"Nasir please put tha gun down, he ain't worth it!"

"Shut up!" he said turning fully towards me.

As soon as he tried to grab me... BONG, BONG, BONG, BONG... 4 shots tore thru his chest causing him to fall to tha ground. My mom ran over to me and held me in her arms. I could hear tha police sirens in tha distance growing closer. I knew I would probably go to jail for a long time but at least my mom would be safe from James. By tha time tha police had come, me and my mom were downstairs sitting on tha couch.

When they came in my mom said, "He's upstairs."

Two of tha cops ran upstairs; when they came back down they had tha gun in a plastic bag.

"He's dead and this is the weapon."

Tha Black cop asked, "Who shot him?"

Before my mom could say anything I put my hand up. Tha same cop who had just asked tha question walked over to me and started saying sum thing about I had tha right to remain silent and I had tha right to an attorney. I later found out that he was reading me my Miranda Rights. It wasn't until he put tha handcuffs on me that I started to cry and so did my mom.

I looked at my mom and asked, "Where am I goin' Mom?"

"To tha police station, I'll be right behind you." And she was tha whole ride; I could see her on her cell phone probably wit my nana.

When we got to tha police station my mom was right there like she said she would be. And within 15 minutes, my nana came marching in wit her pajamas on and rollers in her hair. I felt a sense of calm, for sum reason my nana alwayz made me feel like that even when I knew I was in trouble like now. As soon as she seen my mom's face she came over to me and started wiping tha dry blood from my nose.

"Naz, don't you worry, nana gon' get you a lawyer."

Then she did tha craziest thing, she took out her camera and started taking pictures of me and my mom. Later, I found out that those pictures were of our faces for tha lawyer. If it weren't for those pictures, I would have gotten a lot more time than I did. Since I had no prior charges and wasn't a flight risk, they let me stay out of jail on sum thing called home confinement. That's when they strap this black box to ya leg to monitor your every move. I was only allowed out for school and 2 hours on Saturdays and Sundays.

We had moved in wit my nana and Uncle Charles who was nuffin but a drunk but I liked him. He alwayz made me laugh; Nana was alwayz on his case. I overheard my mom and nana talking about that AIDS thing; my nana told her to make sure she took her medicine.

Tha lawyer told them that tha D.A. wanted me to do juvenile life and that had nana not taken those pictures I would probably have spent tha rest of my life in jail. They both agreed that that was a good deal. My mom told nana to make sure I was alright if she didn't make it; that's when I walked in.

"If you don't make it where Mom?"

She quickly skipped tha subject and started to explain about me goin' to jail for 7 years. Now I knew what jail was but I neva in a million years thought that I would be goin' for 7 years at that.

"Why can't I just keep this on for 7 years instead of goin' to tha Big

House?" As my cousins called it; she explained it to me and I totally understood.

Tha next 3 months flew by and it was time for me to get sentenced. When tha judge said juvenile life I knew he meant until my 18th birthday. Before they took me away, my mom and nana both gave me hugs and kisses.

On tha way to wherever they were taking us, one of tha guards gave us rules. I wanted to say damn this seems more like tha army than jail. I could see now I was in for a long rough stay. We pulled up to this facility with bob wired gates. We had to wait while they checked tha van that we were on; then they let us off one at a time.

Inside, we had to take off all our clothes and put them into a bag. I knew that this would be tha last time I wore those clothes. They replaced my gear wit a pair of tan Khakis and a white T-shirt wit an additional set. They let us know it was up to us to keep our uniforms clean and ironed. Once we had our clothes we were showed our living quarters which was based on our charges. There weren't too many people in here for murder except me, a Spanish kid, and 2 White boys. I could hear people on tha other tiers saying things like Fresh Meat, Momma's Boy, and that they were gon' take my sneaks. I wasn't no punk and nobody wasn't gon' take nuffin from me but a beat down if they tried. I wasn't here to start no trouble, but if it came my way I wasn't backing down. I didn't care who it was or how old they were.

They had what they called phases, as you worked ya way up tha more things you got such as tha phone. Since I was new, I only was allowed two 15-minute phone calls a week. It was actually up to you how you chose to use ya calls. I was goin' to get three 10-minute calls but since I was new I got what they called a courtesy call. So, I called my mom and nana to fill them in about this place. Just as my time was about to be up they called chow. I let them know that I loved them and probably would call tomorrow.

On tha way to tha Chow Hall, I saw two of tha boys who came over wit me; one of them had a fat lip already. I went thru tha line and got my food. There were no rules to where you could sit so I sat in tha first available seat.

As soon as I did, sum guy walked up and said, "You in my seat." I didn't say Shit, I just got up and moved to another table.

Then tha same dude said, "That's my other seat." So once again I moved; I could hear people laughing so I sat at another table.

Once again he said, "That's my seat."

Tha guy looked to be about 15, I stood up then I sat back down and started to eat my food. I wanted to eat as much as I could because I saw where this was headed.

"Yo Lil Nigga, did you hear what I said!"

I stopped eating, looked up and then asked, "Is there any seat in here that's not ya seat?"

"Nah, they all my seats."

"That's what I figured," I said and then started back eating.

Just as he was about to grab my tray tha guard said, "Fatz if you eating you better come on."

"I'll be back," he said as he went to get his tray.

And sure enough like he said he came back and sat across from me. I could tell that he had everybody in here scared of him but I wasn't.

"So you in here for murder? Well, that don't make you tough, it probably was an accident anyway."

I had enough of his mouth so I picked my tray up and moved to another table only to be followed by him but this time he didn't sit down.

"I like those sneaks. What size are they?" He went to grab one and I moved my foot.

"I said, what size are they?"

I stood up and walked over to tha trash, dumped my tray, and headed for tha door only to be cut off by 3 boys who I assumed to be Fatz crew.

One of them spoke up, "I don't believe he was done talk'n to you."

"Yeah, ain't you got no manners," another one said.

"Chow is complete," tha guard said walking over to where we were standing.

I made my way back to tha tier, I got in tha shower and then laid down not knowing what tomorrow would bring. I cried like a baby, I missed my mom and my nana and I knew that I was goin' to have to fight Fatz and his crew.

Tha next morning when tha rest of my tier had gotton up, I was already up. I woke up early so that I could work out and spar like I did every morning at home for tha last 2 years. I had been boxing thanks to my cousin Zook so I was nice wit my hands; I just rather not fight. Tha counselor for our tier came around after breakfast to talk to me.

"Well, you know that you'll be here until your 18; don't you Mr. Jenkins?"

"Yes Mam."

"Is there anything I could do for you?"

"Yes Mam."

"What is it?"

"Well, is it possible that I could finish school?"

"What grade are you in?"

"6, but I was on a 7th grade level."

"I'll be happy to help you obtain your high school diploma as long as you stay out of trouble."

"Ms. Williams, I'm here to do my time nuffin more but if anyone does sum thing to me I will defend myself."

She looked at me then said, "Orlando must have said something to you."

"I don't know any Orlando."

"Well, they call him Fatz around here; he's always trying to bully the new guys. I'll have a talk with him."

"No that won't be necessary, I don't want him to think I told you."

"I guess you're right. Well, just try to avoid him. You seem like a nice kid, I read your file and I could be wrong but I'm normally right. If it was my mom I would have did the same thing."

"Ms. Williams tha funny thing is I don't have any remorse and if I was put in that situation again then I would do it again."

She looked at me, stood up and said, "I know you will, I'll have you on the list to start school tomorrow so just relax for today."

Tha rest of tha day flew by, I decided to wait until after dinner to call home. During dinner, Fatz and his crew tormented tha Chow Hall but they didn't bother me and this how it went for tha next few years.

CHAPTER 2

R.I.P. Mom

Three years later I was in 9th grade and decided to try out for tha basketball team which Fatz and his crew thought they ran. We neva got into a fight but I knew we would before he left. I just did what my mom said and blocked him out, let him talk as long as he doesn't put his hands on me. It didn't matter what he said tha coach was impressed wit my skills on tha court. He let me know not only did I make tha team but I would be starting at tha point guard position. I knew this would start sum thing, especially since I took Fatz spot and he had to come off tha bench.

We had a game in 3 days, your parents were allowed to come but since my mom was sick only nana was coming. I had also found out what AIDS was and where it originated from. Now I understand what my mom meant that day in tha kitchen when she told nana if she didn't make it to take care of me. If you saw my mom you would neva know that she has AIDS. As soon as I saw nana a big smile came across my face.

When tha game started, I just took over. I ended tha game wit 20 points, 10 assist, 10 rebounds, and 5 steals. My first game and I dropped a triple double. I got to talk to my nana for a little while after tha game.

On tha way back to tha tier, Fatz was talking Shit, I just kept it moving. He was mad because he didn't get in tha game. After I showered, me and P.R. sat at tha table busting it up; he had dropped 21.

"Yo, ya boy was on tha sideline salty. He was only gettin' time cause nobody else wanted to play."

"P.R. you know that nigga game is trash."

"I have to agree wit you on that Naz."

That night I couldn't sleep at all. Tha next morning I got up, did my workout but for sum reason my body wouldn't let me stop after my 2 hours like I normally did. Right before breakfast, Tone one of tha thurl guards came on tha tier.

"Naz, Ms. Williams needs to see you in her office."

It was neva good when you had to go to her office but I didn't do anything that I could recall. When I stepped into her office, she had a serious look on her face.

"You need to call your grandmother," she said handing me tha phone.

"Why would she call me to say that?" I dialed nana's number, after tha 3rd ring she picked up.

"Good mornin Nana."

"Same to you Nazir, it actually isn't such a good morning. I have some bad news, your mother has went to be with God."

I didn't understand what she meant so I asked her, "When is she coming back?"

"She's not." At that moment I knew exactly what she meant.

I screamed, "NOOOOOOO! NOOOOOO!NOOOOOO!"

Before I had realized it I was throwing tha chair. Tone came in and yoked me up but Ms. Williams told him to let me go. As soon as he did, I dropped to tha floor and cried my heart out. I could hear her on tha phone telling Nana once she had all tha information to call her so she could arrange it wit tha Warden.

I went back to tha tier, I didn't want to be bothered. I slept until dinner and I only went because I hadn't eaten anything all day. As I walked into tha Chow Hall, Fatz, and his crew started.

I looked him dead in his eyes and said, "Please, not today."

"Awe you upset, what you gon' do cry to mommy?" As soon as he said that I caught him wit a 2 piece; that put him on his butt.

When he got up he said, "I've been waiting for this."

He swung a wild hook which I dodged then came back wit a left hook of my own followed by a right and another left sending him to tha canvas. Tone sat back and let me do my thing. Cal, J.J., and Ears tried to get involved but wit all this rage and anger I had in me they too became victims of my wrath. When I was done, tha 4 of them were stretched out. I had lost my appetite so I asked Tone if I could go back to my unit; he said to go ahead. P.R. said when they came too none of them knew what happened.

"Damn Naz, I alwayz see you shadow boxing but I had no idea you had hands like that. I started coming over but by tha time I did, you had already dusted them off. What made you snap like that today?" I tried to hold back my tears but they just started to pour down my face.

"What's up Naz? I'm ya boy, you can talk to me about anything."

I looked at him then said, "My mom passed away today."

He grabbed me in a bear hug and said, "Believe me, I know what you're goin' thru. My mom died 3 months before I came in here and I still cry about it. You neva get over tha loss of ya mom. It's been 2 years but yet it feels like it's only been a few months. So on days when I seem distant that's why." From that moment on we became tha best of friends.

That night I cried myself to sleep. Ms. Williams talked tha Warden into letting me attend tha whole funeral and not just tha viewing. My nana had brought me a black button up wit black Khaki's and A.C.G. Boots; she even had a pair of black shades for me.

When we arrived at tha church it was packed. Tone said that he would sit in tha back. He neva put hand cuffs on me because he knew I wouldn't run. I walked into tha church and made my way up to tha casket. I just stood there holding my mom's hand not caring about tha people behind me waiting to see my mom. They went around me as I just stood there, I had so much hurt inside. I looked at her, she was so beautiful laying there, she looked like she was asleep.

"Why did they have to take you from me Mommy?" I asked knowing she wouldn't answer.

I felt a pair of hands on my shoulder; I turned to see my Uncle Charles standing there wit tear stained eyes. This was tha first time I had seen him sober. He and my mom were tha closest out of all 8 of my nana's children so I know that it was hitting him hard. Also, he tried to get me to sit down but I let him know that I was staying right where I was at. So he went back to his seat next to nana. When tha people from tha funeral home tried to close tha casket I snapped out.

"No, you are not goin' to close this casket and I mean it so y'all might as well start tha service now!"

My tears started to pour down my face. My nana told me to come sit wit her but I refused.

"No Nana. I'm gon' stay right here by her side; she needs me to protect her."

I could hear tha Rev. tell sum body to get me a chair and that's where I sat. I told my nana that I wanted to sing a song, so when it got to my part my nana handed me tha microphone and gave me a hug.

I turned back around, held my momma's hand and sang, *"We were together just tha other day. Taking life for granted, passing time away. I was there for you, you were there for me. We said we'd be together for eternity. I'm so alone, I miss you. You neva miss a good thing til it's gone. Life goes on but it's not tha same. I can't help at times calling out ya name. Then I realize that you are gone, but my life ain't been tha same since you went away."*

When I finished I held tha mic and said, "Mommy you'll alwayz be in my heart. Your memory will live on thru me."

Then I broke down to tha point where my Uncle Charles had to help me up. I couldn't walk, it felt like my chest was about to collapse. After we buried her, everybody was goin' back to nana's for tha repast.

Tone said, "How about we go get us some of that good food you always talking about." That brought a slight smile to my face.

We went to nana's, bust a grub then headed back to tha detention center. I changed into my Khaki's and tee then headed to my tier. I ran into Ears on tha way but he didn't say nuffin; he just looked tha other way. I asked Tone if I could go to tha gym to work on my 3-point shot. He said it was cool. When I got to tha door I saw Fatz and J.J. playing one on one. I still went inside, I grabbed a ball and started to shoot.

After about 10 minutes P.R. came in, "You a'ight Naz?"

"Yeah, for now."

"Well, you know if you want to talk, I'm here."

"I know Cuz."

"Check ball."

"I don't want to do it to you P.R."

"Nigga check tha ball."

I passed him that ball, no soon as he passed it back, Fatz and J.J. came walking up.

"Y'all want to play 2 on 2?"

I said, "Nah, we cool."

P.R. asked, "For how much?"

"Oh, you want to play for money."

"How much?" P.R. asked again.

"$50."

"Money on tha wood, make tha bet good," I said. They both pulled out $25 and so did we.

"Akeem hold this," I said handing him tha money, "game to 32, straight shoot for first ball?"

"Nah, y'all got it," Fatz said.

Of course he wanted to stick me when he should have been sticking P.R, so I just kept feeding P.R. down in tha post until he got tired. Then I made it rain wit my jumper. They didn't even get to touch tha ball; only to check it up. We had them 28 to nuffin when J.J. called a Bullshit walk.

"Man, that wasn't no walk."

J.J. yelled, "Man you walked!"

P.R. passed me tha ball and said, "Point, check rock."

"Nah, Cuz respect tha call."

"If it was legit I would. Y'all ain't gettin' it like that."

"Well, if you not gon' respect my call, game over!"

"Well, y'all lost Akeem."

"Cuz you crazy if you think you gon' get paid and da game ain't over."

P.R. looked at him, "Yo, don't make me kick ya ass over a petty $25," he said walking towards him.

To defuse tha situation I said, "28 nuffin, y'all ball." Throwing tha ball to J.J.

"Nah Naz, we ain't goin' out like that."

"It ain't bout nuffin P.R., we gon' win anyway."

"Yeah ya right, they ain't even gon' score."

Fatz passed tha ball to J.J., he shot pass P.R. and thought he had an easy layup but P.R. came from behind and pinned his Shit to tha backboard.

"Foul!" J.J. yelled.

"Good call," Fatz said.

"Good call my ass! That was all ball!"

"I called foul Nigga! Now check tha ball," he said throwing tha ball to Fatz.

He tried this weak cross which I anticipated and I stole tha ball.

"Foul!"

"Look, if this is how y'all gon' play y'all can take that $50 and shove it up y'all ass! Y'all need it anyway," I said, "Akeem bring us our money." I gave P.R. his $25 back.

I looked at my watch and we had 30 minutes until rec. was over.

"I need to work on my jumper."

"It looked fine to me tha way you was shootin' his lights." We both laughed but Fatz didn't find it so funny.

"We can play one on one for tha doe."

"I'm good, cause that wouldn't be fair to you."

"Nigga put up or shut up!" he said handing Akeem his money.

"Like taking candy from a baby," I replied also handing over my doe.

"Ya rock," he checked tha ball.

"Game to 32 straight." I was still talking when he went by and scored.

"No bucket! I was still talk'n."

"Well, you shouldn't have checked tha ball; 2 nuffin."

"Don't even worry about it, you won't score over 10."

He tried that same weak cross which I stole then fired a jumper all net. Tha final score was 32 to 8; I went to get my money.

"Akeem you better not give him my money."

"He beat." I snatched all tha money from him.

"Nigga I say!" He went to hit him but I pulled him out tha way.

"I'm tha one who got tha money not him. If you want to hit sum body then hit me Fatz. You ain't nuffin but a fat bully and I tried of ya Shit!" I yelled walking towards him.

"Well do sum thing about it Pussy!"

As soon as I put my hands up Tone yelled across tha gym, "Rec's over!"

I turned around to leave and Fatz stole me in tha back of tha head causing me to stumble forward. I got myself together and quickly turned around to find him coming at me. I dodged his punch then put my hands up; then we squared up. He swung a wild punch, I moved and caught him wit 3 fast jabs. Two dead in his eyes and one in his nose. J.J. tried to get in it but P.R. caught him wit a strong hook that put him on his back. Tone could not stop us so he had no choice but to call tha team.

By tha time they got there, I had punished Fatz, his blood was all over tha place. They wasted no time restraining me then they walked us to tha hole; they had to take them to tha infirmary first. We ended up getting 40 days in tha hole and they got 60 since they started it. Me and P.R. had cells right next to each other so we talked through tha vent all night and slept all day. While I was in there Ms. Williams brought me my schoolwork so I wouldn't fall behind and she also told nana what had happened so she wouldn't get worried. When we finally were let out, I had lost about 5 pounds but it was a good 5 pounds.

It seemed like tha next 2 years flew by; P.R. had 3 months until his 18th birthday.

"So what are you gon' do when you hit tha bricks?"

"I really don't know Naz, my cousin got West Philly in a choke hold. He's been holding me down in here so I might see what's good wit him."

"Damn Nigga, you got to at least give ya self a chance before you jump in headfirst."

"I feel you but on sum real, Naz I ain't got Shit so I got to get ery thing from tha muscle and I refuse to go out there and be in tha way cause ain't no more of this. It's straight to tha county or C.F.C.F. so I got to make it all count."

"I feel you; I just want you to be safe cause we gon' see each other on tha other side of these walls."

"Oh Fo' Sho, I'm gon' keep it gangsta wit you, you tha only nigga I been foolin' wit for tha past 5 years. I can show you better than I can tell you."

"Hold that thought, my nana is here to see me." I left tha tier, headed to tha Chow Hall where they held tha visits.

"Jenkins you have a new pair of sneakers. Do you want your peoples to take your old ones or are you donating them?"

"Nah, I'm sending them home."

I took off tha Air Max I had on and replaced them wit tha new white and red Jordans I asked nana to get. I walked into tha Chow Hall; nana was in there talk'n to sum pretty brown skin girl. I gave nana a hug and kiss then sat down.

"Nazir, I would like for you to meet Ashanti."

"Like tha singer?"

"Yeah, like tha singer," she said.

"I wasn't tryin' to be smart."

"And neither was I so I hope that you didn't take it that way."

"Nah, ma so why is she here?" I asked.

"Because my car is in tha shop and she was nice enough to give me a ride and I wasn't going to have her wait in no car for an hour. Is that Ok with you?"

"Yes Mam, I was wondering why you ain't been bring her."

"Boy she's 19 and you're 16."

"Nana, age ain't nuffin but a number."

"You heard what I said."

"She ain't saying nuffin, you doin' all tha talk'n for her."

"I have to use the restroom. Ashanti, I'll be back so don't let him talk all crazy."

As soon as she left, I started to ask questions. When I was done, I knew all I needed to know.

"When do you get out?"

"On my 18th birthday. Why, you gon' wait for me?" I asked wit a smile, "we can spend tha next 2 years gettin' to know one another."

"You ain't shy at all, are you?"

"Nah, I just go after what I want. Well, how about I give you my info and when you ready you make tha first move."

Once she said Ok I wrote it down. While I was giving it to her Nana walked up.

"Boy what are you doing?"

"Nuffin Nana, just got me a new friend, hopefully."

When tha visit was up I hugged Nana, I extended my arms to Ashanti, to my surprise she gave me a hug.

It was tha day before P.R. was set to leave. His birthday was yesterday but they had to wait until tomorrow before they could release him.

"Yo Naz, did Shorty ever get at you?"

"Nah."

"Well, that's her lost."

"You ain't neva lied about that."

"Mail call Jenkins!" I got my mail, a letter from my cousin and...

"Oh Shit! P.R. you just talked Shorty up." I opened her letter first.

Dear Naz,

Where do I start? I know it took me a minute to write but I had to make sure that I was interested and for tha past 2 months I have been thinking about you hard. I even asked Nana was I wrong for likin you; I am 3 years your senior. She told me if that was what I wanted to do then to go for it, so here I am sending you this letter. I also wanted to make sure it was cool for me to visit. So, let me know and I'll be up there A.S.A.P.

Your Friend Ashanti"

I didn't waste no time responding to her letter which she should get in a few days. When P.R. left it was like a part of me went out tha door wit him. He was tha only person I let get close to me; I don't trust people. It seemed like tha next couple of weeks dragged by, I hadn't heard anything from Ashanti. I was starting to wonder if she had even gotton my letter. I would find out today when nana came to see me.

As I was about to go to my visit, I saw Fatz changing into his street clothes. I didn't say anything I just kept it moving like a drive by. When I got to tha visiting room I didn't see nana.

Tha look on my face must have said it all because tha guard said, "Ms. Tate."

"Who?" Then Ashanti stood up.

"Me Boy."

"Oh Shit, I didn't even recognize you. You look different wit ya micro's in."

I couldn't deny her beauty, 5'6", caramel skin tone, shoulders length hair wit out her braids, hazel eyes, and a fat butt like tha rapper Trina. She gave me a hug then sat down.

"I was starting to wonder if sum body had intercepted my letter."

"Nah, I got it, I just be working so much I don't have a life. Plus, I live by myself so I got to make sure my bills are paid and food is in tha fridge."

"I definitely feel you, a woman wit her priority's in order. So, I guess since you responded wit a letter and a visit that means you at least want to be friends, if nuffin else."

"Tha best way to start out is friends because if tha relationship doesn't work out you will alwayz be friends. See, I'm a little older and I was in a situation that did not work and now I can't stand him. But that was my fault because I rushed into it."

"Well Ashanti, as you already know I'm 16 and in here until I turn 18 for murder. I don't know if my nana told you but I killed my stepfather; he was very abusive to me and my mother. In fact, he's tha reason my mother's not here today; he infected her wit AIDS. Don't get it twisted, by far I'm no killer but when it comes to sum one I love then I will alwayz do what I have to do to protect them. No matter what tha consequences is and I neva had a girlfriend nor have I ever had sex. Not that you needed or cared to know that, I jus believe in honesty."

"Naz, I know that I am 3 years older than you but I look past your age and I ask you this, when you get out in 2 years there are goin' to be so many more females that I know will be interested in you but I ain't worried about that. Well, we gon' just be friends until you get home."

That night all I could do was think about what Ashanti said. I knew she was right about all tha other females that would be out there but that didn't matter, I wanted her. So, if I had to wait then that was all it was.

For tha next year she was up here to see me every week. Nana would come wit her every other week. They even surprised me when they came to my graduation. Nana was so proud of me; she had no idea that I was goin' to school; she just thought I was sitting around all day. Ms. Williams didn't even tell me that people could come. She called and let nana know, who in returned called Ashanti. I gave nana my diploma so she could take it home and hang it on her wall like I know she would wit tha rest of them.

I couldn't believe it, I neva thought this day would come. Not only was it my 18th birthday but Ms. Williams had it set up so that I would leave today. We had grown pretty close in 7 years; she gave me her home and cell number.

"If you need anything do not hesitate to call; no matter what time of day or night it is. If you just want to talk, feel free to call me." Tone walked me to tha front gate, he too had given me his number to call him.

"Amir."

"What up Tex?"

"They say tha boy Cream is having a big party tonight at Club Flo."

"I know, Stylz just hit me."

"You fucken' wit it?"

"Do Muslims make salat? I'mma have to shoot to King of Prussia to grab sum thing to wear."

"You better call Stylz, he was headed there too."

"What about you?"

"I'm cool, I keep sum fly shit in tha walk-in."

"I heard that, well I'll hit you up later."

"No doubt."

"Oh yeah, did Aunt Jean's plane land yet?"

"Yeah, she got in early this mornin."

"A'ight, I'll call her when I'm done shopping."

"Make sure you do; she's been worried about you."

"I'mma call, have you seen Fourty?"

"Yeah, he's wit me."

"Tell him Shorty was asking bout him."

"Tex told me to tell you Shorty was asking bout you."

"I'm not surprised tha way I put it on her."

"Nigga, I told you not to knock her off."

"Yeah, and I told you I was grown!"

"All I know is, you better not Fuck it up for us!"

"She's still goin' to play her position."

"Until you stop fucken her."

"Nah, we already established what tha deal is if we stop fuckin."

"A'ight, I hear you, I'mma get a backup just in case."

"Do what ever you feel you need to do."

"Are you goin' to Cream's party tonight?"

"I don't know, I was think'n about it."

"It's gon' be bitches everywhere."

"What about this Tex?"

"That Shit Hot!"

"I know right."

"I'm tryin' to Fuck sum thing strange tonight."

"Me too, I hope Malaya show up tonight."

"You know she'll be in tha building wit Roxy and tha other chick."

"Hopefully, she'll stop frontin' and get at a nigga."

"You know tha chase is tha best part because once you capture tha prize tha fun and thrill is gone."

"I hope it's worth it, I been tryin' to get at her for tha past six months."

"Damn, and you haven't even got her number yet?"

"All that is goin' to change tonight."

"I've got a feelin' you may be right."

"Come on, let's pay for tha stuff and be out."

"Amir said that work came in this mornin."

"Now that's what I'm talk'n bout, I've got my people in Delaware on a hold for 10 of them things."

"I think I'mma pull tha Maserati out tonight."

"Daaaamn, you pulling out all tha stops to get Mayla ain't you?"

"Nah, if this 'pose to be tha party of all parties I need to come correct."

"You gon' make me pull out my Maybach."

"Go hard or go home is my motto."

"I definitely feel you on that."

"I gotta be at tha shop in an hour."

"Shit let me call Ern, I hope he can squeeze me in."

"You good, I booked us all an appointment."

"What would we do wit out you Tex?"

"Let's hope you'll neva find out."

"Mayla how does this dress look on me?"

"Damn Bitch, that's you all day."

"Wow, Paradise you must be tryin' to catch a big fish tonight?"

"No sense in half steppin'."

"I say that's right."

"Mayla, you know ya boy gonna be in tha building."

"Who, my boy?"

"Bitch stop frontin', you know damn well who I'm talk'n bout."

"If I knew, I wouldn't have to ask who."

"Tex Bitch!"

"That's not my boy."

"You still tryin' to play hard to get, you better stop before sum body else scoops him up."

"I could care less."

"Paradise, you hear this hussy frontin?"

"Umm Hmm."

"Well Damn, who side you on?"

"Family or not, Mayla you frontin' I see tha way you be staring at him."

"What ever."

"You know we right."

"Just cause you wanna get at his boy Amir, don't mean I want Tex."

"You right, but you do want Tex."

"Like I said, Whaaat Eeever."

"We better get to tha shop y'all know how Casey is when you're not on time."

"Just let me pay for my stuff."

"All them other bitches better have their Shit together tonight."

"Even if they do, they not seeing us, we dem bitches."

"I say that's right," Roxy said dappin' Mayla.

CHAPTER 3

Fresh Out tha Box

Ashanti and Nana were waiting out front A.C.G.'s wit a pair of tan cargo pants and a brown and tan black label shirt. I gave them both a hug and kiss on tha cheek.

"I like this car." She had a black on black Dodge Magnum on dub deuces.

"That's tha first thing I'mma do Monday is go get my license."

Tha last year I studied that drivers manual inside and out, so I knew it like tha back of my hand. They ended up taking me to this place on South Street to get sum lunch called Mom Jeans, they had sum of tha best soul food I ever tasted. Afterwards we did a little shopping, I didn't need that much since they both had been buying me things in tha last few months.

When we finally got back to nana's house I was tha first to walk in. I was greeted by surprise and welcome home, all my aunts, uncles, and cousins were there. They have went all out, a welcome home birthday party through tha years that I was locked up. My family let me know that they didn't blame me for what happened because I did what any 11-year-old would have done to protect his mother. Even though they did ask where I had gotten tha gun from so not to tell on my cousin, I had lied and told them I got it from James; that I saw him hide it in tha hall closet.

One of my aunts told me that I looked like a young bodybuilder. I even had to admit, I was cut up like a bag of dope so I had a nice body to go wit my good looks.

"You need to get that hair braided up." She was right, in there I didn't have nobody to braid it so I rocked a ponytail for 7 years.

After everybody had left, Ashanti and Uncle Charles had cleaned up. My Uncle Charles have been sober for 4 years. After my mom died, he just stopped cold turkey, no rehab or nuffin.

"Nana I'll be back later, I'm goin' to visit my mom."

"Okay, take these," she said handing me a set of keys, then she looked at Ashanti, "if he ain't coming home then call me so I won't be worried."

All I could do was smile and say, "Well on that note, I probably won't be home tonight." Then I gave Ashanti a seductive wink which she returned wit a smile.

Tha clock on tha dash said 8 o'clock.

"You know what, I'mma wait til tomorrow to visit my mom. Oh this my Shit, turn it up."

"She got me speedin' in tha fast lane, pedal to tha floor man, tryna get back to her love, her love. Best believe she got that good thing. She my lil hood thing, ask around they know us."

I had to turn around to see what she had in here. Her shit sounded like a marching band.

"I need to stop on Burks so I can get me sum trees."

"That's cool wit me, I could use sum green boy."

"What you know about that?"

"Me and my peeps stayed high on that Sour D."

"Let me find out you was in there blowin' that good green."

"It's nuffin to find out, I just told you."

"Oh, you tryin' to be smart?"

"Nah, I was just joking." As soon as we pulled up on 4th and Burks sum dude came to tha car."

"What up Ashanti wit ya Bad Ass." I didn't say anything, I wanted to see if she was goin' to check him.

"Boy didn't I tell you to fall back."

"Yeah, yeah I know, you got a man and he'll be home soon."

That's when I took tha liberty to speak up, "Nah, I'm home."

He look down in tha car, "Oh Shit my bag Homie, no disrespect."

"None taken, I would be tryin' to holla at her too had I been in ya shoes." That made her blush.

"So you want ya usual."

"Yeah."

He darted into tha alley only to return wit a sandwich bag filled with sum nicks of weed. She handed him six $20 bills which he returned to her a 10 and tha sandwich bag of weed.

"See you in two weeks Tico."

"No doubt once again peeps I didn't mean no disrespect," he said wit his hand in tha window.

I shook it and said, "Naz, I'll be seeing ya around."

When she pulled off I said, "Damn, you been claimin' me already?"

"Yeah why? You got a problem wit that?"

Before I could answer she said, "We've been friends for tha last 2 years, it's time to step it up a notch unless you want to do you. After all, you have been down for 7 years so you might want to explore your options first."

"Ashanti, you been my girl since tha second time you came to see me, you just didn't know it yet." She started laughing.

"Oh, that was funny?"

"No, you just so confident."

"I had to be." All she could do was smile.

While pulling off, I turned tha radio up.

"Here we are, all alone in this room (ooh) And girl I know, where to start and what we're gonna dooo. I'll take my time we'll be all night girl. So get ready babe, I got plans for me and you (wooah). It ain't my first time but babygurl we can pretend (hey!) Let's bump and grind gurl, tonight will never end. Let me take you down, I really wanna take you down and show you what I'm about..." I could tell she was really feelin' this song cause she knew it word for word.

When we pulled up to this house she hit this button and tha garage lifted up. When I walked inside I was really impressed to say tha least. She had very good taste that let me know she was a go-getter and didn't need no man to take care of her unless this was tha benefits from dealing wit a baller. Let me test her...

"Damn, at least that nigga made sure you was Ok before y'all split up, what," I said.

"Nah, I heard what you said, I'm sorry but not only is this my house I paid for everything in here including that car in tha garage." I started smiling.

"What you smilin' about?"

"Cause you real feisty."

"I work at tha bank, I make close to $50,000 a year. I ain't no dumb chickenhead broad and I'm on my 3rd year at Temple. Now what happened?"

"Well excuse me, I wasn't tryin' to down you. I jus wanted to make sure I didn't have any ex-boyfriends who might still want you to worry about."

"Naz, I would neva put you in harm's way. I see, you don't really know me. I thought after 2 years of being friends that you would be able to see."

"Listen Ashanti, I read people real good, very seldom I am wrong. I may have been locked up for 7 years but ain't nuffin slow or dumb about me. If for one second I thought that you wasn't a thurl female, I wouldn't be having' this conversation wit you." With that being said, I walked over to tha stereo and browsed thru tha CDs until I found one that I wanted to hear.

"Is it cool for me to turn this on."

"Sure, do you." I put it in and turned it up.

"My dog went to court they gave him 15. Cracker banned my lil' nigga he was 17. Young nigga don't even know what all that time mean. Pussy ass crackers done shattered my nigga dreams. They holl'in' mandatory they want him to do tha whole thang."

"How do you know that whole song?"

"This my nigga Plies, that's all I listen to, he gets me in my bag."

"You haven't heard his latest CD, Definition of Real."

"Yeah."

"And Da Realist?"

"Not that last one."

She passed me tha Dutch, I took a long pull. It felt good to be able to smoke wit out having to keep lookin' around to make sure nobody was coming. Tha clock on tha wall let me know that it was 11:00.

"Damn," I said.

"What's wrong?"

"I want to take a shower but I didn't bring a change of clothes."

"Come on," she said going upstairs.

When she turned tha light on it was undeniable that she had class and taste; from tha curtains to tha bed sheets was Fendi. She pulled her top dresser drawer open; I couldn't believe it she had made a spot for me and had boxers and socks.

"I'm not wearing no other niggaz Shit," I said wit a smile.

"Naz you better stop playing wit me for you get hurt," she said throwing a punch.

"Let me find out not only are you a pretty mother fucker but you can fight."

"You got a lot to learn, I can go so make sure if you cheat you better make sure she can fight cause I'mma beat her ass then yours."

"Damn, well you ain't got to worry about that."

"Well, if you thought you was goin' to I'm just letting you know. Tha towels are in tha hallway closet."

"Ok."

"I'mma jump in tha other shower."

I wanted to ask her to get in wit me but I stayed in my lane. After I got out tha shower, I walked back into tha bedroom and dried off. I rolled another Dutch, as soon as I lit it up Ashanti came out tha bathroom. She took a took my breath away standing there in a pair of boy shorts and wife beater. Her body was bangin' she sat on tha edge of tha bed. I passed her tha Dutch, she took a few pulls then passed it right back.

"You ain't no real smoker," I said.

"I neva said I was, that's why a bundle last me 2 weeks."

That night we made love, tha next morning Ashanti woke up wit a big smile on her face.

"Sum body's happy this mornin."

"For sum body who neva had sex before I can't front, you put it on me sum thing serious."

"My man P.R. said all you got to do is act like you slow dancing." She busted out laughing.

"Boy you stupid but it worked."

We both looked at one another then embraced; tha next thing I knew it was on. When we were done we both showered and once again she surprised me by telling me that I had a few things in tha closet.

"Hurry up get dressed so we can go eat sum breakfast."

"Babe, do you know any good barbers? I need to get a cut."

"I know you not goin' to cut all that pretty hair off."

"Hell Nah, I'm just tryin' to get a shape up."

"Oh yeah, my cousin he tha Shit, he work at Philly Cutz. Do you want me to call him?"

"Yeah."

"Cause I know you need an appointment." Ashanti pulled out her phone to call her cousin.

"Yo."

"What up Cuz?"

"I can't call it. How many heads you got?"

"2, why what's up?"

"My man needs a shape up and a barber."

"Cuz, you know I'm tha best thing since pants wit pockets."

"I know, that's why I called you."

"Well bring him by, I want to see tha guy who has my lil cuz sprung."

"Shafee shut up, we'll be there in 15 minutes." We paid our tab and rolled out.

Within 20 minutes, we pulled up in front of Philly Cutz. When we walked in everybody spoke to me and I did tha same.

"Hey You," she said to Lil Shafee. He was alwayz in tha shop on Saturdays.

He ran up to her, "Shanti, Shanti." She scooped him up and swung him around causing him to laugh.

"Ashanti put him down, that's why he spoiled now."

"Boy sit down, I ain't tryin' to hear dat."

He looked at Naz then said, "Oh, so you tha one that she been talk'n bout for tha last 18 months."

"All good I hope."

"Nuffin but good," he said extending his hand.

"Naz," I said shaking it.

"Have a seat, I'll be right wit you." Ten minutes later he called me.

As soon as I sat down Ashanti said, "Don't Fuck my baby up."

"Yeah right, I'm tha best barber in Philly. Is it a certain way you want me to shape you up?"

"Listen Peeps, if you as good as you say you are, I'mma let you do ya thing because 9 outta 10 we gon' be locked in ery week."

"In that case, say no more."

"I just want my beard to stay long."

"You Muslim?"

"Nah."

"Don't worry I got you."

Thirty minutes later, he was handing me a mirror. I couldn't front, my thing was so sharp; I was definitely feelin' that razor outline. I stood up and Ashanti came back in.

"Damn, I'mma have to keep a leash on you."

"How much do I owe you?"

"Nah, this one is on me."

"Well, I'll see you next Friday at 1 pm."

"A'ight." We dapped one another and I headed to tha door.

"Thanks Cuz I really appreciate it," Ashanti said.

"No problem, you know you my baby."

"Well, see you later, bye Lil Sha."

"Bye Bye Shanti."

"See you Cuz." Ashanti walked out to tha car, I already had it started bumpin' Plies.

"Boy, you not goin' to Plies me to death."

"Damn, that's how you feel about my boy Plies."

"Now don't get me wrong, I Fucks wit Plies but from sunup to sundown I can't do it."

"I feel you." I changed tha CD.

"I got a bunch of dollars. I can spend them on her. Cause she can be my lady. She can be my lover. Call me on the late night. Get right he ain't acting right. Every super woman needs a super man. Here I am..."

"Now that's what I'm talk'n bout. Do you have anywhere you need to go?"

"Nah, I just want to go by Nana's."

"I'm already 2 steps ahead of you," she said pulling up to Nana's house.

My Uncle Charles was out front doin' sum chatting wit tha neighbor.

"Nana not here, she went into work today. She'll be home in a few hours."

"Ok, tell her to call me," I said handing him a piece of paper wit Ashanti's number on it.

We pulled off. "Oh, I know what we need to do," she said. Next thing I knew we were walking into tha AT&T store.

"Hi, may I help you wit sum thing today?"

"Yes, I would like to purchase an iPhone," said Ashanti.

She went to get tha phone, when she came back she was about to give me tha iPhone spill, but I cut her off..."

"Actually, I just want to add it to my plan."

"Oh, you already have an account wit us?"

"Yes."

"Under what name?"

"Ashanti Tate."

She punched it in on tha computer then asked, "What plan do you want?"

"Tha unlimited ery thing."

"Ok well, that will be $199.99."

"Can I have tha screen protector as well as a case." She reached under counter and came up wit both.

"$226.97."

I pulled out my debit card which she gladly took swiped and gave back. After that, she activated tha phone. We gathered ery thing up and headed back to Ashanti's.

"Babe, I'mma give you tha quick rundown on how to use tha phone."

"That's what's up." When we got in tha house, Ashanti asked if I felt like Chinese or pizza?

"I'll take Chinese, 4 wings fried hard wit shrimp fried rice, no MSG."

While she ordered I looked through tha book on how to use my new iPhone. By tha time she came back I had learned how to do a few things on my own.

"Let me give you a quick run down." She started talk'n all fast.

"Damn Babe, I didn't understand nuffin you just said."

She smiled, "I know, I was being smart but on a more serious note."

By tha time she finished tha doorbell rang. When I looked thru tha peep hole I saw tha Chinese man wit our food. I opened tha door and took tha food.

I guess he wanted a tip so I said, "Next time don't take so long." And shut tha door.

"Naz you so damn ignorant."

"No I'm not, it only came to $18.00. I gave him a dub and let him keep tha change and he still wanted another tip so I gave him one."

"Boy you funny."

"Nah, dem Chinese people funny; all tha money they make off of us and they still want more.

Later that night, we watched a few movies then fell asleep. We slept in all day Sunday until my nana called.

"Hey Nana."

"Boy, I know you ain't still in tha bed."

"No, I'm up," which I was, just not out tha bed, "sorry I didn't call you last night but I was tired when I got in."

"I kinda figured that."

"Nana, let me give you my cell phone number."

"Hold on, let me get me get a pen... Ok what is it?"

I looked at Ashanti, "What's my number?" She said it loud enough so that my nana heard it.

"You get it Nana?"

"I got it Baby. So you two have decided to live together?"

"No we don't live together."

Ashanti looked at me then said, "Oh, so you not moving in?"

Before I could say anything Nana said, "Well, y'all talk that over; I got to get my dinner started."

"Ok, we'll be by later to eat."

"Ok."

No soon as I hung up Ashanti said, "So you not tryin' to move in? I guess I got a key made for nuffin."

"Nah, you know I'm moving in if you really want me to."

"Of course I do, I just didn't want to push you."

Later that night, we ate dinner wit Nana and Uncle Charles.

"So Nazir, what do you plan on doin'?"

"Well, tomorrow I'm goin' to Motor Vehicle to get my license then I'm goin' to fill out a few applications. I got to get me a job."

"Well, you know that it may take a little while so don't get frustrated."

"I know."

After we finished, I when upstairs to get all of my stuff that Nana and Ashanti had gotten me a few days ago.

"I see she got her way," my Uncle Charles said.

That night we talked about tha life we were about to share. We both shared our likes and dislikes; and on this night we realized that we were soul mates wit ery thing in common.

Tha next few weeks were very frustrating, I got my license but I couldn't get a job. Tha only one to call me back was McDonalds. I went to my interview and when I left I had a job at Micky D's. It was cool for tha first few weeks until I got my first paycheck.

"Baby what's wrong?" I showed her my paycheck.

"Damn, all those hours and this is it?"

"Yeah, you can keep it, pay a bill wit it."

"I don't need it."

"Nah, you keep it, I'm good."

For tha next year it was pretty much tha same thing, jobs at fast food joints. One day when I was walking home this nice ass car pulled up; tha boy Doe hopped out.

"What up Naz?"

"I can't call it Doe."

"Damn Naz, you still flippin' brothers at Burgers, I mean flippin' burgers at Brothers?"

"Yeah."

"Man, you gotta quit that Shit; come get sum of this real paper," he said pulling out this big ass knot of money.

"Now I know why they call him Doe."

"Whenever you ready to get this real paper like I said, come holla at me.

Matter fact, take my number." I pulled out my phone, stored his number.

"I see a lot of potential in you Naz. Don't let that Shit go to waste flippin' burgers when you can be flippin' birds." I walked off.

While I was at work, all I could do was think about what Doe said.

"Nazir! Nazir!" My manager brought me outta my daze, "you've been off in tha distance today!" He dropped tha burger on tha counter.

"There wasn't supposed to be any lettuce on this burger!" He was yelling in my face which he alwayz did but today I just wasn't for it.

"Listen Mr. Showell, I wish you wouldn't keep talk'n to me like I'm one of ya kids."

"I'm not tryin' to hear that Naz! You work for me so I run Shit around here!"

"Well, since you said it like that Mr. Showell..." I took my apron off, threw it on tha floor and I yelled, "I Quit!" Then walked out wit out a care in tha world.

Later that night while we were eating dinner, Ashanti must have sensed sum thing was bothering me.

"Baby what's tha matter? Is ery thing a'ight?"

"Nah, I quit today."

"Why, what happened?"

"I told you how Mr. Showell alwayz be talk'n to me and I just couldn't take it today. Then that Prick had tha nerve to say, I work for him, he run Shit; like he pays $10 an hour."

"Baby don't worry about it; you'll find another job."

"Fuck That!" I yelled, "I'm tired of these bullshit low end jobs!"

"Baby just be patient."

"Ashanti, I have been patient for tha past year; I'm at my wits end."

She didn't know but my mind was now made up. After dinner while she was in tha shower, I pulled out my phone and called Doe.

CHAPTER 4

Welcome to tha Game

"Yo, who this?"

"What up Doe, it's Naz."

"Oh, what up Young'n?"

"You."

"Oh, you ready to get this money, huh?"

"Yeah, I had to quit my gig."

"Nigga you should have been did that. So what you tryin' to do?"

"You already know."

"A'ight, I won't be around til tomorrow. This ya number?"

"Yeah."

"I'mma lock you in and I'll hit you around 11 o'clock tomorrow mornin." As I was ending my call Ashanti came downstairs.

"Baby you Ok?"

"Yeah, I'm good, I'm sorry for yelling at you earlier."

"I know you didn't mean it and it may not seem like it but sum thing better will come along."

I took her hands then said, "These past 3 years I have neva lied or kept anything from you and I don't plan to start now." She looked at me wit concern in her eyes.

"I'm about to start hustling."

"Baby, I'm not worried about you not having no money, that doesn't bother me."

"No, but it bothers me. I can't keep sittin' around while you pay all tha bills. I can't sit around."

"Baby that's nuffin, I been on my own for 6 years."

"Yeah, but I feel like less than a man letting you pay ery thing."

"Well Naz, I'mma say this, I don't want you to, but at tha end of tha day you gon' do what you gon' do regardless what I say. Just know that I got ya back no matter what."

"Damn that made me feel good to know that."

"And I do respect that you even told me; just what ever you do, do not bring that stuff into our home."

"I would neva put you or ya house in harm's way."

"Correction Naz, our house. So, how much do you need to get started?"

"Nuffin, I'm goin' to holla at Doe in tha mornin."

"Well, you can just drop me off at work and take tha car."

That night I had a hard time falling asleep, my mom was on my mind. Was that a sign? Was she telling me not to get in tha game or was she giving me as crazy as it may sound her blessing? Only time would tell.

Tha next morning after I dropped Ashanti off I went to Ms. Dolls to grab me a turkey bacon, egg, and cheese on a toasted English muffin. At about 11:30 Doe hit my phone.

"Yo what up Doe?"

"My fault, I'm running late."

"It's cool."

"Meet me around tha way in 15 minutes."

I left tha car at tha crib since tha block was a 5 to 10-minute walk; that's what I did. As soon as I hit tha green box Doe pulled up.

"Hop in Young Boy."

I had neva been in a 745Li before. Once I was in, he pulled off.

"So this is what we gon' do. I know this is tha first time you have ever picked up a pack. You have to get ya clientele up so I'mma hit you wit a G-pack," he said handing me a zip lock bag wit a bunch of caps inside.

"Jus hit me back wit 600."

I had to think, *"If I took shorts, I would probably end up wit about 300 for myself and that wouldn't be bad. Especially, if I got rid of it fast."*

We kicked it for another hour then we went back to tha block. Tha fiends flocked to his car.

"Didn't I tell y'all about rushin' my car when I pull up? Besides, I ain't got it, my young boy got it."

"Nah, we want what you be having."

"It's tha same Shit, he jus got it."

"Well, let me get 5 for 40."

"Nah, you can get 5 for 45."

"Damn Doe, let him know."

"Doe ain't gotta let me know Shit!"

"Either you want it or you don't. I got to get mines now. Once I get right you'll be able to get that but right now I need 9 a cap."

"I'm goin' down tha street," one of them said.

"Go head, you gon' be mad when you spend ya money on that Bullshit!"

"You know he right," the fiend named Wendy said.

"Well, can I get 8 for 70?"

"I'll give you that."

"I got an odd $2."

"This is Wendy, she'll run sells to you. I normally hit her every $60.00. No disrespect Doe, but why do I need her to run sells? If they know I got that Shit they gon' come regardless. So, what I'm gone do is pay you to watch tha corner. I'll pay you 5 dimes a day." Her eyes got as big as golf balls when I said that.

"Hold on, let me get this straight. All I got to do is sit on tha green box, watch out for tha police, and I get 5 dimes a day?"

"Nah, 4."

"Well what ever, I'll take that for jus sittin' on my ass all day."

Doe said, "You gon' blow up in this game Naz. I see it all in you. Well, hit me when you get done."

After he left I put Wendy at her post. I found a sweet spot up in this tree to hide my drugs. And to my surprise, I was done in 3 hours. I called Doe to let him know I was ready. He let me know that he was on his way. This time he hit me with two G-packs.

By tha time I got in tha house it was 1 in tha morning. Ashanti was still up.

"Damn Babe, why you still up?"

"I was waiting on you to come in."

"You don't have to wait up for me; there's gon' be a lot of late nights."

"I didn't want to call your cell."

"Why not? I can do two things at once."

"Why don't you get a burn out to work off of?"

"Damn, that's a good idea."

I counted tha loot I had and I put Doe's money to tha side. I was gon' to end up wit about 600 for myself. It wasn't bad for a day's work, but I needed to think of a better way.

Tha next morning I woke up wit a master plan. I told Ashanti to drive herself to work. It was 9 o'clock when I called Doe.

"What's up Lil Homie."

"I'm ready for you but I need to holla at you."

"My line is secure, talk."

"Do you be selling weight?"

"Yeah, why?"

"I'd rather just get it in weight and do it myself."

I had a few months of Chemistry under my belt from school so it wasn't nuffin for me to do it up.

"A'ight, I'll hit you wit 2 ounces, you just hit me back wit $1,600."

"Cool, I'll be there in 20 minutes."

"Do you got a Pyrex?"

"Nah."

"I got an extra one you can have."

I met him, grabbed up tha work and headed back to tha crib to handle my biz-ness. It just so happens that we had sum bake in tha cabinet.

"Damn, I ain't got no scale," I thought to myself.

I walked around to Hasan's, he had scales and everything else. I didn't need no bags; I was about to turn Philly on to break off. That way I could get all tha money instead of letting it go by. I decided to only put half ounce of bake on it. Once I had tha powder and bake in tha pot, I put a little bit of water in it, turned tha stove on low and let it do what it do. When I was done I sat tha pot in a bucket of ice and ran cold water in it. Within seconds, it was hard as a brick. I took a butter knife, went around tha edges, turned tha pot over, and let tha cookie fall out on tha napkins that I had laid out. When it was dry enough I dropped it on tha scale, it weighed 63 grams; I was cool wit that. Lastly, I put it in 3 sandwich bags and headed to tha block. Wendy was already there at her post; I broke her off a nice nick to wake her up.

"What's this?" she asked looking at tha rock in her hand.

"It's a little sum thing to get you started."

"I'm not talk'n bout that; why you ain't bag it up?"

"Cause, I'm not doin' tha bag thing; I got break off."

"What is that?"

"As long as they got 3 dollars or better I'm taking it."

"Damn Naz, you tryin' to get all tha money. Let me hit this, I'll be right back."

While she was gone I had served a few people. When Wendy finally came back, she was high as a spaceship.

"Naz, this is way, way, way better than what you had yesterday. Shit, truth be told, I ain't had no coke this good since tha 70s. Doe steppin' his thing up."

"Nah, I did this up myself."

I made Doe's money back off tha first ounce plus and extra duece. I stayed out until I finished my work; it was still early. I called Doe so I could re-up, I had a total of $3,500. I told Doe that tha way it was moving' that I needed him to hit me wit a little more this time; he hit me wit 3 ½ ounces. I let Wendy know I would be back when I finished making it tha same way; they were goin' crazy over that Shit. When I got to tha house Ashanti was just finishing up dinner.

"Babe, you just in time to eat."

"I need to cook this work up; it's only temporary until I find another spot, Ok?"

"Yeah, just don't have nobody knocking on our door."

I gave her that look that said yeah right, I wish sum body would. I pulled out what I needed; Ashanti stood there as I handled my biz-ness.

"So not to be in ya biz-ness, how much do you have to give Doe back?"

"$2,800."

"How much coke is that?"

"3 ½ ounces, I make 1,800 an ounce."

"So, you're making 9,000 of that."

"Yeah, but I'm only seeing 6,200."

"That's good for only hustling 2 days."

"That's not including this," I said pulling out 2,900. Then I went into tha freezer and pulled out tha other 600.

"Damn, you doin' ya thing."

"Yeah, I'll end up wit 9,100."

"Well, why don't you just buy ya own?"

"Because I want to stack my money."

"Then I'mma do me," Wendy said.

"When I do it, it's gon' be way better than what Doe was hittin' me wit."

I ate then went back on tha block. God Damn, I couldn't believe it, there were about 30 fiends all standing around waiting on me. I had just served tha last 3 when Doe pulled up. Shit, I had sold a whole ounce in less than 5 minutes and nobody spent less than $50. I hit Wendy wit a dime so she could do her.

"Damn Baby, you got tha block jumpin' and you only been out for 2 days. I came to give you this," he said handing me a .40 Cal, "this is in case them stick up kids come lurkin' or niggaz try to beef cause they fiends is coming around here to get that shit you got."

"Yeah, they loving this blueprint."

"I heard, I came thru a little while ago and they were lined up. I tried to pump my couple of dimes I had on me but they told me that they were waiting on you. They wanted that Good Shit you was breaking off. I had to get Wendy to explain to me what that was. Damn Young'n, you really tryin' to corner tha market and make it hard for ery body else."

"In reality Doe, they think they gettin' more but they not. It's a mind thing."

"Naz you holding?"

"Yeah, what's up?"

"I got 150.00, can you strap me?"

"Yeah, I got you. Show me what you gon' give 'em for that."

I ran to my stash spot, when I came back and showed him, all he could say was damn. So, I hit Mark wit his Shit.

"Oh Shit, you strap me, good lookin' Naz, I'll be back." And he walked off.

"Damn, it is a mind thing that wasn't even a six tenth."

"I know plus wit tha product being what it is."

Five fiends walked up and asked, "Naz you holding?"

"Yeah."

"I got 100."

"I got 50."

"Me too."

"So do I."

"I got 200."

"Hold up..." I dipped off again, came back served them and they went on their way.

"Damn, you definitely got it poppin' like Chris Brown. Well, hit me when you ready."

"A'ight, it should be in about 2 hours, 3 at tha most."

When I finished it was 11o'clock, I called Doe he said that he would be by and tha next 30 minutes, so I decided to wait. He finally pulled up wit 2 broads in tha car.

He rolled tha window down and said, "Climb in Young'n."

I slid him his loot then he introduced me to tha 2 broads. He told them that I was one of his workers. That Shit pissed me off; he could have just said I was his young boy. I felt like he was trying to belittle me in front of these broads because they started laughing.

I laughed too then said, "Damn, I'm a worker, huh."

After he slid me tha work he said, "3,600." I didn't say Shit, I just got out.

"You done for tha night?"

"Nah, I'm out all night tonight."

"I'll be back in a hour tops."

"Ok, I ain't goin' no where."

I got in tha house and went straight to work turning 4 ½ to 6. Since I've been doin' tha work I been have making 2 grand off every ounce. So, I was bound to make no less than 11 stacks off this 6 ounces. Before I went back outside I went upstairs and kissed Ashanti who was asleep.

When I was walking out tha room she said, "Be careful Baby."

"A'ight," I replied.

I had to find another spot to stash my drugs. When Wendy saw me her face lit up like a Christmas tree.

"I didn't think you were coming back."

"One thing about me, I'm a man of my word. If I say I'mma do sum thing then that's all it is. Let me ask you a question, do you live around here?"

"Yeah."

"Where at?" She pointed across tha street.

"Do you live wit sum one?"

"No, why?"

"I need a spot to pump out of."

"I wouldn't care what you did outta it but I don't have no electric."

"Why? Is tha bill to high?"

"Yeah, my mom died and left me that house."

"So how much is tha bill?"

"It's a stack, it was more than that. I've been paying on it every month."

"Well, I'mma give you tha money to pay it so we can set up shop."

"Ok, when you want to do that?"

"In tha mornin, you know I'm goin' to take you. Not that I don't trust you, I just need it on ASAP."

My phone started to vibrate when I answered Ashanti asked, "You Ok Baby?"

"Yeah, what you doin' up at 4 in tha mornin?"

"I had to use tha bathroom and you wasn't here so I had to make sure you were a'ight."

"I'm good, tryin' to get this money right plus after this I'm doin' my own thing." I told her how Doe tried to son me in front of 2 broads.

"I know you was mad."

"Yeah, but I ain't say Shit."

"Why don't you wait for another couple of flips so you can be all tha way straight."

"On sum real Baby, when I finish this I should have 17,200."

"Are you serious?"

"Yeah, dead serious."

"And you only been in da game for 3 days."

"I'm just tryin' to get in and get out."

"Well, be careful out there this late."

"After tonight I'll have a stash house to hustle out of."

She asked me, "What you talk'n bout?" So I told her about Wendy.

"You better not give her no stack."

"You must didn't hear me; I'm driving her there. Not only that, you only get one chance to Fuck me over."

"Naz, you need to get ya self a pistol."

I took my .40 Cal out my waist, "Already ahead of you."

"Where you? Neva mind, I don't want to know. Jus be safe."

"When you ready in tha mornin if I'm not there call my phone."

"Ok, I love you."

"I love you too."

Tha whole time I was on tha phone I was serving fiends. It was almost 8 o'clock when Ashanti called me.

"Good mornin Beautiful."

"Good mornin to you too, I was about to call Ms. Dolls for a breakfast platter. Do you want anything?"

"Yeah, order me turkey bacon, fried potatoes wit cheese and eggs fried hard platter."

"A'ight, I'll be around in 15 minutes."

I had a little over an ounce left but by tha time she pulled up I had a half left. I hit Mark wit another 100 piece then told Wendy to come on. When we got in I told Ashanti to drive.

"Hey Ms. Wendy."

"Hey Girl," she replied.

Ms. Wendy use to run wit her aunt until she had an overdose.

"I should have told you to order Wendy sum thing to eat."

"Oh that's Ok Naz, I'm not hungry."

"When was tha last time you ate?"

"Yesterday, lunch time."

"Well you gon' eat sum thing."

"If she not hungry, she not hungry," said Ashanti.

"I ain't tryin' to hear that. Wendy if you gon' be on my team you gon' have to clean ya self up and first thing is eatin'. I don't care if I got to take you to breakfast, lunch, and dinner. Were you serious when you said you did not want to get high tha rest of ya life?"

"Yeah."

"So when do you want to stop? Don't answer that, you just let me know and I'll help you. If you want to be on a winning team, I need you clean and sober cause I'm goin' to tha top."

"Well Naz, if that is how you want to do it give me 30 days and I'll go to rehab."

Ashanti pulled up to her job, we both got out. I gave her a kiss and told her l love her.

"I love you too, see you at 5 o'clock."

I told Wendy to get up front, 15 minutes later we pulled up in front of tha electric company. I passed her tha money and she went in. She took so long that I had dozed off. When I woke up she still hadn't come out yet. I was starting to think she had pulled a fast one on me until I saw her diddy boppin' out wit a big smile. She got inside tha car and went to hand me tha receipt.

"Nah, you keep it, put it up. Neva throw it away ya receipts."

"They said it should be on in an hour."

I shot to tha Gallery, took Wendy in, and bought her a few sets before we went back to tha hood. I made a stop at Basking Flowers and ordered a dozen of white long stem roses to have them delivered to Ashanti. He asked me if I wanted to have them sent in a vase or box; I let him know that I wanted a vase. Inside tha card I wrote, *"i hope that you know sum days will be better than others so i hope that today is one. Know that i love you,"* signed Naz.

"So, what do you say about stopping to get sum lunch?"

"A'ight, I am a little hungry." I didn't feel like waiting so I swung by McDonald's.

"Let me get a Number 1."

Then I looked at Wendy, "Get me a Number 4."

I continued my order, "And let me have a Number 4 wit a Sprite and Orange." I pulled up to tha first window and it was a bad chick in tha window.

"12.97," she said. I passed her a dub then pulled up to tha next window.

As tha lady was passing me my food tha other chick said, "You didn't get ya change."

"Nah, that's you ma."

"Well thank you, take my number," she said.

"I would but I got a girl."

"Damn, I respect that, it ain't too many around like you."

"What's like me?" I asked.

"A faithful man."

"I heard that."

"Well, take my number anyway so whenever you're free get at me and by free, I mean no significant other."

"A'ight," I said pulling my phone out, "what is it?" After she gave it to me I pulled off.

"Naz you a'ight wit me," I turned my head to look at her, "you kept it real wit homegirl and she still hit you wit tha number."

"Damn!"

"What?"

"I didn't even get her name."

"Well, call and ask." I pulled my phone back out and touched send. After 3 rings she picked up.

"Who dis?"

"Damn, that's how you answer tha phone?"

"Who dis?"

"Stop giving ya number out and you would know."

"Stop playing, who dis?"

"It's Naz."

"Who?"

"Tha boy you just gave ya number to."

"Oh, what you wanted to make sure I gave you tha right number?"

"Actually Nah, I neva got ya name."

"Heaven."

"It fits you."

"Thank you for tha compliment."

"Well, let me let you get back to work and ya money."

"Oh you got jokes; nah cause, I was gon' let you know this is my second job on my days off when I'm not at tha law firm."

"Oh excuse me, but you seem like good peeps."

"I am."

"Well, anytime you want to bust it up or just need an ear to listen, hit me up."

"You got my number now too." She said a'ight then hung up.

"Boy you sum thing else; look at all these people out here waiting on you."

"Damn, I need to call Doe."

"Why you empty?"

"Nah, but I don't got a lot left."

"Naz one thing you need to remember, neva run out. Alwayz keep work, so if you buying ounces when you get to one, re-up."

Before I got out I called Doe; he said he would be thru in 20 minutes. By tha time I had finished Doe was pulling up. I hopped in tha car.

"Yo, you ready for sum real work?" he asked.

"Listen Doe, I'm bout my paper. I'm ready for what ever."

I passed him his money and he passed me tha zip lock bag. As I was getting out he said 7,200. I walked over to Wendy's when I got to tha door she pulled it open. I was surprised at how nice it was.

"Damn Wendy, you got a nice spot."

"I didn't alwayz get high. Truth be told, I only started gettin' on when my mom passed away 18 months ago. That's what made me start. My mom was like my sister/best friend." I could tell that was an emotional topic so I switched tha topic.

"Is it cool for me to chef up?"

"Boy go ahead."

I decided to stay on tha block, I'll just hold that work in here and play it at night. I weighed it out; it was only 3 grams off but I would let him know so he wouldn't try it again.

CHAPTER 5

My Boo

I couldn't believe it Naz was really trying to help Wendy get herself together. He wasn't tha average hustler because anybody else would neva do what he's doing. Including paying her high ass electric bill even if it is of benefit to him. He could just hustle out of there during tha day then relocate outside when it gets dark. Even though I really don't want him in tha game I know he is goin' to blow up. Hell, he has only been in tha game for 4 days and he already has 17 stacks. I guess I would too if I hugged tha block from sunup to sundown. Shit, tha only time I have seen him is when he's dropping me off or picking me up. I know that once he gets himself fully established that will change.

"Ashanti, Ashanti!"

"Oh, I'm sorry Ms. Walker I was sum where else."

"I can see that; would you like to go to lunch wit me today?"

"Sure, cause I am gettin' hungry."

"Alright, I'mma run to tha ladies room then I'll be ready."

"Ok, let me do tha same."

I got up from my desk and went to use tha bathroom. When I was done, I grabbed my jacket, closed my office door, and we went to lunch. By tha time we were done lunch Ms. Walker told me not to call her that, she wanted me to call her Nancy. She told me that we had been co-workers to long for me to be calling her that. Even though I was tha supervisor, she was tha H.B.I.C. (Head Bitch in Charge).

We walked into tha bank and put our coats on tha coat rack. A man walked in with a vase filled wit a bunch of beautiful white roses. Nancy assumed they were for her because her fiancé is alwayz doin' sum thing nice for her.

"I'll take those," she said as everyone in tha bank looked on in awe.

"Oh, are you...," he looked at tha card, "Ms. Ashanti Tate?"

"No, but she is," pointing to me.

He walked over then handed me tha vase. I was speechless, no one had ever done anything like this for me before.

"Well, sum one loves you. Are you goin' to read tha card? When I didn't answer she took tha card out and read it to me.

I hope you know that sum days will be better than others so I hope today is one. Know that I love you. Naz

I tried to hold back my tears but they were already flowing.

"Here take these, I was tha same way when I got my first flowers too so I know exactly how happy you feel."

I took tha card then walked into my office shutting tha door behind me. I couldn't believe it, Naz went thru all this trouble for me, just as I was about to pick up my phone and call my phone rang.

"Hello. First USA this is Ms. Tate may I help you." When I finished my call I looked at tha clock then decided to wait and see him.

When I got off, for tha rest of tha day I didn't get any work done due to tha fact that I couldn't get my baby off my mind. Tonight he would have to put hustling on hold.

CHAPTER 6

Ery Body Down!

(BOOM!) was tha sound tha door made when I kicked it off tha hinges.

"Ery body down on tha Fucken Ground!" One of tha boys tried to make a move. BONG, BONG, two shots hit him in tha chest causing him to drop instantly.

"Now unless you all want to end up like ya mans, I suggest you do as ya told!" I bent down and pulled one of tha broads up by her hair.

"AAAH!" she screamed while I had a handful of hair wrapped around my hand.

"Bitch! You better shut up, it makes me no difference if you live or die," I said puttin' my pistol in her face, "now I'mma ask you a question and it would behoove you to answer correctly. Now where are tha drugs and money?!"

"I swear I don't!" (SMACK)

"Wrong answer! Next time it won't be my hand you'll get hit wit! Let's try it again! Where is Ery thing!"

Before she could say anything one of tha other niggaz said, "She really don't know nuffin."

"But I suppose you do!"

Sticky said, "Yeah."

"Well, talk then!"

"It's in tha basement inside tha furnace."

"Go check it out!"

After about 5 minutes he came back wit a black duffel bag. He nodded to me and wit out warning we both opened fire on tha two girls and two guys that were left. When it was all said and done there were no witnesses left to identify us. Just to make sure we tore tha house up and it's a good thing we did because we found another duffel bag in tha Attic. We left out tha back, hopped a few gates, and were back in our car in no time.

"Damn, I love my job."

Let them make it and we take it that was my motto. We had been sticking niggaz for as long as I could remember. Tha pay off was alwayz lovely; we didn't do it unless there was a nice payoff in it for us. Just that simple.

"Yo Cannon, what up wit ya peeps?"

"Who?"

"Ya peeps Doe."

"What you mean what up wit him?"

"Do he still want us to do that job for him or what?"

"I don't know but now that you mention it I'mma ask him later."

When we got ery thing together, we had ended up wit $40,000, 44 ounces of coke, 3 pounds of weed, and 5 ounces of heroin. That was a good take, we were Damn near millionaires behind tha robbery game. Even though I had all that money it was my job and tha only way I'm goin' to stop is if a Nigga or Bitch pop my top. I remember when we robbed this broad from Cambridge Maryland. I got word from a legit source that this babe was eatin' crazy down there. So, me being tha predictor that I am, I went down by myself and scooped her out for about a month to get her schedule down pack. I knew ery thing about her, I even knew how many times she went to tha bathroom every day. I couldn't believe how much bread she was gettin'. I hit Sticky wit all tha info I had on her.

Tha hit went good until that Bitch got cocky. We took her to all 3 of her houses. It was tha last house that she tried sum Dumb Shit. I had to give it to her, she was a soldier. She even gave me sum thing to remember her by; a nice hole in my side before Sticky rocked her to sleep like a baby.

"Aye Cannon, what up?"

"Yo, my peeps got sum thing sweet for us up Jersey."

"You know I'm down wit that."

"I'mma check it out then back wit you."

"Ok, that's what's up and I'mma do tha same wit Doe."

We gave each other dap and went on our way.

CHAPTER 7

Moving Up in tha Game

By tha time I'd finished chefing up tha work, I had 12 ounces. I started doin' tha math in my head since I was sum thing like a human calculator. If ery thing went right, I would have an even 28g's. I'mma deal wit Doe for another few months then branch off and do my own thing.

I hit tha block until it was time to pick up Ashanti. I could not believe how I had tha block jumpin' in 5 days. I had my own block and I wasn't goin' to let nobody take it from me. Doe didn't even have this block jumpin' like me; my block was doin' numbers. I walked back to Wendy's to put my work up and let her know that I will be right back after I picked Ashanti up from work.

I sat at tha table counting up my money, "WOOOOOOO!" I yelled.

Wendy came in running from tha back, "What's wrong?" I smiled and pointed to tha money on tha table.

"Naz I changed my mind about tha 30 days," but before I could say anything she said, "I just got off tha phone wit Henrietta Rehab, they told me that I can come in Monday which is in 5 days. So, I'mma go for tha 120-day program. I'm tryin' to get sum of that," she said pointing to tha same pile of money that I had a few minutes ago.

I put tha money in a bag and stood up.

"Naz, I don't think you should be walking wit all that money and I also don't think that you should have it in here nor ya house. You need to get ya self a safety deposit box. Naz you been out here for 5 days and you got this block jumpin. Doe wasn't even doin' it like this and you need to be on tha watch for Cannon and Sticky."

"Who dat?"

"Cannon is Doe's cousin, Sticky's his right-hand man but they are tha ones that let you eat then come get it."

"Oh I see."

"Yeah, and tha way you got this block it won't be long before they come."

"Well, if they do they'll be robbing Doe."

"Between me and you, he's tha one who sends them."

"Well, he won't get paid. Wendy one thing for sure two things for certain, I ain't no punk. Ain't no and I mean no body taking Shit from me and gon' to live to tell about it. I put that on my dead momma."

I looked him in tha eyes and beneath those brown peaceful eyes I could see a true murder.

"Wendy, I'm tha nicest nigga you'll ever meet but I will get down for mines and my family. And I consider you family. By tha time you come back home I'mma have Philly in a choke hold."

"I just want you to be safe while I'm gon'. Oh, before I forget," she handed me a key.

"Would you be a'ight if I put an alarm on tha house, as well as a few cameras?"

"Now why would I be mad about sum thing that's gonna benefit tha both of us?"

I looked at my watch, "Shit!"

"What's wrong?"

"I got to get moving' if I'm late I'll neva hear tha end of it."

"Well, you might get away wit it considering you sent her those lovely roses earlier."

"You right but I don't want to find out." I walked out and to our house where I put tha money up.

As soon as I pulled up, she was coming outside wit her boss.

"Hello Nazir," Ms. Walker said, "love tha flowers."

"Thank you," I replied. Ashanti got in.

"Hey Baby Girl, how was ya day?"

"Thanks to you, I didn't get any work done."

"What did I have to do wit you not gettin' no work done?"

"Because, once I got those beautiful roses I couldn't stop think'n about you. I hope you don't plan on being out tonight."

"She must have read my mind cause I'd had planned on being in tha house early. I need to recruit me a squad of young boys so I won't have to be out all night. Hopefully, within tha next 3 weeks I'll have a strong team."

"Naz, Naz..."

"Yeah."

"Where you at?"

"I was just think'n bout sum shit."

"Baby, I need you to open a safety deposit box for me."

"A'ight, when?"

"Right now."

"I was already in route to tha train station."

"How much money can you put in one of those things?"

"A lot."

"Well, what's a lot?"

"1, 2, 3 million."

"Damn, I know you ain't make that much in 5 days."

"Nah, but I will."

"I just don't want to have no money in tha house or Wendy's."

"You must have heard about Cannon and Sticky."

"Yeah, Wendy put me down."

"But like I told her, ain't nobody gon' take Shit from me or hurt anybody I love."

"Well, you just need to be careful and you need a squad." I pulled up to tha train station.

"You go ahead, I'mma wait here," I handed her tha money, "get an extra key."

While I was sittin' there sum dude trying to park hit tha back of my car. I started to get out but they didn't hit it that hard but when they did it again I hopped out.

"Yo! What tha Fuck! You can't drive! You hit my Shit twice!!"

"Damn, my fault."

When tha nigga got out tha car I was like, "Oh Shit! What up My Nigga, I been tryin' to find ya Punk Ass. I thought you forgot about a nigga, tha letters just stopped."

"Hell Nah, I was in tha joint, they tried to charge me wit this murder. I sat for 2 ½ years waiting to go to trial. It wasn't bout nuffin, as you see I beat it. So what's up wit you?"

"Hey Man, you know what it is."

"Oh, so you hustling?"

"Yeah."

"What ya numbers like?"

"I ain't gon' front, right now I'm gettin' fronted 9 ounces."

"That's it?"

"I just started 5 days ago."

"Well that's good."

"Give me 3 weeks, right now I got this block jumpin. I can't front, my block doin' major numbers." Ashanti came out.

"I see you locked in wit Shorty." I turned around and Ashanti was getting in tha car.

"Let me hit you wit my number so we can bust it up." I gave P.R. my number and took his.

"Yeah, we got to get up. I know sum folk that got that Shit for tha low but you got to have ya loot right; they only deal wit birds."

"How much they go for?"

"24 stacks, but I can get 'em for 18 to 20 stacks."

"Like I said, I'll be ready in 3 weeks tops." Ashanti honked tha horn.

"Hold up Babe! So what you doin'?" He pulled up his shirt exposing his Glock, "you a hit man for hire?"

"Nah, I stick niggaz that owe my folks money and don't want to pay."

"Let me get her home. What you doin' tomorrow?"

"Nuffin."

"Give me a call."

We gave each other a pound and hug. As soon as I got in tha car she wanted to know who was that.

"That's my man P.R., we was bidding together," she passed me both keys, I handed her one back, "that's yours."

That night we made love as if it were tha first time. Tha next few days flew by, before I knew it I was driving Wendy to Henrietta Rehab. I was happy for her, plus I knew once she got herself together she would have a spot on my team.

"I know I already said it a thousand times but thank you Naz for helping me."

"It ain't about nuffin; I want to see you on top."

Wendy wasn't no ugly woman by far, so I know wit tha help of rehab she would get her weight back in no time. We talked for a few more minutes then I walked her inside.

"May I help you?" tha receptionist asked wit a smile.

"Yes, my aunt is scheduled to check in today."

I said her name, she replied looking down at her clip board. Wendy gave her name.

"Ok Ms. Curtis, I need you to fill tha first 2 pages out."

She sat down and did just that. She returned handing tha woman tha papers she filled out. After 15 or 20 minutes, sum one came from tha back and called her name.

"Follow me."

"Ok." I stood up then let her know she was on her own from here.

I gave her a hug, "If you need anything just call." I watched as she walked to tha back.

"You really love ya aunt, huh? I said, you really love ya aunt."

"Why you say that?"

"I can just tell." I smiled.

"Excuse me, before I leave, are they allowed to have visitors?"

"Yes, twice a month and every other weekend."

"Ok thank you." I turned to leave.

"So I guess I can expect to see you again," she said in a seductive tone.

I just gave her tha thumbs up and kept it moving. She wasn't bad looking for an old mom. I later found out she was 34 and stacked like tha International House of Pancakes (IHOP). Not to mention, she had a crush on me.

It had been two months since Wendy had been in rehab. I made sure I went to see her every visiting day which she more than appreciated. It didn't take her long at all to gain her weight back; I couldn't front she was fat to death. I knew it all along, I could tell she had it goin' on before she started gettin' high. Even though Doe and a few other people had told me also.

Today, I was bringing her a new pair of white on white Air Ones and a few sweat suits. I checked in wit Lez.

"Naz, when you gon' stop playing and get wit me?"

"Lez you know I got a girl."

"Yeah, that's what you keep screaming and like I keep telling you I'm 34, I don't do that young girl shit. You don't have to be scared, I'm not tryin' to become as you young people say wifey." All I could do was smile.

"Well, let me think about it," I said while goin' to tha visiting room. Wendy was already there.

"Hey Nephew." She stood to give me a hug then we sit down.

"I brought you a few things."

"Boy, I got too much as it is. They said I have to send sum stuff home."

I had been bringing her clothes, sneaks, and shoes every visit. I just wanted to make sure she stayed sharp.

"So what's goin' on wit you?" she asked.

"Well, you know I got tha block doin' stupid numbers wit tha coke and weed."

"Oh, so you pumpin' weed now too?"

"Yeah."

"Did you get ya self sum help?"

"Yeah, I got a real strong team."

"Well, who are they? I might be able to give you sum insight."

"Well, I got my peeps P.R. that I was doin' time wit and tha young boy Tico."

"Is he from Burks?"

"Yeah, why?"

"Nuffin, he good peeps and he a gun on tha low."

"Tha boy Dirk from Allegheny?"

"I know him, he's a stand-up dude."

"Chopz from Fairfield?"

"Know him too Naz. You know why they call him Chopz?"

"Unh, Unh."

"He play wit dem choppers." I knew, I just wanted to see if she knew.

"Esco, Louis's son."

"I don't know who his mom is."

"I know he bout dis paper and my cuzin Gunz."

"He ya real cuzin?"

"Yeah, my mom and his mom are sisters."

"I could tell you stories about him."

"Well, like I told you, by tha time you come home I'll have Philly in a choke hold."

"So, how are you pumpin' ery thing?"

"Well, I'm still breaking off wit tha coke. I'm think'n bout also selling halfs and bundles cause a lot of hustlers be tryin' to get double ups or buy weight."

"Oh, so you got weight?"

"Nah, Doe only hits me wit 9."

"Well, that's only because he don't want you to blow pass him."

"I was think'n tha same thing. I be calling this dude like 2 or 3 times a day for 9."

"Yeah? Shit Nephew, it sure didn't take you long at all. So you got ya own block and you doin' way more numbers than when I was home. If you ask me, I think it's time you got a new plug. Sum body that can handle ya order."

"Funny you said that, my peeps is introducing me to his folks today."

"Good, just watch out for Doe; he not gon' like that."

"Well, that's too bad. I don't owe him or anybody else Shit!"

"So is tha weed good?"

"Yeah, I got that Kush jumpin' wit da 20s and 50s and they loving it. Let's just say that 8th and Indiana is where it's at from sunup to sundown."

"What about tha neighbors?"

"Oh they cool, you know they all old so I went to all of them and let them know what was goin' on. At first, they wasn't wit all tha cars and traffic on tha block but at tha end of tha day money talks. So not only is it gon' cost me 20 stacks a month but I get to spread tha work out in their houses."

"Did you say 20 stacks a month?"

"Yeah, I told them I would hit them wit a stack apiece."

"Oh you got it all figured out."

"Listen, right now I do no less than $21,600 a day. Well no, I'm lying, $43,200 a day. So if I do that a day then I'mma see $1,189,600 after I hit them off a month. As far as tha green, I see $50,000 a day, $1,400,000 a month." I could tell she was doin' tha math in her head.

"Shit!" she yelled causing all tha other visitors to look, "oh I'm sorry Naz, you bringing in $2,589,600 a month."

"Well, probably about 2 mill after they get their $98,266."

"Hold on, Hold on, so you mean to tell me that they get close to 100 grand a month?"

"Yeah, but once I get this new plug we'll all see a lot more."

"And you been doin' this for tha last 2 months?"

"Nah, just this month."

"You got that block doin' stupid numbers. I hope you didn't forget what I said about Cannon and Sticky?"

"Nah, I didn't but I'm prepared for that. I got 4 niggaz on tha rooftops Capes, Man-Man, Rell, and Az in case anybody try to come in wit that stupid Shit. So they got 11 guns at least to worry about."

"Sounds to me, you got it all under control. When do you plan on tellin' Doe?"

"Once I make sure this plug is official."

"I know, compared to what Freeway, Ricky Ross, and Rayful Edmonds were making it's peanuts. Boy you did that in 2 ½ months."

"Yeah, cause Ricky Ross was doin' a mill a day. On a good day that's serious money."

"Yeah, but where they at now? You don't want to blow too fast and have dem boys on ya heels." After my visit, I walked pass Lez.

"Sum body's smilin', must have been a nice visit. Oh, so you don't want ya license?" she asked now standing showing her fat ass in those Baby Phat jeans. I couldn't help but stare which she noticed.

"See sum thing you like or want?" All I could do was smile.

I grabbed my license off tha desk and shot for tha door.

"Umm, Umm, Umm, I'm gon' get that young boy. Just tha sight of him makes my panties moist."

"I needed to call P.R. to check tha status of our supply and meeting."

"Well, we runnin' low so you might want to call ya man so he can hit you. As for tha meeting, we have 45 minutes."

"Cool, I'm on my way."

Doe let his phone ring 6 times before he finally picked up.

"Yo."

"Damn, what up Doe you ready?"

"Nah, I'm taking care of biz-ness right now; hit me later."

"I need you now."

"Nigga did you just hear what I said!" Then he hung up.

That was tha last straw even if P.R. peeps wasn't talkin' right, Doe was officially cut off. By tha time I got there, damn near all tha work was done.

"Let's roll P.R."

"We still got 30 minutes."

"Nigga come on! Alwayz be early, neva late."

We pulled up to tha restaurant, got out and walked in.

"Damn!"

"What's tha matter?"

"My cuzin Juan is already here."

He went first to tha back table where tha waitress was putting sum thing on her tablet, smacked her on tha butt then walked to where Juan was seated wit another gentleman.

"Juan, Uncle Migel."

"Hello P.R.," they both said giving him hugs.

"This is my boy Naz I told you about."

"Nice to finally meet you," Juan said wit his hand extended.

"Likewise," I said shaking his hand as well as Miguel's.

"Please have a seat." Tha waitress that P.R. had smacked came over.

"Can I get you two anything?" she asked.

"Water," I said.

"And you?"

"Yeah, but what I want might get you fired," P.R. told her.

"Well, I get off at 10 and you know where I live."

"Yup, sure do." She left.

"You still think you a playa I see," his uncle replied.

"It runs in my blood." They all laughed.

"So let's get down to biz-ness. What are you tryin' to cop?"

"Well, it all depends on tha numbers."

"What are you paying now?"

"To be honest wit you, I been in da game 2 ½ months," they both gave me that look that said so what do you want wit us, "tha dude I was dealing wit would only front me 9 ounces. Now let me clear one thing up, I wanted more but all he would front me is 9, so I would re-up 2 or 3 times a day."

"If you don't mind me saying and asking, it seems like this guy didn't want you to get ahead of him since you were dumping damn near 27 ounces a day."

"Not to sound rude, but it is what it is."

"So who is this guy?"

"Sum nigga name Doe."

"Doe from 8th and Indiana?"

"Yeah, you know him?"

"I now know why he was only giving you 9 ounces. He's only buying a half a brick and he's gettin' it from us. What was he charging you?"

"7,200."

"We were giving it to him for 4,000."

"Damn, well I ain't mad, he had to make his."

"I was wondering who he was dealing wit cause he has been calling us 2, 3, and 4 times a day."

"So how much you gon' charge me a brick?"

"15 stacks."

"Well, let me get 7 to start wit."

After we discussed how we would conduct biz-ness and exchanged numbers I knew it was about to be on.

CHAPTER 8

Just Friends

"Hello."

"Hey Stranger."

"Who this?"

"Damn, you don't have me programmed in no more?"

"Of course I do, Heaven."

"I was gonna say, damn ya peeps be checking ya phone like that, that you had to erase me out?"

"Nah, I was just joking. How I'm not goin' to know ya voice and we been cool for a few months."

"Now I heard that you got a lot of shit wit you Naz."

"Why you say that?"

"Cause you do."

"Where you work at? Oh, flippin' burgers."

"No, at tha law firm."

"Do y'all have any good lawyers?"

"They all good."

"Well, which one would you recommend?"

"Depends on what you want tha lawyer for first."

"I want a all-purpose lawyer."

"Smart Ass."

"I wasn't being smart."

"I know you didn't pick up no case."

"Nah, I just want to have one on deck for me and my squad."

"I feel you. Well, I would go wit Troy Banks, he's one of tha best in

Philly."

"Is he free today?"

"Hold on, let me check his schedule. Yup, but it's for 1:30 pm." I looked at my watch, it was 10 o'clock.

"Where are you located?" She hit me wit tha address.

"I'll see you when I get there." Within 15 minutes I was there.

As soon as I got out tha meter maid was walking up. I put 3 quarters in and went about my biz-ness. When I got to tha desk, Heaven was on tha phone jotting sum thing down.

When she looked up and saw me she said, "Girl, let me hit you back."

"Well, do you do anything besides talk on tha phone?"

"Yeah, but I'm on my lunch break."

"Oh, I see."

"Well, let me let Troy know that you're here," she picked up tha phone, pushed a few buttons then said, "Troy your 1:30 pm is here... Ok, I will. Go ahead back."

"Where is back?" I asked.

"Oh, I sorry, follow me."

"I would gladly do that watching her butt tha whole time. That might be why I neva saw her stop."

"Oh Shit, my fault."

"If you wasn't watchin' my ass then this wouldn't have happened," she opened tha door, after knocking, "Troy this is your 1:30."

"Thank you Heaven." She walked back out.

"Have a seat," he said pointing to one of his chairs, "so what can I do for you?"

"I just want to retain you in case I or any of my peoples need you."

"Oh I see, you're in the drug business."

"I'm not saying that."

"Listen, let's get one thing straight, if I am to become your lawyer you have to keep it 100 with me."

I went into my front two pockets and pulled out 5 stacks, 50 hundred-dollar bills.

"Is this enough to retain you?" I asked putting tha money on his desk in front of him.

After he counted it he wrote me a receipt.

"I'll be hittin' you once a month." Which he had no problem wit.

We talked for another hour then I stood to leave. After shaking his hand I grabbed 10 business cards then headed out. On my way I stopped to talk to Heaven.

"So let me say thank you by taking you to dinner tonight."

"You gon' get ya self in trouble."

"How? We just friends."

"Well, if that's how you want to play it, I'm fine wit that."

"What do you mean if that's how I want to play it? We are just friends unless you know sum thing I don't."

"Naz it ain't no secret that I'm feelin' you and you might be okay wit that but I'm starting to catch sum feelings for you. Now don't get it mistaken, I don't love you, I just like you a lot."

"So are you saying that you don't want to go to dinner?"

"No, I'm not saying that at all. I just wanted to let you know where I was at."

"I respect you keepin' it real."

"I also don't want to disrespect your girl in no way and me being who I am I know that I don't usually fall for a man that's already taken. That's why I really don't understand; maybe it's because you were honest from tha jump which in my book is a big plus. I said all that to say, I would love to have dinner wit you."

"Do you have any special place that you like to eat at?"

She looked at me then asked, "Have you ever been to tha Hotel DuPont in Wilmington?"

"No."

"They got sum good food."

"Well, that's where we'll eat."

"Ok."

"I'll make reservations for 9 o'clock."

"A'ight."

"What's ya address so I can pick you up?"

"Here." She wrote it down on a piece of paper.

"I'll see you at 8."

As I was on my way out I turned around and blew her kiss which she grabbed out of tha air and put it on her cheek. I just smiled and kept moving.

Later that night, I swung by to pick her up. She let me know that we had to take her car because she wasn't goin' to let me drive her in Ashanti's car. I knew that I was goin' to buy me a squader this weekend. I parked and got inside her car which was nice. She had a 525I Wagon red wit peanut butter guts or dubs.

We got to Delaware in 20 minutes. We got out and tha valet parked our car. We enjoyed our dinner and conversation.

"If I didn't have a girl, I would definitely make you my girl."

"Stop, you got me blushing."

"Nah, I'm serious though."

I found out that she was tha same age as me and she was a spoiled brat who still lived at home wit her mom and dad. She didn't have to work but she didn't want to depend on her parents for everything. I told her about tha 7 years I spent in tha box and why I had to. I even told her about my mother dying; that was still a rough topic for me so I quickly changed it. All in all, we had a good topics that we busted it up about.

"So back to what you said earlier, would you really make ya girl if you wasn't wit ya girl?"

"Yeah."

"Well, here's sum thing for you to think about. I'm willing to play tha side jawn, mistress, or what ever you call it. But for sum odd reason I'm really feelin' you and you don't have to worry about me running my mouth."

"Heaven you deserve to be sum body's wifey not mistress."

"I know but I don't know... just forget it."

We ate tha rest of our meal in silence. I thought about what she said. I loved Ashanti and I was neva gon' leave her. Now on tha other hand, Heaven is also a bad chick that I was feelin' as well. I don't know, I'll think of sum thing.

"Damn," I thought to myself, *"did I just play myself by saying that. I don't want him to think of me as a smut for saying that. I feel so dumb right now."*

When tha waiter came wit tha bill we paid it, tipped him, and then went back outside waiting on tha valet to bring tha car back around. When we got in she put a CD on and turned it up.

All you heard was, *"Heard about my past. Things I used to do. The games I used to play, the girls that didn't last. I know what's on your mind, think I'm doing wrong. Can I say what is real? You are the only one. When I'm not around, do you think of me? Or what the jealous ones are claiming me to be. You should know by now, that it's gonna take a lot of trust from you for us to make it through."*

This was my song so I was singing it word for word. I thought I sounded better than Jon B. When it went off she turned it down.

"Where did you learn to sing like that?"

"I was born wit this voice," I told her.

"Wow, you got a gift."

"Thank you," I said modestly.

When we pulled up at her crib she wasted no time jumping out heading to tha house.

"Hold up for a sec Heaven." She turned around and I walked up to her.

"Look, I thought about what you said at dinner and I'm willing to try it."

"Naz we talked about so much, I don't know what you are talkin' about." I lied, I just wanted him to say it.

"When you said you would be wifey #2."

"Oh? I said don't worry about it." I knew she was trying to play hard-to-get so I decided to play wit her.

"Well is it cool if I call you tomorrow?"

"That's up to you," she said walking up tha steps to her house.

I didn't say anything else, I just got in my car and pulled off.

"Damn, what was I thinking about. I hope me tryin' to play hard doesn't come back to bite me in tha ass. I'll just have to wait and see. I'm not goin' to call him, he's gon' have to call to hit me up. That will let me know if he's really serious or not."

CHAPTER 9

Jealousy

It had been 2 ½ months since I've heard from Naz. I know he has another plug; I just don't know who yet. I can't believe that in 4 months he has a whole block. Let me find out he's doin' numbers.

While I was at tha light a '74 Olds 98 sittin' on 26-inch Forgiato's. What really got my attention was tha cranberry paint wit tha white guts piped out in cranberry and tha driver none other than Naz himself. I blew my horn to get his attention. When he looked over I put my hands in tha air to say what's up. He motioned for me to pull over.

As soon as tha light changed, I pulled up behind him. I thought he was about to pull over but he kept going. I assumed that since we were by tha hood that's where he was headed. And sure enough, I pulled into a spot down tha block while he parked in front of tha fiend Wendy's house. I haven't seen her around, they said that Naz put her in a rehab. If he did that he must be knocking her back out to do that. I walked up to where he was at.

"I was tryin' to get at you but you neva hit me back."

"Nah, I dropped that Shit in da toilet and Fucked it up. I couldn't get no calls or retrieve none of my numbers so I just got another one."

"I been lookin' for you, you ain't been around."

"Yeah, I had to leave town on sum family shit."

"Right, I feel you on that," *let me pick his brain to see what tha deal is wit him and Wendy*, "so where's Wendy at? She still holding you down?"

"Yeah, she still playin' her part. She out of town right now."

"Oh, she went to visit her peeps, huh?"

"Why is this nigga so worried about Wendy?"

"So I guess you found another plug."

"Yeah, but I do appreciate you helping me get to tha top."

"I see you got this block doin' major numbers, I only been standing here for 20 minutes and it's nonstop money. I should have done this."

"I wanted to say, since you know who gave you ya start, let me get a piece of this block, but I held back because da boy Esco came up."

"What up Doe?"

"What up Young'n, I see you got ya weight up," I said looking at his 8th Chain.

"Yeah, I'm a'ight, you might want to get at me now," he said.

I started laughing, "Nah Young'n, you got a ways to go to get to my level."

"Damn this cat be frontin'. I wanted to say, nigga we got tha same connect. You only gettin' a half bird but I didn't want to rain on his parade. Damn, I can't believe Esco tried to play me like that. I'mma get 'em back."

"Aye Naz, you need to call ya mans, we low."

I was only grabbing 15 bricks but I was also thinking bout messing wit those E-pills. I told them to spread tha word to see how many people would actually buy 'em before I spent my money on them.

"Oh yeah, I think you need to put those E-pills in effect cause they been coming all day for them." Just then a broad walked up.

"Hey Esco, let me get 2 50's of Kush, 2 bundles and 10 E-pills."

"We ain't got no E's yet but I got you on tha rest."

I let her know we would definitely have tha E's on deck by tonight or tomorrow at tha latest. I couldn't believe it, Naz had tha coke, E's, and weed jumpin'. I was about to say sum thing but he was already on his phone putting in his order. I was tryin' to hear exactly what he was gettin' but all he said was I need to holla at you, yeah tha same then he said let me get a thousand E-pills just to see how they move. If they go quick then I'll grab a lot.

Oh, he must really be eating; I'm goin' to put Cannon and Sticky on it. He probably got all tha doe and work in there. I know he does. When he got done I let him know that I was happy to see him doin' his thing. I asked him what his plug was letting tha birds go for. He said that he wasn't up to a bird.

"Nigga as much as this block is making. I know you coppin' heavy."

"Nah, it ain't that I can't, I just don't want to have a lot of work in Wendy's..."

"Bingo! I knew that's where tha work was at. Well, I'mma get at you," I said dappin' him then walking off. He don't know that he is now Prey!

CHAPTER 10

Home

That nigga Doe must think I'm slow, stupid or both; I read through all that bullshit. That's why I told him tha work was in Wendy's house just so he could tell Cannon and Sticky.

"Them niggaz gon' get top popped if they think they gon' get a dime."

"Nah, Nah, I'm gon' let them get 10 stacks."

"What nigga, you crazy. Yeah, you must've hit ya head or sum thing. Why we gon' just give away a free 10 stacks?"

"Cause if we do that, they gon' come back and when they do it's all over."

Gunz looked at me then said, "I got a better plan."

"What's that?"

"Why don't we just get rid of them two niggaz."

"I'm wit that."

"Me too, sounds like a winner."

"Damn, I neva thought about that cause if we off them on tha block it's gon' be too much heat and none of us need that." Tico had just finished putting tha last stack in tha envelope.

"You all know Wendy will be home next week."

"Oh word? Do you think she gon' be able to be around all this work and not be tempted to get high?"

"Yeah, I put her through a couple test and she didn't bite. So I do believe that it won't affect her. She is goin' to be hands on wit tha money."

"Oh, so she gon' be sum thing like an accountant."

"Yeah."

"A'ight, well if anybody doesn't have anything to say or add let's get this money. Esco make sure ery body gets there money."

"No doubt."

Tha next few days flew by, I was sittin' on tha stoop jus watching tha block when one of my phones went off. I started not to answer since I didn't recognize tha number but I did anyway.

"Hello."

"Well, Damn Stranger, I see how it really is." I knew it was Heaven but I played it off like I didn't know.

"Who is this?"

"Oh, so now you don't know my voice. But then again, it has been damn near 3 months since we last spoke." I smiled to myself.

"How you been Heaven?"

"Fine, tha question is how you been?"

"I can't complain, I did not think I would hear from you again."

"Well, if my memory serves me correctly, you were suppose to call me."

"Well, to be honest wit you, after you said to forget, I just figured that you meant us. So I said to myself, if you wanted to talk you would call me but you neva did."

"Oh I see, is that why you been sending ya friend Ricardo to bring Troy money."

"Yup, I didn't want to see you knowing I couldn't have you." I lied but it sounded good.

"Well, you should have called. Truth be told Naz, I can't get you off my mind that's why I had to call you. So if tha offer still stands, I'd like to take you up on it."

"You know my memory is fucked up and it has been a few months since we last talked."

"Look Naz, are we gon' cut tha bullshit or we gon' go through tha same thing again!"

"Damn," I thought to myself, *"I better stop before I let her get away again and for good this time."*

"Well since you put it like that, what do you say to a nice dinner tonight?"

"That's fine wit me."

In tha middle of our conversation my other phone went off; I knew it was Ashanti by tha ring tone.

"Hold up Heaven (CLICK)

"Hello. Yeah, when? I got a few things to do later. How bout if I swing by for lunch?"

"A'ight, give me 20 minutes." (CLICK) "Hello."

"Damn, you should have told me to call you back."

"That was my peeps. So I'll see you at 8, you can pick where you want to go."

"Ok." When I hung up, Doe was hittin' my phone. *"Now what does this nigga want."*

"Yo."

"Hey Lil Homie, what's tha deal?"

"What can I do for you?" I asked skipping through all tha Bullshit.

"So that's how you feel?"

"Nah, I'm just a little busy."

"I need to know if you got a half joint. If so, how much?" Juan had already told me that he raised tha price on him to 14.4.

So I said, "I got it but my numbers is high."

"How high?"

"15."

"Damn, you raping a nigga."

"Nah, that's sweet considering this recession that's goin' on."

"Yeah, I guess ya right. Let me get it."

"Meet me on 9th and Indy."

"A'ight."

"I'll be there in 30 minutes."

I called Capes and Rell to let them know where to be positioned in case this nigga was trying to line me up. I don't trust that nigga no more plus Da Game Ain't Fair.

Within 30 minutes Doe was pulling up. He motioned for me to get in, so I motioned for Capes and Rell to watch my back. I hopped in, slid him tha work and got tha money.

"Do I need to count this?"

"Now you being disrespectful."

"Ain't nuffin personal, it's just biz-ness." I got out, he rolled tha window down.

"Do I have to weigh this?"

"You can, I ain't gon' do to you like you use to do me." All he could do was smile then pull off.

I had Esco count tha money. When he called me back he said it was 1,500 short. *This dude got it twisted!* So called him, tha first time he didn't answer. So I waited then called back.

"Yo."

"I asked you did I need to count it?"

"What you talk'n bout Homie?"

"Tha count was off by 1,500."

"Nah, you might need to count it again."

"I did, 3 times."

"Or check tha nigga you got counting it."

"Look, I'm not gon' play this game wit you. Where you at so I can get my loot?"

"Man it was all there!"

"You right, my bag." I hung tha phone up.

Next time he calls I'mma take his paper and he ain't gettin' Shit. I put that on my mom.

"Damn, I knew Naz was a sucker but that was sweet. I even made him think it was all there."

That night I took Heaven to dinner. I couldn't believe how beautiful she looked wit her pink and cream Donna Karen dress. There was no way I was letting her go this time. By tha end of tha night, she was my thing on tha side.

Tha next morning, Ashanti went wit me to put money in my safe deposit box. Then we went to pick Wendy up from Henrietta's, this would be her first day home. I just hope I was right about her being able to be around all those drugs and not be tempted to get high. When we pulled up Wendy was already standing out front wit Lez.

"Hey Nephew, hey Ashanti," said Wendy.

Wendy was back, I had come to visit her one other time before wit Naz.

They had developed a close relationship. I think Naz had started lookin' at her like an aunt because she was alwayz trying to keep him on tha right track and was in his shit when he was in tha wrong.

"Hey Naz," tha other chick said.

"What up Lez."

"Shit, you make sure you take care of Wendy."

"Girl, I got ya number so I'll be in touch wit you. We gon' hang out I promise." Wendy gave her a hug then got in.

"Naz let me holla at you for a sec."

"What up Lez?" Ashanti was watching tha whole time.

"I know ya girl is staring so get my number from Wendy and get at me so I can give you sum of this good pussy."

I gave her five and said, "Sold." We both started laughing.

Wendy pulled down tha window, "Come on give her tha number so we can go!"

I looked at her like she was crazy until she said, "Cause I'mma make sure you got tha right plug.

"Well, hit me when you ready."

"You still didn't give me tha number." I hit her wit tha number and winked.

"I got it." Ashanti wasted no time.

"Why didn't you just get her number?"

"Cause when she wants to cop she can call me. I don't call nobody, especially to buy work."

"I feel you." We hit South Street did a little shopping then headed to tha block; when we pulled up tha block was jumpin' as usual.

"Well Damn, you wasn't playing when you said tha block be like a block party." I pulled into a spot behind my old school.

"Is that tha car you was telling me about?"

"Yeah, that's my baby."

"I like that, I can't wait to drive it."

"Nah, I don't let nobody drive that, nobody," I said looking at Ashanti.

"He don't even let you drive?" Wendy asked.

"Nope, that's why I got this 72 Impala so I wouldn't have to drive his."

"Oh, but he can drive yours. Well, yours is better if you ask me," I said winking at her.

It was nice, white on white wit pink piping and rims sittin' on duece fours. We all got out, everybody ran up to me giving me hugs and welcoming me home. I'd been gone for 4 months but it seems like a lot longer. A few neighbors even came out, they let me know that I looked good and they were proud of me. That was a low point in my life and I vowed I would neva ever go down that road again. I walked into my house and it felt good to be home. Once I put all my things away I opened my closet to get tha chest box that I kept in there out. I opened it then smiled even harder.

"I figured you would no longer need that stuff so I did tha honors."

Wendy looked at me, "Naz, I know I've thanked you a million times but I really want to thank you for caring enough to do what you've done for me. I owe you my life."

"No you don't, all you owe me is to just stay clean."

"Well, I want you to know that I don't want anything handed to me. I want to work for it like everybody else."

"Oh you are," he said wit a smile.

"Well, you just let me know what I have to do."

"Your job is an Accountant."

"What's that?"

"You just count tha money."

"That's it?"

"Yup, it's not as easy as it sounds, you'll see. We make a lot of money every day."

When we got back downstairs Ashanti was feeding one of tha money machines.

"I don't see how you could do this all day long."

"There's nuffin to do, tha machine is doin' it all for you." Naz looked at me then Ashanti.

"Babe, she think that's an easy job."

"I use to think that too when I first started working at tha bank, you'll find out. I'll give you three days.

And sure enough, 3 days later I was tired of seeing money let alone counting it. I needed to come up wit a better system since this was my primary job. Instead of counting it twice a day, I did it every time one of them brought in tha money. Because I noticed every 5 stacks they bring tha money in, so I started to count it like that.

It was tha beginning of May and it was hot already. Naz was having a block party for tha neighbors and kids to show his appreciation. I had only been home for 2 weeks and already made a nice piece of money just for counting money. Ever since I came up wit this new system my job has been a whole lot easier.

I walked outside to da smell of hamburgers, hot dogs, chicken, and steak. Tha DJ had tha music thumping and tha money was still flowing like water. I had to look twice to make sure my eyes weren't playing tricks on me.

"Now I know these niggaz ain't about to do no dumb shit."

"Nah, they probably tryin' to see how it's goin' down." I alerted Naz's phone.

"Yo holla at me Aunty."

"I want to let you know Cannon and Sticky are in tha area scooping shit out."

"Okay, good look." I watched as he walked over to them.

"Man, I ain't for no dumb shit, let me see what these dudes want."

When I got to where they were I said, "I see y'all came to get sum of this good food."

"Yeah, niggaz is starving round here." I read thru all tha bullshit.

"I heard you got this Shit on smash round here."

"Believe none of what you hear and half of what you see."

Sticky looked at me then said, "We want in."

All I could say was, "What did you say?"

He said, "We want in."

"We cool, we got enough people around here."

"So you saying we can't get no money around here?"

P.R. walked up, "He ain't tryin' say Shit, he said it right."

"That's what's up."

They didn't want no smoke wit P.R. They knew his work and had bear witness to one when he off Sticky cousin after he tried to rob him. They tried to get sum payback but that wasn't a bright idea. Sticky ended up shot

3 times and Cannon 2, courtesy of P.R.

"Well, thanks for tha food cause like I said niggaz is starving and we will eat."

"So what are you tryin' to say?" I asked now wit an attitude.

"Like ya man said we ain't tryin' to say nuffin, we said it."

"I heard that."

"All I got to say on that is tell ya family you love them." Then turned and walked off.

"Is you threatening us!" I didn't respond.

I hit up Esco, Gunz, and Chopz and told them what needed to be done. I sat back and watched as Naz talked to them. If they even acted like they wanted beef I was gon' cook that Shit and make sure it was well done. I would risk my life for Naz, that was on sum real shit.

Once tha food was gon' or should I say given away because there was so much left over. Naz had even took a lot of it to Center City to feed tha homeless. He's so generous, I know he's gonna last a long time in this game.

Tha next few days was pretty much tha same. Me and Lez had become close friends, we alwayz went to tha clubs together. She was constantly asking me about Naz so I decided to call him while she was standing right there. When he picked up I wasted no time. By tha end of our conversation, I had set it up so that he would be over her house later that night for dinner.

"Damn, Wendy you put me on tha spot."

"Oh well, I'm tired of you talk'n my head off about if you had tha chance or you only need one night. Well, tonight you get ya chance so you better make it count."

"I am, let me go to tha supermarket so I can grab sum steaks."

"I might as well go wit you; I need to grab a few items myself for tomorrow."

"What's goin' on tomorrow?"

"Nuffin, Sunday dinner."

After Wendy dropped me off, I went in and started dinner. I was almost done when my doorbell rang.

"Just a minute," I said while turning tha oven off. I opened tha door to find Naz standing there in his peach linen wit a single rose; I was stunned.

"Damn this young boy was sharp."

"Are you gonna invite me in?"

"Oh, I'm sorry, please come into mi casa."

I walked in her house and it was laid. I could tell she did not have any kids from tha cream and peach furniture.

"UMMM sum thing smells good."

"That would be dinner. What time do you have to be home?"

"Let me find out you got jokes."

"I wasn't being funny; I know you don't stay out all night." Just as I was about to say sum thing my phone went off.

"What up Baby Girl? Nah, I'm tied up right now, I'll hit you when I'm done. Probably in a few hours. Ok." I sat down to eat.

"Who told you this was one of my favorite meals, Wendy?"

"No, I just had a taste for steak, shrimp, baked potato, and salad but thanks for sharing that." After dinner I asked if it was a'ight if I watched tha game, Boston and Dallas was playing.

"Sure, I'mma take a shower and slip into sum thing more comfortable."

"You can come down nude as far as I am concerned."

While I was goin' upstairs I thought about what he said. That did not sound like a bad idea considering I'd planned on taking off what ever I put on anyway. I got out tha shower, dried off then lotioned up wit sum of that cucumber melon from Bath & Body Works then headed back downstairs.

I turned around when I heard Lez coming down tha steps. My mouth dropped open when I saw her.

"Damn, you tryin' to give me a heart attack?"

"You said come down wit nuffin on."

"I didn't actually think you would do it."

"Ain't nuffin shy bout me, plus, I'm not one of those in tha dark chicks."

"And what's that?"

"You know, one of those broads wit a fucked-up body that can't or won't take their clothes off unless tha lights off." I busted out laughing.

Even though she was right, her body was flawless. To say tha least, she was in damn good shape. She probably had a lot of young girls beat. To make a long story short, after a few hours we both were breathing hard. I couldn't front, she had put it on me in a serious way but I wouldn't let her know that. I could neva let her get one up on me. Now don't get me wrong, I love Ashanti to death and her sex is tha bomb but she didn't have nuffin on Lez.

"So was it worth it?" she asked.

"Yeah, you got that."

"So then you'll be back?" I know I put it on him and he did tha same to me."

"I'll definitely be back as long as you let me." We locked in.

"Well, that's all it is then."

I looked at my watch, it was 11:30. I picked up cell then dialed Heaven's number. She answered on tha first ring.

"Damn, you waiting on sum body to call?"

"Yeah, you."

"They said you would say that."

"Who's they?"

"Just a saying, don't wreck ya brain. Well, what you doin'?"

"On my way out."

"Where you headed cause I was think'n bout goin' to Palmers."

"Well, go ahead, holla at me when you leave."

"A'ight, I probably won't be there long."

"You might see me pop up."

"Yeah right, you don't do tha clubs."

"You neva know."

"Well, I'll see."

"You will, just don't get all drunk."

"I don't drink to get drunk."

"I hear you." I could hear a horn honking in tha background.

"That's my ride, if I don't see you then I'll call when I leave."

"A'ight."

As I was hanging up I was pulling up on tha block. P.R., Esco, and Dirk were all on tha stoop while everybody else was still scrambling.

"We were about to hit ya phone. You tryin' to go to Palmer's tonight and have a few drinks?"

"Yeah, let me run in here, take a shower, and change real quick."

"Nigga ya real quicks be like an hour."

"It ain't gon' take me long."

"You still talk'n, you could have been in tha shower," Dirk said.

"A'ight, I'll be right back." Wendy was at tha table putting money in a bag, on her phone.

"Come on it's ready."

I knew she was talking to Tico letting him know to come take tha money to one of tha stash houses on tha block. I shot up stairs and within 30 minutes I was back down, dressed in a pair of black Affliction jeans wit a tight black Affliction fitted shirt, black A.C.G. boots, and black Prada frames.

"Damn Sharpy, where you headed?"

"Nowhere special, just Palmers."

"So how was dinner?"

"Bangin' and desert even more bangin," I said wit a smile.

P.R. opened tha door.

"Damn Nigga come on!" I grabbed my 8th Chain off tha TV since they all had theirs on.

"I'll talk to you tomorrow cause I'll be in La La Land when you get back, so be safe."

"Alwayz," I said exposing my .40 under my shirt.

"You driving," P.R. said to me.

"We gon' follow y'all."

"That 4 deep Shit is corny unless you puttin' in work."

"I definitely feel you on that plus I wanna show off my whip," Esco said wit a smile.

He had an 84 box Crown Vic black on black on duece fours wit a marching band. When we pulled up in front of Palmers it was 12:30 in tha morning and it was still a long ass line. P.R. knew tha bouncer that was at tha door. I didn't know he had already called him to reserve two spots directly in front of tha club, I was parking there anyway. All eyes was on us when we pulled up. Both cars were bangin', sum thing different.

I scanned tha line in search of Heaven before I got out. When I finally did get out, P.R., Esco, and Dirk were making their way to "as they call it" cut tha line. I followed suit hitting my alarm. I could hear bitchez whispering saying who them dudes. I saw one broad who alwayz comes thru for weed & E's.

Then she said, "That's Naz and them from 8th & Indy."

"Oh that's them?" tha other one shot back.

"Yeah."

"They sum fine ass niggaz. We'll see 'em inside that's if we ever get in."

Once we were in I went straight to tha bar to order me Bombay wit pineapple, they all wanted Remy straight. We all had about 300 on us. I told them to neva come to tha club wit more than that because sum niggaz come to tha club just to scope out their next pray. I was hesitant on wearing my chain because it's sure to draw attention. I had neva been to Palmers. Shit, I've neva been to any club for that matter. We went upstairs to tha second floor to be met by tha sounds of Jim Jones *"Byrd Gang"* tha broads were goin' crazy. After that song went off, we went upstairs to tha 3rd floor. As soon as I came thru tha door, Heaven's girl spotted me and I acted like I didn't see her. I went to tha bar and ordered another round for all of us then headed to tha dance floor.

"Let's take sum flicks."

"Nah, y'all go head, I don't do tha picture thing."

"Why not Man?"

"If tha Feds ever get on you they can find you wit pictures they might have a name wit no face. But pictures give them a face."

"Damn, I neva thought about that."

"Nigga, cause you was neva seeing this much cake."

"Yeah, you right about that."

"Sum body need to pay for tha next round," I said holding up my almost empty cup.

Dirk said, "I got it." We went back to tha bar.

"Aye Naz, ain't that ya shorty by tha DJ Booth?" I didn't turn around to look.

"Yeah, she in here. I saw her girl when we first came up."

"Lisa, there dey go," one chick said.

We got our drinks then slid back to tha dance floor only to be followed by those same 3 chicks.

"Excuse me," tha one who was doin' all tha talking said.

"What up ma," Dirk responded.

"My girl wanted to know ya name."

"Well, tell ya girl to ask for herself."

"She a little shy."

"So am I." We all laughed.

"So that's funny?"

"Nah."

She came up to me and said, "I'm not shy, what's ya name?"

I smiled then said, "Taken."

"My name Nina."

We all busted out laughing even harder. She must didn't get it. I could see Heaven watching me. Nina finally caught on.

"Wow, that's how you gon' handle me?"

"Nah ma, my name is Naz but I am taken."

"Oh, she must be in here; I feel you. Well, I'll give my number to one of ya boys. You can get it from him."

"That's all it is then."

When *"She Got a Donk"* came on, Heaven made her way over to me, turned around, and just started shaking her fat ass all on me. I could feel my nature starting to rise so I turned her around.

"Damn, I thought you was a good girl."

"What gave you that impression?"

"You a mess."

"Unh, Unh that's you. All tha babes tryin' to get at you."

"Yeah right."

"I knew you was in here cause before y'all came up a group of girls came up talk'n bout y'all."

"How do you know they were talk'n bout us?"

"Well let's see, nobody else is wearing no icy 8th Chains and let me quote one of them. Tha one wit tha long braids looks like a Dominican, I would love to have him. Look at you blushing."

"I been called a lot of things but Dominican is a first, people say anything."

"I know but she was right."

Nina walked back by, "Hey Taken." I just smiled.

"What was that about?" Once I told her about tha conversation we had Heaven started blushing

"You only said that because you seen me over there."

"Nah, actually I didn't because if I did I would have come over there."

"Oh this my Shit!"

She turned around and started shaking that ass again. As tha DJ played Mike Jones *"Drop and Give Me 50"* she had my shit hard as a brick.

When tha song went off I said, "We ain't gon' keep doin' this."

"Doin' what?"

"Don't worry about it."

I knew exactly what he was talking about; Naz didn't know it but he was goin' to get sum of this tonight.

It was about 2 in tha morning and I was past ready to leave. P.R. let me know he was riding wit Heaven's peeps and he asked if I could give Heaven a ride home. I knew that meant he was gon' knock her down. I asked Heaven was she ready and she said yeah.

"I feel a little drunk."

"I thought you don't drink to get drunk."

"I don't but tonight I had too many." I let Esco and Dirk know I was about to pull out.

"Come on Heaven we out."

When we got outside it was j-peep. I hit tha alarm and automatic start. When I was about to get in Nina walked by and winked. I returned it wit a smile. Heaven was in tha car half sleep so she didn't see anything which was good. I put my Chris Brown CD in, turned it up and let tha sounds of *"Say Goodbye"* came blaring out causing Heaven to wake up and start singing. When I was about to pull up to her house I turned tha music down.

"Why you come here?"

"Don't you need ya over nite bag?"

"Ok, I just wanted to make sure you wasn't tryin' to drop me off."

"Just hurry up." She went in, 15 minutes later came back out.

"You lucky, I was about to pull off."

"Yeah right, you ain't gon' get in trouble for staying out all nite are you?"

"Nah, she'll think I'm on tha block or that I fell asleep in Wendy's house."

"She won't come looking for you?"

"Nah, we don't do that. We gon' to tha Sheraton, you need ya own shit cause we ain't gonna be doin' this often."

"Boy this couple of ones ain't gonna hurt you. Shit what?"

"I hope I got enough cash on me. If not, I can just use my credit card. But seriously, you neva thought about moving on ya own?"

"Yeah, that's why I'm saving all my money so I can have my first months' rent, security deposit, and enough to furnish my shit. I should have it by tha end of tha year."

"How about you find a place and I'll do tha rest. All you have to do is pay tha rent every month."

"I don't know, I want to do it on my own that's why I didn't get tha money from my parents."

"I respect that. Well, you do that and I'mma get Wendy to find me another spot so when you feel like staying wit me we can go there." That night I gave her tha biz-ness to make sure she wasn't goin' nowhere.

CHAPTER 11

Envy

"Aye, that nigga gettin' a lot of bread and he keeps in that junkies house."

"Are you sure?"

"Yeah, when they had that block party I saw them take tha money in there."

"Ok well, when y'all gon' get at 'em soon."

"We gotta do this Shit tha right way!"

"A'ight, just get at me before y'all do it."

"Aye you know what we can hit tha nigga for sum work. No Mask No Nuffin!"

"Fuck him and them niggaz he run wit because it's gonna be hard to get in tha crib cause it's alwayz sum body out there so we might have to line him up wit a few bricks. I'll give you tha doe to cop ½, you off that and give me my cash back. Then cop 2 but this time he ain't gettin' Shit!"

"A'ight I'm down wit that."

"I'll be ready in a few days, I gotta go down VA to do a hit. I'll hit ya phone when I touch down."

I couldn't believe this nigga Naz was eatin' like that in only 6 months. Then he gon' tell me I can't get a piece of tha action. If it was not for me, he'd still be flippin' burgers. Then he got tha audacity to charge me these High Ass numbers. I'mma give him one more chance to let me in. After about 6 rings he finally picked tha phone up.

"Damn Nigga, you wasn't goin' to answer."

"What's tha deal Doe?"

"I'mma need ½."

"I won't be ready until later or tomorrow. I have to finish what I got."

"Just hit me when you ready."

"Aye."

"Naz before I forget, let me buy in."

"What you talk'n bout Doe?"

"Let me buy in on that block."

"Nah, I can't do that. It's already too many of us now."

"Right, I hear you."

"But I'mma call you when I finish this shit up." (CLICK)

"This nigga got tha game all twisted. I'mma hit his ass every chance I get. I made that nigga. I'm tha man around here, alwayz have been alwayz will be. Matter fact, I'mma show him who run this shit!"

I went outside jumped in whip and made my way to tha block. When I pulled up there was this light skinned chick standing on tha corner, I got out.

"Hey, you holding?" she asked.

"Holding what?"

"You know, halfs and bundles." I didn't but I would sell her a double up.

"What you need?"

"3 bundles."

"How much you guys Shorty?"

"300."

"Hold up," I said sliding back in my car to get her 6 dimes. Once I had them counted out, I put them in one bag.

"This that drop, right?"

"Yeah."

"A'ight I'll be back." I was down on tha corner killin' 'em when Chopz walked up to me.

"Damn Doe, you down here doin ya thing, ain't you?"

"Aye Man, I'm just tryin' to do me."

"Not right here you ain't. You gotta take that Shit sum where else!"

"Y'all still gettin' y'all's."

"It don't matter, we built this Shit up. You had ya shot, you chose not to do nuffin wit it. Nah, actually you did, you put Naz on and he turned this block into a gold mine. So now you think you gonna reap sum of tha benefits?" As he was talk'n Naz pulled up.

"Aye."

"Yo, Naz come here for a sec. If he say it's cool, then do you. But if he say otherwise, you gots to roll."

"Yeah what ever, you gon' see." When Naz came over he spoke and so did I.

"What's up Chopz?"

"Ya man right here," he said pointing to me, "down here grinding. I let him know he had his chance to have this block. He chose to put you on. He just didn't know that you were goin' to blow this much so fast."

"What ever, I put him on cause I saw potential in him. Nigga you got me all Fucked up! I ain't no hater Homie!"

"Fuck all that you talk'n Doe. Naz is it cool for this nigga to get paper right here?"

"Yeah, he cool for today but after this, Doe you gonna have to set up shop elsewhere."

"This little bit of money I'm gettin' down this end ain't hurting ya pockets."

"That's not tha principle, if I let you do it then all kinds of niggaz gon' try. Then tha block gon' be hot from all types of bodies droppin' round here."

"I'm just tryin' to finish my work so I can get at you." I tried to throw that in to see if he would bite.

"I feel you but like I said you good today but after this ain't nuffin." Then he walked off.

"I got a lot of respect for you Old Head so I would hate to send you to tha boneyard," Chopz said then slid off also.

"What tha Hell was he talk'n bout sum boneyard?"

I would later find out thru Cannon that he was referring to da cemetery when he said boneyard. We just gon' have to do what we gon' do cause I'll be damn if I let all this money go by and not get none of it. I need to come up wit a plan they won't be able to run this Shit wit out Naz. I have to get him out of tha way permanently so I can take this Shit over. I know just who to call. I opened my phone, found tha number I was looking for then pressed send. Within seconds, it was ringing.

"Hello."

"What up Easy Hawk?"

"I can't call it. What's good wit you?"

"Shit, you still workin' for those people?"

"Yeah Man, they got me on this lifetime plan. Why, what up?"

"I need a serious favor."

"Nigga, last time you needed a favor it almost got me killed."

"Well, this all you to do is..." I put him down wit my plan.

"Damn, you a rotten nigga."

"Look who's talk'n, this shit don't come nowhere near close to what you do to niggaz."

All Easy could say was, "Yeah, I know and that shit be messing wit me. I lose sleep at times, it ain't easy being a Rat."

"You should have neva signed that contract wit tha Devil."

"Who you tellin', ery time I try to get out they keep threatening me wit all this jail time."

"Well, look at it like this Easy, at least nobody knows you're a Rat. Shit I only found out because I had one of tha Fed's on payroll. But that's jus between us."

"You don't have to worry about your secret gettin' out. So when do you want me to put it in motion?"

"I'll give you a call in a few days."

"A'ight, just hit me up. Oh yeah, I'mma need 5 stacks for this."

"Damn Easy Hawk, we suppose to be peeps."

"I know, that's why I'm only charging you 5g's."

"Well, it ain't bout nuffin, I got you."

A part of me so bad but Fuck that Naz had to go so that I could take my throne back and whoever didn't like it that was just too damn bad. I finished tha rest of my work then rolled out.

"Who are these people in this photo Agent Sharp?"

"The one in red is Fourty, the one in black is Stylz, the one in blue this Tex, and you already know that's Amir."

"I'm not 100% percent sure, but I think he gets his shipment on Wednesdays. I'm hoping to get some pictures of them with the work."

"How do you plan on doing that?"

"I don't know but I'll figure something out."

"Agent Sharp don't compromise yourself or your job."

"Chief trust me, there's nothing I want more than to see Amir behind bars rotting in jail for the rest of his life."

"So, do I but you need to be safe Agent Sharp."

"I have it all under control Chief."

"A'ight, if you need anything you be sure to let me know."

"Since you mentioned it, I could use a few of those micro cameras."

"Make me a list of everything you need, and I'll have it first thing in the morning."

"OK thank you Chief." As I left tha building I couldn't help but smile at the thought of bringing Amir down.

"Yo Buck ain't that homegirl coming out tha federal building?"

"Who?"

"Homegirl?"

"Nigga I don't know you talk'n bout."

"Neva mind, I'm probably tripping. Sasha told me to let you know she wants to holla at you."

"Oh, now she see a nigga gettin' at a dollar she wanna give a nigga sum rhythm."

"You know how they do."

"I sure do and I'm good, Fuck her!"

"That's what I would do."

"Nah, I'm not goin' to give her tha satisfaction. Speak of tha Devil," I said seeing Sasha as we pulled up to McDonald's on Broad.

"Hey Buck."

"What up Sash?"

"Hey Twist."

"Sash."

"Did you tell him?"

"Tell me what?" I asked acting like I didn't know what she talk'n about.

"I told Twist to tell you I wanted to holla."

"Listen Sash, you wasn't tryin' to get at me before I was gettin' this paper."

"I know and that's because you was buck wild."

"I still am."

"No you're not, you've calmed down a lot besides, I could care less about ya money."

"That's what ya mouth say."

"And its tha truth Sweety."

"It's only one way to find out," Twist said before either of us could say anything.

"Mind ya biz-ness."

"Now it's mind my biz-ness, you was not saying that when you wanted me to tell him you was tryin' to holla."

"Thank you but I got it from here."

"I'll order ya food while you talk to Sash."

"Just get me a Number 3 wit a Strawberry milkshake."

"So what's up Buck?"

"This paper, that's what's up."

"Nigga I'm talk'n bout wit me."

"I don't know, what's up wit you?"

"So, you do have a sense of humor."

"Sorry, but I wasn't being funny," I said in a serious tone.

"No need to get all serious I was only joking."

"Yeah, so was I."

"Are you goin' to take my number?"

"No, but you're more than welcome to have mine."

"Can you at least put it in my phone?"

"I can do that." Once I put my number in her I-phone she asked if she could take my picture.

"Fuck you tryin' to line me up?"

"Boy no, I just want to put it wit ya numbers, so it will show up whenever I call, or you decided to call me."

"In that case, go ahead." Twist came out while she was talk'n my picture.

"Fuck was that about?"

"Do you ever mind ya biz-ness Twist?"

"Not when it comes to my boy his biz-ness is my biz-ness."

"Not this time."

"He'll tell me."

Sash looked at me then said, "Damn that's how you get down?"

"Nah, he just messing wit you."

"A'ight I gotta go, I'll call you later."

"You do that." I watched as Sash walked away ass bouncing like crazy.

"UNH, UNH, UNH."

"What?"

"She fat to death."

"You ain't gotta tell me."

"I know you gonna hit that."

"Damn right and I'll tell you all about it."

"Damn, they alwayz puttin' all this mafuckin' salt on their fries."

"Take 'em back."

"I'm not goin' through all that."

"Then stop complaining, you alwayz do that."

"Did Jake pay you that doe yet?"

"Yeah, he hit me this mornin."

"I'm bout to holla at Fourty."

"I think we should just grab 25 from now on."

"We can do that since we dumpin' that every three weeks anyway."

"A'ight, let me make tha call."

"Buck, see if you can get us sum of that good green they got."

"To smoke?"

"Yeah and to put on tha block since people alwayz asking for it."

"Damn, I neva even thought about that."

"Nigga we might as well get all this money, ain't no need playing wit it."

"Fo' Sho."

"Well, I'll hit you on tha way back."

"You want me to send Shanky wit you?"

"Nah, I'm good I'mma take tha Honda."

"Oh yeah, I keep forgetting Fourty hooked us up wit those stash boxes."

"Dog, proof it don't get no better than that."

"Who you tellin'."

"Before you leave go holla at Mrs. Dee, she needed to see you."

"I was on my way to holla at her anyway."

"Nigga you hittin' that?"

"Shit, I wish I was, she fatter than a Mafucka."

"Mrs. Dee, Twist said you wanted to holla at me."

"Yeah I did."

"You did, or you do?"

"I do. I respect tha way you take care of ery body on tha block."

"It's tha least I can do, wit out y'all me and Twist wouldn't be able to do what we do."

"I'mma be up front, I could use sum extra money and I hear that you could use another place for ya stuff."

"Actually, I do."

"Well, I'll be willing to help you out if tha price is right."

"I'm willing to give you a stack a week."

"A stack?"

"You don't think that's enough?"

"Hell yeah, I'm just surprised you'd be willing to give that much up."

"Why not, you're doin' me a huge favor, so I have no problem showing how much I appreciate it."

"Say no more."

"I'm on my way to grab sum shit now so I'll be back in a minute."

"Here take this key and get a copy."

"I'll bring tha money back when I come back."

"What's up Nephew?"

"I need 25 and what's tha number on sum of that good green y'all got?"

"Personal or sell?"

"Both."

"850 a pound."

"Let me get 10 of 'em."

"A'ight, same place 30 minutes." When I pulled up Fourty was already there.

"How long you been here Unc?"

"I just pulled up right before you. Make sure you call ya mom she's worried about you."

"I actually sent her sum flowers and was taking her to dinner."

"That's good cause I told her I hit you wit a nice piece of money, so you wouldn't have to be in tha streetz."

"Good lookin' Unc."

"Buck, I don't like lying to ya mom so at sum point you gon' need to come clean wit her."

"I know but not right yet."

"A'ight but jus make sure you do it."

"Damn Unc, I know you not scared of big sis?"

"Nah, but we don't lie to each other either."

"I respect that and I'm sorry for putting you in this position."

"When I do tell her, I won't say you knew, she'll probably tell me to deal wit you anyway."

"You're probably right."

"Come on, you know my mom's."

"Yup, sure do and if she doesn't find out from you we'll both be in for it."

"Jus give me two weeks. Oh yeah Unc, I need one more of these cars for Tweet."

"No problem give me a few days. Buck, I didn't want for you. I do what I do so you would not have to."

"Unc I know but it was time for me to get my own bread and not depend on you."

"I understand and I am proud of you for being ya own man standing on ya own two feet."

"I just took ya advice about think'n before reacting."

"That explains why tha body count is down in tha city."

"Come on Unc, that wasn't all me."

"I know, you and Twist," he said wit a smile, "I'm just glad you're on my side."

"Well, you can rest assure I'm on this paper chase right now unless a Mafucka cross me."

"Hopefully, that will not happen, if it does call me I got people to handle that."

"No doubt, I'll hit you up Unc."

"Cool be safe."

CHAPTER 12

Happy Birthday

It was 3 days before Ashanti's birthday, I had Wendy find out what she wanted. She let me know that all she wanted was this tennis bracelet and matching necklace but I had done sum thing better. I went to Ralphy's on Market and had her a bracelet and necklace made wit her name both all diamonds. I had a nice piece of change for them but she was well worth it. Even though I did my dirt, I still loved her to death and I neva disrespected her. No matter what I'm doin, home alwayz comes first.

I wanted to throw her a party so I had Wendy and her best friend Shauna help me. We decided to have it at Club Fusions; Shauna knew sum body that could do tha flyers. We just had to give them out and hope that she wouldn't find out about it. Tha flyers were hot, they had a big picture of Ashanti's face on tha front wit Surprise Birthday Party and on tha back it had all tha information. You had to have that shit on, no sneaks or Timbs. It was goin' to be tha party to start tha summer. I had her thinking we were goin' to tha 40/40 for her birthday so we both got sum hot ass Gucci shit made. Ery thing would be Gucci from tha frames to tha shoes.

I couldn't wait to let Heaven know that she was more than welcome to come. I knew that she wasn't petty but what I didn't know was would she be able to handle me and Ashanti hugged up all night. She said she could but saying it and seeing it is totally different. Lez was even goin' to be there. Nina had also gave me a call to ask if she could come. I had knocked Nina off a few times as well. Tha question was would I be able to handle all of them at tha party at tha same time? Heaven was my number 2 wifey while Lez and Nina was my jump offs.

Shauna had hit my phone to see if P.R. was wit me. She alwayz did that when he either didn't answer his phone or didn't come home. And judging by her tone he didn't answer his phone. I let her know he was handling sum thing for me.

"I kind of figured that but he knows how I worry."

She wasn't lying, she worried so much it was starting to rub off on Ashanti. I hit P.R, I could tell he was in tha middle of breaking off one of his many smuts.

"Listen Nigga, you better start taking time to answer ya phone when Shauna call. You should neva disrespect home especially wit a Bitch that's only in it for tha money. P.R. you got to tighten up as far as Shauna goes."

"I know, I know you right Naz."

"Well, make sure you call her. I'll holla at you later I'm about to take wifey to breakfast then pick up our clothes for tonight."

"A'ight hit me later." Before I hung up I said call Shauna.

"Baby I'm ready," Ashanti yelled upstairs.

"Oh Shit! I hope she didn't already look outside. Nah, cause she would have been a lot more happier than that." I came downstairs, I had to admit she was beautiful.

All I could say was, "Happy Birthday Beautiful."

"Thank you Baby."

"So what do you want to do today?" I asked after we eat breakfast.

"I have a hair appointment."

"Well, you'll be in there all day."

"No I won't, Sady knows it's my birthday and I'm not tryin' to be there all day."

"Well, let's go eat."

When she opened tha door all she could scream as I said Happy Birthday again. I handed her tha keys, she immediately hit tha alarm and jumped in. I had bought her a navy-blue wit peanut butter guts on a set of shadow dub dueces S600 Mercedes Benz equipped wit ery thing including tha marching band.

As soon as she turned tha key, *"Love, never knew what I was missin' but I knew once we start kissin', I found, found you."* Tha sounds of Keyshia Cole came blaring out. She put tha car in drive.

"Babe, ain't you gon' take tha ribbon off?"

"Oh Shit!" she said putting tha car back in park. Once she had it off she put it in tha trunk.

"Now we can leave."

"Babe is it cool if I listen to Plies."

She looked at me and then said, "I don't care what you listen to."

I said, "Plies Definition of Real, Track 6 Volume 10."

When *"Somebody Loves You"* came on, I looked at her.

"Yeah, it's voice activated." She swerved trying to kiss me.

"Hold up! Don't crash already, I still owe 10g's."

After we ate she wanted to know if I had anything to do. I let her know that I was headed to tha same place she was, to get a haircut.

"I know you not cutting ya hair off."

"Hell No!"

"Oh, I just asked cause you got it in that ponytail."

"I need to get it done."

"I'll do it when we leave here," she said pulling up to tha shop.

When we got out everybody in tha shop was staring. Shafee came to tha door.

"Damn Naz, you killin' 'em wit tha new S600."

"Nah, that's ya Cuz not me."

"Wow, that's all I can say Cuz."

She smiled, "It was a birthday present."

"It is ya birthday? Happy Birthday."

"Thank you." We went in, everybody was telling me they like my new whip and tha 22's set it off.

"Well, maybe I need to get me one of those for myself." Sady looked at Ashanti then high five her.

"Girl, you must got tha bomb shot and head to get a birthday gift like that." All tha women started laughing.

Shaffe told me I had 2 in front of me which was cool. Ashanti went straight to tha chair which was even better. That meant we would be done around tha same time. By tha time Shafee was done cutting me, Ashanti was already putting her coat on. When she was outside everybody said they would see us tonight. Everything was goin' according to plan. She still had no clue about her party tonight.

For tha remainder of tha day we went to King of Prussia to do sum shopping. I was glad we did because I found a pair of Gucci loafers that were better than tha ones I had and a Bad Ass Gucci watch. Ashanti had gotton herself sum costume jewelry. I hadn't given her tha necklace or bracelet. I was goin' to wait until after she was dressed to surprise her wit it. When we got back home it was 7 o'clock.

"Naz, go upstairs and get tha comb and tha black rubber bands."

I had to put them on tha end of my braids or they would come out. No matter if she braided it all tha way to tha ends or not. While she was braiding my hair all I could think about was *Heaven, Lez, and Nina coming to this party tonight. I hope they all will play their part. Well truth be told, tha only one I was worried about Heaven. Ever since I got my spot on tha side she practically moved in. Then had tha audacity to get mad when I told her she might as well let me buy her a crib since she was alwayz at mine.*

"Naz."

"Huh?"

"Boy where you at? Did you hear what I said?"

"Nah, what did you say?"

"I said after I'm done these last 3 braids I need a shot, I'm horny."

CHAPTER 13

Creeping

"Damn, I can't believe Ashanti acted like that in front of all those people. I'm goin' to teach her ass a lesson, I'm not goin' home for a few days." As soon as I got in tha car my phone started to ring.

"Yo."

"Am I goin' to see you tonight or do you have to go home and playhouse?"

I just hung up; I wasn't for her Bullshit either. She called right back. I turned my phone off since that was tha only number she had. As if on cue, my other phone rang.

"Hey Daddy, can I see you tonight?"

"Where you at now?"

"On my way home."

"I'll be there in 15 minutes." Lez was on tha other line.

"Hello."

"You Ok?"

"Yeah, I'm straight."

"Well, she didn't mean it, she was venting cause she wanted you to go home wit her."

"That wasn't tha way to go about it."

"I know but that was tha Remy talk'n."

"Well, she don't need to drink cause she can't handle it."

"Naz."

"Yeah."

"Go home."

"Nah, she beat for a few days."

"A few days?"

"Yeah, she really embarrassed me. I don't tolerate that from nobody. Are you gon' be up in an hour?"

"I should, why you coming over?"

"Yeah, I just got to holla at my peeps real quick."

"Well, I'll put tha key in tha mailbox just in case I doze off and if I'm sleep like Beyoncé said tap me on my shoulder and I'll roll over."

"Sounds good to me. Oh, do me a favor."

"What's that?"

"Don't have no clothes on."

"Like you don't know I sleep in tha nude anyway."

"Well a'ight, I'll see you in an hour," I said pulling up to Nina's house.

I went in and went straight to work. 45 minutes later she was dead sleep. I washed up then bounced on my way to Lez house.

When I got there tha keys was where she said they would be. I could hear soft moans as I made my way up tha steps. When I got to tha bedroom Lez was handling her biz-ness.

"Damn, you couldn't wait for me," I said causing her to jump.

"Nah, I just was gettin' her ready for you."

I took my clothes off; I gave Lez one of my best performances yet which she enjoyed letting me know that she had reached 8 orgasms. Once we were done, we talked for a while. Tonight was tha first night that Lez opened up to me.

"Naz I need you to know that I know we said that this was nuffin more than sex but I find myself in love wit you. And I feel bad about it because after tonight I know how much Ashanti loves you. I think we need to stop."

She had totally caught me off guard wit that. Now don't get me wrong, I was feelin' Lez like a Mother Fucker. I just wasn't at tha love stage yet anyway but here she was telling me that what we had was now over.

I didn't say a word, I just listened until she asked, "Did you hear me Naz?"

"Yeah, I heard you."

"Well, why didn't you say anything?"

"What is it to say Lez, you said it all. So no matter what I say your mind is already made up."

"So you don't think we should stop?"

"Do you really want to know what I think?"

"Yes I do."

"Well, I think that I would be lying to you if I said I didn't care about you or have feelings for you. But, if you want to end this there is nuffin I can do about it. Evidently, you have thought about it for a while."

"Actually I haven't, not until I gave Ashanti a ride home. Now I'm no young girl and I knew what I was gettin' myself into from tha jump. So regardless how I feel about you, I would neva put you in a position where you had to choose because I would lose. So if I had to be tha as you young'n say 'tha jump off' I know my place."

"Let me say this Lez then you can make tha choice. I've neva treated you as just a jump off. I honestly respect you and at tha end of tha day, this is more than just sex for me." Wit that said, I turned over only for Lez to scoot right behind me and start rubbing my man which brought him right back to life. This time I took my time wit her making sure to hit every spot imaginable wit slow strokes. If this was goin' to be tha last time, I made sure she would alwayz remember me.

When I was done, all she could say was Damn Naz then she drifted off to sleep. Normally, I would take a shower which I did and slide out but since I wasn't goin' home and I knew Heaven was at my other spot I just climbed back in bed wrapped my arms around her and went to sleep.

"Damn, he must really care, normally he would have left. Who am I kidding, I ain't goin' nowhere especially not after tha way he just put it down. I have to get sum in tha morning. Maybe I'll wake him up wit a good shot of head in tha morning."

Tha next morning I was awaken by one of tha best feelings in my life. I opened my eyes to see Lez wit all 9 inches of my penis in her mouth. I guess this was her way of saying goodbye.

By tha time I got to tha block I had to call Juan because Wendy let me know that we were low. Juan answered on tha first ring.

"What's up Lil Homie, I need to place an order."

"Same thing?"

"Nah, I need 15 chicken sandwiches and double my other order."

"A'ight, give me an hour." I walked to Wendy's.

"I see you haven't been home."

"Nah, I'm about to jump in tha shower."

"Well, Ashanti has been calling my phone all mornin lookin' for you."

"If she calls while I'm here, don't tell her I'm here."

I turned all my phones off so that I could take a shower in peace. After I was done, I turned them back on. It's a good thing I did, Juan was calling.

"What up Juan."

"You ready for me?"

"Yeah."

"I'm goin' to Jakes to grab a bite to eat."

"As soon as I finish putting my clothes on I'll be right there."

I called down to Wendy. When she came up I told her to be ready we were goin' to meet Juan.

CHAPTER 14

Things Done Changed

I came walking down tha block after leaving my old heads house. I needed a shot of Remy so I stopped at tha bar on tha corner. When I got in, I saw my peeps Hop.

"What up Gunz!" he called out over tha music.

"I can't call it."

"*Is that Lil Bobby?*"

I walked over to where they were sitting. One of tha dudes looked familiar, I just couldn't remember.

"Lil Bobby look at you all grown up."

"It's me Dimes."

"Oh a'ight. I heard you tha man now. I remember when I used to send you to tha store for a dollar. How long you been locked up?" I asked, "10 years, right? A lot has changed since then."

"Oh I see," he said reaching in his pocket coming out wit a 10-dollar bill, "well, take this and get me 2 Dutches, you keep tha change." Bub started laughing.

I jumped up, grabbed my pistol, and smacked tha Shit out of Dimes wit it. He hit tha floor, I cocked my .40 and stood over top of him.

"Like I said, a lot has changed in 10 years," Bob went to move, I pointed my .40 his way, "give me a reason." He knew I would put his brains all over that table even if he blinked wrong.

"You been gone a long time; you better ask around about me. And by tha way, tha name is Gunz. If you don't want to find out why they call me that then I'd suggest you know ya position. Now if you need a job, ya mans know how to find me."

I looked at Mr. Rudy, "Sorry bout tha commotion," I said tossing him a hundred-dollar bill.

I backed out tha door wit my .40 still in hand. Once outside I tucked it back in my waistline. I got to tha block and it was people everywhere.

"Damn Nigga, where you been?" Tico asked.

"Man, I had to smack old head Dimes that nigga tried to play me."

"You talk'n bout Dimes that just came home from doin' 10 years?"

"That's him, Nut Ass Nigga."

"What happen?"

"He thought I was still sum young boy that he tried to send to tha store wit a 10. Talk'n bout keep tha change so I smacked him wit my .40."

"He was by his self?"

"Nah, he was wit Clown Ass Bub."

"I don't like that nigga, I think he workin' wit dem people."

"What y'all over here talk'n bout?" I schooled Naz.

"Damn Cuz, I would have popped his top for that, word."

"Yeah, I can't take nuffin."

"You think he gon' try to come back at you?"

"On sum serious shit, I don't know but if he do, he better come wit his game cause I'mma tag his toe."

I walked across tha street to sit on tha stoop. It had been a week since I talked or seen Ashanti or Heaven. They both have been calling I just haven't picked tha phone up.

"Damn," I thought to myself as I watched Ashanti swing tha corner in her Benz.

I wanted to get up and dip in tha crib but I'm pretty sure she saw me as her car came to a slow stop.

She rolled down tha window in a weak but firm voice she said, "Can I talk to you for a minute?"

"I'm listening."

"Can you get in or do you want me to park and get out?"

"That's up to you, I'm sittin' right here."

She pulled over, when she got out at that moment I realized I missed my baby but I wouldn't let her know it.

"Is it a'ight if I sit down?"

"Do you."

"I don't want to argue wit you; I just want to talk."

"I'm listening."

"I know I was wrong for screaming at you, especially in front of all those people but I wanted you to go home wit me. This past week I have been in tha world of pain wit out you. I haven't been able to sleep not knowing if you were okay or not."

"Well, you should have known I was cool if Wendy or one of tha fellas didn't call you to say otherwise."

"Nah," she said puttin' her hands on mines, "what is it goin' to take for you to forgive me?" I looked into her beautiful hazel eyes.

"All I need from you is understanding. You know what I do so you need to understand in this biz-ness I'm like a doctor, alwayz on call. But no matter what I alwayz..."

BONG, BONG, BONG, BONG!

I threw Ashanti to tha ground while pulling my gun out. BONG, BONG,

BONG! I looked down tha block.

"Yo y'all a'ight?"

"Yeah, we cool, tha one time we ain't strap niggaz try sum funny shit."

"Either of you see who it was."

"Nah, I didn't."

"Me either."

"Well, I did."

"Who was it?"

"That cop nigga Bub and probably tha nigga Dimes.

"They weren't tryin' to hit shit, jus shooting."

"My Baby could have been hit so now it's personal. A real nigga ain't gon' shoot up tha block; they gon' run down on who they want. Where them niggaz be at?"

"They probably over on Clearfield."

"We gon' let it die down then ride on them. In a few days, call Capes, Man-Man, Rell, and AZ, tell 'em they need to be on tha rooftops: all day, every day. Nobody should be able to shoot up this block and not leave wit out a toe tag." I was pissed off!

"Them niggaz won't live past tha weekend; I promise you that."

Later that nite, I decided to handle them niggaz on my own. I got word they were on tha block, I knew just how to get them.

I parked my car about 5 blocks away. When I was a block away, I could see both of them just standing on tha corner talk'n to sum hood rat. They neva even noticed me walking up. I pulled my mask down... BONG, BONG, BONG, BONG, BONG, BONG! Were tha sounds that had escaped my twin Glocks. Both of them hit tha ground, I walked up to them, they were both trying to crawl. I kicked Bub in his head. BONG, BONG! Wasn't no need to play, I hit both of 'em in tha head taking tha life out of them. Instantly, I turned around and walked back tha same way. I came wit out any hesitation, I pulled off slowly not to cause any unwanted attention to myself.

For tha rest of tha night I went home to be wit Ashanti. She had no idea I was even coming home because we neva got to finish our conversation. Heaven had been blowing my phone up for tha past hour. I still didn't answer her phone call. As much as I dug her, she was starting to pluck my nerves. For sum reason, she thought that I was suppose stop what ever I was doin' to cater to her. I had to let her know that she would neva be able to take Ashanti's place. That had pissed her off but I had to let her know tha truth.

After I got out tha shower, Ashanti asked if we could finish our conversation. I really didn't feel like arguing so I let her talk while I just listened at tha end of tha conversation. We had come to tha conclusion that no matter how busy I was. If I wasn't goin' to make it home I should call and let her know and she would respect what I did. Over tha next few days rumors spread that sum female had set Bub and Dimes up to get killed. Then they said it was tha girl who did tha hit. But tha one that took tha cake was that an 11-year-old kid had pop their top. I

didn't let anyone know that I was behind this. In fact, I asked Gunz if he did it or had anything to do wit it. I knew he didn't but I had to play it off. I had killed my stepfather 8 years ago so it wasn't my first time but it didn't feel tha same. I knew that if need be, I would kill again.

Tha next few months tha block had really picked up; even though it was cold tha money was coming in at a fast pace. So I needed to invest sum money in a few legal ventures to make sure if anything happened I would have sum thing to fall back on. After much thought, I decided to invest in real estate and open up a women's and children's store. I had an inside connection to put me down wit a few people to help me get started on both biz-ness ideas.

CHAPTER 15

It's Time

"Yo what up Cannon?"

"I can't call it."

"Where you been?"

"I been on sum outta town shit. I can't keep running around here on sum bullshit not gettin' no real paper."

"Yeah, I feel you on that. On another note, I got a hit for you worth about 6 figures. When you coming back?"

"In a few days, I'm handlin' sum thing down this end."

"A'ight, you just make sure you hit me when you touch down this end."

"No doubt, I got you Cuz." (CLICK)

"Damn that nigga alwayz on a mission."

Lately, I have been on tha grind. Easy Hawk had called me but I let him know I wasn't ready yet. I had this new connect where tha coke wasn't as good as tha shit Naz had but tha price was a whole lot cheaper. So until I get my loot all tha way back up I would deal wit him. I need to get Naz out of tha way so I can take over tha block. It's time to put my plan in motion.

"Easy Hawk what up?"

"You."

"Aye, I'm ready to do what we talk about."

"I just thought you told me you wasn't ready yet?"

"I changed my mind."

We went over all tha details, it was set. I would call him once ery thing was in place. Later that night, I had done what I need to do. I gave Easy Hawk a call and he let me know that he would handle it from here.

CHAPTER 16

Tha Set Up

I had just left my apartment and I finally had started speaking to Heaven. I let her know that she knew her position when she got into this and if she couldn't respect Ashanti then she should move on. When it was all said and done, she let me know that she wasn't trying to be selfish but she felt like I was neglecting her; and I was. I pulled up to tha light on 7th & Girard when my phone rang.

"Hey Baby, I'm on my way home now." She was about to hang up when all of sudden my car doors were being pulled open.

"Put that car in park and put your hands on tha steering wheel!"

I could hear Ashanti yelling, "Baby you alright, What's goin' on!"

That's when I asked, "What's goin' on? What's this all about?"

They took me out of tha car then while putting handcuffs on they read me my Miranda Rights while three of them searched my car.

Tha one that had put tha cuffs on me asked, "Is there anything illegal in the car we should know about?"

"Hell Nah! Ain't nuffin..."

Before I could finish one of tha cops said, "I found it."

I looked then said, "Found what?" He held tha gun up so that other cops could see.

"Oh Hell Nah! Y'all not gon' put that Shit on me!"

"Bag that, let's take him down to the station."

By now there was a crowd that gathered, Wendy happens to be one of them who was on her way towards us.

"Hold it right there Mam!"

"That's my nephew!" Tha cop that had me told him to let her thru.

"What is goin' on?"

"I shouldn't be telling you this but we got a tip that Mr. Jenkins had killed someone and the gun would be in the car."

"No, No, No! That can't be right! My nephew wouldn't do anything like that."

"Mam he's no saint, he just did time for murder."

"He was 11 and that was self-defense."

"Damn, did sum body see me kill Bub and Dimes? They would have to prove it and I ain't saying Shit! Call Troy, tell him to come to tha station A.S.A.P." She pulled her phone out, tha whole squad had him on speed dial.

"Excuse me, Sir."

"Yes."

"Can I take my car?"

He looked at tha other plainclothes cop then asked, "Do you have a license?"

"Yes I do." I wanted to say sum thing smart but my better judgment told me not to so I didn't.

"Go ahead," he said tossing me tha keys.

I had to leave Troy a message since he didn't pick up his phone. When I pulled up Ashanti was coming out tha house.

"I think Naz has been arrested."

"He has, I just left from around there..."

I was interrupted by my cell phone. As soon as I picked up Troy wanted to know if everything was a'ight. I explained to him what I knew, he let me know that he was on his way to tha station. Before I could say anything else tha line went dead.

"Get in, we going to tha police station."

By tha time we got down there Troy was already there.

"I need to speak with my client and if I may ask, what is he being charged with?"

Tha plainclothes cops said, "First Degree Murder, they had ran the gun and it was the same gun that had killed two men a few days before."

"Well, did you test for fingerprints or DNA?"

"We're doing that now."

"Where is my client?"

He led me to one of the interview rooms where Naz was being held. I walked in and sat down. The first thing he said was I didn't do it; I'm being set up. I asked by who and for what?

"I don't know, all I do know is I didn't kill nobody."

"I have to let you know that you are most likely going to be held without bail."

"How long am I goin' to be held wit out bail? How long am I goin' to have to sit?"

"I can't say, hopefully, it won't make it past preliminary. Just don't say Shit about this to anyone."

"Well, that won't be hard since I don't know Shit."

"Good, because a nigga is always looking for a way out. Don't let it be you they get out on."

We talked for a little longer before they came in to process me. As I walked to be processed I saw Wendy and Ashanti standing by tha detective who was handling tha case.

"Baby don't worry we're gon' get you out of here!" Ashanti yelled wit tears in her eyes.

Once I was done being processed, they took me back into tha room where I just was.

"What that Hell is goin' on?" I kept asking myself, *"who would go through all this trouble to set me up? Even to plant a gun wit a body on it in my car. I couldn't think of anybody that would want to do this to me."*

Tha detective came into tha room followed by my lawyer; they both took a seat. Tha detective put his folder that he had on tha table.

"Mr. Jenkins, do you know why you have been placed under arrest?"

"He does," my lawyer said. Tha detective gave him a look that said he can talk.

"Well, in that case," he opened his folder then placed 2 pictures in front of me, "do you know either of these men?" I looked at Troy who nodded letting me know it was cool to talk.

"Nah, I don't know 'em."

Which was tha truth, I didn't. I had seen them before but that was it. Then he took out another two pictures of tha same dudes. Only this time they were both face down in a pool of blood with holes that size of quarters in their heads; before tha detective could utter a word that door had opened. A cop walked in and whispered sum thing to him and walked back out. Tha detective whose name was Lyon started smiling.

He put tha pictures back in his folder, looked at Troy then asked, "Would you like to negotiate a deal? The gun we found was a match," then he looked at me, "we got you by the balls."

As he was walking out Troy said, "Pick 12, if we even make it that far."

Once he was gone Troy said, "Don't worry about nuffin, no prints, no DNA, no case."

Another cop came in to say they were ready to transfer me to C.F.C.F. Troy said he would be to see me in a few days. Detective Lyon said that I could have 10 minutes to talk to Wendy and Ashanti. When they came in Ashanti ran and wrapped her arms around me.

"Baby, who could have done this?"

"I don't know. Tell P.R. and Esco to come see me A.S.A.P. Wendy I need you to hold Shit down while I'm here. Call Juan let him know tha deal and that you will be handling shit until I come home."

"Jenkins lets go!"

"Baby I'll be there tomorrow after I come from tha doctors."

"A'ight."

"I love you Naz."

"And me you."

After I got to C.F.C.F. all I wanted to do was lay down. I had a terrible headache and I was tired as Hell. I was shown to my tier and I went straight to my room to lay down. After about a half hour I was awaken by my celly turning on his radio. I rolled over to say sum thing to him but when I saw who it was I sat up.

"What up Fitz," I said.

"Yo Nigga, what you doin here? Last I seen, you had 8th & Indy doin' numbers."

"Yeah, I still got that Shit. Oh, this where you been?"

"Yeah Man, why else you think I didn't come holla at you? I got this bullshit case, my sons mom told tha police I had pulled a gun out on her."

"Damn Nigga, that's how you doin' it?"

"Come on Naz, I would have just smacked her. What I look like pulling my shit out on a Bitch; my sons mom at that. She just mad cause I got this new bad ass Chinese chick so her motto is if I can't have you nobody will. I'mma beat it, I just got to wait it out since they hit me wit this ransom bail. What tha Hell you in for?"

"They charge me wit First Degree Murder." Tha look on his face said it all.

"Who they say you earthed?"

"I don't even know their names."

"Damn, it's two people."

"Yeah, but tha gun they found in my car doesn't have my prints or DNA."

"Hold up, Hold up! Did you say tha gun they found in ya car."

"Yeah, sum body set me up, I ain't worried, I got tha boy Troy Banks."

"Oh, you good, he tha Shit. Expensive but tha Shit. Anything in here you more than welcome to." He had a nice supply of commissary.

A female guard came to tha cell.

"Hey Fitz."

"What up Mimi, you got that?"

"Yeah," she said looking around.

When she was certain nobody was watching she went into her pants then tossed him a sandwich bag. Fitz opened up his radio and took out tha money that was inside handing it to her. She said thanks, see you next week then walked off as if nuffin had occurred.

"Damn, that's how you doin' it?"

"Yeah, I sell this Shit to keep me right while I'm here."

"How much can that radio hold and what do you charge?"

"To answer ya questions, probably about a quarter pound and 5 dollars an ace." He began to roll tha weed.

"Check this out, will Mimi bring that much in?"

"Hell yeah."

"I'mma have my peeps give her A.Q.P. plus 5 hundred and we gon' sell them 10 dollars a Ace because this gon' be Sour D so let ery body know next week this is what it is. Who else on this block got tha weed?"

"Nobody just me."

"That's even better. Can you get sum of that coke in here?"

"Yeah Fo' Sho, they be wanting that shit more than weed. Is she gon' bring it in?"

"Yeah, when you gon' talk to ya Folk?"

"I'll be hollering at her tomorrow at tha visit. My Chinese chick is her sister."

"Oh, that's even better. When P.R. comes thru tomorrow I'mma put him down. We bout to get major paper in here." That night I could not sleep at all.

Tha next morning, they woke us up for breakfast. I had just fallen asleep so I told Fitz to go head I was sleeping in. By tha time he got back I was up taking care of my hygiene.

"Aye Fitz, what day do?"

"Y'all go to canteen on Friday's."

"A'ight, I need to make a call so I can tell my girl to bring a nickel so I can have it on my books."

By then tha phones were on now. I went on tha block all 4 phones were occupied so I had to wait. When one was free I got on, it rang 3 times before sum one answered.

"This is a collect call from Naz. If you accept this call do not use 3-way or call waiting or you will be disconnected. This call will be monitored, to accept this call dial 5 now. Thank you."

"Hey Baby, how you feeling?"

"Dealin' wit tha circumstances, I'm straight. I need you to bring 500 when you come plus I need you to tell P.R. to come to tha visit wit you."

"He is, we'll be there. I'm on my way to tha doctor's that's why it took so long to answer tha phone. I had to get it out of my pocketbook."

"Oh, you got tha calls transferred?"

"Yeah." We continued to talk.

"You have one-minute remaining."

"I love you and I'll see you later."

"A'ight, I love you too." Tha phone went dead.

I walked over to where Fitz was standing.

"Yo, it should be a go once I get my visit."

"Did you tell her to bring tha money?"

"Yeah, I didn't talk about nuffin else, you can't trust them phones."

"I know, that's why I don't use them too often. Visit or letter, that's how I do it. You know how to play Spades Naz?"

"Yeah, why?"

"I need a partner for this money."

"Nah, I ain't doin' no gambling til after my visit."

"Awe Nigga, I'mma put you up. If we win we split if we lose we split tha bill."

"A'ight."

"Yo, we got winners."

Tha short dude said, "Don't go too far this almost over. We playing 2 dollars a man."

"Damn, that's all," I said.

"We can raise tha stakes as long as you got tha money."

"We'll be right back, let's go smoke this Ace."

"Damn Fitz, you back in?"

"Yeah, you know it."

"Why you ain't say sum thing? Bring me back 2."

"Me too, you can bring me 4."

"A'ight. Oh yeah, starting next week I'mma need 10."

"What? You must got sum Fire."

"Yeah, Sour D."

"Oh, you can get that?"

"All day! It ain't about nuffin."

"I know it ain't to a baller like you."

We got to tha room since it was no C.O. on tha block we could just smoke wit no hassle.

"Aye, ya boy got doe?"

"He talk like he do plus he alwayz gambling and buying weed."

"Well, we gon' play 5 dollars a man. You wit that?"

"Hell yeah, I alwayz play 3 or better. I jus neva have a partner wit money or that can really play."

"Well, you ain't got to worry about that."

"A'ight, let's get this money."

By tha time we got back to tha table it was tha last hand. Tha little dude was down and they went 10. I sat back and observed how they played tha hand. That was all I did in tha joint was play Spades. I could set tha deck whether I cut or dealt they just made 10. Little dude whose name was Messy was talk'n cash shit.

We sat down, "Is 5 dollars a man to steep?"

"Not at all. Before we start let's set tha rules so it won't be no bullshit 10, firsthand double set, firsthand game Boston, firsthand triple. Anytime during tha game it's double if you caught cheating game. We good?"

They all shook their heads, "first Diamond deals."

They flipped tha cards and tha first Diamond came to me. I did my thing and Messy cut them just tha way I knew he would. I wanted them to start off in tha hole so I dealt us a Boston. Fitz could not hold his smile.

"How many you got Naz?"

"2."

I lied just to see what they would go. Messy said he had 2 and Boy-Boy had 3. I knew they didn't have 5.

"How many you got Fitz?" He started counting, when he was done he said, "7."

"If you got 7, I'mma count ery thing. Give us 10."

A crowd had gathered Messy said, "Y'all will neva see it."

All I had was Spades and Clubs. Boy-Boy started wit tha Ace of Diamond.

"That's one," he said.

When it got to me, I cut it wit tha 3 of Spades then I ran Trump. After I played Joker Joker, I let Fitz finish 'em off. Once all their Spades were gone, he ran tha rest of his Diamonds down their throats. We had 10 books, they started to throw their hands in.

"Hold on! We might have a Boston," I said.

"Oh, y'all ain't got no Boston."

It was on me, I played tha Ace of Clubs. I could tell Fitz was wit me so I came back wit tha 10 of Clubs. He played tha King then came back wit tha 6. I played tha Queen.

And tha on lookers said, "Damn, they ran a Boston!"

"So, are we playing pay as you go?"

"Yeah," Fitz said, "go get that 30, we need that."

Tha cats that just lost said, "And we play Rise and Fly."

"Nah, we locked in."

"We can play Rise and Fly, I want ery body's money."

While they went to get that money, we started a new game. By tha time they came back tha game was over. I cut us a 10.

"Yeah, go get that dub."

"Tha next few games went tha distance but we still came out on top. When it was all said and done, we had both won 45 dollars. Tha guard came to get us for our visit. When I got there, Ashanti and P.R. were both sitting at tha table.

"What up Honey?"

"I can't call it," I said giving him dap.

"Hey Baby."

"Hey ma," I said hugging her and laying a big kiss on her, "it's only been one day and I miss you already."

"They said you can get 3 visits a week so I'mma take full advantage of that."

P.R. spoke to Fitz and I put him down wit what I needed to be done. As far as Fitz girl and tha block, I had a lot of trust in P.R. so I knew that he as well as Wendy could hold it down until this thing blew over which I hoped would be soon.

By tha end of tha visit it was all a go. Fitz had his girl on point. She would holla at them outside. I told P.R. that Mimi was a bad broad and if he could knock her off it would be even better for us. Of course I didn't say it around Ashanti since Shauna was her girl. Not that she would say sum thing, I just didn't want her to assume that I was talk'n to other broads.

"Oh yeah, before I forget, I'm 8 weeks pregnant," she said wit a serious look on her face.

I didn't know how to respond. I was happy but at tha same time mad. Happy that I would be a father, mad that I was in jail for sum bullshit. She must have sensed it.

"Did you hear what I said?"

"Yeah, I heard you. I'm happy as shit, this is a time when you need me most and I'm here for sum thing I didn't do!" I said getting mad and throwing tha chair.

Tha C.O. stood up, "Visit over."

I held Ashanti like it was or would be tha last time. She tried to hold back tha tears but to no avail. I watched as they left, before she was totally out of tha door she turned around and told me that she loved me then blew me a kiss. Truth be told, I was devastated. My baby was having my baby. I went back to my room to lay down.

Fitz came in, "Ery thing a'ight wit you? I see things got crazy at tha V.I."

"Nah, I just found out that I'm about to be a dad."

"Congratulations, that calls for a celebration," he said rolling up a Fat Ass Ace, "you know them niggaz want sum get back."

"I don't feel like playing right now."

"I feel you. Damn, ya whole life is about to change. Take it from me, I got 2 kids and their mom as you see is a vicious broad. Alwayz calling for sum thing and tha minute you say you don't got it "BOOM" she goes crazy."

"Nigga, not every broad is like that. Let me ask you this, when you first met ya kids mother was it love at first sight or was it just a Fuck thing?"

"It was just a Fuck thing."

"That's why sum times you have to be friends first. First get to know tha other person, find out their likes and dislikes; with me and Ashanti we were friends for two years. Now maybe because I was locked up but it was a good thing cause once I got out we were one. I do my dirt but at tha end of day, month, and year I love her."

"Damn Naz that sweet."

"Awe Nigga, Fuck you." We both started laughing.

Tha next few days all I could think about was Ashanti and my baby that she's carrying.

"Jenkins!" I heard tha guard call my name; I walked out my cell.

"Your lawyer is here to see you."

I came down tha steps into tha office that was off to tha side of tha tier.

When I walked in Troy had his hand extended, I shook it then sat down.

"How are you doing?" I looked at him.

"Not so good, I just found out that I'm goin' to be a father. I need to make bail."

"Well, I'm afraid they're going to hold you without bail; your preliminary is next week. Hopefully, they'll drop it but if not, I'll see if I can get you a bail."

"So how is it lookin'?"

"The only evidence they have is that gun that doesn't have your prints or DNA."

"Will their snitch have to come to trial to testify?"

"Yes."

"Well, that's a good thing, I'll be able to see who it is that lined me up wit this Bullshit."

CHAPTER 17

Part of tha Team

I had to put tha paper down and smile to myself. Right there on tha front page *"Man Charged in Double Homicide."* Once I was finished reading tha article all I could think about was all tha money I was soon to make. So I thought I knew that Easy Hawk will be calling me for his money soon. It didn't matter that was 5 stacks well spent. I know that when they run out of product it's a wrap. There's no way that any of them knows tha connect and that's when I'll step in. But in tha meantime, let me see what it's lookin' like over there but first I needed to hop in tha shower.

Once I was done I threw on a sweat suit and headed to tha block. It was jumpin' just like tha time before this time. I parked in tha middle of tha block. As soon as I got out P.R. walked over to me.

"What up Doe?"

"Yo, what's up wit Naz? I was reading tha Inquirer and Naz was on tha front page for 2 counts of First-Degree Murder. Why would he still have tha gun in tha car at that."

"Man, my peeps ain't do that shit!"

"Well, they said they got tha gun."

"Sum body set him up."

"I hope he got a good lawyer cause it seems like tha deck is stacked against him but I know he gon' make it out. So I know you didn't come up here for that."

"Actually, I was suppose to meet Naz to discuss sum biz-ness but I guess it's been a change of plans."

"What kind of biz-ness? Maybe I can be of sum help."

"Nah, I was suppose to join tha team."

"Yeah well, I'll holla at him next week at tha visit."

"Doe, you better not be lying cause if you are I won't hesitate to shoot you for tryin' to play me."

"Damn, I need to go up C.F.C.F. to holla at Naz before this nigga does. I'll shoot up there later today."

"Yo, in tha meantime do you."

"This nigga don't even know what I'm about to do, he better be lucky I'm gon' still let him hustle out here."

"Yo, what you doin around here?" Esco asked.

"Chill Young'n, I got a pass from Naz to be out here. P.R. gon' holla at him."

"Yeah, I sure am and if this nigga lying..." he put his hand up to imitate a gun.

Esco pulled out his Desert, "Man Fuck this Nigga!" He cocked his Shit back...

"Hold up Young'n! Man put that Shit away. He got a pass until I holla at Naz next week."

My mind was made up once I officially take this shit over this little Bitch nigga goin' straight to tha boneyard.

Later that day while I was on my way to C.F.C.F. to see Naz, one of my little Shorty's called.

"Hey Doe."

"What up Roz."

"You. Where you at?"

"On my way to holla at my folk."

"Can I have sum of ya time when you done? I have a itch that needs to be scratched and only you can scratch that spot." Damn, just hearing her talk like that gave me an instant erection.

"Yeah, well give me a hour and I'll be there."

"You not goin' to be here in no Damn hour so stop lying."

"A'ight, A'ight, make it a hour and a half."

I pulled up to tha prison and there were a few bad females goin' in. I'll get at them on tha way out. I let them know who I was here to see. After about 5 minutes Naz came out. I could tell by tha look on his face that he was more than surprised to see me. I stood to shake his hand as he returned my dap.

He asked, "What do I owe this visit?"

"Listen, I'mma get straight to tha point. I wanna be on tha team. I didn't know until I picked tha paper up this mornin that they had you on this Shit."

"I had planned to holla at you on tha block but you know Doe I really don't have a problem wit you joining tha squad but I know that you have another motive."

"Nah, I'm just tryin' eat. I was tha man but I have no problem taking a back seat. Truth be told, I like money and I don't have to be tha boss to get it."

"Well, I'm goin' to let you get down because if it wasn't for you I wouldn't be where I'm at today. So wit that being said, all you gotta do is holla at P.R." When tha visit was over I felt like I had just won a championship fight.

"I also left you a nickel on ya books. That should hold you down, even though I know you are already sittin' high." We dapped each other and I headed out.

Once in tha parking lot I noticed a note on my car window.

I see I wasn't tha only one lookin' if you're interested here's my number. Call me A.S.A.P.

I got in then pulled my cell out tha glove box wit out wasting any more time I dialed tha number that was on tha paper. After 3 rings she picked up.

"How did you know which car was mine?"

"I didn't, I went off assumption. I must've been right since you called."

"What's ya name?" I asked.

"Angel."

"It fits. What would ya man say if he knew that you gave ya number out to a perfect stranger that was checking you out at a visit?"

"Well, first of all I don't have a man if I did we wouldn't be having this conversation. Secondly, my brother told me you were checking me out."

"Oh Damn, my bag I thought that was ya dude."

"Nah, that's my older brother. Do you think I would've been lookin' if it was? You must be use to lookin' or need I say dealing wit chicken heads."

"So I look like a chicken head type of dude?"

"Now you puttin' words in my mouth."

"Nah, you might as well had said that."

"Let me find out you one of those Uh... sensitive type of dudes." All I could do was laugh.

"Did I say sum thing funny."

"Yeah, you did. Well, what part of Philly you from."

"North."

"What do you know so am I. Would it be asking too much to ask you to join me for dinner tonight if you're not busy of course?"

"Well, I did already have a dinner date but I can alwayz cancel."

"You don't have to; we can do it another time."

"Nah, tonight's fine. My girl won't mind and before ya mind starts wondering I'm talk'n about my best friend."

"I wasn't goin' to say anything. Well, you make sure you lock my number in so that you won't have to say who is this when I call," my line started to beep, "hold up for a sec Angel." (CLICK)

"What up Roz."

"Where you at? I'm laying here ass naked playing wit myself waiting for you. How much longer do I have wait?"

"Chill, I'm on my way right now," I clicked back over, "hello."

"Damn, I was bout to hang up. I don't do tha hold on thing. You might want to call up En Vogue for that."

"You ever thought about doin stand up?"

"Yeah but wit my nursing job it didn't pan out." All I could do was laugh.

When I pulled up to Roz's I told Angel to be ready by 8 o'clock and I would call her when I was on my way. As soon as I walked in Roz was coming down tha steps ass naked. Damn, she has a body like a stallion. No stretch marks, no cellulite. Her body was flawless and ass was so fat that Beyoncé didn't have shit on her. She wasted no time pulling down my pants and inserting my whole penis in her mouth. Within seconds, I found myself stroking her mouth as if it were her vagina; that's how good it felt. Long story short, after a few hours I hit tha shower then peeled out and headed to tha block to get sum money before my dinner date wit Angel.

CHAPTER 18

Missing My Baby

I had just gotton off tha phone wit Naz. He had only been in there for two months yet I missed him like crazy. I was now 18 weeks and I was showing. I had been spending more time wit Nana since she found out I was pregnant. She had called me in tha middle of tha night saying she had a dream about fish. At tha time I had no idea what she meant. I just rushed her off tha phone once she let me know she was a'ight so I could go back to sleep. But she had called me back in tha AM to explain what she meant. I told her that was an old myth and that I wasn't pregnant but Nana being Nana she knew I wasn't telling tha truth. So I started crying then admitted to her I was indeed pregnant and I didn't want to raise my child alone. She assured me that as long as she had breath in her body that she would be there for me. From that moment on Nana made sure she called me every day and that I stopped by.

"I can't believe they didn't let my baby go at his preliminary even after his lawyer proved that he was set up."

"That's how them people do it if they think they can get a conviction or a plea out and most people do."

"I think tha Damn judges and prosecutors work together!"

"Chil they do, especially when tha defendant is Black."

"I leave it in tha Lord's hands."

"Nana there's no way a jury will find him guilty. This whole thing has me so stressed out."

"Well, you don't need to be doin' no stressin' that's not good for tha baby. Did you find out what you having yet?"

"No, I don't find out til next month on tha 23rd."

"Ain't no need in me asking what you want cause I know you want a boy."

"Yup Nana, sure do. It's gettin' late I better be on my way."

"Chil you know you more than welcome to stay here."

"I know but I got a visit to see Naz in tha mornin."

"A'ight you call me when you get in so I can know you made it home Ok, love ya."

"Nana love ya too."

On my ride home I listened to Musiq Soul Childs *"Love"* before I realized it tears were rolling down my eyes at a steady pace. I couldn't help but think about Naz. These past few months seemed to alwayz have this effect on me.

By tha time, I got in tha house all I wanted to do was take a nice hot bath so I could relax my mind and body. As I sunk down inside tha tub I couldn't help but think bout Naz and wonder if he was think'n about me like I was him.

"At this moment they can't take my baby away from me. What will we do wit out him?" I asked rubbing my stomach talk'n to my child. After 30 minutes, I washed up then got out.

Tha next morning tha sound of my alarm woke me. I was still sleepy but I knew if I didn't get up now that I would not get up at all. So I got up and dressed. After my visit I planned on doin a little shopping because all my clothes were gettin' to small. So I was gonna shop til I drop.

It was 1:30 when I made it to my visit. I was tired, it seems like I've been extremely tired as of late and this is only tha beginning. I still have 4

½ months left. As I sat there waiting for Naz to come out all I could think about was who tha baby would look like.

"Damn, I don't get no hug, kiss nuffin? Wow."

"OOOOH I'm sorry Baby," I said as I stood to hug him, "I was just think'n about who tha baby is gonna look like."

"As if you don't already know, I did all tha work."

"Boy please, don't flatter yourself."

"So how you been doin?"

"I should be asking that, you haven't called in a few days."

"Two of tha phones on our tier are broke and I'm not tryin' to beef over no phone. You didn't get my letter?"

"I haven't checked tha mailbox in 2 days."

"Well, I'm glad I didn't need you to do sum thing."

"If it was that important you would have called. Nana sends her love."

"You been spending a lot of time wit Nana."

"I get lonely Naz plus Nana checks on me around tha clock."

"You growing out of those."

"I'm 2 steps ahead of you, did that this mornin. You know they say great minds think alike."

"Is that right," he said smiling.

"Baby, I miss you."

"And I miss you."

"How much longer before trial?"

"Ashanti you know these kind of cases could take up to 2 years."

"Damn tha baby will be 2 when you come home." Tha tears rolled my eyes.

"Baby don't cry."

"Can't ya lawyer get a faster court date?"

"He's working on that."

"I hope that he's able to do it cause we're gonna need you. I'm gettin' my tubes tied after this."

"Nah Babe, I want a boy and girl then you can tie 'em up."

"What if it don't happen like that? What if I have 2 boys or 2 girls?"

"Well, then we gon' go head and tie, burn, or clip them shits."

"Boy you crazy," I said wit a smile on my face.

"There it go."

"There what go? What you talk'n bout?"

"That pretty smile of yours." That made me smile even more.

"You sure no what to say."

"I just don't like to see you upset or stressed that can't be good for tha baby."

"Now you sound like Nana."

"Besides, I do enough of that for tha both of us in here."

"I know, I'll just be glad when this nightmare is finally over."

Tha guard let us know that visits were over. I gave him a hug and kiss that lasted until tha guard let us know that we had to break it up. I told him that he had better call me tonight. I got back to my car and before I pulled off I just sat there rubbing my stomach.

"Don't worry Daddy gon' be home soon." I pulled off to my destination to home to get me sum much needed sleep and rest.

CHAPTER 19

Shit Don't Stop

"Yo you a'ight? You been quite since you came back from ya visit."

"Yeah, I'm cool. I was just think'n about how Ashanti is starting to show. I need to be there for her. I hope Troy can get me court date soon."

"I feel you on that."

"Twist sum thing up Nigga," I said tossing him tha Dutch as well as tha Sour D, "and don't roll up no little ass pin Dutch like you be rolling."

"Go head Nigga, I just tryin' to make this shit last."

"Awe Man, we gon' alwayz be straight. Oh Shit! I almost forgot to tell you that my girl said that Mimi and P.R. are hot and heavy."

"I know, P.R. said that tha pussy and head is a definite keeper so as long as she play her part we gonna be crazy straight."

"Fitz! Naz!" I went to tha door it was Messy.

"Yo, you Niggaz tryin' to play sum Spades?"

I held up tha Dutch then said, "Yeah, hold up! Shit I'm on my way up."

Over tha last two months I had gotton cool wit Messy and Boy-Boy. I even turned his cousin on to 8th & Indy so he could score sum good weed and Caine for a nice price. He was holding Messy down until he beats his case which was Bullshit. They had him for robbery 1st and assault 1st. His lawyer got tha video tape which had caught tha whole thing but tha guy in tha tape was about 6'8" while Messy was only 5'6" if that. Like me, it was all a waiting game. Him and Boy-Boy walked in, I moved my bed to let them sit in tha chairs. Fitz was already on my bed; he had given me tha bottom bunk a week after I was here which was fine by me. I did not feel like that jumping up and down thing.

"Damn Naz, you be rolling ya shit like you still on tha block."

"You know Shit don't change."

They had started buying quarters off me. I was charging them a 180 dollars for a quarter which they were sending to Wendy every week or their peeps would just drop tha money off. I had tha 2 stacks that were allowed on tha books which I neva spent because we had more than enough food in our room from tha weed and Caine we were pumping. Not to mention, tha store we were also running. In just two months, I had our block and a few others jumpin'. I was making a lot of money in here just like my team was out there. At first, it was hard to get Mimi to bring in all tha weed and Caine I needed to supply everybody. She was scared that she would get caught. But once I let her know all she had to do was leave it by tha trash can she was cool wit that.

Fitz had an uncle who had off ground status who would bring in our shit every week just as long as we kept his books tight which I made sure he kept a stack on there. We had a spot where we kept it because there was no way we could fit all that into our radio. I also had a few other guards on tha take. Truth be told, there was more money in jail then on tha streetz. I made sure everybody was a'ight so nobody would hate and start snitching. It was around 7 o'clock.

"I hope you came wit sum good news."

"I have good news and bad news. Which do you want first?"

"Give me tha bad news."

"You have a court date for July 8th."

"Damn, that's 8 months away."

"I know but it's better than January."

"No it's not, that's next month."

"No, I'm talk'n about next January."

"Oh, you got a point there."

"Now, for the good news, the prosecutor is just tryin' to draw this out. 9 outta 10 in July it's goin' to be dropped. They have no case."

"Then why won't they dismiss tha case?"

"Well, the attorney general is hoping that you cop out."

"They can forget it, I ain't copping out to no Shit I didn't do. I can wait it out. I need to tell my girl."

"Oh, before I forget," he opened his briefcase then handed me this Razor cell phone and a charger,

"Naz, don't get caught wit it. It's a prepaid, so it can't be traced," P.R. said, "don't worry about minutes, he got you." I tucked tha phone and charger in my pants then we both walked out.

"Aye, did P.R. give you that 15 thousand?"

"Yeah, he been gave me that."

"Alright Naz, if you need anything call me."

"A'ight."

"You should give Heaven call," he said as he walked out.

I hadn't talked to her since I told her Ashanti was pregnant. I guess she was mad, I don't know. I do know that I got too much Shit gon' on to be worried about her being mad about my wifey being knocked up. Not that I expected her to be happy, I just wanted her to hear it from me opposed to tha streetz and I damn sure wasn't goin' to call her. She knows where I am; she can write or visit me. I went straight to my room to call Ashanti when she picked up I could tell she was sleep.

"Do you want me to call you back?" I asked in a low voice.

"Who is this and how did you get my number?" Since she didn't have a clue it was me; I decided to test her even though I knew she wasn't cheating.

"I got ya number from a friend."

"Is that right?"

"Yeah."

"Well, it couldn't have been that much of a friend."

"Why would you say that?"

"Besides they would have told you that I have a man."

"Girl, what ya man have to do wit me?"

"Listen, who ever you are please don't disrespect me or my man by calling my phone again!" (CLICK)

Before I could say it was me she hung up. I called right back. After 5 rings she answered.

"Look, you must have not heard me!"

Before she could get tha rest out I said, "Ashanti it's me Naz." I guess she caught my voice.

"Where you at?"

"In jail."

"How you call straight thru?"

"P.R. sent me a cell phone."

"Oh Shit! He did tell me he was sending you a phone."

"Well, I have a little of good and bad news." I filled her in on what Troy had told me; she was happy as Hell.

"But you won't be here to see tha baby born."

"That's Ok, I'll have Nana or Ms. Tracy record it so I can see it when I come home in July. At least he'll only be 3 months."

"How you know it's a boy?"

"I just do, trust me."

"I alwayz do." I heard Fitz talk'n.

"Hold on Babe."

I put tha phone under my pillow. Once he was in he asked if I was staying in for tha night.

"Yeah, I'm chilling."

He closed tha door and once he did I pulled tha phone from under tha pillow. He didn't see it, he jumped on his bunk.

"Damn, pass me that lighter Cuz."

"Baby my fault."

"It's Ok, I know you got to do that."

"Yeah."

"What you say Naz?"

"Nuffin Fitz, I ain't talk'n to you."

"I know you ain't stressing like that now you talk'n to ya self. I'mma have to tell Ashanti about this."

"Oh he must don't know I have a phone. Nah, he don't know, I don't know what Fitz ask lookin' down now."

"Oh Shit! I know that's not what I think it is." He quickly jumped down.

"Baby let me call you back in a few."

"A'ight but tell him don't be long ." I started laughing.

"I guess you do know me."

"Yup, sure do. Love you."

"And I you."

"So, that's how you gon' do; hold out on ya peeps?"

"Nah, I just got it tonight."

"Oh, ya lawyer, huh?"

"Yeah."

"We should have been thought of this. Let me call Kima."

"Here, you got a hour," I said handing him tha phone.

As soon as he was done, I called Ashanti back.

"It took you long enough."

"Come on Babe, you know I had to let him get his quality time in wit Kima."

"I know, I'm just playing wit you. I miss you."

"I miss you too. When is ya next doctor's appointment?"

"Next week."

"Ain't Christmas next week?"

"Yeah, but I go to tha doctors on tha 23rd." We talked for another hour then I let her know I would call tomorrow around 6.

Tha next morning, I woke up and started back working out to make sure I stayed in shape. In case, sum body try to try me in here or out there. By tha time Fitz came back from chow, I was just finishing my workout. I grabbed my stuff and headed to tha shower.

While I was drying off, I heard tha guard say, "Everybody lock in! Shake down!"

I stepped out tha shower then put my clothes on. Tha whole pod was filled wit guards. When I got to tha room, Fitz had just finished making sure ery thing was in order. When our door opened, Mimi and Ras told us to step out. I knew we were good but truth be told, I would rather it had been 2 regular guards to see if our spots were really official. I told them to search as if they were in sum body else's cell. So they did and didn't find shit. At that point, I knew we would be cool. When they finished, we had to put ery thing back in order. After about 2 hours they were done; finding nothing. We came out to Rec.

"Hey, y'all feel like playing sum cards?"

"Why not, ain't nuffin else to do but take y'all money. Now don't get me wrong, we lost too but not more than we won."

Tha next couple days I stayed in my room, I wasn't feelin' too good but I knew that Ashanti would be by to visit today but I wasn't feelin' well at all. I got tha cell and dialed.

"Hey Baby, I'm bout to leave tha house now."

"Nah, don't come."

"Why? You still sick?"

"Yeah, I don't know what it is but I'm fucked up in tha game. Before I knew it, I was at tha toilet throwing up. When I finished I got back on tha phone.

"EEL Baby, you need to see a doctor."

"I ain't goin' to none of these fake ass doctors in here. I'mma call you later, I need to lay down."

"A'ight, before you hang up, you were right."

"About what?"

"It's a boy, love you." Then she hung up.

Even though I knew it already, I was still happy to be having a lil me, Lil Naz. I closed my eyes and in seconds I was fast asleep. When I woke up, Fitz was on tha phone smoking a blunt.

"Damn Nigga, you must really be sick you slept thru lunch and dinner. I thought you had a visit today?"

"I did, I told her not to come since I wasn't feeling good."

"Nigga, you been fucked up for damn near a week. You must have food poison."

"I'm feelin a little better now." I looked at my watch, it was close to 6 o'clock.

"Jenkins!" tha guard yelled," I went to tha door, "you got a visit, let's go man!"

"Shit, I just told her not to come."

I brushed my teeth and went downstairs. When I got to tha visiting room, I didn't see Ashanti anywhere. It wasn't until Heaven stood up that I knew who came to see me. When I got to tha table she must of thought she was gettin' a hug. I sat straight down.

"Well, hi to you too."

"Hello Heaven, I didn't hug you because I'm sick and didn't want to pass my germs to you."

"So you not still mad?"

"Mad about what? You're tha one who left tha visit."

"But you didn't write or call me?"

"Why should I? You walked out."

"I wasn't ready to hear what you had told me."

"Heaven lets be real, Ashanti is my girl. We have sex unprotected so it was only a matter of time until we had a son."

"Oh, so you're having a boy?"

"Yeah, Lil Naz. You gon' babysit?" I asked wit a smile.

"I might," she replied wit her own smile, "well Naz, I'm sorry about that."

"Listen Heaven, that's tha second time you've done that; tha next time it's over. I don't have time to play these childish games that you keep playing. You knew what it was from jump and no I'm not saying this to hurt ya feelings, but I have to keep it 100 wit you." She looked like a child that had just been scorn.

"Now don't get me wrong, I do care for you but I have so much on my mind right now that I don't have time for all tha drama."

"Naz, I know that and that's why I had to come here to see you. Plus, I think I know who set you up."

"What!" I yelled causing tha guard to get up.

"My fault, did you just say..."

"Yes, you heard me correctly."

"Well, who is it?"

"Do you know Easy Hawk tha boy from Jefferson Street?"

"Yeah."

"Well, between me and you, he working wit them boys."

"How you know?"

"He mess wit my cuzin and I overheard him telling her that he set sum boy up on 8th & Indy."

"Did he say who or why?"

"Nah, but he did say he got paid 5 stacks and you tha only one from ya set that got set up."

"Who else you tell this to?"

"Nobody."

"Good, keep it to ya self. I'll be out in a few months so I will able to find out more."

After my visit, I sat in my room thinking about what Heaven had said.

"Why would Easy Hawk set me up and for who? I swear on my mom when I do find out may God have mercy on their soul. Tha police are gonna need a new rat cause Easy Hawk is a dead rat walking; he just didn't know it yet."

That night I didn't get any sleep, what Heaven said kept playing over and over in my head which only built up rage inside of me. So at 4 in tha morning, I got up and worked out. I wasn't feelin sick anymore; it's like my sickness was replaced by anger. When Fitz got up for breakfast, I was still working out. I normally workout every other day but since I was sick I hadn't even did so much as a push-up.

"I see you back."

"Yeah."

I didn't tell Fitz what Heaven had told me. When I kill him, I didn't want anything to link him back to me. Not that I didn't trust Fitz, I just didn't see tha need to tell him.

"Yo, you goin' to chow?"

"Nah, I'mma finish my workout."

Once he left I finished up my workout then hopped in tha shower. I didn't feel like being bothered so I decided to stay in my room all day.

CHAPTER 20

A Matter of Time

"I had been out here for 3 months and they still were able to score; I had them thinking I was only pushing their work. When in fact, I was pushing my own as well. I couldn't front, this block was a gold mine. I had accumulated a hefty amount of money for myself in just 3 months. So I know if I was running this shit what tha take would be. I was tryin' to be patient but I didn't know how much longer I could be. There was no doubt that this team Naz put together would ride for him and this block. Half of them didn't want me up here. As it was, I might need to call Easy Hawk and start plucking them off one by one."

"Damn Nigga, you must be in deep thought."

"Huh," I said startled by P.R., "I didn't even hear you."

"I know."

"Nah, I was just think'n about my lil cuzin that got killed in that shootout wit tha police in West Philly."

"That was ya peeps?"

"Yeah."

"I tip my hat to that little nigga; he was a true solider trained to go. If you got to go out that's tha way to do it."

"Nah, that was sum nut Shit. Nigga is you high? He was bangin out wit sum niggaz and they called tha man. When they came they didn't ask no questions they just started shooting so he returned fire. It was either them or him."

"Yeah, and it was him."

"Shit! He took 4 of 'em wit him."

"Fuck what you talk'n Doe that nigga will forever be known in tha streetz as a legend."

"Man, he was 16, he had his whole life to live."

"Nigga, you sound like a Fucken preacher."

"Aye P.R., why this nigga alwayz in sum body biz-ness?" I asked referring to Esco.

Even though it was no secret that he didn't like me nor did I him. I knew we were on a crash course collision, I just wanted to make sure I'm tha only survivor.

"Damn, why y'all alwayz bickering like two females?"

"Cause, I don't trust or like this nigga," Esco said bluntly.

Now that was tha one thing I did like about him; he didn't hold or bite his tongue even if that was gonna be his downfall.

"Check this out Young'n, I don't give a Fuck if you do or don't like me but you will respect me," I said walking towards him.

P.R. stepped in between us as we were about to face off like Cage and Travolta.

"I swear, if you two don't knock this Shit off I'mma shoot both you Motha Fuckas!"

Esco looked at me then said, "Make that ya last time Nigga. Next time P.R. ain't gon' be able to stop what I'mma throw at ya Bitch Ass!"

"You threatening me!"

"Nah, I don't make threats," he said then walked off.

"Listen Doe, to avoid any future shit just don't say shit to him."

"I didn't say nuffin to begin wit, me and you were having a conference."

"I know, I'm bout to go say sum thing to him." My phone started to ring,

I waited until he walked off before I answered.

"Hello."

"Long time no hear."

"What up Cuz, what's good wit you?"

"I can't call it, just calling to make sure you good."

"Yeah, I'm bout to take over this block."

"What block?"

"I been on 8th & Indy tha past few months eatin' all crazy."

"Damn, Naz let you in."

"Yeah, but he in C.F.C.F."

"He got knocked wit sum Caine?"

"Nah, murder."

"WHAAAT!"

"It's a long story."

"I got time." I filled him in on what I had Easy Hawk do.

"Damn Doe, I thought I was grimy when I send niggaz to tha boneyard but you sent a nigga to tha bing for life."

"I could have sent him to tha boneyard but I'd rather see him in jail watching me run tha block he started."

"Well, if he letting you pump out there and you crazy up, why not keep it like that?"

"Cause, I see how much this block generates and I want it all."

"I feel you on that. Well, I'mma hit you up."

"No doubt."

"Be safe."

"You do tha same." As soon as I hung up Angel had called.

"What up wit you ma?"

"Shit, calling to see if you wanted to catch a movie later."

"How come we can't catch one now?"

"I thought you were probably busy."

"Nah, I'm just finishing up. I can be there in tha next 30 minutes."

"Ok, just hit my phone when you get close."

"A'ight, I got ya." (CLICK)

I let P.R. know that I had a date and I would be back later.

CHAPTER 21

Tha Plan

"Listen Nigga, tha next time you come up short wit my doe I'mma..."

BONG, BONG, BONG, BONG! Before he could finish, I pulled out my .357 and hit him four times in tha chest.

As he laid there doin' a dying man's version of tha Harlem shake I said, "Nigga you have been disrespecting me too long! I should and would have been killed ya Bitch Ass! I just needed to know where all tha money and drugs were being kept. Now that I know, like Nino told Smitty on New Jack City, ya service is no longer needed!" I put my .357 up to his temple, BOOM!

I watched what little life he had left instantly leave his body while I was retrieving ery thing. I heard sum body come in.

"Shit!" I said to myself, *"if Sticky was here who ever it was would have neva made it inside but since I had no idea this was gonna happen, I wasn't prepared."*

I stood in tha closet wit tha door opened just enough to see who was in tha house. When they came upstairs after about 5 minutes I could hear sum body coming up tha steps; wit my finger on tha trigger I held my .357 in my hand ready to shoot whoever it was. When tha person finally got to tha room I was more than relieved to see Sticky standing there.

"Nigga I thought I was gonna have to kill you," BONG, "hold on Nigga it's me," I said already on tha floor because I knew that he would shoot first.

"Mother Fucker you almost got killed."

"How did you know I was here?"

"Because I thought I saw you get in tha car wit that nigga. I just wasn't sure so after you didn't come back for a minute, I decided to come here."

"How did you know where to come?"

"I do my homework too Nigga."

"As you should."

"We better get out of here before sum body comes home."

I grabbed tha duffle bag then headed downstairs out tha front door. We had walked away wit close to 400 thousand and 2 bricks of Caine. We had already gained a nice bit of clientele so there was no need to run back to Philly. Especially, since I had just killed tha man who ran VA. So it was time for us to take over. I know there are goin' to be a lot of bodies on tha way.

Three weeks had passed by, a lot of blood had been shed, but at tha end of tha day we were at tha head of tha table.

"Listen Cannon, when Pow was alive he was letting them things fly at 26.5. Now you tryin' to charge 28."

"See, tha difference is tha work he was giving you is no where near as good as this," I said handing him a brick."

I had used my resources; I could get them for 20 so why not sale 'em for 28. They really had no choice but to pay my price, nobody else had them. I will have to let my cuzin come down to run this. Tha drug trade wasn't my thing, I just didn't want none of these other niggaz trying to cut in. I pulled out my phone and dialed Doe's number and within 3 rings he picked up.

"What up Lil Cuz."

"You."

"I heard that. I got a few questions for you."

"What's that?"

"You running that block yet?"

"Nah, it's taking' longer than I anticipated."

"Are you interested in running ya own city?"

"Nigga what kind of question is that?"

"Well, how much money do you have saved up? And I'm talk'n about ery thing, don't hold back on me Cuz."

"Truth be told, I got about 250g's saved up, give or take 300 when I'm done my work."

"Are you willing to spend it all?"

"Why? What you tryin' to do?"

"Nigga all you tryin' to spend it all or not?"

"Yeah."

"That's what I wanted to hear. As soon as you done ya work hit me."

"A'ight."

"Doe."

"Yeah."

"As soon as you done, I'll fill you in when you hit me back but one thing for sure, two things for certain, you'll see way more money than that block you tryin' to take over."

"A'ight, I should be ready in a few days. I'mma hit ya phone."

"Make sure you do that. Don't miss out on this once in a lifetime opportunity." (CLICK)

As soon as I hung up, I knew that he would follow through. Doe was my older cuzin and I had a lot of love for him. I owed him my life, he alwayz had my back no matter if I was right or wrong. So since I was now in a position to really have him on top, that's where he will be. I'mma turn him on to my peeps so he can get 15 birds for his money. Just thinking about him running VA had me excited. Plus, wit me and Sticky by his side, how could he lose?

Tha next few days came and went. Just when I started to lose faith, my phone rang bringing an instant smile to my face.

"Hello."

"My fault Cuz, I got tied up."

"I was starting to think you didn't want to get down."

"Nah, Nah, you know I'm alwayz gamed to make doe. That is my name Fo' Sho. So what's this big plan you got?"

"Do you know how to get to Richmond?"

"Yeah, you know I got a young jawn down in Richmond."

"That's even better. When we hang up, call her and let her know that you bout to move down."

"Whoa, Whoa, who said I was moving down there?"

"Once you see what's goin' on, Philly will be a afterthought, trust me."

"Well, let me pack a few things then I'll hit you when I'm close."

(CLICK).

It was about to be on and I couldn't wait. Sticky walked in.

"What you so happy about?"

"Nuffin, Doe's on his way down."

"Oh, he decided to take tha offer?"

"Actually I haven't told him yet but I'm sure he will. He'd be a fool not to."

"Yeah, you right about that. Come on let's grab a bite to eat."

CHAPTER 22

On My Way

As I was packing my clothes Angel had called.

"Shit! I forgot about her." When I answered tha tone in her voice let me know that sum thing was wrong.

"Hello."

"Doe we need to talk."

"Yeah I know, I was about to call you." I was lying but it sounded good.

"Well, you go first," she said.

"I'm leaving town for a while if things go right it would probably be for good. I need to branch out and spread my wings. I've been in Philly my whole life; it might be time for a change."

"Where are you goin'?" she asked.

"Richmond."

"That's not far, it's only about 3 ½ hours away. I know, I have family in Richmond."

"Oh yeah?"

"Yup, my aunt, and 2 cuzins, Shizz, and Beauty."

"As soon as I heard Beauty's name my heart skipped a beat. What were tha chances that my young joint from VA would be Angel's cuzin?"

"Doe, Doe."

"Huh?"

"Did you hear me?"

"Huh, yeah."

"Why tha change of voice?" I neva lied to her so I wasn't about to start.

"Now Ang."

"Yeah."

"I need to tell you sum thing else."

"What's that?"

"Ya cuzin Beauty was my young jawn." What she said next surprised me.

"I know, she had told me awhile back that she messed wit sum dude from up this way named Doe. It didn't dawn on me until we slept together that it was you. So I called her to see if she had feelings for you because if she did, I would have backed off. But she said y'all were just bed buddy's. So don't think you can go down there and smash. I do respect ya honesty though. So what did you have to tell me?"

"Well, truthfully, I don't know if I want or even should tell you now since you leaving town."

"Ang, you been dealing wit me for a few months and you still don't know me?"

"I'm pregnant," she said then got quite probably waiting for my response.

I knew not to ask if it was mine because we have been having unprotected sex and she's not tha type to sleep around.

All I could ask was, "Are you tryin' to visit ya peeps?"

"For a little while, are you saying you want me to go wit you?"

"Only if you want to go."

"Stop playing, I get to visit my peeps and spend time wit you. Shiiiit! When we leaven?"

"About an hour."

"How long we staying?"

"Pack enough clothes for 2 weeks."

"I have about 2 weeks' worth of vacation, so I'll call my job."

"Just be ready in a hour."

When I hung up I called Cannon to let him know about what just played out. He couldn't believe that Ang and Beauty were cuzins or that I was goin' to be a daddy. Shit, I couldn't even believe it. He told me to bring her down. I was already 2 steps ahead of him.

"They still riding them Buicks down there."

"Yeah why? You coming down wit ya old school."

"You know it, let me go pick Ang up then I'm on my way."

"A'ight Cuz, it's 6 o'clock see you around 9 o'clock."

I finished putting my clothes in my Gucci luggage bag then went into my garage to bounce out. I wanted to take my 745 but since I was trying to blend in. I hopped in my watermelon on white 62" Impala wit tha 26 inch spinners. I had tha top cut and replaced wit a soft white top. Tha inside was piped out in watermelon and TVs in tha head rest, 17 inch flip down wit tha marching band, 4 6-9's across tha back deck, 4 6 ½ in tha doors, 3 15 inch in tha trunk. I went old school, ery thing pioneer even tha 3 amps I had pushing it. I pulled out of tha garage in route to Angel's.

When I pulled up I didn't have to call or honk tha horn. She heard me coming and was already out front. I popped tha trunk so she could put her bags in. When she got in and saw my wraps she asked if I wanted her to drive so I could roll my trees. I let her know that I could drive and roll at tha same time.

"Can I watch my movie?"

"Look, you not goin' to mess up my flow."

"You can still listen to Plies; I Just Want to Watch Belly." I put it in and pulled down tha visors.

"Oh, tha dash TV don't work?"

"Yeah, it works."

"So why you pull that down?"

"I thought you would rather look at it on that."

"I'm good."

We were damn near there and it was only 7:55.

"We making good time."

"I know we are, you been doin 110 tha whole ride."

"Have I? It didn't even feel like it."

"I know, I just happen to look at tha dash a few times."

When we arrived it was only 8:30. I called Cannon to let him know that I was in town. He said he was in front of Beauty's house wit Shizz which was good because that's where I was taking Ang. I pulled up right behind him, when I put my high beams on they both jumped out tha car.

When they saw it was me Shizz said in his Southern drawl, "You almost got this pretty shit shot up Cuz."

"Awe Nigga, you wasn't gon' do Shit!"

"Is that my Cuz you got wit you?"

"Hey Shizz."

What up Angel, come give ya cuz a hug. Damn Girl, you picked up sum weight since tha last time I saw you."

"That's cause she's knocked up," Cannon said smiling.

"Oh Snap, lil cuz having a baby." Shizz was so loud that Beauty and her mom came to tha door.

"What is all this noise out here?"

When they saw Angel, Beauty ran out, "Oh My God! Why didn't you call to say you were coming? I know I would have cooked a big dinner."

"It was a spare of tha moment thing, I didn't even know."

"What's up Doe," Beauty said to me wit a smile.

"Aye Mom, guess who's pregnant?"

Before Ang could speak, Beauty said, "You alwayz running ya mouth," we all looked at her then she asked, "so how many months are you?" All I could do was smile, then I let them know I was only 8 weeks.

"Well, come in, it's chilly out here."

"Y'all go head, we need to talk."

As they were walking back to tha house this 92 Grand Marquis on 22s pulled up bumpin' that Clisp Vagina. Beauty quickly turned around.

As soon as dude got out tha car he said, "What up Cannon, Shizz."

"What up Meat?"

"I can't call it. God Damn, this pretty Mother Fucker you?" he asked pointing to my whip.

"Nah, that's my cuzin Doe Shit."

"Oh, what up my Nigga? Shit what's them 24's?"

"Nah, 26's."

"Whoooo you sittin' pretty."

"Thanks."

"Hey Baby," he said to Beauty.

"Hey Daddy," was her response.

"Why didn't you call to say you was stopping by?"

"Cause I came to holla at ya brother and Cannon."

"Umm excuse me, you just make sure you come in before you dip off."

"I got you," he said smacking her ass. He turned around to catch me lookin', I just smiled.

"Aye Cannon, you ready for me? I'm bout to put you down wit my cuzin, this who I been gettin tha work from. I figured I would introduce y'all that way we don't have to do this middle man shit no more."

"I'm down wit that cause you probably been pocketing a few ones off of us anyway."

"Nah, he been charging y'all 28 a brick; ery body else been paying 30," Shizz said.

"I know but considering that recession is still goin' on, that's good."

I looked at Cannon then smiled, "I see what he was doin."

At that point, my mind was made up. I was moving to Richmond, me and my baby momma if she was down. After we finished kicking it wit Shizz and Meat, Cannon wanted to take a ride.

"Hold up, let me tell Ang I'll be back." Instead of knocking I chirped her phone.

"Yes."

"I'll be back."

"Where you goin'?"

"To check into a hotel."

"For what? My aunt said we can stay here."

"Nah, you can but I'mma get a room."

"Well, I'm staying wit you. Don't be all night."

Beauty said, "There's a party jumpin' tonight."

"A'ight, give me a hour, at tha most."

"Before you pull off let me get sum thing to wear out my bag."

"Come get tha keys, I'm riding wit Cannon." I gave her tha keys then bounced.

"I ain't letting you stay in no hotel; you can use one of my spots."

"That's what's up. Where's Sticky?"

"He wit one of his broads. Did you bring tha money wit you cause we need to holla at my peeps tomorrow so we can get tha ball bouncing. Listen Doe, tha nigga who was running this Shit is dead and you already did it. I could easily take over this Shit but hustling ain't me. I'd rather let them niggaz make it while I take it. So me and Sticky figured we would just bring you in so you can run this shit. My mans will sell you birds for 20 a pop. You let them go for 28 or 30."

"I feel you, but none of these niggaz don't know me."

"But they know me and wit my help by tha end of tha night they'll know you. That party they was talk'n bout, all tha major players and money getting niggaz along wit tha smuts and dimes will be in da building. So I hope you packed one of ya good suits like I told you."

"Of course."

"And we driving ya Shit. They gon' be on you when we pull up in that."

"These Bama Ass Niggaz don't do it how we do it up North."

"You might find a few people wit 24s, but nobody got 26s or a pretty ass old school like that."

He took me to tha spot where he was gonna let me crash. Then we shot back to Beauty's house.

"Hit my phone when you get dressed."

"Ok."

As he was pulling off, Ang was coming to tha door. Damn she looked good wit her cream & brown Christian Dior dress wit matching stiletto's.

"You might as well get dressed here it's 10 o'clock."

"Yeah, you right."

I went in my trunk and got what I needed then headed to tha house. Ang showed me to tha bathroom. Once I was showered and dressed, I had to admire myself in tha mirror. Brown Gucci button up, Gucci jeans, Gucci blazer, and Gucci loafers. Of course, I had to throw my Gucci frames on. I gathered my things then stepped out tha bathroom.

"Damn my nigga that shit is airborne." They had tha craziest slang.

"I like ya Shit too." I lied but I had to say sum thing.

These niggaz are dressed like straight Bama's. I would neva put on a orange suit and shoes looking like a Sunkist orange. When we came downstairs, Meat had on a purple one lookin' like a Black Barney.

Ang said, "Y'all got a crazy dress code down here." Then started laughing. Meat took offense.

"What so funny."

"Nuffin." She was laughing so hard tears were rolling down her face.

"Y'all don't know style up north."

"Ery body gon' be dressed like this?" She kept laughing.

That's when Shizz said, "Ya man like my suit." She looked at me then laughed even harder.

"You right, if you call that style; we definitely don't know nuffin about style."

Beauty dressed like she was from up North. She had on a black Liz

Claiborne dress that showed every curve. Ang stop laughing when she caught me lookin' at Beauty.

"Let me call Cannon, I couldn't dial his number fast enough."

"Yo, you ready Cuz?"

"Yeah, that's why I called."

"Where you at?"

"Over Shizz house."

"We'll be there in 15 minutes."

Sure enough, they were pulling up. They both were dressed in Prada button ups and blazers wit Prada shoes.

"Meat, I'mma ride wit you and my sis if it's cool."

"Sure."

I had already hit tha automatic start so when we got outside my car was already running wit tha system bumpin' that Plies, Keep it to Real. Cannon and Sticky hopped in tha back while me and Ang jumped in tha front and pulled both visors and tha flip down so that tha cars behind me could watch Belly. I didn't have my shit up loud so I could hear Meat's shit pumpin'.

"I know ya Shit is louder than this."

"Stop tryin' to play me."

"Well turn that Shit up!"

"Put my anthem on," I said, "Definition of Real, Track 3, Volume 20."

When Bushes came on dem niggaz said, "God Damn!"

We pulled up to tha club and it was j-peed, tha line was around tha block. I slowed down since everybody was staring. Might as well let them see who was behind tha wheel of this fly ass whip. It was sum nice whips but my shit was by far tha hottest. I found a spot. When we hopped out, all eyes were most definitely on us.

Ang said, "Damn, these niggaz can't dress."

"You ain't neva lied about that," Sticky said dappin' her.

"I know that's why they alwayz on our shit." And tonight was no different.

"You know I'm not waiting in this long ass line."

We walked to tha front, Cannon slid tha bouncer sum money and we went straight in to be greeted by T-Pains, *Buy You a Drink.*

"Excuse us for a minute," Cannon said leading me towards a group of niggaz.

"What up Folk? What it is Kin?"

"Sup Cannon." They all spoke.

"This is my peeps Doe that I was telling y'all bout." They all spoke.

"I know we came to have a good time but you gon' be ready in tha mornin. Doe we need 9 of them things. We got da 270 stacks?"

"Yeah, I'll definitely be ready."

When we slid off, Cannon smiled then said, "What I tell you?"

"Yeah Cuz, I owe you big time for this."

"Naw, you don't owe me Shit."

"Well, I need to buy me a crib."

By tha end of tha night, I knew all tha major niggaz and had tha bricks sold already. My man was definitely gonna have to come down on tha price.

A few of tha females were all over me but there was no way I would say anything to them while Ang was there. She was still a little mad about me staring at Beauty. I'mma let her know that she needs to understand that we had a thing and me being a man I'm goin' to look when I see any female in sum thing that accents her body, I'm goin' to look. Just like if she sees a nigga that looks good she's goin' to look, just like she's doin now.

I walked up to her, "Fine sum thing you like?" She jumped.

"My fault, didn't mean to startle you."

"Boy go head, I ain't Fuckin wit you."

"Why? Because I was lookin' at Beauty?"

"Yup!"

Listen, I told her what needed to be said. I also let her know that I was not trying to disrespect her in anyway. When it was all said and done she understood.

It was 3 in tha morning when tha party was over. There was sum commotion goin' on outside near my whip. So I hit my automatic start. When my car came to life. *"Gilly's Get Down On tha Ground"* was blaring out. Everybody looked to see who had just started it up. Two dudes were arguing over sum broad that was just standing there saying nuffin.

"Doc, I know you not out here playing ya self arguing over no broad."

"Nah, I'm just letting this nigga know tha next time he put his hands on my sister I'mma bust his ass!"

"Real talk, Man you gon' be wasting ya time cause she still gon' be wit him anyway."

BOOM, BOOM, BOOM! Were tha only sounds that could be heard. Everybody was running and screaming. Ang was already in tha car. We all hopped in, I wasted no time mashing out. I seen sum young boy standing there holding a .45 in his hand wit a big smile on his face.

"Stop tha car for a sec Cuz." I looked at Cannon like he'd lost his mind.

"Nigga stop tha car!" When I did, he rolled down tha window.

"Reep, what tha Fuck you doin'? Get ya Dumb Ass in here!" He diddy bopped to tha car wit out a care in tha world like he wasn't just shooting.

Once he was in I asked, "Cannon what tha Hell was that about?"

"I was just letting Crate know that if I wanted him I could have got him."

"I thought that Shit was over."

"So did I, but he told his baby moms that I wanted to kill him."

"You still hittin' that?"

"Nah, I just drop by occasionally to get a shot of that super head."

"Oh Shit! My bag I didn't see tha lady in tha front. This is a nice whip. Who they?" he asked pointing to me and Ang.

"Oh how rude of me, Reep this my cuzin Doe and his wifey Ang."

"What up y'all. At first, I thought you was this sexy ass broad named Beauty; y'all kinda favor."

"Nah, but that is her peeps."

"No wonder they look alike. So what you 2 niggaz bout to do?" he asked talk'n to Cannon and Sticky.

"I got to drop him off then I gots to handle sum thing. Why you want to roll?"

"You know it."

Reep only looked to be about 16, no older than 18. I pulled up to Shizz house to let them out.

"Aye Sticky, you better get ya Bitch Ass up or you gon' sleeping in tha car."

"Nigga I'm up, I ain't sleep." Once they were out I asked Ang if she had her bag.

"Yeah, I neva took it out."

"Is you staying wit me or..."

Before I could finish she said, "Don't play wit me, you must be tryin' to go holla at one of dem gold diggers that was sweating you."

"Oh word, broads were on me?" She punched me in tha arm.

"That's it! No Pussy for you tonight."

All I could say was, "Ya lost not mine." Then started laughing.

"I don't know how a long distance relationship is gonna last."

"What you talk'n bout?"

"I'm moving down here."

"Well, you better find a place big enough for 3," she said pointing to her stomach.

"Oh, so you moving down wit me?"

"I know you didn't think you was goin' to start a new life wit out us, did you?"

"Truthfully, I was hoping that you were goin' to say that. Otherwise, I would have went to court to get custody of my child."

"Well, you would have one Hell of a fight on your hands if you thought I was goin' to just give my first and only child up."

"I would have just gave you a hundred grand." I pulled up to tha crib.

"Listen, if you plan to be wifey, we need to get a few things straight."

"I'm listening."

"We can talk when we get inside."

After we finished talk'n, we handled our biz-ness until tha sun came up.

CHAPTER 23

Holding it Down

"I knew I should have peeled that nigga cap back when I had tha chance."

"It ain't bout nuffin, he ain't take Shit from us."

"Still he running around yapping his mouth like we pussy's. Next time I run across him..."

"Next time you run across that nigga you ain't gon' do Shit!"

"A'ight, I bet you see his boys wit 'In Memory' T-shirts," he said then walked away.

"Esco, why you do that? You done got that nigga killed. He ain't gon' wait to run into him, he gon' go look for that nigga as soon as tha sun sets."

"Fuck that nigga! He should of kept his big mouth closed. Truth be told, if Gunz ain't do it, I would have been tha one to do it. See, if you let one Mother Fucka disrespect you and don't check 'em then ery body else gon' think they can do it. A lot of niggaz fear us cause they know we bout our biz-ness, Stone Cold Killers. Then to be killers wit all tha bread we got now, Mother Fuckas don't know how to take us but one thing about me P.R., I put my own work in. Why pay another joker to do sum thing I can do on my own."

"I definitely feel you on that. So what's tha deal wit ya boy Doe? I ain't seen him around in a few months."

"I don't know, I heard he moved down South sum where. I ain't really sure."

"It don't really matter to me, that's one less nigga I got to send to tha boneyard."

"What's tha beef wit y'all?"

"I just don't trust that nigga; my heart tells me he ain't right so I play him to tha left. I'm bout to go holla at Naz to let him know what tha deal is; you need me to tell him sum thing?"

"Nah but give him this." He pulled out a wad of money, then peeled off 5 hundred dollar bills.

When I pulled up to tha prison there were a few news vans outside, I couldn't help but wonder what was goin' on that would bring Channel 6 and 10 News. I walked in tha lobby and when it was my turn I handed them my ID then let them know I was here to see Nazir Jenkins.

"You can have a seat; we'll be ready in 10 minutes." One of tha news guys were in tha middle of an interview wit a guard.

"So do you think that his death was really a suicide?"

"Yes, I have no reason to believe that sum one would kill him."

"Vasquz, this way." I walked into tha visiting room and Naz was already waiting; that was a first.

"What up my Nigga?"

It had been 30 days since we last saw one another, even though we talked on tha phone.

"I wanted you to come up here because you know my trial starts in less than 3 months. I want you to check on Ashanti every day since she's due any day now!"

"Nigga I been doin that anyway. You know I'mma hold you down."

"I know, you been doin that since day one."

"Biggie said it best, 'Real Niggaz Do Real Things' I like to consider myself real." We both started laughing, for tha rest of tha visit I filled him in on tha daily operations of da block.

"So nobody still hasn't seen or heard from Doe?"

"Nah, but word is he down South sum where doin his thing."

Tha visit came to an end, we dapped each other then went our separate ways; him back to his tier and me outside. When I got back to tha block it was little after 5.

Wendy came to tha door, "Hey P.R., when you get a chance let me talk to you for a minute."

"A'ight Wen, Give me a second I'll be right in." I walked up tha block to see what all tha commotion was about.

"I'm tellin' you I gave you 1400."

"Nah you didn't. I didn't go nowhere, I'm showing you how much you gave me."

"You need to recount that Shit; I'm tellin' you!"

"I wouldn't try no Bullshit, I alwayz come straight."

"I know and it if it was only 100 short I wouldn't give a Fuck, but this is 300 off!"

"Well, just give me 1200 worth." Tico stepped off to get his product.

"Ery thing cool down here?"

"Yes, just a little misunderstanding nothing major."

Tico came back, "Here Dash, I even put a little extra in there for you."

"Good lookin'," he said. As we walked back to his car.

"Oh Shit!" We both turned around to see Dash heading back our way.

"Tico, Tico!"

"Yo."

"Hold up for a sec!"

We both stopped. I put my hand on my .45 I had in my pocket just in case this nigga was gon' to start shooting.

"My fault, you was right," he said handing Tico tha other 300, "it must of fell out when I got out my car, luckily nobody picked it up."

"I know."

"Let me get tha rest."

"A'ight, I'll be right back."

"Damn! I feel stupid as Shit."

"We all make mistakes, no need to beat ya self up over it though." Tico came back hit him off, then we finished walking down tha block.

"Yo, let me go holla at Wen, I'll be right back."

"A'ight, I ain't goin' nowhere."

When I walked in Wen was at tha table doing what she alwayz did, counting money.

"So what's up Wen?"

"Listen, I don't know if you know or even noticed it at all but between us out here and Naz in there we have been running thru ery thing; so I'm goin' to up ery thing."

"To what?"

"Instead of 15 bricks I'mma get 30, 30 pounds of Sour D and 8 thousand "E" pills. I also noticed that a lot of people been coming thru for heroin. So what I'm gonna do is buy just an ounce to see how it moves."

"I don't know nuffin about that dope."

"No, but I do; all I need you to do is go to tha trophy shop and tell them you want a stamper wit tha name Exclusive. I already talked to Juan, he told me I could get tha ounce for 3 stacks."

"Damn!"

"That's cheap, you really don't know nuffin bout dope. Off of 3 stacks we gon' see 10 easy."

"10g's Damn!" He phone rang 3 times before she picked up.

"Hello, yeah when you want me to leave?"

"Now."

"A'ight, I'll be there in 15 minutes." As soon as she hung up she put all tha money in a duffle bag then headed to tha door.

"I'll be back in a few, hold it down."

Don't I alwayz? Oh, go get that stamper."

I pulled up to tha storage spot, slid my card in, and once tha gate opened I proceeded to pull my car around to 527. I had rented this space a few months ago. I would either meet Juan here or just drop tha money off and pick tha drugs up, but today I needed to holla at Juan to see how good this heroin really was. As soon as I pulled around to tha garage I spotted Juan goin' in. I grabbed my duffle bag then slid in.

"Hello, my Lady," he said to me. I dropped da duffle bag on tha floor.

"You know Juan, you at least drop tha price considering all tha money we spend wit you."

"Maybe if you would go on a friendly dinner date wit me I would."

"If that's what it's goin' to take then I'll gladly go on a friiiendy and I emphasized tha word *'friendly'* dinner date." Juan had been trying ta get in my panties ever since tha first time Naz introduced us.

"When you ready you can give me a call but if you don't call before it's time to re-up, I'm calling you." We both busted out laughing.

Truth be told, tha only reason I wouldn't give him any is because I don't mix biz-ness and pleasure, it neva works out. After we finished I let him know if tha heroin was good I would need more. If you do just call me. I put tha work in tha secret compartment of tha car then drove off.

As soon as I saw Wendy pull up I walked into tha house. I had 2 people coming up from Delaware to grab 4 bricks at 30 apiece. When she came in wit tha duffle bag I wasted no time opening it up.

"Damn Nigga! Let me put tha bag down first!" My phone started ringing.

"Hello, yeah I'm ready for y'all. Are y'all already up this way? Look meet me at tha same spot in 30 minutes."

When I pulled into tha Super Fresh parking lot KB and Rob were parked where they alwayz park at. I pulled in next to them and motioned for one of them to get in. Once KB was in I backed out, I didn't have to tell Rob to follow us, he knew tha routine by now.

"Is this tha same work?"

"Yeah."

"They loving this shit down my way. If you come down on da number we'll cop more."

"Nigga we still in a recession, you getting' 'em for da low."

"I know ery body else want 36 and tha Shit is trash." I pulled over to let him out.

"I'ma holla at you when I'm done, be safe."

"You do tha same down ya end wit all them snitches."

"Man who you tellin'?"

I pulled up to tha light on 8th & Spring Garden; tha next thing I knew BONG, BONG, BONG, BONG! TAT, TAT, TAT, TAT, TAT, TAT, TAT!

I stepped on tha gas and at tha same time pulling my .45 out and firing out tha window. BOOM, BOOM, BOOM, BOOM! One of my shots hit tha passenger in tha face and tha driver turned off. I wasn't trying to hear that so now I was tha predictor on tha heels of my prey. BOOM, BOOM, BOOM! I let off another 3 shot shattering tha back window. I could tell that I had killed tha passenger by tha way he was slumped down. When tha driver turnt around to see if I was still on his ass, I caught a glimpse of his face. BOOM, BOOM, BOOM! I was trying to tear this niggaz head off. I could hear tha police sirens so I slowed down then turned off.

By tha time I made it back to da block I was pissed off. My car looked like Swiss cheese.

"Fuck! I just got this, 600."

"What tha Fuck happen to ya Shit?" I got out and damn near passed out. My adrenalin was running so I neva even felt tha bullet hit my side.

"P.R. who did this? Dem niggaz from Delaware you went to meet?"

"Nah, that Bitch Ass Nigga Ralo that was talk'n shit to y'all. I killed one of them though. Go get Wendy so she can take me to tha hospital. Take my car sum where and set it on fire, my insurance will pay for it." Wendy came out.

"Shiit! Let me get a sheet so you won't bleed all over my Shit! What you gon' tell tha hospital? You know they gon' call tha jakes."

"I got car jacked and you just happen to be right there."

"Sounds like a winner to me."

"Esco don't retaliate until I come back."

"I'm gon' try to stay put for as long as I can; them niggaz crossed tha line.

By tha time we got to tha hospital, I had lost a lot of blood. Once they put me on tha gurney ery thing after that was a blank. When I finally came around to find my uncle and cuzin along wit my team all standing around my bedside.

"Damn Nigga, you gave us all a scare."

"Yeah, we almost lost you."

"Nah, you know I ain't goin' out wit out sum get back."

"Well, you gon' have to put that on hold; tha doctors said you gon' be in here for a few weeks."

"A few weeks! What tha Fuck!!" Tha nurse came running in when she heard me yell.

"Is ery thing alright in here?"

"Sorry bout that, my nephew had moment," my uncle told her. She looked at me then smiled.

"Damn she was phat, I would be hittin' that before I checked out."

"If you need anything just push tha button," she said pointing to tha pad on tha side of my bed then turned and walked off.

"Listen P.R., since you gon' be confined to that there bed for a few weeks, we gon' handle that situation."

"Nah, Nah, I want to do this Shit, it's personal now. Them niggaz tried to send me to tha boneyard."

"Ricardo we already got Maria on tha job."

Maria was a broad that my uncle used to line niggaz up that owed doe or when beef was on. Hearing her name made me smile. I remember when I first met her at my uncle's store; she had on a pair of skintight jeans wit a apple bottom shirt. She had a fat ass; I mean fat buffy tha body fat. I spit my game at her, but she wasn't trying to hear it. I came at her wit everything I had. She just wasn't goin' for it, so I gave my unc his cash then left out wit out saying bye to her. Later that night, she had called my phone. I didn't know tha number so when I asked who it was she hit me.

"Damn, how many Bitches got ya number?"

"Not too many, that's why I asked who this is."

"Maria!"

"Who? Oh, how you get my number?"

"Ya uncle gave it to me, I hope you don't mind."

"Not at all, I'm just surprised that you asked him for tha number tha way you kept shooting me down."

"It wasn't that I was shooting you down, I like ya persistence."

"Nah, you liked tha fact a nigga was sweatin' you."

"Boy pleeease, I get that all tha time."

"Oh do you?"

"Yup, sure do."

"So what's up wit you?"

"Check this out, we gon' skip thru all tha extra bullshit."

"What you mean by dat?"

"You want sum Pussy, don't you?"

"Damn, this was my kind of broad, straight to tha point."

"Yup, I sure do!"

"Well, meet me at tha Marriott by tha airport at 8 o'clock. P.R..."

"Yeah."

"Don't be late." Then she hung up.

"Damn, sounds like this Bitch tryin' to line me up. Let me if call my

uncle to see what's up wit her. If anybody would know he would."

Once he told me that she works for him and I had nuffin to worry about. I knew it was on. Long story short, I gave her one of tha best Fucks of her life just to assure that I could smash anytime I wanted.

"P.R.! P.R.! P.R.!" my cuzin shouted, bringing me back to tha present.

"What up Nigga yelling like that?"

"I said ya peeps goin' ta handle it, you just get ya rest; we'll be back tomorrow." As they were walking out Juan turned around.

"Sum broad by tha name of Mimi came by and called about 5 times. So make sure you call her fine ass," he said while winking at me.

"If I know him, he probably tried to holla at her. Shit, I would have if tha shoe was on tha other foot."

"Awe, now that they left, will sum body tell me what's really up wit this beef wit Ralo?"

"You know what we know, tha nigga still mad cause Gunz knocking his baby mom off."

"Tha crazy thing bout it is, I ain't knocked her off in damn near 2 months."

"Yeah Right!"

"Real rap, I ain't say she didn't give me no head. I just ain't knocked her down."

"It has to be sum thing else then. You ain't pillow talk'n wit her about him are you?"

"What? Nigga don't be disrespecting my gangsta like that!"

"I'm just asking, no need to take it personal."

"It don't even matter, that nigga dead!" Esco's phone went off.

All he said was, "Uh, huh, Oh right, uh huh, we on our way but if he leave before we get there, hit my phone. Come on Gunz we gotta go."

"Where we goin'?"

"Don't worry about it, just come on." They left wit out saying anything else.

"Wendy don't tell Naz about this, he already has too much to deal wit."

"To late, he already knows. You know jail finds out about ery thing." Mimi came in.

"Well, I let you talk P.R., I'll be by tomorrow."

"A'ight, bring me sum real food please."

"Hey You, glad to see you. You finally came around."

"Yeah."

"My uncle and cuzin said you been by a few times."

"You know I had to check up on my Boo-Boo."

Mimi was a bad ass chick, if it wasn't for her chinky eyes you would neva know she was Chinese. She was 5'5", gray eyes, short Anita Baker style haircut, a fat ass like tha broad Free that use to host 106 & Park. She was tha first Chinese I ever saw wit brown skin; maybe because her dad was Black.

"P.R. I know that you have a girl but since I been dealing wit you these last 6 months I haven't been wit anybody else, not that I had anybody else before you. I didn't know if I should tell you this before, but after seeing you in this bed I realized that life is too short. So I said all that to say, I'm in love wit you."

"Shit! Did she just say what I thought she said?"

"Did you hear me?"

"Yeah."

She said what I thought she did. I was falling for her too, I'm just a playa at heart. I neva thought I would feel this way about anybody except Shauna.

"Well, to be honest wit you Mimi, I'm diggin' you like a hole. I just don't know if we can take it to another level because I already have a girl."

"I know you do and I'm not asking you to leave her, especially not for me."

"Mimi let me ask you a question."

"I'm listening."

"Why would you want to be wit a person like me when you deserve a lot better?"

"I respected ya honesty from tha door. You didn't have to tell me you had a girl but you did. P.R. I neva planned for my feelings to evolve tha way they did this fast."

"As long as you know ya position, we can ride this thing til tha wheels fall off."

"That's all it is, me and you against all odds."

"Don't you mean, against tha world?"

"What ever!"

Shauna walked in, before she could say anything I said, "Hey Babe."

"Oh, so this is tha girl who stole my cuzins heart," Mimi said wit a big smile. So I followed suit.

"Yes, this is her. Shauna this is my cuzin Mimi, vice versa." They both extended their hands.

"Well, I better get goin', I don't want to be late for work. I love you Cuz," she said reaching over to plant a kiss on my forehead.

"Love you too Cuz." When she left Shauna said that dumbest Shit.

"Y'all do look alike." I couldn't help it, I had to laugh.

"What's so funny?"

"Nuffin, I just thought about what Esco said."

CHAPTER 24

It's Time

I was due any day now and I couldn't wait. I had gained over 30 pounds. Naz had told me not to come see him til after I have tha baby. He didn't want me goin' into labor in tha visiting room. Ever since he had gotton his cell phone, we were alwayz on tha phone every night. Since I'm due to have my baby any day, he's been calling all day every day. My cell started ringing, *"I'm Locked Up They Won't Let Me Out"* all I could do was smile.

"Hey Baby Daddy."

"Oh, so I'm just ya baby daddy, huh?"

"Naw, you know you my Boop-Boop."

"That's what ya mouth say."

"Boy sit down. Naz ya son is driving me crazy, all he does is move around."

"If you been trapped in a small space for 9 months wouldn't you want to get out?"

"You damn right, I want him out just as bad as he wants out."

"Woman go through a lot to have a baby; y'all definitely get props from me."

"I finally got tha rest of his stuff."

"That's what's up."

"Naz, he got so much stuff it don't make no sense."

"I bet he do between you and Nana."

"Naw, between P.R., Esco, Gunz, and da rest of them; Shit he won't need no clothes til he gets about a year." He said that P.R. had told him they had gotton him a few things.

"Well, if that's a few, I'd hate to see a lot. They all made their selves Lil Naz's God father's."

"Did they?"

"Yeah, we won't have to worry about him needing nuffin."

"Babe, we ain't gon' have to worry bout that anyway. I'm his dad remember! Ashanti, I'm call you in a few hours they bout to do count."

"Ok, I love you."

"Love you too."

After I hung up Nana called to tell me that she had made my favorite lasagna, "I'm on my way."

On tha way I felt a sharp pain, I just thought it was Lil Naz kicking again. As soon as I pulled up to Nana's I felt it again.

"Damn Boy, you better calm ya bad ass down." Nana met me at tha door, when I walked in he did it again this time I had to stop.

"Baby you Ok?"

"Yeah, he just kicking me every few minutes."

"Sounds like you might be having contractions. You might need to go to tha hospital." Just then it felt like I was pissing on myself.

"Chil' you bout to go in labor, ya water just broke."

"AAAAAH! SHIIIIIT!" I doubled over in pain.

"Charles!" Nana yelled, "come drive us to tha hospital, it's time!"

Charles came running down tha steps, "Damn!"

Near falling, he helped me to tha car wit Nana on our heels. We made it to tha hospital in 10 minutes flat, by that time tha pain had become unbearable. Tha kicking was less than 2 minutes apart. By tha time they put me on tha stretcher, it felt like he was coming out. Tha funny thing was

Nana had tha camcorder out tha whole time.

"Push! Chil' Push!"

"AAAAAH, AAAAH! OOOOH!"

"He's coming, I can see his head! Push a little harder!!" I gave it one last hard push.

"WAA! WAAAA! Were tha first sounds my son made." Nana cut tha umbilical cord.

After they cleaned him up, I finally got tha chance to hold and see my son.

"Hey mommy's baby." Nana was crying.

"What's wrong Nana?"

"He looks like Cassy." Cassy was Naz mom.

"I can't believe it; God has sent my baby back in tha form of my great grandson."

Charles came in, "Wow! He looks just like Naz and Cassy."

"Yeah, he does cause Naz looks just like his mother."

Uncle Charles pulled out his digital camera, he took so many pictures that Nana had to tell him to put tha camera away.

"I need to make sure Naz has plenty pictures of his son, SHIIIT!"

"Chil' watch ya mouth!"

"Sorry Nana, but I forgot to forward my calls."

"Chil', dat boy gon' be a'ight, if he can't get you, he'll call my house."

"Yeah, but you here wit me."

"Charles will be there so he can either forward tha calls or call on 3-way." Nana didn't want to put Lil Naz down, she didn't even want tha nurses to touch him.

I only stayed in tha hospital for 2 days. Naz neva called maybe he's in tha hole. I decided to go see him, he didn't know that I had a 7 pound 6 ounces baby boy.

It was hot out considering it was tha middle of May. Lil Naz had too many clothes, so I decided to put him in his Gucci shorts and tank top wit his Gucci sneaks to match. When I arrived at tha prison, there were more cars than usual.

"I'm here to see Nazir Jenkins." He took my ID and gave me a visitors pass then told me to have a seat.

After 15 minutes tha guard came to escort me and tha other visitors to tha visitors room. When we got there, Naz was already standing. As soon as he saw me carrying Lil Naz he ran over.

"Let me see my son."

"Unh, Unh, you ain't called in 2 days."

"These Fuckin' Niggaz had us on lock down for 2 days."

"Well, why didn't you use ya cell phone?"

"They were doin sum bullshit, I got word from Raz not to use tha phone for a while."

"You know I was worried, I even called up here to make sure you were a'ight." I handed him his son and he did tha same thing Nana did when she first saw Lil Naz.

"DAAAMN! He looks just like my mom."

"I know, Nana did tha same thing when she saw him."

"Maybe. Nah, neva mind."

"What? Say what you were goin' to say."

"Don't worry about it."

"I know what you was gon' say."

"What?"

"That God sent ya mom back in tha form of Lil Naz."

"Yup, how you know?"

"Nana said that same thing."

"Look at my little man in his Gucci, damn you sharp like ya Mom-Mom; may she Rest in Peace." I had to admit, my son was a dime; I knew he was goin' to get dark by his ears.

"Look at all this pretty hair he got; I wonder where he got it from?"

"Not you," I said smiling as I looked at both my men.

Naz had really been working out; his body was more cut up than before.

"What color are his eyes?"

"You not goin' to believe me."

"Try me."

"Green."

"Stop playing."

"I'm serious."

"Where did he get those from, ya side?"

"Naw, we all got hazel eyes."

"So do we."

"Nana said her sisters has green eyes."

"I wouldn't know, I neva saw them or if I did, I was too young to remember."

When tha visit was almost over, Naz let me know that his trial was moved up to July 1st instead of tha 27th.

I looked at Lil Naz, "You hear that? Ya Daddy will be home in a month."

"Visits over!" Before we left Naz wanted to show tha guard his son.

"Aye, Naz you better get a paternity test," I was about to cuss him straight out until he said, "cause that lil nigga too sharp to be ya son." Then started laughing.

"Nigga you just mad cause none of ya kids this sharp." We all started laughing.

Naz kissed us then we left. Tha whole ride home I was feelin good. My son got to see his father for tha first time.

CHAPTER 25

Not Guilty

Tomorrow was tha start of my trial.

"Jenkins, ya lawyer is here to see you." I got my legal work and headed to tha counselor's office to holla at Troy.

"Big day tomorrow, you ready?"

"Troy I been ready since I got here."

"Well, tha A.G. isn't tryin' to drop tha case so I'll just have to make them look stupid."

"See, that's tha problem wit them people uptown, they know they ain't got no case yet and they still want to try dey luck."

"Don't worry, there's no way I'mma lose this case."

Soon as Troy left, Raz was coming to take me to my visit to see wifey and my lil man. They were already waiting when I got there.

"Hey Sexy," I said.

"Hey Baby."

"Damn this nigga gettin' big. How much he weigh, 50 pound?"

"Don't be talk'n about my son!"

Ashanti keeps him in sum thing tight. Today was no different, she had him in a pair of Ralph Lauren khaki shorts wit a Ralph Lauren button up to match, and a pair of RL sandals.

"Are you ready for trial?"

"You already know I'm more than ready."

"Me, Nana, and Uncle Charles will be there. Do we have to bring ya clothes here or to tha courthouse?"

"To tha courthouse."

"Ok, we just wanted to be sure."

"Troy said they want to go all tha way wit this."

"That's crazy when dey have nuffin on you."

"Babe you know how dem folks uptown play."

"Don't worry," Troy says, "he got them by tha balls." When tha visit was over we all said our goodbyes as well as I love you's.

Tha next morning, I couldn't sleep so I got up and started working out. By tha time I was finished tha guard was coming to get me up for court. She was cool she let me bust a shower before they came to get me.

Once I got to tha courthouse, one of tha guards let me change into tha suit that Ashanti had brought over. I could tell that tha guard was hating, who wouldn't. I had a black Christian Brothers suit wit a white button up, a pair of black Prada loafers and a black tie.

It seemed like I was downstairs forever. When they finally called my name. Tha guard put tha cuffs on me then escorted me upstairs.

"You sure you got enough people?" tha guard asked me.

I didn't know what he meant so I didn't answer him. It wasn't until I got in tha courtroom and saw all my peoples that I understood what he was saying. I walked in and sat next to my lawyer. Tha judge let us know that this was tha stage where we got to pick tha jurors. We got to pick 6 and so did tha prosecutor.

After 2 hours, we had a mixed jury of White, Black, Hispanic, Oriental, Mexican, and Italian jurors. I was satisfied that tha ones we picked were bias and would be honest in making any decisions.

It was 12 o'clock and tha judge took a recess for lunch. I let Troy know that I didn't want to go back downstairs so we went into tha room on tha side until tha judge and ery body else was back in tha courtroom. Tha prosecution had their chance first to present their case. They kept saying that confidential source (C.S.) led them to tha guns but they neva produced this C.S. Tha only witnesses they had were tha arresting officers and tha medical examiner. My lawyer ate them for dinner. Troy was as good as he said he was. By tha time it was our turn, tha judge recessed until 9 tha next morning.

As they were taking me out, Ashanti said, "Babe, do you want me to bring you a different suit tomorrow?" I nodded yes and kept it moving.

That night I couldn't sleep at all. I grabbed my cell out of tha radio.

"Hello."

"Hey Baby."

"What time is it Naz?"

"I don't know, I couldn't sleep."

"Me either, I just dozed off."

"Where's my son?"

"He's at my mother's house. I didn't want to be rushing in tha mornin. You know I got to pick Nana and Uncle Charles up."

"I didn't expect to see all those people in tha courtroom today."

"Ery body wanted to show their support as well as loyalty."

"They've been doing that for tha past 9 months."

"I know, Nana didn't know that they were all your friends until court was over."

"What did she have to say?"

"That she hopes you weren't doin anything illegal." We talked for another hour before I told her to get sum rest.

"You do tha same."

"I will."

"I love you Naz."

"I love you too."

I was already up when tha guard had come around to wake me up for court.

"Good luck."

"Thanks Fitz."

When they got me to court my clothes were already waiting on me. Today I had a pink Ralph Lauren button up, Ralph Lauren jeans and a pair of brown loafers.

As soon as I was dressed they took me upstairs. It seemed like it was more people today than yesterday. Lez, Nina, and Heaven were all in attendance today.

"Mr. Banks, call your first witness."

"I'd like to call Ashanti Tate."

I was surprised he called her. Judging by her face so was she. Once she was sworn in he began. He asked her tha basic questions. I was starting to wonder why he called her.

Then he said, "During the week of August 14th to the 28th, where were you?"

"Objection! What does this have to do with this case Your Honor?"

"If he would let me finish, I'll show you."

"Overruled!"

"Now, where were you?"

"Punta Cana."

"Where and what is that?"

"Tha Dominican Republic, an Island."

"Where you alone?"

"No."

"Who was with you?"

"Naz."

"Would you be talk'n about the defendant Nazir Jenkins?"

"Yes."

"No further questions."

"Does the prosecution have anything for this witness?"

"No Your Honor."

"Ms. Tate, you may step down."

"Your Honor, I'd like to recall the state medical examiner." After he was sworn in Troy began.

"Did you find any fingerprints or DNA on the weapon found?"

"There were none."

"What date were these men killed?"

"August 18th."

"No further questions."

"Prosecution."

"No questions Your Honor."

"You may step down. Call your next witness."

"Nothing further Your Honor."

"Take a 15 minute recess then we'll hear the closing arguments."

When we came back tha prosecutor began. Once he was done Troy went.

"Ladies and Gentlemen of the jury, I'm going to make this brief and to the point. True, they found a gun in my clients car, that was used in a double homicide. My clients prints or DNA weren't found on the weapon. The prosecutor would have you to believe that my client wiped tha gun clean. Why would he go through the trouble of that and still have the gun in his car? Wouldn't it have been easier to just get rid of the gun? They also say, they had a tip from a confidential source. But he neva testified for the state. The most important thing is Ms. Tate testified that her and my client took a 2 week vacation from the 14th to the 28th. Yet, the state's medical examiner testified that the murders occurred on the 18th. We have proved beyond a reasonable doubt that my client was set up and did not commit this act. So with all that said, I hope you all reach a verdict of Not Guilty."

Troy walked back and sat down beside me. Shit, I felt like standing up and applauding him. Tha judge told tha jurors that they could be excused to deliberate.

After about an hour tha verdict was in. I came back to tha courtroom to find tha jury already there. I looked at Nana and Ashanti who both had a look of concern on their faces.

"Has the jury reached a verdict?"

"We have Your Honor." They handed tha Bailiff tha paper who then gave it to tha judge. Once he read it, he sent it back.

"Would the Foreman please read the verdict?"

Tha Black lady stood up, "We the jury find the defendant Nazir Jenkins Not Guilty on the first count of First Degree Murder." Tha courtroom went crazy. Tha judge banged his gavel down.

"Order in the court! Order in the court!" After ery body calmed down tha jury read tha rest.

"On the second count of First Degree Murder, we the jury find the defendant Nazir Jenkins, Not Guilty."

Tha courtroom really went crazy. After tha judge got ery body to calm down, he let me know that I would be released from prison before tha day was out. He let me speak. I let tha jury know that I was thankful that they were able to see past tha set up.

It was after 5 when I got back to tha prison. Raz wanted to know how ery thing went. *All I could say was what Cassidy had said, "Did My Time (in a) county jail (Just When) just when things (started) going well. I'm an innocent man."* Then I said, "Not Guilty Y'all Can Not Feel Me!" Fitz, Boy-Boy, and Messy ran over to me.

"I knew you was gon' beat that Shit Naz."

"Me too."

"That's what's up; you should be outta here in a little bit."

"Don't worry, I'm a man of my word. I'mma hold you niggaz down."

"We straight, as long as you keep ery thing flowing."

We had let Messy and Boy-Boy get down wit us since we were making so much paper.

"Don't worry about that. Now y'all can stack sum doe."

"Yeah, cause I'm tryin' to be holding when I beat this Bullshit."

"I feel you on that Cuz. Let me get my Shit so when they call me I'll be ready."

As soon as I was done they called me bag and baggage. Tha only thing I was taking was my mail and flicks from Ashanti. Ery thing else I tore up and threw away.

"Aye Naz, be safe out there and see what's up wit Easy Hawk."

"No doubt, that's top priority. Y'all keep ya heads up. I'll see y'all on tha other side soon enough.

When I got to tha receiving room, I just grabbed my stuff I didn't need change. I got outside to find Ashanti waiting arms wide open. I walked right into them.

"Baby please don't leave me again."

"I would have neva left if nobody set me up."

"Ya lawyer is tha Shit."

"You ain't got to tell me. Did you know he was goin' to call you on tha stand?"

"No, I was shocked like you was."

We talked all tha way home. I was mad that my son was wit her mother, but I understood she wanted to get sexed down. We wasted no time doin tha nasty. When we were done she let me know we were headed to Plush. While we were in tha shower we went at it again. After about an hour we finally got out.

"Baby why don't you put on this?" she said walking out wit a pair of

Gucci jeans and Gucci fitted shirt.

She must've bought this for me to wear. I can't recall having either of them.

"Babe, I would, but I don't have no footwear."

"Not to worry," she said coming back out wit a Gucci box.

When I opened tha box I was really feelin' tha Gucci sneaks. By tha time we both were dressed it was 10 o'clock.

"Damn!"

"What's wrong?"

"I need to call P.R. and tha crew."

"Baby you can holla at them tomorrow, tonight is for me and you."

We pulled up to Plush it was j-peed. We let tha valet park our car. Tha line was long.

"Ashanti, Ashanti." We both looked up to find Shauna at tha door.

"Excuse us, Excuse us." I could tell that people were mad that were cutting tha line.

"What up Naz? Welcome home Nigga." As we were walking in tha music stopped.

"I want to give a special shout out and welcome home to Naz!" I looked at Ashanti, she shrugged her shoulders.

"Yo, welcome home my Nigga. We held it down for you."

I looked only to see Esco wit tha mic and a bottle of Ace of Spades. P.R. grabbed tha mic.

"All this for you." After tha DJ put tha music back on ery body made their way over to us.

"Welcome home Nigga," Esco said handing both a bottle and chain wit NJ in white and yellow diamonds.

"I'm not from New Jersey."

"That's ya initials, ain't it?"

"Oh I see."

"I hope you like it; we paid a grip for it."

"I can tell, all this ice."

For tha rest of tha night we partied like 1999.

CHAPTER 26

Shoot Sum Thing

"Hello."

"Did you handle that situation?"

"Yeah."

"Why didn't you hit me?"

"My fault, I got caught up."

"Where you at now?"

"On my way back across town."

"Meet me at tha tavern in 15 minutes."

"A'ight."

I pulled up at tha tavern, there were a few people outside. In only 2 months, I had locked Richmond and Norfolk down. I kept Reep on my hip like a pistol. Niggaz were terrified of Reep. Not to mention, I put in work so that they wouldn't even think about tryin' me. You know if you don't show you bout it, Jokers will try you when ya gun ain't around.

"What up Doe? When you gon' put me down?"

"In bout 3 more years."

"Come on Man, in 3 years I'll be on top?"

"Nah Young'n, I don't want to be responsible if sum thing was to happen."

"Look, just because I'm 14 don't mean I don't know nuffin. Shiiiit, I been in these streetz since I could walk. All I'm asking for is a shot. I got a few ones to come to tha table wit."

"Check dis out Murder, take my number and call me at 6."

"No doubt, I'll hit you up tomorrow evening at 6."

"Nah, 6 in tha mornin."

"DAAAAMN, that early."

"Yeah, you know what they say early bird gets tha worm."

"A'ight, I'mma hit you."

That will show me how serious he really is. I heard he bout his biz-ness that's how he got his name.

Reep was already at tha bar when I got inside. I spoke to a few people then made my way to tha bar.

"Where's my drink at? Double shot of Bombay on tha rocks wit a splash of pineapple please. So what's tha deal wit Murder?"

"Da young boy Murder?"

"Yeah."

"It depends on what you mean."

"He wants to get down."

"He's definitely a gat. That's why dey call him Murder. Shit, he got more bodies than me."

I turned to face him, "Yeah, I know." He knew what I was thinking, I didn't even have to say nuffin.

"Reep has over 50 bodies from what I hear."

"How can a nigga be so young like Murder and have that many bodies?"

"Doe all that nigga know is tha streetz. His mom and dad were killed in a home invasion."

"WOW!"

"His dad was a big time drug dealer. Sum niggaz ran in his house lookin' for money, when they didn't find any they killed him and his wife. Tha only reason Murder still alive is cause he hid in tha basement."

"How long ago was this?"

"4 years ago."

"Did they ever find out who did it?"

"Yup, that was tha start of his body count."

"Oh Shit!"

"I'm tellin' you, don't let that innocent face fool you."

"It sound like we can use him."

"He's definitely a gat and trustworthy."

"What about as far as hustling?"

"To be honest, I really don't know. What I do know is he be grinding on tha low."

"He got my number; I'll see how serious he is; if he calls me or not."

"So you gon' put him on?"

"I'mma give him a shot. Ery body deserves a chance." Cannon and Sticky walked in.

"Y'all just in time to buy me another drink."

"You got it. Shay another round please."

"What brings you two gangsta's down here?"

"We was cruising by and Sticky spotted ya car. I see, you got my young'n out front holding you down."

"Who Murder?"

"Yeah."

"Actually, he was here when I got here."

"He said he was wit y'all."

"Yeah, he down here wit me," Reep said.

"Why didn't you say that when we were talk'n?"

"Didn't think it was important."

"So he be runnin' wit you?"

"Sum times."

"It doesn't matter." BOOM, BOOM, BOOM, BOOM! Ery body in tha bar took cover.

"Don't ever disrespect me you Fucken Rat Ass Nigga!" I knew by tha voice it was Murder.

"Just in case you want to tell tha police..." BOOM! Me and Reep jumped up ran outside to find Miz laying in his own blood.

"What tha Fuck you doin?"

"This Rat Ass Nigga gon' tell me to take a G Pack and hit him wit 900! He must've thought I was sum Dumb Ass Nigga! I laughed it off at first, then he had tha audacity to say I was goin' to hustle for him or else." There was alwayz shooting or sum body getting killed. That's why tha police neva came fast.

"Come on let's get outta here!"

"What you doin Murder?"

"Making sure ain't no witnesses."

Once he was sure that it wasn't any he made his way to tha car. I let Reep know I would get up wit him at about 10.

"Angel, Angel!"

"Yes, I'm in tha kitchen. Why you doin' all that yelling?"

"If you turn that music down I won't have to yell."

"What you cooking? That smells so good?"

"Turkey chops, Spanish rice, green beans, and cornbread."

"Umm, Umm sounds like a winner to me."

"Well, dinner will be ready in another 15 minutes."

"A'ight, let me get ready."

"Honey, can you keep an eye on my cornbread while I use tha bathroom?"

"I got you Baby."

When I first met Ang I didn't think she could cook since we were alwayz goin' out to eat. Tha cornbread was done so I took tha butter out tha fridge. By tha time she came back down her plate was on tha table.

"Damn, what you have to do Shit?"

"If I did, so what!"

"EEEL you smell like poop too Baby."

"I'll remember that next time you want sum."

"Wow, you can't even take a joke."

"I thought you would see it my way."

"Woman sit down and feed my seed."

"Yes Sir." We discussed possible names if it was a boy or girl.

"Why can't we just name him after you if it's a boy?"

"Because, I don't like my name."

"So why wouldn't you want ya first son wit ya name? Besides there's nuffin wrong wit tha name William."

"Look, I don't like it and that's that!" There was more to it, but I wasn't goin' to press him about it, not tonight anyway.

"Do you want me to help you wit tha dishes?"

"Nah, I got it."

"Well, I need to handle a few things. I'll be back in an hour."

"Ok be safe."

"Don't I alwayz?"

No soon as I got into my car my cell started ringing.

"Yo! What up Nigga."

"What up Reep? You still playing house?"

"Nah, and don't be tryin' to play me."

"Nigga stop gettin' in ya feelings, I'm only joking wit you. Where you at?"

"On my way to tha crap house."

"I'll meet you there, I'm tryin' to win sum money anyway."

"I heard that."

When I pulled up there were more cars than usual. Tommy's was an after hour spot where most people came to drink or gamble.

"Doe over here!" I spotted Reep talk'n to Murder.

"How much money you bring out wit you?"

"10 stacks."

"Ok."

"Why you ask me that?"

"Nah, just in case I might need to hold sum thing. I only brought 5 stacks out."

"Well, you should be good as long as you bet wit me, I feel it tonight."

"Murder you stay out here and hold us down."

"Damn Reep, I wanted to shoot craps too."

"I feel it tonight also."

"Fuck it, come on but we got to hold each other down."

"Niggaz know better than to try us."

"Yeah, but you know how niggaz get bold when that liquor start talk'n to 'em."

There was a big dice game goin' on. Sum nigga named Yetti was on tha bones.

"What's point?" I asked.

"10!" Sum body yelled.

"Well, bet."

"I'll take a 150 to 100 lay."

"Bet."

"You got another one," Murder said.

"It's a bet. You want to bet to Reep?"

"Bet it." After 3 rolls he hit his point.

Da nigga that was fading him said, "I got to go get sum money."

Nobody wanted to fade him so I said, "I'll fade him."

"Bet 20."

"Nah, bet 50 Nigga."

"Bet it." He hit 3 door blows.

"You might not want to fade me, I'm hot."

"Well, shoot a 100."

"It's a bet." We were tha only ones betting against him.

After he hit a few more points he crapped out. I was down $2,500. Yetti was feelin' real good about his self.

"Nigga, bet 200 from tha door."

"Bet it."

"You two niggaz wanna bet sum thing? What ever you want to bet."

"Fuck it, bet 300."

"It's a bet!"

For tha next 30 minutes I hit just about every point. I was up $1,500 when I crapped out. Yetti told me to go back. That was a no-no, one thing I learned is when a person is hot you neva let them go right back. I threw a few snake eyes then caught a 10. Everybody jumped on it. I had bets all around tha table.

I yelled, "Flowers in tha spring time!"

Sure enough, 2 and 5's showed. Within an hour I had damn near all his money.

"You just about broke now Yetti."

"Nigga it ain't about nuffin, I can alwayz go get more money unlike ya self."

"Now why would I feed into that? This is what you do, loose that rest of ya money. Then go home or wherever you got to go and get sum more money."

"Nah, all I have to do is make a phone call." He pulled out his phone and dialed a number.

"Hello, bring 10 grand to Tommy's." (CLICK)

"You want to borrow sum thing until ya money comes," Reep asked.

"Nah, I'm cool."

"Well, who got me faded?" Nobody said anything.

"Don't get scared now Motha Fuckas!" I peeled off two 20's.

"Murder get us a drink."

This bad ass chick came in wearing a skirt exposing her ass it was so short. Everybody was looking.

"What tha Fuck did I tell you bout coming out tha house like that!"

"Boy beat it, you ain't my man or my daddy!" Murder came back wit tha drinks.

"Hey Murder," she said.

"What up Britney?"

"Nuffin."

"What you doin in here?"

"Just came to bring my brother sum thing." Murder looked her up and down.

Yetti cut in, "A'ight I see you."

"Nigga I'm grown, so fall back."

"Anyway, what you doin later?"

Yetti was shooting darts at Murder which he paid no mind. Once Murder realized ery body was still staring at her.

He said, "Let's go outside and talk."

"You need to take ya grown ass home."

"Fuck you Yetti! I swear he makes me sick. I'm 18 Fucken years old, not 10."

"He just tryin' to look out for you."

"Fuck him, what's up wit you?"

"Nuffin."

"You ain't got no girl?"

"Nah."

"As sharp as you are, nobody ain't snatched you up?"

"Nah ma, I'm what you might call a freelancer."

"Well, take my number."

"You sure you want me to have it?"

"Boy, I been on you for a while. You just hard to catch up wit. Why you lookin' like that? Oh, you see sum thing you like?"

"I might." She turned around started making her booty, shake sum thing serious.

"Britney you better stop for I catch a charge out here."

"You ain't gon' catch no charge, I'm gon' give it to you."

All I can say was Damn when she bent down and touched her toes exposing her entire ass. I had to grab a handful which she more than enjoyed.

"Let me get back in there."

"Make sure you call me when you leave so I can throw this on you."

By tha time I went back in Yetti had lost damn near all his money. Doe rolled a 6.

"I like 'em 300." He done got personal he only betting Doe.

"Oh, he must be losing like a Motha Fucka."

"You know it," Doe said.

"Well, you did say you was feelin it tonight."

"This ain't nuffin but chumps call ya peeps back and tell her to bring sum real paper." After another hour he was broke.

"Anybody want to fade me?"

"Shoot sum C-10."

"We can do that too. If I knew you knew how to shoot C-10 we could have been played." Once again he pulled out his phone.

"Brit bring me another 10. What? It don't matter, just do what I said!"

"You want to hold sum thing til ya money comes?"

"Nah, go head, she not gon' be long."

Sure enough 20 minutes later she was walking thru tha door. This time her short skirt was replaced by a pair of Tweety Bird pajamas and a matching tank top.

Murder came over, "Y'all gon' be good."

"Yeah, but I'm bout to go take care of sum thing. Doe, Reep, I'mma hit y'all up in tha AM."

When I walked outside and Brit was right behind me.

"So you gon' come by when you get done handling ya biz-ness?"

"Nah, I coming over now. You is what I got to handle."

"That's what ya mouth say."

"Are you allowed to have company this late?"

"Don't disrespect me, I live by myself."

"Excuse me."

"Well, come on then."

"How far you live from here?"

"Right around tha corner." We started walking.

"Let me ask you a question Murder."

"Go head."

"How old are you, 15?"

"Nah ma, I'm only 14."

"WHAAAT!"

"That's too young for you?"

"Nah, age ain't nuffin but a number."

"I heard that, Aaliyah said it best." We got to her crib and she wasted no time getting naked.

Two hours later, I was headed back to Tommy's. When I got there, Reep and Doe was still inside.

"4, 5, 6 Baby!"

"You still hittin'?"

"Does a fish swim in water? Damn, what time is it?"

"Five minutes to three."

"I'm bout to be out. I don't feel like hearing Ang's mouth." 3 minutes later my phone rang.

"Point 5," I said as I was answering my phone.

"I knew you were gambling."

"How did you know that?"

"Because, it's 3 in tha mornin and you still ain't home yet."

"I'm bout to be out in tha next 30 minutes."

"A'ight, I love you."

"Me too."

"Oh, too many people around for you to tell me you love me?"

"Nah, it ain't bout nuffin, I love you too Ang."

"Bye Boy, hurry up home, I'm horny!" All I could do was smile at her words. Ang was only 4 ½ months but she was starting to blow up.

After I hit Yetti for about 30 grand, he was more than ready to leave.

"You got dat Doe."

"Aye Man, you know to bet wit me, not against me."

"I ain't mad, it goes like that sum times."

"I know that's right. Yo, I'mma hit you in tha AM cause I need to get wit you anyway."

"That's a bet." I let Reep and Murder know I would get wit them in tha morning then rolled out.

CHAPTER 27

Sum Thing New

"Yo, what up Easy Hawk?"

"What up Naz?"

"Let me holla at you for a sec."

"What's good, pull over."

"Hop in, let's take a quick ride." I could tell he was a little uneasy.

"Nah, pull over I'm out here trapping."

"Ain't nobody gon' steal ya Shit, if dey do I got you."

"A'ight, let me put my Shit down." I saw this as a come up. Just in case let me grab my .380.

"Damn Nigga, you all scared."

"Nah, I just didn't want to get in ya whip dirty."

"Right, Right."

"So what's up Naz? What you want to rap about?"

"Check this out, I'm gon' get straight to tha point. You not gon' need that gun you brought wit you first of all. If I was on sum bullshit you would already be dead."

"That's how you feel?"

"Fuck all tha extra Bullshit! I know you had sum thing to do wit me goin' to jail."

"Nah Naz, I don't know where you got ya information from but I didn't have Shit to do wit that." I could tell he was lying but I needed to know who paid him to do it.

"Naz if you want, I could look into for you."

"Yeah, I would definitely appreciate that and it would be worth ya wild."

"This nigga ain't smart as I thought. I'mma let him know it was Doe. Fuck that nigga I don't owe him Shit."

"Like I said, give me a few weeks and I should be able to get a name for you."

"A'ight," I said as I was pulling back up to where I had first picked him up.

When he did come wit tha name which I'm sure he already knows they're both dead!

When I pulled up to tha daycare, Shana was coming out wit her daughter.

"Hey Naz."

"What up Shana?"

"I can't call it. Did ya boy tell you what I said?"

"Nah," I lied I just wanted to hear it from tha horse's mouth, "what was he suppose to tell me?"

"Nuffin, don't worry about it."

"Must not have been important."

"What ever!"

"Seriously."

"You probably lying, I know P.R. told you."

"I just told you he ain't tell me Shit!"

"You don't have to be nasty."

"My bag, I wasn't tryin' to come across nasty. So what did you tell him?"

"All I told him was that I thought you were cute."

"Is that little boy cute or grown man cute?"

"Boy you funny, it's grown man cute."

"Here take my number, call me when you find time."

"You're tha one wit tha girl, I'm single and able to mingle."

"Do you want my number or not?"

"You to Damn smart," she said as she pulled out her phone, "what is it?" I read her off tha seven numbers.

"This better be tha right one." All I could do was laugh.

"Do you actually think I would go through tha trouble of giving you tha wrong number?"

"I don't know what you might do." I started walking towards tha daycare.

"Just call me."

"Oh you better believe I am!"

As soon as I got into tha daycare Ms. Faith said, "You here to pick up Lil Naz already?"

"Yeah."

"He's in his room." When I got there Ms. Heidi was putting his pamper back on.

"Hey Lil Man," I said wit my arms extended. Lil Naz started smiling flapping his arms like a bird.

"Sum body's happy to see their daddy." I put his stuff in his diaper bag then headed to tha door.

Lil Naz was 4 months but he looked like he was 6 months. I decided to take him to tha park so we could hang out for a little while. While we were at tha park this bad chick walked up wit her 2 kids.

"Hello."

"Hey, hi you doin'?" I responded.

"Is that ya son?"

"Yeah."

"He's adorable."

"Thank you." We talked for a minute before my phone went off.

"Excuse me."

After I finished my call I let her know that it was nice meeting her and if I was lucky I would run into her again. She told me that she had a friend but that we could still be friends. Then I stood to leave.

"Are you gonna give me ya number?"

"Only if you really want it."

"I wouldn't have asked if I didn't, now would I?"

"275-1696, don't hesitate to call me." She gave me that look that said, yeah right.

I couldn't front, Janelle was bad, 5'6" long hair, caramel skin tone, brown eyes wit a ass like tha singer Fantasia.

As I was walking away she said, "Nice Ass." I turned around then said, "Vice versa."

On my drive home all I could think about was my new friend Janelle. Ashanti was pulling up at tha same time we were.

"Hey Babe, how was ya day?"

"Stressful!"

"You want to talk about it?"

"Maybe later, right now all I want to do is take a nice hot bath and eat."

"Well do you, me and Naz gon' fall back out ya way. Are you feelin' well?"

"I'm good. Why you ask me that?"

"Cause you're giving me a break."

"I alwayz do."

"Yeah right."

Later that night, I was sitting on Wendy's stoop when Esco walked up.

"What up Naz?"

"I can't call it."

"What you doin out here?"

"I ain't allowed to sit out here?"

"I wasn't saying it like that. Oh, I know what I meant to ask you."

"What?"

"My cousin called me today asking if I knew you."

"Ya cousin who?"

"Janelle." That brought a smile to my face.

"Why would she call you and ask about me?"

"She knows I'm in tha streetz real heavy."

"Yeah, I met her in tha park today."

"Well, I told her you got a girl and about 3 chicks on tha side you deal wit."

"Damn, that's how you handle me?"

"Hey Man, that's family, she like my sister."

"I respect that."

"Naw, I'm bullshitting, I told her you was my man and I deal wit you like that. Which I should not have said."

"Why?"

"Man, you know she wanted to know ery thing about you." All I could do was smile.

"Well, if she calls I'll make sure not to mention this conversation."

"Good, cause she made me promise I wouldn't tell you she wanted to know all that stuff."

"What about her friend she has?"

"Awe that nigga is a straight lame capitol! She's been tryin' to leave that nigga. Look Naz, I know you got a wifey and a few chicks on tha side. I just don't want my cuz to get hurt."

"Come on Esco, that ain't my style. You know I'm gon' be honest wit her."

"I know you will."

"I had to stop dealing wit Nina and Heaven. Even though I let Heaven have tha crib, she was just too damn sneaky. Messing around and even had tha nerve to have sex wit sum nigga from West Philly in my house while I was in tha bing. So I just made up sum shit about us just being friends. She assumed it was because I wanted to be a family wit Ashanti and Lil Naz."

My man showed me how to hop that train to N.Y.C. and how to stretch that Cain, make 5 outta 3!" My phone took us out of tha conversation.

"Hello."

"Hey, may I speak to Naz."

"Who dis?"

"This is Janelle."

"Oh what's up ma?"

"Nuffin, were you busy?"

"Nah, just bustin' it up wit my boy Esco." I took tha phone from my ear to let Esco know it was his cuzin.

"Don't tell her what I told you." When I put tha phone back to my ear she was asking me did I hear what she had said.

"Nah, I lost service. What did you say?"

"Are you free later?"

"Yeah, I can be."

"How about dinner? I know this nice spot in West Philly, they have tha best soul food on tha planet."

"I'm down wit that."

"Let me you give my address so you can pick me up. You do have a car," she said.

"Nah, but I'm sure I can borrow one from one of my boys. So what's tha address?"

She gave me her address then said, "Get my cuzins car, I like his it's old school."

"We'll see, I'll call you around 8." I put my phone back in my case.

"Yo, ya peeps is crazy; she asked me did I have a car." Esco started laughing his ass off.

"No she didn't."

"Yes she did, then she told me to get ya car."

"Yeah, she likes old school cars. I had sold my other one and bought a 63' Chevy Impala, navy blue on white wit a pair of 30-inch Talinky's wit all tha works to go wit it."

I looked at my watch, it was a little after 8.

"Shit," I said as I pulled out my phone. After 3 rings Janelle answered.

"First let me apologize."

"No need."

"Do you still want to have dinner?"

"I just ordered a pizza."

"How about tomorrow then?"

"Nah, I'm gonna eat a microwave dinner."

"Wow, I said I was sorry for calling 15 minutes late Damn!" She started laughing.

"Boy I'm joking, how long is it gon' take you to get here?"

"Another 10 minutes, I'm in route now."

"A'ight, call me when you get out front."

"You'll hear me."

"What?" I didn't answer, I just hung up.

"Guess what I did today? Those were the words I said to you. It was last May, don't know the exact day. In my hand there was a ring..."

Janelle came out tha house looking good wit a pair of Baby Phat jeans and shirt on.

As soon as she climbed in she said, "Turn that down." Once I did, she let me know that she loved my car.

"I know who ever let you use this made you pay them."

"Nah, I only paid when I got ery thing done to it," tha look on her face said it all, "so you really thought I didn't own a car?"

"My girl must've had you mixed up wit sum body else."

"So you asked ya girl about me?"

"I wanted to make sure I wasn't goin' out wit no stalker or serial killer."

"You real funny, you know that?"

She gave me that address which I punched in tha Navy. Plies, Definition of Real, Track 11, Volume 10; within seconds, *"Bust it Baby"* came out.

"You got state of tha art Shit, huh?"

"I only deal wit tha best."

"Oh really?"

"Yup, so next time you want to know sum thing about me ask me!"

"Like you would tell me if you were a stalker."

"I would, I'm an honest man."

We pulled up to tha restaurant, since there were no spots we pulled into tha parking lot around tha corner.

Once inside tha waitress showed us to a nice booth in tha back.

She handed us a menu and asked, "Would you like something to drink while you look over the menu?"

"Water for me."

"I'll have a Ice Tea wit extra lemon please."

"I already know what I want," said Janelle.

After about 10 minutes our waitress came back.

"Are you ready to order?"

"Yes, can I have tha Turkey Chop platter?"

"What sides?"

"Mac & Cheese and Collard Greens."

"Biscuit or Cornbread?"

"Cornbread."

"You Sir?"

"Let me have tha Chicken Breast platter wit tha same sides."

"Will that be all?"

"Let me also have a side of your Southern Fried Shrimp and a slice of Carrot Cake."

"Ok."

"So as you were saying in tha car, just ask you."

"Yeah, nobody would know tha correct answers but me."

"Sure ya right. Would you mind if I ask a few questions?"

"Not at all."

"Well, let me see. Do you have a girl?"

"Yes."

"Do you love her?"

"Yes."

"If you do then why are you here wit me?"

"Truth be told, I'm a man and as long as home is taken care of that's all it is. As far as you go, I find you attractive."

"But I'm tha one that asked you for tha number, remember?"

"I don't be hollering at broads, I play my position, you know."

"I hear you. So how many broads as you say are you knocking off?"

"You want to know tha truth?"

"Of course I do."

"One besides wifey."

"Damn, I would've thought you would say at least 5."

"Nah, just one."

"Are you a hustler?"

"Yes."

"Not that it matters, but are you a in tha way hustler?"

"What's a in tha way hustler?"

"You know, a nigga that's in tha way."

"Oh you mean a nigga that ain't gettin' no money."

"Yeah."

"Well, if you call running a block, making more than a few mill a month in tha way, then yeah."

She smiled then said, "Damn, so ya boss pays you good if you run a block that's doin' numbers like that."

"I don't know if you heard me or you just don't understand."

"Maybe I don't."

"How can I say this so you can understand."

Before I could say anything tha waitress came wit our food. I couldn't wait to eat, I was starving.

"As I was saying."

"Don't talk wit ya mouth full."

"Anyway, I'm my own boss. I run 8th & Indiana, ery body on that block is my team."

"So they work for you?"

"If you want to say it like that, yeah."

"Wow, you big league."

"Nah, I just do what I need to do to eat. Do you have any more questions?"

"Yeah, do you like ya food?"

"Love it, this is my new favorite restaurant."

"Now let me ask you a few questions."

"Uh oh."

"Is your relationship serious?"

"It was once."

"You say once?"

"He had a baby on me and like an asshole I accepted him back, only for him to cheat on me again and again and again." I could see she was hurting just talking about it.

"You must have really been in love to put up wit that."

"Yeah and dumb."

"That doesn't make you dumb, you just followed ya heart. So what's tha deal wit you two now?"

"Nuffin. He doesn't want to just be friends."

"Wow, you got ya self a stalker."

"I can't even have friends wit out him chasing them away."

"He ain't gon' shoot my car up when I drop you off, is he?"

"I hope not."

"For his sake me either."

We finished our food, paid tha tab then left. On tha ride back to her house, I put on sum Keith Sweat.

When we pulled up Janelle said, "Fuck."

Before I could ask what was wrong this nigga was walking towards my car wit his hand in his pocket. I reached under my seat and grabbed my .45.

"Naz, can you pull off?"

"I want to see what he wants."

When he got to tha car he tapped on my window on her side. I rolled it down.

"Janelle what tha Fuck are you doin and why didn't you answer ya Fuckin' phone?"

"First of all, I told you not to be dropping by unannounced."

"If you would have answered ya phone. Who is this nigga?"

"My friend." I just sat quite since she had it under control.

"Ya friend?"

"Yeah, my Fucken Friend!"

"How long y'all been friends?"

"Does it matter?" I was starting to get tired of all his questions.

"Aye Yo, my Man, You Fuck my girl!?"

"I'm not ya girl."

"Check this out, it seems to me that Nell doesn't want to be bothered wit you."

"Nigga you don't know me!" he said raising his voice.

"You're right. Truth be told I wouldn't want to know you." He started reaching in his waist.

"If you about to pull that .38." out I would advise you to use it." He had a look on his face that said how did you know I had a. 38?

"Champ, why don't you just leave me alone. Look Champ, I don't want any problems wit you. It's obvious that you haven't gotton over Nell. Don't tell me that you don't have any other broads that you deal wit."

"Nigga you sound like sum type of Dr. Phil ass nigga."

All I could do was laugh which made him madder. I could tell he really wanted to pull out his pistol. Nell looked at me wit this sad look on her face. I turned my car off, opened my door and got out. I put my pistol in my waist band. As I was walking around to her side Champ was backing up. I quickly came to tha conclusion that all her other friends had let him scare them wit his mouth. I opened her door and helped her out.

"What tha Fuck are y'all doin'?" I stepped dead in his face.

"Listen Champ, from what I understand Nell has let go so I suggest you do tha same. Let's go Nell," I said holding my hand out.

As she grabbed my hand she said, "Please don't bother me again Champ."

We headed towards her house. Tha next thing I knew I felt a sharp pain in tha back of my head; I almost blacked out. This nigga actually smacked me in my head wit his gun. Janelle screamed, when he tried to hit me again but I caught tha gun in midair. Wit my right hand on tha gun, I used my left to punch him square in tha nose. He instantly let go of tha gun. I handed it to Nell then beat tha dog shit out of him. Before I realized it I had my .45 in his mouth.

"Naz don't! He's not worth it!"

Hearing Janelle scream brought me back to reality. I took my gun outta his mouth then smacked him across his jaw wit it.

"Nigga if I ever see you around here or even hear about you bothering her again. So help me, you'll be goin' straight to tha boneyard and Janelle won't be able to save ya Sorry Ass!" I chose to keep his gun which I later threw in a dumpster.

When we got in her house I let her know that I usually didn't do all this on a first date. We both laughed.

"Do you want sum ice for your head?"

"Sure, that would be nice."

"I'm sorry about all of this, I really am."

"No need to apologize, sum body had to check that nigga or you'd be goin' thru this forever."

"Yeah, cause ery body else was scared of him."

We chatted a little while then I said, "Let me leave."

She surprised me by saying, "You have to leave already?"

"Nah, but don't you have to go to work in tha mornin."

"No, I had took off, I have an appointment tomorrow."

"Well, I can stay a little while longer if you like."

"What I would like is for, oh neva mind."

"Say what you was gonna say."

"Neva mind."

"I hate when people do that."

"Do what?"

She knew exactly what I was talking about but I told her anyway. She ended up skipping tha subject. Long story short, I ended up staying tha night but didn't even try to have sex wit her. I know she thought I would try to. That had to earn me a few more cool points.

It was 7 in tha morning when I got up to leave.

She startled me by saying, "Can I call you later?"

"That's up to you." I made it home in time to see Ashanti and Lil Naz off.

"You need to get sum rest, those all-nighters catching up to you."

"I know."

My head was still a little sore. I gave them both a kiss then went upstairs. I jumped in tha shower then laid down.

CHAPTER 28

Give Me tha Loot

(SMACK) "Shut tha Fuck up Bitch!" (SMACK)

"I told you I don't know where nuffin is." (SMACK)

"Bitch stop lying!" I hope Sticky was having better luck than I was.

"You don't want to talk! You willing to die for these niggaz money?" I had to admit she was a trooper.

"I'm goin' to give you one chance to talk. If you choose not to that's up to you. You will have to live wit tha death of ya baby." At tha mention of her baby she was now more ready to talk than ever.

Jus as I was about to say sum thing my phone went off.

"Yo, what's up?... You did?... How much?... That's all?... There's more than that. Fuck it! I'm bout to kill his seed then I'll hit you back." When I hung up I let her know I was about to kill her child.

"NOOOOOO! PLEASE NOOOO! DON'T HURT MY BABY PLEASE!

"Where's tha money at?"

"Downstairs in tha basement." (SMACK)

"Bitch stop lying, I already looked there!"

"No there's a fake wall." I pulled her to her feet.

"How bout you show me."

I was tempted to kick her down tha steps. But decided against it. Once we were in tha basement she immediately went to tha wall and began to push on it. Wow was all I could say when tha wall moved. I'd had seen a lot of things but this might have took da cake. I ran back up tha steps to get my duffle bag. When I came back down she looked like she was trying to get free.

"Now why do you want to get shot," I asked her.

I proceeded to empty all tha cash into my bag. I left 10g's for her.

"I would advise you to put this in a bank account then leave his ass. He let us know that we could kill you. He didn't care." I made my way back upstairs and out tha house.

"Where you at Sticky?"

"Same place."

"Did you get any more money?"

"Naw, only tha 20 stacks I told you about tha first time."

"Well, let him know that his son had to die before his girl told me where tha money was." I could hear him saying that he didn't believe me.

"Ask him about tha fake wall in tha basement."

I heard him yell, "That Bitch!"

He was a cold Mother Fucka, he didn't even care that his son was dead. All he cared about was his money. I'm gonna do her a favor.

"Sticky."

"Yeah."

"Send that selfish piece of Shit to tha bone," before I could get tha last word out (BOOM!) "then, I'll meet you at Tha Diamond."

By tha time I got to tha spot Sticky was already there.

"What took you so long Nigga?"

"I had to make a stop."

I dumped tha money on tha bed. We counted out 380 thousand, not including tha 20 that Sticky had confiscated.

"Cannon I neva would have thought these niggaz in Fayetteville was gettin' cake like this."

"Me either, but I do my homework to make sure. Doe took over Richmond and Norfolk and hasn't looked back."

"He better not plus he got Reep and Murder."

"I know, real live wires that will ride out wit him. Truth be told Sticky, dem niggaz will probably ride on us if it ever came down to it."

"That will be tha day they go straight to tha boneyard."

"Put that Shit in tha trunk, we got one more stop to make before we head back to VA."

"You ready to do this?"

"Yeah."

"Now remember, in and out."

I put 3 fingers up then took them away one at a time. When I got to tha last one, we kicked tha door in.

"N.C.P.D. Ery body Down!"

Just as we thought, there were 3 people at tha table breaking down birds. We hog tied them. We really looked like police, we had mask on so they couldn't see our face. We put tha drugs in tha bag. I went upstairs to search to see if tha money would be where they said it would be.

"BINGO!" I yelled.

I bagged it then headed downstairs. When I got there Sticky had ery thing ready.

"Nice doin biz-ness wit you guys. Oh yeah, Porky said he'll see you in Hell."

Porky was tha guy from tha first sting. He had told us about these dudes in hopes to keep his money and his life. Of course, we doubled crossed him. It's all in tha game, I was raised by wolves! All in all, we made out wit 750g's. I love this life, see what a few weeks of studying gets you. As long as niggaz hustle we'll alwayz have a job.

CHAPTER 29

Hello

BOOM, BOOM, BOOM! 3 shots hit him in tha center of his chest. I spun around BOOM! 1 shot in tha center of his forehead. I hid behind tha wall to wait for my next target. As soon as he popped up BOOM, BOOM! 2 shots to tha head and chest. When my clip was empty, I went to tha desk to get another round.

For tha last few weeks I had been coming to tha range to sharpen up my skills. When I was done I handed my .40 Glock into tha desk clerk.

"How did you do today?"

"85."

"This time next month you'll be at 100."

"Yeah, I should be. Did my check come back yet?"

"Nah, but it should be back by next week. I told you it takes a second."

"I know, I just want my permit so I can have a gun."

"I'll see you next week."

"Ok Naz, you be safe out there."

"You know I will." I jumped in my hoopty then mashed out.

When I pulled up on tha on tha block it was jumpin'. Wendy was sitting on tha step looking over tha block.

"Hey Nephew, where you been?"

"I was at tha range."

"You been gettin' a lot of practice in lately."

"Yeah, I want to make sure my arm is accurate."

"Short or long range?"

"I hear you."

"So what's tha deal wit that boy who set you up?"

"I don't know, he hasn't gotton back wit me yet."

"You still ain't heard from Doe?"

"Nah, word is he down South sum where bubbling."

"He'll surface."

"He don't owe me no money so it doesn't make me any difference whether he does or not. Wendy have you been putting ya money in tha bank like I told you to?"

"Why would you ask me a questions you already know tha answer to?"

"Gotta keep you on top of ya game."

I spotted Esco up tha block, "Excuse me for a sec Wendy."

"Esco, Esco!" I motioned for him to come here; we met in tha middle of tha block.

"Damn, I heard about ya incident tha other night at Janelle's."

"Man that bitch ass nigga hit me in my head wit a pistol."

"I know, Janelle said you beat tha dog shit outta him."

"If she hadn't stop me that nigga would be on a T-shirt as we speak."

"Yeah, she said she thought you were gonna kill him."

"I was, but then I would have had to kill ya peeps too," he gave me a are you serious look, "I couldn't afford her to testify against me."

"Well, I'm glad you didn't. She really likes you. She said that Champ hasn't been around since."

"Matter of fact, I haven't talk to her since I left da next mornin." No sooner as I said that my phone started to ring.

"Hello."

"Hey Stranger."

"Who dis?"

"Damn, what you took my number out?"

"Nah, you didn't sound like ya self."

"Well, why haven't I heard from you? I thought that maybe you needed time to get ya head right."

"Well, you thought wrong."

"Do I detect sum hostility in ya voice?"

"You tell me!"

"If I did anything wrong or to offend you then I apologize."

"Nah, you didn't do anything."

"So when can I see you again."

"I don't know, your tha one wit tha job."

"Are you busy now?"

"If you call talk'n to Esco busy then yeah."

"Tell him I said hi."

"Janelle said hi!" I yelled up tha block to him.

"He says tha same. Give me a half hour and I'll be thru."

"Ok."

When I pulled up to Janelle's house there were two kids out front. At first I thought they were her kids. Then I remembered that she only has one child and he wasn't that old. I hopped out my car.

"Checks on that car," one of tha kids said.

"I already called it," tha other one said.

"No you didn't"

"I did so." Janelle came to tha door.

"What's goin' on out here?!" she yelled.

They both tried to out talk tha other one.

"Naz, I didn't even hear you pull up."

"That's because I didn't have my system up," I looked at tha two kids, "y'all both called it." As we were going in Janelle wanted to know what I was talk'n about.

"They called checks my car." All she could do was laugh.

"My nephews are crazy."

"You did it when you was young."

"I know, that's why I laughed. Funny how sum things don't change. Kina this is Naz, Naz this is my sister Kina."

"Hey ma." She walked up to me then gave me a hug.

"Thank you. What exactly did I do to deserve that?"

"You got rid of Champ. I don't know what Janelle seen in him anyway."

"Kina don't start."

"Tha truth hurts."

"What ever."

"Janelle you were right, he does look Dominican."

"Kina shut up please."

"Actually, I wouldn't mind hearing what else she had to say."

"She also said that you were tha perfect gentleman." Even though I knew tha answer I still asked anyway.

"Has Champ been around since?"

"Nah."

"Not to be nosey but don't you two share a child?"

"Hell to tha No!"

"Kina I believe he was talk'n to me. No, I had Faheem before I met

Champ."

"So there's no strings attached then?"

"Nope, none at all." My phone started ringing.

"Excuse me for a second." I walked into tha other room.

"Bitch he is sexy as Shit. You better get him before I do."

"Please, I told you he's already got a woman."

"Well, it must doesn't mean too much to you."

"And what's that supposed to mean?"

"If you don't know neither do I. Shiiiit I wouldn't care if he had a girl or not. As long as I get mines."

"See that's cause you a bonified freak."

"And you know it." I walked back in to find them high fiving.

"Did I miss sum thing?"

"I was just tellin' my sister that she better not let you get away."

"So I guess tha high five meant you wasn't."

"Kina you got a big mouth, you can't hold nuffin."

"Hey, it's not my fault you scared to tell him you feelin' him. Right Naz?"

"Well, I'm glad you told me or I may have neva know."

"Naz please, so you think I let any man stay tha night wit me?"

"Hold up, you didn't tell me about that. Now I know why you been talk'n my ears off about him."

"Nah ma, it ain't even like that."

"You stayed tha night and nuffin happened? Is that what you tellin' me?"

"Yes."

"Bitch you whipped and you ain't even get non yet. Wow! Look at him blushing all hard."

"I have to make a run."

"Can we do dinner later?" If you're not busy."

"Of course y'all can do dinner, I'll watch Faheem for you tonight."

"Well it's settled, I'll pick you up at 8:30. Dress regular, we goin' back to that soul food restaurant."

"Janelle must have turned you on to Ms. BB's."

"Yeah. I'll call you before I come," I said walking out tha door.

"Aye ya car started up by itself," Travis said, "can you take us for a ride around tha block."

"Ain't nobody got time for that!" Kina yelled.

"Awe Man!" Seeing that they really wanted to go for a ride I told them to climb in.

"Damn this is one mean Motha Fucka."

"OOOH I'm tellin' Mommy you cussin'."

"Chill Lil Man, no need to tell."

"He just like his dad, a snitch."

"No I'm not."

"You alwayz tellin' Mommy ery thing. If you do that then what you gon' do when pressure come?" I sat back and listen to Keenan school his younger brother.

When I pulled off Keenan wanted to know if I had any Meek Millz.

"What you know bout Meek young'n?"

"I'm 13, who don't know bout him?" I put sum Meek on then took them for a ride.

"I thought you had a banger in here."

"I don't want to bust y'all ear drums."

"Man please! Aunt Janelle's last friend had a marching band in his whip. Is you gon' turn it up or what?" Travis asked.

"A'ight," I turned it up a notch to 15, "is that good enough for you?"

"No. But if that's how loud it goes, it's cool."

"Young'n this ain't even halfway."

I put it on 25 then watched as they both enjoyed tha loud music. When I pulled back up I looked over at them boppin' to tha music. Just to show off, I turned it up a few more notches causing Janelle and Kina to come out. When I turned it down Keenan let me know that I had tha loudest system he'd ever heard.

"You ain't hear nuffin, I still had 30 notches left."

"DAAAAMN!" Travis yelled.

"Boy you better watch ya Fucken mouth!"

"And you wonder why they cuss," Janelle said.

"I'm grown though." I waved, turned my shit back up then slowly pulled off. I went home to spend sum quality time wit Ashanti and my lil man.

"Aye Yo P.R., let me holla at you for a second."

"What up Gunz?"

"What's up wit you and Shorty from across town?"

"Who Rhonda?"

"Nah Dalinda."

"She good peeps, ain't nuffin serious. You can smash if you want."

"Nah, I'm cool, I just wanted to tell you to watch that Bitch. They said she be lining niggaz up."

"It's funny you said that cause she been calling my phone. Asking if she can come to my crib."

"Now you know why."

"I swear, I'll send that smut to tha boneyard."

"You still got that crib ya peeps left you?"

"Yeah."

"Take her there then see if it gets hit. If it does then well, you know it was her." As if on cue my phone started ringing.

"What up Shorty?"

"You, why you ain't been answering ya phone?"

"I just got my phone fixed." I lied but it sounded good.

"Well, can I see you tonight?"

"Yeah."

"We goin' to ya house or you gettin' a room?"

"I don't know. Why you keep tryin' to go to my crib?"

"I was tryin' to save you sum money!"

"Well, don't you worry about my money."

"Excuse me."

"I'll hit you later."

"I'mma be sittin' at ya peeps house just in case she is tryin' to line you up."

"I don't think that they gon' come while we there."

"Well if they do, I'll be waiting on them. Believe that."

"Hey you, I miss you."

"Do you?"

"Of course I do."

"I can't tell, you haven't returned any of my calls."

"I just got back in town."

Truth was, I had to fall back from Mimi. She was catching a lot of feelings and I didn't want to break her heart. Especially since I didn't feel tha same way she did.

"Can I see you after work tonight?"

"What time do you get off?"

"I get off at 12 o'clock."

"Yeah, just hit me up."

"Why don't you just meet me at my house. You still have ya key don't you?"

"Sure do."

"Well, let ya self in."

I had a few hours to kill so I shot to tha mall to grab those new Jordans that just came out. Before I left, I called Dalinda to let her know I was on my way. She let me know that she would be ready by tha time I got there. I grabbed a bite to eat before I left.

"Yo, I'm out front."

"I'm coming out now."

"Damn this broad is phat to death."

As soon as she got in tha car she asked, "Are we goin' to your house or you gettin' a room?" She was pissing me off.

"Why tha Fuck you keep asking me that Shit?!"

"I don't know who you think you talk'n to; you can take me back home!"

"Bitch you right!" I turned around.

"Where you goin'?"

"Dropping you back off."

"I was just playing wit you Damn!" She changed her tune quick.

"I don't know what type niggaz you use to dealing wit but I'm a boss. Don't you forget that Shit either."

"That's exactly why I'm lining ya Dumb Ass up!" she thought to herself.

I made sure to drive slowly so that she could get tha directions and streets right. I hadn't used this spot in a while. I neva kept any money here because this was where I did all my smutting and tricking. We got out then went into tha house.

"This is nice, you live by ya self?"

"That's a dumb question. Would I bring you here if I lived wit sum body else?"

"I don't know, I thought that's why we alwayz went to tha motel."

"Good thing you don't get paid for thinking."

"What ever." I looked at my watch, it was 10 o'clock.

"No need to waste any time, I have to be sum where in a couple hours."

"You so ignorant."

"Nah, I just don't play no games."

Within seconds, my pants were down and she was deep throating all 9 inches. She was a pro Fo' Sho. When we done, I jumped in tha shower.

"Wake up, we out."

"You goin' back home?"

"Yeah." I made it back to her house in record time.

"I'll call you." I pulled off wit out saying nothing.

15 minutes later, I was pulling up in front of Mimi's house. She was already home. I walked through tha front door, only to be greeted by tha sounds of Alicia Keys. I went straight upstairs. Mimi was in tha shower singing along wit Alicia Keys getting her right for me; she jumped.

"Boooy you scared tha Shit out of me! I didn't even hear you come in."

"Bad Boys move in silence. I thought you know that?" She pulled tha shower door open exposing her nudeness.

Damn she was beautiful wit or wit out any clothes on. I couldn't deny tha fact that Mimi had it goin' on. Tha fact that she was independent was an added bonus.

"Hey Baby, I missed you."

I wanted to tell her I missed her too but I didn't. I settled for did you really. I couldn't help but stare as tha water rolled down her body.

"Well, at least sum body missed me," she said wit a smile looking down at my erect penis. All I could do was smile.

I walked back to tha bedroom. There was sum thing different but I couldn't put my finger on it until Mimi came in.

"You like tha way I switched tha room around?"

"I knew it was sum thing different about tha room." I sat there and watched as she finished drying off.

"P.R. can you put sum of this on my back?"

She knew that cumber melon was my favorite. I took my time applying tha lotion on her back. I made sure to caress and massage her at tha same time. Once she let out a soft moan, I knew I was doin' my job.

"That feels so good P.R. it's been a few weeks since you have done that to me."

Next thing I knew, Mimi had spun around and put her tongue in my mouth. Now I didn't play tha kissing thing, but wit Mimi I didn't mind. He lips were so so soft. Before I knew it my pants were off and those soft lips were now wrapped around my penis. She had sum of tha best head I'd had ever gotton in my life.

2 hours and 4 orgasms later, we both laid there sweating and breathing like we had just run 2 games of full court basketball. I looked down only to realize that in tha heat of tha moment, I didn't have a condom on.

"Shit!"

"What's tha matter Baby?"

"I forgot to put a condom on."

"No you didn't," she said looking down at my semi erect penis, "well, I'm not on tha pill."

"Why not?"

"First of all, for tha past year I haven't been Fuckin' nobody but you!" She emphasized tha word *you*.

"Now you on tha other hand, probably have been Fuckin' ery thing that's not nailed down."

"Wow, that's what you think about me?"

"P.R. I've heard ya name a few times at tha hair salon. I just stayed in my lane since nobody knows were Fuckin'." Hearing that made me wonder who tha broads were but I wouldn't dare ask.

Instead I just said, "Don't believe ery thing you hear."

"Oh believe me, I don't. If I did, well let's not go there."

"Nah ma, finish what you was gonna say."

"Don't worry it's not even important."

"Fuck it then."

She started rubbing on my chest and within seconds my man was standing at full attention. I didn't know whether to put a condom on or not. I knew I was taking a chance on her getting pregnant but what tha Hell.

No soon as I finished my cell phone started to sing, *"Here we are, all alone in this room, and girl you know where to start what we gon' do."* I knew that it was Shauna.

"Hello."

"I just wanted to know if you were coming home for a change."

I looked at my watch, "Shauna it's damn near 5 in tha mornin. You should be sleep."

I couldn't help but to smile at tha conversation P.R. was having wit his girl. To make matters worse, I pulled his penis thru tha slit in his boxers. As soon as I took him in my mouth, he moved tha phone from his mouth.

"Shiiiit!" I couldn't believe it; she was trying to start trouble.

"Listen Shauna I'm on tha block, I probably won't be in for another couple hours."

"You know what P.R., I'm tired of your Shit!"

"So what are you saying?"

"I'm saying it's over! Your Shit will be on tha front porch!"

"If that's tha way you want it. Fine! Don't come running back this time either!"

"Fuck you Ricardo!" And tha line went dead.

Mimi just looked at me. "Well, you got what you wanted."

"And what's that P.R.?"

"Shauna just left me."

"You don't seem to upset about it."

"Nah, I'm cool wit it. Truth be told, I love Shauna but I'm not in love wit her no more."

Damn, I was happy but I wasn't goin' to get my hopes up high since I knew that they would probably get back together anyway. Another round of applause for tha head game. Mimi had given me; I fell into a deep sleep.

CHAPTER 30

Fitz

I was finally out of that Hell hole. I had left ery thing to Messy just like Naz had told me to. My uncle was suppose to be here to pick me up.

"Damn, where is this Motha Fucka at? Shit, I ain't tryin' to be waiting out here all day."

Just as I started to walk this 645 CI pulled up alongside of me. Out of habit, I reached for my pistol. Shit, I just got out what am I thinking about. Tha dark tinted windows rolled down.

"Nigga you ain't holdin' nuffin. Get ya scared ass in da car." I breathed a sigh of relief once I seen it was Naz.

"Damn Nigga, you done that much dirt?"

"Nah, I ain't got no beef. But I don't trust no cars wit tint that I can't see inside."

"I feel you on that Cuz."

"I know you glad to be out of dat Bitch."

"Fo' Sho, Fo' Sho. I sat for 18 months behind that dumb Bitch. You know how that goes when they push ya dates back."

"Yeah."

"So did you school Messy to ery thing?"

"Yup."

"Did you tell him how much to hit us wit off each score?"

"Yup."

"Well, let's get this paper then. First you need sum gear."

"I got clothes at my son's mom house."

"Man let her keep that Shit, you don't want no smoke wit her. One thing for sure, two things for certain, if she did it once, she don't got no problem doin it again."

"I know that's right."

"We gon' shopping."

"I need to stop by my uncle's to grab up sum loot."

"Don't worry about it, I got you covered."

Our first stop was tha Gallery. We hit a few spots then headed to South Street. By tha time we had finished Naz had to have spent 6 grand easy. Naz let me know that I had a spot on his roster. Which was fine by me, considering tha way my cuzin Chopz was eatin' all crazy.

"Aye Fitz, you need to get ya L's."

"I already got 'em."

"In that case, you need to get you sum wheels to get around in."

"I got my hoopty that I had before I fell. My uncle put it in his garage for me."

When we pulled up to my uncle's house Kima's car was parked out front.

"Handle ya biz-ness then hit me up when you're done."

"No doubt, thanks for tha gear. I really appreciate it Naz."

"Fitz that's tha least I can do for you. When I first came to C.F.C.F., you looked out for me."

"Yeah, but then you locked that Shit down. C.F.C.F. bringing in numbers like tha block. If it wasn't for you, my doe wouldn't be up like it is." Before I got out, Kima was coming outside.

"Well handle ya B.I., jus make sure you hit me later."

"Don't worry, I'mma hit ya phone."

"Nah, just come to tha block, that's where I'll be."

I grabbed all my bags out of tha car then headed towards Kima. She grabbed me and squeezed me so tight.

"Damn Baby, I just got out. You tryin' to kill me already?"

She let me go, "I'm sorry Baby, I'm just so happy to have you home."

"I know and I'm happy to be home after 18 months of being caged up. They'll bury me before I go back to that Hell hole!"

"I guess you won't be needing my clothes I got for you."

"Shiit I don't know why I don't. You can neva have enough clothes not to mention, I don't have Shit."

"Oh yeah, how could I forget that. So you gon' just let her keep all ya stuff?"

"You damn right he is," my uncle said coming out of da house.

CHAPTER 31

Twisted

"There he go right there." Reep just sat there.

"Yo, did hear me?"

"Yeah."

"What's up wit this nigga Doe? He been distant all Fucken day."

"I got a lot of things on my mind, that's all."

"Well, you better get ya head right. One slip could send anyone of us to tha boneyard."

"There goes Rope."

"We gon' get 3 birds wit one stone."

"Actually a few stores, I plan on emptying my whole clip in one of them Fuck Ass Niggaz. Dey got da game all messed up."

"They must've thought we were soft or sum thing."

"That's Bullshit, they tryin' to get a rep off us."

"Well, that Shit cost 'em dey life."

Once Joe went in we were ready. We all put on our vest then made sure we had our pistols off safety.

"Reep, Murder, y'all take tha back door, I'll take tha front. When you get in position twirk my phone."

"That Shit to loud."

"Not if you put it on silent. Once you hit my phone I'll count to 3. When I hit 3 we go in, capice."

"We got you."

"Once we were all in position, Reep hit my phone."

"A'ight 1-2-3." (BOOM)

As soon as we hit tha door all Hell broke loose. BONG, BONG, BOOM, BOOM, POP, POP, POP! As fast as it started it was over.

"Reep, Murder, y'all a'ight?"

"Yeah we straight." Out of tha corner of my eye I saw sum thing move in tha closet.

"Come out now before I empty tha rest of this clip in there!"

Tha door opened slowly. We all had our guns aimed at tha door, just in case sum body started dumping at us. When I saw who it was I couldn't believe it.

"Ranay what tha Fuck are you doin in here!" Reep yelled.

"I was here wit T.J." I could tell she was shaken up.

"What tha Fuck you doin' messing wit T.J.?"

"This is why I been stressin' all day. My mom said she hasn't been home in 2 days."

"Ranay where do they keep ery thing at?" Murder asked.

"Upstairs in tha backroom under tha bed." Murder ran up tha steps to retrieve it.

"You know Mommy is worried sick about you."

"Reep I'm not a little girl anymore. I can handle my own biz-ness."

"Ranay you won't be 18 for another few months. So until then, you need to abide by Mommy's rules."

"I hope y'all gon' break me off since y'all Fucken my score up." I looked at Reep.

"What do you mean ya score?"

"You didn't think I was dealing wit him because I liked him, did you?"

"Actually, yes I did."

"Pleeease be fo' real, you should know me Reep."

"I thought I did, but I don't know now."

WOOOW!

We all took off running upstairs. When we got there I couldn't believe my eyes.

"I know we bustin that down 4 ways," Ranay said.

We didn't have to rush because gun shots were a regular around here. By tha time we got all that money into tha bags, it was time for us to get out of there.

"Reep, wipe down any and ery thing ya sister touched."

Once that was done we headed back to one of our many stash house. Reep was tha first to speak after we counted our take.

"Ranay we gon' give you 10g's."

"What!" she yelled.

"You heard me loud and clear."

"Nah Reep, we gon' bust down 4 ways. Wit out her, we would have neva found that spot. This is yours," I said pointing to one of tha piles of money. Her face lit up like a Christmas tree.

"I get all this?"

"Yeah, so spend it wisely."

"As soon as I turn 18 I'm buying me a house."

"Well, you better get a job then so you can pay ya bills. And I want a key."

"You sound like her dad Nigga."

"Mind ya biz-ness Murder."

"Awe Nigga, I know you just tryin' to make sure lil sis a'ight."

"Who you calling Little? You younger than me."

"Damn Nay, why you alwayz got to take ery thing to tha heart. You know I wasn't saying it like that."

"Y'all be tripin' fo' real."

"I'm starting to think they like each other," Reep said wit a smile.

"Pleeease, he's just a baby!"

"That's what they all think until I pull this big .45 out."

"Don't get me wrong, I know you bout ya work."

"Ok, as long as we got that clear." We all started laughing.

Reep had put me on tha spot once again. He knew that I told him Murder was cute. Shit he even surprised me when he had said he would hook me up. Of course I declined, Reep alwayz was over protected of me. I told him when Murder turned 18 then we would see. Until then I would admire him from tha sideline.

"Nay, let me ask you sum thing."

"I'm listening."

"How many other people have you lined up?"

"3, but it wasn't for no real money."

"I don't want you doin that Shit no more. If you want sum money ask me or get a job. Murder drop Nay off at my mom's for me. I have to handle sum thing."

"I smiled to myself, Reep knew what he was doing. I bet he didn't have Shit to do."

"Come on Shorty let's go."

"Boy don't be rushing me."

"Reep before you roll let me holla at you."

"What up Doe?"

Once I was sure Murder and Nay were gone I said, "You tryin' to play match maker wit them two?"

"Not really, I just know Nay likes him. If anybody messes wit her I rather it be Murder. Because I know he'll make sure she a'ight."

"So why you been linin' Niggaz up?"

"Money why else you think?

"So why not get a job?"

"What's this 21 questions?"

"Nah, I was just wondering that's all."

"Anything else you were wondering?"

"As sexy as you are why don't you have a man?"

"I don't have time for a man."

"Oh I see."

"Once I get out of school I babysit my neighbors kids."

Nay was sexy as Hell. 5'6", bronze skin tone, shoulder length hair, brown eyes and a ass like J.Lo. If she ever gave me tha time of day.

"What you think'n bout?"

"You," I said just to see what she would say.

"What about me?"

"Nuffin really."

"I know Mr. Mouth all mighty ain't shy."

"Not hardly, I was just wondering if Reep would be mad if I started messing wit you?"

"You ain't got to worry bout that cause it'll neva happen."

"Stop playing ya self Nay. I see da way you be lookin' at a nigga. Now I may be young, but I'm from da hood."

"What's that suppose to mean?"

"If you don't know then I don't either." I left it at that.

When I pulled up to her house before she got out she let me know that if I was a few years older.

So I hopped out, "If I was a few years older what?"

"Maybe I would holla at you."

"Nay you only older than me by two years."

"3, I'll be 18 in 2 months."

"I'll be 16 next month. So like I said two years."

"Well take my number, we'll see what happens. Matter fact, get tha number from Reep."

"Why I gotta get tha number from him?"

"If you get tha number from him then that means he approves." I pulled out my phone.

"What you doin? Didn't you hear what I just said?"

I didn't say nuffin, I just dialed. When Reep picked up I put it on speaker.

"You drop Nay off?"

"Yeah, but I wanted to know if it was cool if I hollered at her?"

"Do you, she likes you anyway."

I looked at Nay, "Oh, do she?"

"Yeah, just don't hurt my lil sister Nigga."

"I won't, you got my word."

"I know that's why I don't mind you talk'n to her. A'ight, I'm on my way back to tha block."

"Was that good enough for you?"

She didn't say nuffin. She just took my phone and programmed her number in it under wifey. When I looked at her, she smiled then asked if I had a problem wit it.

BOOM, BOOM, BOOM!

CHAPTER 32

Down Goes Easy Hawk

"Hello."

"What's good Naz?"

"Who this?"

"Eazy Hawk, I found out that info that you wanted to know about."

"I forgot all about that."

"I don't want to talk over tha phone. Meet me at tha McDonald's on Broad."

"A'ight, I'll be there in 15 minutes."

When I pulled up I spotted Eazy Hawk talk'n to two females. I motioned for him to come inside.

"You want sum thing to eat?"

"Nah, just a soda."

After I ordered, I got my food then went to a table in tha back where nobody was around.

"So who set me up?"

"Listen, I'mma tell you this but you did not hear it from me."

"I'm listening."

"A very reliable source told me that ya man Doe set you up."

"Bullshit, why would Doe set me up?"

"Word is, he wanted to take over dat block you got."

"That Mother Fucka!" Ery body turned to look at me; I didn't give a Fuck.

"What tha Fuck y'all lookin' at! Are you sure about this Eazy Hawk?"

"Let me just say my source is 99% right all tha time. I know you want to kill him." I wanted to say you damn right, y'all both dead.

But instead I said, "Nah, I ain't Fucken wit him."

"You just gonna let him slide?"

"Yeah, he ain't in town no more anyway."

"You got a point there." We stood to leave; I went in my pocket to hand him sum money.

"This for ya help."

"No doubt, good lookin' Naz."

He would be dead within 24 hours anyway, Rat Ass Nigga.

As I drove back to tha block, my mind was on Doe. I couldn't believe this dude went through tha trouble of setting me up just to take over a block. I need to put my ear to tha street to find out where Down South that nigga is. While I was sittin' on tha stoop P.R. walked over.

"What's tha deal Naz?"

"Yo, I need to find out where at Down South Doe is."

"Why? He owe you sum money?"

"Nah, that Mother Fucka tha one that set me up. I'mma kill that Bitch Ass Nigga, I put that on my son."

"That's probably why he went Down South to begin with."

"Nah, he did it so he could take over tha block. That Shit wasn't goin' to happen."

"Well, let me check wit a few people to see if I can find out where that Snake is at. How did you find out?"

"Eazy Hawk."

"How did he know?"

"He's tha one that set me up."

"Say no more, I know what needs to be done."

"Don't worry about it, I already have that taken care of."

"Well, I want in, you know I can't stand that dude anyway."

"A'ight, meet me at tha spot no later than 9 o'clock."

When P.R. finally arrived it was a after 9.

"Nigga didn't I say 9 o'clock!"

"Relax, it's only 10 after."

"A Mother Fucka could have been ready to blow my brains out if you wasn't on time wit a ransom. I would be in tha boneyard right now!"

"If that was tha situation I would have been here early."

"Well, I'm ready to get this Snake. You got ya vest?"

"You know it."

I pulled out my two .40's, made sure they were fully loaded and ready to go. Chopz had hit my two way to let me know that Eazy Hawk was at Nite on Broad. A known strip club on Broad Street.

When we pulled up, I got out to get in position. After what seemed like an eternity, Eazy Hawk was finally coming out.

"Excuse me, could you spare sum change?"

"Tha time it takes for you to ask for sum change you could be out finding a job."

"Well, I don't think there's anything open this late. Do you have sum spare change or not?" He pulled out his .38.

"Who tha Fuck you talk'n to?"

"Hey Man, I don't want no problems, just sum change."

"Yeah, that's what I thought," he said putting his gun away. As soon as he did, I stood up wit my two .40's in his face.

"What tha Fuck!"

Before he could say another word I let my .40s tear through him. As he laid there shaking, I stood over top of him.

"Neva judge a book by its cover."

I put my gun to his forehead and fired a single shot that took what little life he had left outta him. I drew up a hawker and spit in his face.

"Rat Ass Nigga! Doe will be joining you soon." I walked off as if nuffin ever happened.

"Damn Nigga, I thought we were goin' to have to help you out when he pulled that .38 out. Shit, I didn't even know you shot him until he went down."

"Yeah, I had my silencers on. I knew they would come in handy one day. What do you say we go to Palmer's to have a much-needed drink?"

I'm down."

"Me too." I couldn't believe it, Palmer's line was long and it was 2 in tha mornin.

"Aye Naz, I'm goin' to cut tha line."

"Oh you thought I was goin' to stand in this long-ass line?"

"Nah, I just wanted to make sure we were on tha same page."

"What up fellas?"

"I can't call it Mohammed."

"Excuse us, but can we get thru?"

"Be easy ladies, we tryin' to get in also."

"You do know that it's an extra dub to get in this way?" Mohammed asked.

"We know."

"Yeah, and you said that to say what?"

"Damn, no need to get defensive," Chopz said.

"You mind ya own biz-ness."

"Hold on ladies, my boys didn't mean no disrespect. So to show you I got y'all," I handed Mohammed a 100 and a 50-dollar bill. He moved aside to let us by.

"If you don't mind me asking what's y'all name?"

"Chopz and P.R., and I'm Naz."

"I'm Iissa, this is Sandy, that's Jazz, and that's Kendra."

I couldn't help but to stare because Iissa was beautiful; 5'6", bronze skin, hazel eyes, and an ass that would make Beyoncé jealous. I ended up paying tha cover charge also.

"Since you paid our way, at least let me buy you a drink?"

"Now you sound like T-Pain. It's not too often that a beautiful female offers to buy me a drink. So I guess I better take advantage of this."

We went to tha bar on tha first floor so that we wouldn't have to wait in line. After I had my drink I said thank you then walked off.

On my way up to tha second floor Iissa said, "Next round on you."

"Not a problem, just come find me." Chopz had P.R. were busy talk'n to her girls.

"Damn Naz, I know you not goin' to let her get away." I walked to tha bathroom followed by P.R. and Chopz.

"Yo, you crazy Nigga."

"Man chill out, I know what I'm doin. Don't sweat dem let dem sweat you."

"Niggaz gon' be all over her."

"So what, let 'em."

"Fuck it then, let's go have a ball." We walked into where tha DJ was playing Jamie Foxx's *"Blame It On tha Alcohol."*

"Damn it's hot as Shit in here." You could smell tha weed that was being smoked.

"Chopz light that Sour D up so we can get high." No soon as we lit tha weed a bunch of chicken heads flocked around us.

"OOOH dat smell like sum bomb Shit. Can I hit dat?"

"Fall back Shawty, you don't even know us."

"I don't got to know you to know you blowing dat Shit."

"How you know it ain't lace wit sum thing?"

"Y'all don't look like da type to do no stuff like dat." I could tell they were ghetto just by tha way they were acting

"Y'all sum cuties, y'all got girls?"

Before I could respond Iissa was pulling me saying dis one spoken for. I looked at her and smiled.

"No disrespect, I was just wondering." I couldn't help but laugh when she looked at P.R.

"Nah Shorty, I got a woman."

Then he grabbed Jazz who was more than happy to be on his hip. She turned her head towards Chopz.

"Sorry ma, these two are more than I can handle," he said grabbing both Sandy and Kendra by their arms.

"Shit, all tha good ones are alwayz taken," she turned to her girls, "come on y'all." As soon as she left I let Iissa know I appreciated that.

"No problem."

"Now I'm ready for my drink." I gave P.R. that look that said see what I mean.

For tha next hour we danced and bust it up. When all tha lights came on I knew it was a rap. Tha night air felt good compared to tha inside of tha club.

"Where y'all parked at?"

"Right over there next to that 750."

"Ok, I'll walk you to your car since you parked next to me. So where y'all from? I ain't seen y'all in Philly."

"That's because we from Trenton. So Mr. Naz, what are y'all about to get into?"

"Nuffin."

"Well, there's this club in Exton that doesn't stop jumpin' til about 7."

"Is that an invitation?"

"Only if you accepting."

"We'll follow y'all."

"Why don't I ride wit you."

Chopz smiled, "I'm jumping in wit dem if dats cool."

"Sure is Sandy," said wit a big smile.

We pulled up to this club called tha Paradox. There were cars and people everywhere.

"Is it alwayz this packed?"

"Yeah, they don't open til 3 am."

"Iissa ain't that ya nephew up front?"

"Sure is, come on. Excuse us, Excuse." She said that until we got to where her nephew was standing.

"Aunt Iissa, what you doin out this late?"

"Boy I'm grown. Question is, what are you doin here?"

"You know my peeps be at tha door. Plus, I got this," he said pulling out his fake ID, "who you here wit?" he asked looking back at me.

"Don't worry about it."

Tha door opened up and they let us inside. There were even more people inside then there was outside. We were all basic except for our 8th Chains.

"I'm surprised they didn't say anything about y'all-white T-shirts."

"Bitch, you know they don't care what you wear on Friday's."

"Well, for tha record, we normally get dressed but we were fresh off tha stoop." She didn't hesitate to ask me what tha stoop was.

"Tha block," I responded wit.

"In other words, you hustle?"

"You can say that."

"White T-shirts, blue jeans, and butters is ya block attire?"

"Sum times."

"If you don't mind me asking but are you mixed wit Dominican?" All I could do was laugh.

"What's so funny?"

"I knew you were goin' to ask that. Nah, I'm all Black, 100%."

"You sure?"

"Positively."

It was 5 am and I was ready to go. Chopz and P.R. had dipped out wit Iissa's girls. I thought that she would have wanted to leave when she asked me if I had a girl. Of course I told her tha truth. Her response took me by surprise.

"I don't mind sharing. I'm starving."

"Me too."

"I know an all-night spot that we can get a bite to eat from."

While we ate I got to find a lot out about Iissa. When it was all said and done, I stayed tha night wit her. I didn't have sex wit her. I wanted to but I didn't.

CHAPTER 33

Getting Ready for Beach Weekend

I couldn't believe it when I picked up tha Philly Inquirer. *Federal Informant Found Shot to Death in Front of Strip Club*. I know this ain't Eazy Hawk they talking bout. But as I read it was confirmed. At first I thought that it might have been Naz who had done it. Eazy did call me to let me know he was home. As I read on, once I read that they said he had an altercation wit sum one in tha club. I knew Naz wasn't tha one who killed him.

"You still reading tha Inquirer Baby?"

"Yeah, this tha only way I can stay up on what's goin' on up top."

"Well, is there anything in there?"

"Remember tha boy Eazy Hawk?"

"Yeah."

"He got killed last night in front of a strip club."

"Damn, he didn't seem like he had beef wit nobody."

"He was probably drunk talk'n Shit."

"Does that say Federal Informant?"

"Yeah."

"Oh My God! Eazy Hawk was a rat? I had no idea he was on tha Feds payroll."

"I got shooters to my left, shooters to my right. Real niggaz that won't hesitate to shoot on sight!" I picked up my phone.

"What up Reep? Fuck I forgot all about beach week. Give me a half hour, I'll be ready."

When I hung up Ang said, "I'm goin' to beach week too."

"You ain't goin', not wit that big stomach."

"Yes I am, me and Beauty will be there pregnant and all."

"You know what, do you. Just don't get out of pocket."

"Nah Nigga, don't you get out of pocket!"

"What ever Ang."

"You heard what I said Doe. By tha way, I need sum money to get a few outfits." I went into my pocket and pulled out tha money I had.

"You better make this enough." I watched as she counted. Hell, I didn't even know how much it was.

When she finished counting she smiled then said, "Thank you Baby."

Now I was curious as to how much I had just given her. I made a few rounds but neva counted tha money.

"If you need more just let me know."

"This 2,600 should be more than enough. I will need spending money though." There was a knock on tha door.

Ang yelled, "Come in Beauty!" When she opened tha door she was looking like her name.

"Hey Doe."

"What's good Beauty?"

"I can't call it. Ang you ready?"

"Yeah. I'm riding wit you."

"No problem cause you driving to beach week."

"Bitch yeah right!"

"Nobody wants to drive so doesn't look like you'll be goin'."

"Yeah, you would love that, wouldn't you?"

"Ang it doesn't matter to me if you go or not. Even though I don't think you should being all pregnant."

"Well too bad cause I'm goin'."

"Hey that choice is all yours."

"Let's go Beauty before he changes his mind."

We all walked outside only for us to go our separate ways. When I pulled up to Reeps, him and Murder were out front waiting.

"Y'all ready?"

"Yup."

"I need to stop by one of tha stash houses to get sum doe."

"I thought you said that you just made a few rounds when we talked earlier?

"I did but Ang hit me up for money."

"So you letting her go to beach week?"

"Yeah."

"Nigga you crazy or jus dumb?"

"I know you neva take sand to tha beach. All those people that's gonna be there, what are tha chances of me getting caught up?"

"Yeah, I guess you got a point there."

After a few hours we were done shopping.

"Girl you know Doe is gon' to flip if he sees you in that little dress."

"Well, I don't have to worry about that."

"And why not?"

"What's tha chances that we'll even see him?"

"Wow, I neva thought about that."

"Well, I might as well live on tha edge."

"What that's suppose to mean?"

"Since I know my man will be wit them I'm goin' to buy a few small items as well."

"I know you can't wait to drop that load."

"Girl who you tellin'? As soon as I drop I'm goin' on vacation."

"Where you goin'?"

"I don't know, maybe Punta Cana. I'm hungry."

"Me too."

Since we were in tha Gallery all we had to do was go downstairs to tha Food Court. Funny how they had a mall called tha Gallery like we had in Philly. While we were standing in line to get sum Japanese. These two guys walked up.

"Excuse me but I was standing over there and I could help but notice you two lovely ladies."

"I have a man."

"And so do I."

"Well, they must be fools to let you come out by ya self."

"Not fools, jus trusting."

"If you don't mind me asking, how far along are you?"

"Seven months."

"Well, you two ladies enjoy tha rest of your day."

"We will, thank you."

"Doe better be lucky I'm faithful Bitch."

"Who you tellin', they both were sharp as shit."

"So you really not driving this weekend?"

"I don't want to. I thought we would look better hopping out that candy red S600 than my Honda."

"We still can take my car as long as you drive."

"Then it's settled, we taking' ya car."

"Yo Reep, I think you should grab that Gucci shirt and sneaks."

"Murder you ain't playing no games, are you?"

"Man I'm just making sure my shit is tight."

"I can see wit all that Gucci, Prada, and Ralph Lauren you purchased. Ranay gon' have to keep a leash on you."

"Nigga go head wit dat bullshit."

"I'm just saying, you and my sis been goin' hard."

"Shit Reep, he been spending more time wit Nay than he has wit us. Speak of tha Devil." We turned around to see Nay and one of her girls walking up to us.

"I see y'all ain't playing no games for this weekend."

"Sis, you know we do it big when we do it."

"I hear you, y'all not goin' to have my baby down there tricking."

"What! They don't make me do Shit. I see you came to get you sum new gear."

"And you know it."

"Hey Reep, you can't speak?"

"Sup Linda?"

"You."

"That's what's up."

"Maybe I'll finally get to holla at you on a one on one this weekend."

"Maybe."

Linda had been telling my sis that she wanted to holla at me. I jus be so busy I haven't had time to get at her. She looked like Eva Mendez body and all. There was no doubt I would be tappin' that, if not this weekend, real soon.

"Well, I'll hit ya phone later, Murder I got a surprise for you."

"A'ight."

We finished shopping then headed to tha strip to collect sum money.

BOOM, BOOM, BOOM!

CHAPTER 34

Virginia Beach

"Y'all ready for Virginia Beach?"

"You know it."

We were shutting down tha block for tha weekend. My whole squad was goin' down, all 12 of us. We were riding 2 deep, so we would be driving six cars. We all decided to drive our exotic whips down to show off. I was pulling out my Alphine white on white Murcie Lago Roadster Lp 640 on 20-inch Wizcott's. While P.R. would be driving his midnight blue 599 GTB Ferrari. Gunz with his pearl red Aston Martin, Chopz wit his money green Ferrari 430 GT, Dirk wit his pearl black Ferrari 360 Spider and Tico wit his cream Ferrari 360 Spider. Everybody made sure their rims and cars were clean as a whistle. There was no doubt that my team would outshine all of tha competition. Not to mention, we would all be taking at least 15 grand a piece. When you work hard you play even harder.

Ashanti, Wendy, Liz, and Shauna were goin' down together. Ashanti had tha new Caddy Truck on 30s so she wanted to show it off. I let everybody know that we would be leaving in 3 hours.

For tha next hour it was biz-ness as usual. I let Fitz know that he would be riding wit me. We had reservations in one of tha hotels on tha main strip. And since it was only a 3 ½ hour drive, we decided to leave at 2 pm so that we wouldn't get caught in tha 5 o'clock traffic. We were all packed and ready to go. I had doubled even tripled check my luggage to make sure I wasn't forgetting or leaving anything behind. We all had our 8th Chains on to represent our block.

"Damn, y'all tryin' to get all tha attention this weekend."

"Now why would you say that Wendy?"

"Umm let me see, y'all pulled out tha exotic whips for starters and y'all look like y'all upgraded those pieces. And if I know you ya gear is Gucci, Louis Vuitton, Prada, and ya boy Ralph Lauren." All I could do was smile. Wendy knew me like tha back of her hand.

"Oh, did I tell you that you look nice?"

"Thanks Wendy."

"When are you guys leaving?"

"Tomorrow mornin, we have a few more things to do." While me and Wendy were talk'n Lez pulled up.

"Hey Naz."

"What up Lez?"

"Well, I know who will have all tha attention this weekend."

"Let's go Naz, we ready to hit tha road."

"A'ight. Wendy I'll see you down there."

"Maybe, maybe not."

"What's that suppose to mean?"

"Nephew there's goin' to be so many people don't be mad if you don't see us." She winked and smiled at me.

"Do you have enough money?"

"Don't be asking me no dumb question like that."

"My fault, no need to snap." P.R. and tha rest of tha squad started honking their horns.

"Y'all better hold tha Fuck up!" Wendy snapped.

We were rolling on tha highway hitting speeds up to 180 mph. Tha other cars were staring at us as we zoomed pass. A 3 ½ hour trip turned into a 2

½ hour trip.

"Damn Naz, it's j-peed out here."

There were all types of cars but there was no doubt we would have tha hottest whips in Virginia this weekend. We pulled up to our hotel and all eyes were on us. While chicks looked on in awe, tha niggaz looked on wit envy. There were six reserved spots in front just like we asked for. We all got out only to be greeted by stares. Once we had checked it we got our bags and headed to our rooms, which were all on tha same floor. Gunz and Tico wanted to change their clothes. I was straight I had on a white Ralph Lauren tank top wit a pair of peach Ralph Lauren Capris and white and peach RL sneaks to match. Me and Fitz shared a room.

"Let's go out and get sum Bitches."

"Hey Naz, ain't you forgetting sum thing?" he asked holding up my frames.

"No doubt, good lookin' Baby Boy."

"Damn, look at all these honey's out here."

"Man who you tellin'?"

There was a large group of girls gathered around our cars. We all hit tha remote start to our whips. Within seconds, they came alive.

"Excuse me, I didn't mean to startle you. Wow Sexy Man pushing a sexy car."

I just smiled and jumped into my car. I couldn't say tha same for tha rest of my squad.

Shorty tapped on tha window, "I know you not one of those stuck up Niggaz."

"Na ma. But I'm also not tha type to sweat no female either."

"I definitely feel you on that cause I don't sweat no niggaz either. I got and get my own bread. So you from Philly?"

"Yeah, and you?"

"I'm from Jersey."

"What part? I have peoples in Camden."

"Sorry Boo, I'm from Brick City. So those ya girls my boys gettin' at?"

"Fo' Sho, they call us tha Pretty Pussy Click."

"I don't even have to ask why they call y'all that."

"So you got a girl?"

"Yeah, and you?"

"When I want to have one."

"Must be a lame if you don't want to claim him."

"Actually he's not, but he thinks just because he gets money he can Fuck around."

"Oh I see. Basically two can play that game, huh?"

"Don't do it if you don't want it done to you is my motto."

"Well, sounds like y'all need to fall back or jus be committed to one another. So if you don't mind me asking. What are you down here tryin' to find?"

"A friend. Why you interested?"

"Maybe."

"Well, take my number then."

"Nah, but you can take mine." She pulled out her iPhone and stored my number.

"Where are y'all staying at?"

"Right here."

"Well, hit me up later. Maybe you can stop by for a drink. Come on girls," she said heading to this white Bentley coupe. Tha other broads fell in line.

"What was Shorty talk'n bout?"

"Nuffin really, just how she gets her money and doesn't sweat no niggaz."

"Shit, I can't tell tha way she was all on you."

"I am sum thing like a chick magnet."

I'M LOCKED UP THEY WON'T LET ME OUT. When I picked up tha phone I already knew it was Messy from tha ringtone.

"What up Nigga?"

"I can't call it, same shit just behind these walls. What's tha deal on ya end?"

"You know, down Virginia Beach doin what we do."

"Who you go down wit?"

"Tha whole squad."

"That what's up. No wonder Fitz didn't pick up his phone."

"I'mma make sure we flick it up so you and Boy-Boy can have sum flicks."

"Yeah, do that and make sure you got sum bad ass Bitches in tha flicks."

"Now you being disrespectful, I don't Fuck wit no ducks only swans." We both started laughing on that.

"So did you get tha re-up?"

"Yeah, it came through this mornin. I noticed it was more than tha usual."

"Yeah, since you been running thru that Shit I figured I would send more this time and see how long it takes to dump it."

"A'ight, you know I'm wit you."

"I know you are, that's why I'mma make sure you straight for that punk ass 3 years you got left."

"No doubt, I know you will Naz. Tell Fitz I said I'll hit his Bitch Ass later or tomorrow."

"He right here, you want to holla at him?"

"Nah, they bout to do count."

"A'ight, hit me back later." (CLICK)

"Yo, that was Messy. He said he hit ya phone."

"Shit, I didn't know it was on silent. I missed 10 calls."

"Let's hit tha strip, see what we can get into.

CHAPTER 35

Doing it Big

"Doe you ready to roll out?"

"Yeah, I don't think tha beach is ready for us this weekend."

"I know we gon' have tha dopest whips." So they thought anyway.

"Meat you talk to Shizz?"

"Yeah, we suppose to meet up at tha Wawa."

"Let's roll then cause Sticky and Cannon gon' meet us there too."

We were driving our old schools, this would definitely turn sum heads, if not all. We pulled up to tha Wawa, Sticky, Cannon, Shizz, and Doc were already waiting on us.

"Took you Niggaz long enough."

Cannon was in black on black 62 Skylark on 26s. While Shizz had his 73 red Impala on 26s. Reep brought out his green apple 69 2LI Camaro on 26s. As for me, I pulled out my cannery yellow 66 Fairlane GT sittin' on 28s. We were only 45 minutes away from tha beach but we still got a room for tha weekend. I opted to get a hotel that wasn't on tha strip just to make sure Ang wouldn't see me. Not that she would wit all these people.

It was only Thursday and it was already j-peed out. Once we were checked in, we wasted no time hitting tha strip.

"Look at all these broads. I'm glad I let y'all talk me into coming," Doc said.

"This ain't nuffin, wait til we hit Miami for tha All-Star weekend in a few months."

"Shit, you can count me in."

Later that night, we headed to this club called Whispers.

"Doe this line is long as a Motha Fucka."

"I know, that's why we gon' cut to tha V.I.P. line."

"Oh Shit! Uncle Ned what you doin?" Reep asked.

"Working, what it look like Boy?"

"Me and my peeps tryin' ta get up in this piece." Reep pulled out sum money and slid it to his uncle.

"You was alwayz my favorite nephew."

"That's because I'm ya only nephew." We all started laughing.

"I don't wear skinny jeans cause my knots don't fit!"

That was tha sounds that we were greeted by upon entering tha packed club. We headed straight to tha bar to order sum drinks.

"Damn this Motha Fucka is jumpin'."

"Who you tellin'."

We had a ball, by tha end of tha night we were all drunk. I ended up taking this bad ass Spanish chick back to tha room. She did things that I had neva had done to me before. I definitely had to get her number; she lives in DC, about a hour drive from VA.

By tha end of tha weekend, I was partied out. Marisol had did her thing on me all weekend. I knew she would be seeing more of me in tha future. I could have sworn I saw Gunz and Chopz in a Ferrari and Aston Martin. Them niggaz ain't got that kind of bread for no whips like that. So I just shook it off. They say we all have sum body that looks like us. Plus, Naz would have been wit them.

CHAPTER 36

Gotta Go

"Damn, these niggaz keep blowin' my phone up."

I decided to fall back and chill wit Cessely. Finally, I answered tha phone after Gunz kept calling.

"What up Nigga? Why you blowin' my shit up?"

"You not goin' to believe who I jus saw."

"Who Beyoncé?"

"Nah Nigga, Doe."

"What!" I could tell that Cessely was startled by my sudden outburst, "what did he say?"

"I was riding down tha strip and he was goin' in tha opposite direction. By tha time we made a U-turn, he was gone. He was driving a yellow Old School."

"Where tha Fuck did he go?"

"I don't know."

"You would think wit that bright yellow car we would have spotted him. Where y'all at now?"

"Still lookin' for that Rat Ass Nigga!"

"If you find him hit my phone back."

"Gotcha."

"Is ery thing a'ight?"

"Yeah, my nephew hasn't been home and they jus saw him."

"Oh." I wasn't about to tell her tha truth.

For tha rest of tha night and weekend I couldn't get Doe of my mind. I even spent tha remainder of tha weekend searching for him. Only to come up empty. Cessely told me to give her a call so we could hook up.

"Yo, you a'ight? You been quite tha whole ride back." I didn't respond, I just kept driving.

"Naz, Naz."

"Yo, we gonna catch up wit that nigga. If I would have seen that nigga I would've act like nuffin was up."

"Take all his money then kill him. Cause he doesn't know that I know it was him. You don't think Easy Hawk told him you know?"

"Nope."

"Well, that's a good thing. He won't expect anything when he sees you or any of us."

For tha next few months it was biz-ness as usual. Ery thing had picked up for us as well as Messy. Tha All-Star weekend was coming up, and we were preparing ourselves. Especially since tha festivities are in Miami this year.

"Naz we got a problem."

"What kind of problem?"

"Remember those two dudes I told you about?"

"Tha ones that tried to open up shop around tha corner."

"Yeah that's them."

"So what's tha problem?"

"Well, they got tha same stamp that we got."

"I told them what they did around tha corner was their biz-ness. As long as they didn't involve us."

I went in Wendy's to get my .45, "I'll be right back."

"Man you think that I'm goin' to let you go around there alone?" When we got around there they were sitting on these steps.

"So what's up wit y'all niggaz? Listen, I told you to do y'all jus don't involve us. So why would you use tha same stamp that we use?"

"What stamp is that?"

"Exclusive!"

"We didn't know you used that. We bought that stamper from tha shop."

"Well, now that you know could you please stop using it. That Shit y'all selling is puttin' a bad name on our Shit."

"We'll see what we can do."

"I don't think you understand."

"Nah Cuz, you don't understand."

"I'mma just say this and leave it alone. If you continue to use that stamp then I won't be at fault for tha outcome!"

"Are you threatening us?"

"I don't make threats only promises." Wit that being said, we walked off.

My phone started ringing.

"Hello."

"Hey You."

"What up Janelle?"

"You!"

"I heard that."

"What you doin'?"

"Shit."

"Why don't you stop by?"

"A'ight, give me a hour."

I haven't been in tha mood to play games wit Janelle. It's been over seven months and we still haven't had sex yet. It's like we were playing this cat and mouse game. When I wanted it, she didn't and when she did I didn't.

I pulled up to her house.

"Hello. Hey I'm out front."

"Are you goin' to come in? Open tha front door it's unlocked."

When I walked in tha soft sounds of Jaheim filled my ears. Janelle came down tha steps wearing a black teddy and pumps.

"It's time to stop playing games. Don't you agree Naz?" I was speechless.

"Close ya mouth and come on."

When she turned to walk back upstairs. My mouth really fell open. Jus seeing her bare ass caused an instant erection. I was goin' to give her tha best sex she ever had.

As soon as we got into tha bedroom I told her to take her teddy off. When she did, I began my foreplay. I took my time to make sure I had her at her highest peak. As I slowly licked her nipples, I used my hands to caress her love nest. I could feel her warm juices running down my fingers.

"OOOOH NAAAZ OOOH That Feels So GOOOOD!!"

Once I put my tongue in between her thighs that sent her into overdrive. "Oh My God," was all she could say. I began to flick my tongue in and out of her in circular motions. As soon as I hit her clit she started shaking uncontrollably.

"Whaaat you doin'? I'm ready to cum." That's when I took tha opportunity to suck on her clit like a lollipop.

"OOOOOOH NAAZ OH SHIIIIT I'M CUMMIN!!!"

Once her body jerked I could feel her cum in my beard. I smiled to myself knowing no one had ever ate tha pussy and made her cum before.

"Naz put it in! I want to feel you inside of me." Not thinking, in tha heat of tha moment I slid in wit no condom on.

"Damn Baby, I been waiting for this," she said.

Long story short, Janelle neva knew she could cum that many times. When we were done, we both collapsed. They only sounds were our hard breathing.

"Why did you do that?"

"Do what?"

"Fuck me so good, I've neva cum so many times before. Shit, truth be told, I don't even get to nut once before it's over."

"Nah ma, I got to make sure you get at least two before I even think about one."

"Two? Try six," she said wit a big smile, "a girl could get use to this."

Wit that said, we went for round two.

An hour and another 3 nuts later we were both sleep. Tha constant ringing of my phone woke me up!

"Yo!"

"Damn Nigga, what tha Fuck you been doin for tha last few hours?"

"Can't a nigga get sum sleep?"

"Like you tell me, you can sleep when you die."

"I heard that. So what's so important that you keep calling?"

"We need to deal wit that situation from earlier."

"A'ight, give me a few minutes," I looked over at Janelle who had that look in her eyes, "matter fact, give me about an hour."

She didn't even wait for me to hang up before she saddled up on my horse. Since I learned where her spot was I figured I'd make this quick. 30 minutes later she was more than done.

"How do you make me have multiple orgasms like that?"

"If I tell you then you won't need me. Now will you?"

"You Fucked it up for anybody else who might be lucky enough to get sum of this."

"Well, I don't have to worry about that anytime soon. I got to handle sum biz-ness. I'll call you later."

"Awe, I was hoping you could come back."

"Only if you want me too."

"Boy stop playing. I'm not goin' to front, Naz you got me really Fucked up now."

"You got me blushing."

Janelle was well worth tha wait. Her shot was tha bomb, but I was not about to tell her that.

After I got out of tha shower, I put my clothes back on then headed out tha door. When I pulled back up to tha block, P.R. was already out there.

"I didn't think you was coming."

"You know how it is when you in sum Good Pussy."

"I sure do. So what's tha deal wit those two niggaz?"

"They bout to get a First-Class Ticket to tha boneyard; courtesy of Mr.

Smith and Wesson."

"I'm wit you on that."

"Nah, if they see you they gon' know what it is."

"They don't know me."

"You right."

"I'mma act like I want to buy sum dope."

"Well, I'mma be on tha corner just in case you need me."

"A'ight."

When I stood on tha corner, I made sure to stand behind tha wall so they couldn't see me. I watched as P.R. got close.

"What up poppi? Yo, this where they selling that Exclusive?"

"Yeah, what you need?" I could tell that neither were packing.

"How much for a log?"

"600."

"Let me get 2 logs. I'm gon' be spending a lot of doe wit y'all if it's proper."

"Oh, you'll be back."

"But will y'all be here?"

"We ain't goin' nowhere." When his man came back, I looked to make sure he didn't have a pistol on him.

"1200."

"You two shouldn't be out here wit no heat."

"These niggaz round here ain't bout puttin' no work in."

"I wouldn't be so sure of that."

"Fuck 'em."

"Well, since you feel that way." I pulled out my Smith and Wesson.

"What's tha matter? Looks like you seen a ghost." By this time, Naz had walked down tha block.

"Now I tried to be nice about it. But I guess you didn't think I would make good on my promise."

"Actually, they said that you niggaz is soft and ain't about puttin' no work in."

"Wow, well who said that?"

He pointed to tha one who went to get tha work. I pulled my .38 out. One shot to tha center of tha forehead.

"Now is that puttin' in work or what?"

His boy guessing he was next tried to make a run for it. BONG, BONG, BONG! P.R. hit him wit 3 shots. Tha first one killing him before tha other 2 had had a chance to hit him. We calmly walked back to tha house as if nuffin ever happened.

"Pretty good shooting."

"Yeah, tha range is paying off."

"I told you I don't care how good of a shot you think you are. Tha range will only improve ya shot."

CHAPTER 37

Welcome to tha M.I.A.

"What tha Fuck did I tell you Nigga?" (SMACK)

"You just a hardheaded Motha Fucka ain't you! I told you as long as you cop from me you could sell ya Shit out there."

"I found a cheaper price."

"You may have but you're not goin' to sell that Bullshit around here."

"Listen Doe, I don't want no problems wit you, but I am goin' to continue to sell my Shit whether I buy it from you or not." (SMACK)

"Wrong answer Motha Fucka! This is my last time tellin' you. If you don't buy from me do not and I say it again, do not hustle around here! Do I make myself clear!?"

"What ever." BOOM!

"Nigga I was wondering when you was goin' to do that."

"You didn't think I was letting him leave here alive did you?"

"I don't know, we should have jus hit him on tha block."

"We don't need that type of heat."

"You still goin' to Miami next week?"

"Now why would you ask me a dumb question like that?"

"Nigga you know how you change ya mind at tha last minute."

"Not for sum thing like this."

"Did you get all ya Shit?"

"Jus about, I want to grab me a nice fox colored mink."

"Where's Murder at?"

"Like you told me, why you ask me a dumb question like that?"

"Is him and Nay real hot and heavy?"

"Yeah, Shit he's wit her more than wit us."

"Awe, do I detect a little bit of jealousy?"

"Stop tryin' to play me Doe. And if you real like me, throw ya hands in tha air so tha whole wide world can see last of a dying breed."

"Speak of tha Devil. We just spoke you up."

"Who is we?"

"Me and Doe, who you think?"

"You know y'all tha only niggaz I fuck wit."

"True Dat, True Dat. So what's tha deal wit you?"

"I'm jus finishing up my shopping."

"I didn't think you were still goin'."

"Shiiiit, I wouldn't miss this for tha world. So Nay letting you go?"

"Damn Reep, you gon' handle me like dat?"

"I'm just saying, she been on you like a gnat on Shit."

"It ain't even like dat. Besides, her and Linda flying down."

"I should have known."

"What's that suppose to mean nigga?"

"Hey, I alwayz say, neva take sand to tha beach."

"Check this out Reep. I can't tell her where she can and can't go."

"Why can't you wear tha pants in tha relationship? Or do you?" He started laughing which made me mad.

"Look Murder, Nay is my lil sister and I love her to death. But you my nigga so don't go gettin' all soft on me."

"One thing for sure, two things for certain, I'll neva go soft Reep. I'm a Motha Fucken killer, don't ever forget that!"

"I heard that. Tell Nay I said pick Mommy up sum thing." HA! HA!

HA!

"What you laughing at? How you know I'm wit Nay?"

"Come on Nigga, this Reep you talk'n to. She said that you gon' give her money back when she sees you."

"A'ight."

"Hit my phone when you finish boot loving." HA! HA! HA! Before he could respond, I hung up.

"You keep Fucken wit dat nigga."

"I need to dump this body and finish up my shopping."

"Throw him in tha ocean."

"Nah, I'm goin' to chop and bag him."

"Just make sure you don't put no holes in tha bag this time."

"Yeah, cause last time that Shit was crazy. If it wasn't for that damn cat they would have neva found tha body."

For tha next 3 days, I took care of biz-ness. Making sure that all my peeps were taken care of while I would be in tha M.I.A. for All-Star weekend. Ang wanted to go but her mom was out of town. And Beauty's mom was wit her so there was nobody to watch Lil Doe. Ang had him on New Year's Eve. He weighed 7lbs 8 ounces, brown eyes wit straight hair. He looked like Ang to me but everybody else seemed to think he looked like me.

"Baby can we take a trip sum where next month?"

"We'll see."

"That means no. Anytime you say we'll see we neva go."

"Ang you know I'm a busy man."

"Yeah, not too busy to do what you want when you want though, huh?"

"Listen, I don't feel like this Shit right now."

"You neva feel like it when it's about you." I didn't even respond, I just grabbed my luggage and headed out tha door.

I scooped Meat, Shizz, Reed, Murder, and Doc up then went to tha airport.

"FLIGHT 141 HEADING TO MIAMI IS BOARDING AT GATE 16."

"That's us y'all, let's go."

"WOOOO Miami Pretty Bitches here we come," Doc said all excited.

Tha other people in tha airport just looked on and shook their heads. We all tried to get drunk off tha cheap gin they served on tha plane.

"PLEASE BE SEATED AND FASTEN YOUR SEAT BELTS."

When we exited tha plane we were greeted by tha warm Miami sun.

"Damn, if it feels like this in February I can imagine what tha spring and summer must feel like." We walked over to tha rental car place.

"Reservations for Walker please."

Tha lady handed me two sets of keys. I figured these were tha keys to tha two Bentley's I rented. Miami had any kind of rental you could think of.

"What tha Fuck! I know you didn't rent these Bentley's?"

"When we do it, how we do it?"

"BIG!" They all said at once.

"We gon' have a ball this weekend. Look at all tha Bitches in our hotel."

We waited for tha elevator to open up. When it did, I was surprised to see Allen Iverson and Rasheed Wallace coming out. We said what's up and kept it moving.

"Oh Shit, do y'all know who that was?" Meat asked.

"Yeah, but we ain't no male groupie niggaz."

"I wasn't saying it like that cause I'm a celebrity too Nigga." We all laughed at him.

"I don't find nuffin funny about that."

"This nigga alwayz in his feelings like a broad."

"What ever Motha Fucka."

"Both y'all chill tha Fuck out, Damn. I know every time we go sum where y'all alwayz gettin' into it," Murder replied.

"I ain't tryin' to hear that bullshit, I came to have fun," Meat said giving me and Murder sum dap.

Truth be told, Meat and Doc didn't like each other. Meat said Doc didn't know what if felt like to struggle. He was born wit money and he just wanted to be down that's why he got into tha game. Which is true but he's half ass a'ight, so unless he crosses me then he cool. Once we were situated in our suits, we headed out to see tha town of Miami.

"Excuse me, Excuse me don't I know you from sum where?" I turned around to see who was talk'n.

"Oh Shit, what's tha deal Mami?"

"Why didn't you say you were coming down here?"

"Because it was a last-minute thing. Where you staying at?"

"At my grandparents beach house."

"WOW, lucky you."

"Marisol, you not goin' to introduce me to ya friends?"

"My bag, Doe this my cousin Tooty and my cousin Juicy."

"Hello ladies, these are my boys Reep, Murder, Doc, Shizz, and Meat."

Tooty and Juicy wasted no time picking who they wanted. Unfortunately for Juicy, Murder was already spoken for.

"Nigga is you stupid?" Reep asked.

"Nah, I just don't get down like that."

"Fuck that, I'm not goin' to tell on you."

"I'm not worried about that shit Reep, you should know that."

"I'm just saying, how often do you get to come to Miami? Nigga you better live it up while you here."

"Like I said, ma I'm good."

"OOOH too bad papi, we could have had so much fun this weekend," she said wit a devilish but seductive smile.

Doc stepped up to tha plate.

"I'm not taken ma."

She looked past him to Meat, "I hope you're not taken too."

"Nah, I'm all yours, even though I don't like to be chosen second."

"Papi don't take it personal, I'm sure you do it all tha time."

She did have a point. Not to mention she was 5'6", green eyes, long natural curly hair and an ass that would make any bitch jealous.

"So where are y'all headed?"

"Jus sight-seeing."

"I'll be happy to show you around. This like home away from home for me. I don't want to cramp ya style though."

"How could a beautiful woman such as ya self cramp my style? For anything, they gonna be hating cause I got tha baddest chick in tha M.I.A.!"

"You know how to make a girl feel good."

"They say tha truth works all tha time."

"They ain't neva lied about that."

"If y'all done wit all that mushy, gushy shit I'm tryin' to sight see."

Meat seen his chance to one up Doc.

"Do I detect a little bit of, what's tha word I'm looking for?"

"Jealousy, papi jealousy."

"Yeah, that's it." Everybody laughed which only pissed Doc off.

"Fuck all y'all," he said and walked off.

"I don't know about y'all but I'm hungrier than a hostage."

"I didn't know you was a physic too."

"And I didn't know you was a comic."

"Come on, I know a nice spot to grab a bite to eat from."

She took us to this place called Justin's which was Puff Daddy's restaurant. Tha food was remarkable.

"Shit I'm stuffed."

"Me too. I think I got niggaitis." Tooty asked Reep what he was talking about.

"You know after you give a nigga a good meal they don't want to do shit." We all had to laugh at that.

"I think I need to take a quick nap."

"No, No, there's plenty more of Miami to see. You can sleep tonight after we go clubbing."

"Yeah right, like I'm goin' to get any sleep then."

"I suppose you are right about that. Well then, let's do a little shopping."

"Sounds like a winner, we were goin' to do that anyway."

We paid tha tab then headed out tha door only to bump into Diddy himself.

"Hope you enjoyed ya meal. Please come again."

"Sure did and will."

CHAPTER 38

All-Star Weekend

We arrived in Miami tha temperature was 75 degrees which was warm for February. We had reserved tha 3-bedroom suites in tha best hotel in Miami where all tha stars will be staying at. So I wasn't at all surprised at tha plush room when we walked in. Me, P.R., and Gunz were sharing a suite. Of course, I took tha master bedroom.

"I'mma jump in tha shower real quick."

"A'ight, we'll be downstairs in tha lounge having a drink or two."

"I shouldn't be that long."

Since we were goin' to be here for a whole week; I packed more than enough clothes. I decided since tha weather was really warm to throw on my pink Ralph Lauren capris wit my all-white Ralph Lauren shirt wit tha RL in pink and white RL tennis shoes wit tha pink stitching.

Once I was dressed, I gave myself tha once over in tha full length mirror. I went back to my room and threw on my NJ piece princess cut earrings, Bovoli watch and my Ralph Lauren frames. Now I was ready to go.

By tha time I got downstairs tha whole squad was more than ready to roll out.

"About Fucken time Nigga."

"Man, you worse than a broad. We done had 4 drinks waiting on ya ass."

"Fuck y'all! Y'all could have left."

"Now you sound stupid. What we look like leaven you?"

"Well, stop complaining, it takes time to look like this." HA! HA! HA!

"Now that was funny."

Since P.R.'s uncle and cousin lived up here we don't have to rent any cars, they hooked us up. They had left tha keys at tha front desk for us. There was no way that I wasn't goin' to push tha convertible white on white Rolls Royce. P.R. wanted tha black on black Maybach which left Esco wit tha platinum on platinum Flying Spur.

"Naz, my cousin said to give him a call later so he can show us a good time while we're here. First, let's go to Justin's to grab a bite to eat."

Tha waitress seated us then let us know she would be back to take our order. Tha service in Justin's was fast and good. By tha time we finished eating I was stuffed like a turkey.

"Let me call my cousin to see if he's done doin' what ever he was doin'."

"Hello. What's up Juan? I was just about to give you a call."

"Where you guys at?"

"We about to leave Justin's."

"Meet me at tha house in 15 minutes."

"See you there." (CLICK)

"Yo follow me."

15 minutes later, we were pulling up in front of this mansion. We had to wait to be buzzed in. Once we were, we drove around to tha front of tha house. Then we were greeted by two armed bodyguards.

"P.R. hi you doin? Long time no see. Where you been?"

"In my hometown Killadelphia."

We were all patted down to make sure we didn't have any weapons. Juan came to tha door wit this bad ass Brazilian chick on his hip.

"Naz, what's tha deal wit ya?"

"Just here to live it up for this All-Star weekend."

"Speaking of that, do you have tickets for tha game or tha celebrity game?"

"Nah, I wish."

"Lucky for you, my dad knows sum powerful people in powerful positions. I got you tickets to both games. Let's go out by tha pool to have a few drinks before we leave."

I couldn't believe it, there were about 15 chicks running around wit damn near nuffin on.

"I don't know about y'all but I'm in Heaven." We all looked at Rell and busted out laughing.

We sat around drinking and getting to know tha girls. Before we realized it, it was 10 o'clock.

"I don't know about y'all but this Bombay has me feelin' it and ready to party."

Juan looked at me then slurred, "I'm wit you on that Naaaz."

"You sure you gon' be able to hang?"

"This is nuffin, I'm at my best when I'm drunk."

"Well, on dat note, let's go tear tha town up."

"We want to come papi," one of tha girls said.

"No, you girls stay here. We'll be back at tha end of tha night."

"You promise?"

"Sure do."

Capes grabbed a handful of her ass then said, "It will be worth tha wait mami."

"Sí papi sí!"

We pulled up to V.I.P. in front of this club called Pleezer's.

"Damn, look at this long ass line."

"We don't wait in no line, straight to V.I.P."

"Shit, that line is just as long," Tico said.

Juan walked to tha front of tha line wit us on his heels.

"Hey Juan. How many?"

"Me," and he turned around to count, "16."

I had to turn around; I know it was only 12 of us. But when I spotted tha four females, I had to smile. I turned back around in time to catch Juan winking at me.

Once we got into tha club tha four ladies that we had helped get in walked up to us.

"Thank you, how much do we owe y'all?"

"I'm goin' to take that as total disrespect!"

"I wasn't tryin' to disrespect you in no type of way. Well, can I at least buy you a drink?"

"No, but you can let me buy you a drink."

Juan looked at me then said, "Smoove."

"So, can I buy you that drink or what?"

"Only if you promise to let me buy tha next round."

"I can't make that promise ma."

"Why not? If you don't mind me asking."

"Because, I neva make a promise I can't keep."

"I see, well I guess you can buy me a drink."

"You from Miami?"

"Yeah, Dade County. And you?"

"Nah, I'm from Philadelphia."

"Oh, you from Philly?"

"Yeah, I'm down here for tha All-Star weekend."

"You're early ain't you?"

"I decided to get a jump on tha competition."

"What competition?"

"Tha ones that will be competing for you. By tha way, I'm Naz."

"I'm Nafeeza. At first, I thought you were from New Jersey," she said pointing to my chain.

"No, just my initials."

By tha time tha bartender made her way to us, I was more than ready to drink.

"Can I take ya order?"

"Let me get a bottle of Bombay Sapphire."

"What you know bout that drink?"

"That's all I drink."

"Me too."

"In that case, make it two."

"Wit two cups wit ice and pineapple juice," she said before I could say anything, "WOW, a gentleman, good looks and you drink Bombay. Where have you been hiding?"

"Philly," I said. We both laughed.

"You might need to visit Miami more often."

"Besides this, I neva had to come to tha M.I.A."

"Well, hopefully when you leave, you'll have a reason to come back," she said.

Feeza was definitely worth a trip back to Miami. 5'7", bronze skin, hazel eyes, short Anita Baker styled haircut, and a body that was perfect. To say tha least, she was nothing short of a dime. I could tell that Feeza was feeling me as well. Her girls were on tha dance floor cuttin' up.

"I don't want to hold you hostage if you want to go and get ya party on."

"You not holding me hostage."

"Do you know how to dance?"

"I know how to two-step, if you consider that dancing."

"OOH, this is my Shit! Come on!"

She grabbed my hand and led me towards tha dance floor. They had that song *"Swagger Like Us"* playing. I did my thing. I could tell she was impressed. When they played that song *"Donk"* Feeza turned it all tha way out. Damn she was phat and soooooo soft. I know she felt tha hard on that grew inside my pants. She kept looking back at me wit a big smile on her Sexy Ass face. I made my way back to our table so that I could have another drink.

"Excuse you Sinclaire."

"Bitch what?"

"Why you drinking my Shit?"

"Well, Chopz said it was cool, that Naz wouldn't mind."

"Don't worry about it Feeza. Chopz was just about to go get two more bottles. Ain't that right Chopz?"

"Yeah."

"I'll go wit you."

"She gets on my nerves wit that."

"Don't let it bother you ma. It ain't about nuffin."

"I see ya friend is drunk," she said pointing to Juan.

He staggered over to our table.

"Me and Capes bout to be out."

"Where y'all goin', it's only 12 o'clock?"

"Nigga, we goin' back to tha house."

"A'ight, be safe."

"I know another club we can hit, if you up to it."

"I'm down wit what ever."

"Let me round up tha rest of my crew."

15 minutes later, she came back wit her girls followed by P.R. and Esco.

"Yo, we bout to be out."

"Damn, tha night is young, Feeza bout to take us to another spot. Let me use tha bathroom before we mash out." When I walked into tha bathroom all I smelled was weed.

"My man, I got that Kush and E-pills."

I didn't know if this nigga was a cop or not tryin' to sell me drugs in tha bathroom of a club. Not that they don't do this all tha time in Philly.

"No disrespect peeps but are you tha police?"

"Fuck No! Do I look like tha police?"

"I just need to make sure. It's not every day sum body ask me to buy drugs in a bathroom."

"You not from Miami, are you?"

"Nah, just in town for All-Star weekend. Let me get a quarter of Sour Diesel."

"I got Kush."

"Well, let me get a quarter of that. What kind of E-pills do you have?"

"Blue Dolphins, Dr. Thunder Bolts."

"Let me get two Bolts." Chopz came into tha bathroom.

"Yo, what tha Fuck you doin' in here?"

"I had to grab up sum of that Kush."

"Did you get enough?"

"Yup, enough for me."

"Peeps you got any more of that?"

"Yeah, what you need?"

"Give me a half ounce."

"Ok, we ready."

"I thought you fell in." When we got outside tha line was still long.

"What time they stop jumpin'?"

"Normally 4 o'clock but since it's All-Star weekend probably 6 o'clock."

By tha time we finished partying it was close to 7 in tha morning.

"I hope that I'll be seeing more of you before you leave."

"That's up to you."

"I would love that."

"Here's my number, maybe we can hook up when you get up to do lunch."

By tha time I hit tha pillow I was out.

8 hours later I was awakened by a knock on my door.

"Come in."

"Nigga get up! You gon' sleep tha day away? It's 4 o'clock."

"I'm gettin' up now. Let me jump in tha shower real fast."

"You know it's about 78 degrees out today."

"What am I goin' to put on today?"

I didn't want to get out tha shower it felt so good. I kept it basic, Gucci jeans, and fitted shirt wit my tan Gucci sneaks. I grabbed my frames and headed out tha door to tha lobby.

"This is a first."

"What you talk'n about Esco?"

"It only took you 30 minutes. Hey, Asia called me, wanted to know if we wanted to do dinner. You can't front, they bad as a motha fucka. Her girl was all over Naz."

"She's down to earth. If tha shot is good, I'll be back to visit more often."

"Me and you both," Chopz said.

For tha next few days all we did was party from sunup to sundown. Before we realized it, it was Friday. We had good seats for tha rookie game, tha three-point and slam dunk contest. To my surprise, Feeza and her girls had tickets also.

"Are you following me?"

"Nah, this is tha reason we came in town."

"You didn't think we would miss this, did you? Truth be told, I was hoping that we did bump into y'all."

"And why is that?"

"These last 5 days have been fun."

"That's a good thing, right?"

"Sure is."

After tha game was over I went down to take sum pictures wit tha future stars of tha NBA.

"Dwayne Wade is throwing a party tonight."

"Is that an invitation?"

"Only if you want to go."

"You already know a long as you there so am I."

"Say no more then." My phone was goin' off. I knew that it was Ashanti from tha ring tone.

"Hello, you."

"Hey, Babe. What you doin'?"

"Just finished watching tha rookie game. About to go get my party on."

"I was just checking up on you. Enjoy tha rest of ya weekend; see you when you get home. Love you Naz."

"And me you." When I hung up Feeza was smiling.

"What?"

"That was sweet. She's one lucky broad."

"I don't know about you but I need a drink."

We ended up at Dwayne Wade's party. Feeza asked if I wanted to come back to her place for a night cap.

"My girls said they're goin' to another spot wit ya boys."

"Well, give them ya keys or do you want to drive?"

"It's up to you."

"Well, I'll just ride wit you."

"Chopz, I'm gonna fall back and hang out wit Feeza. So here are tha keys."

"We not riding six deep in tha Rolls? Well, here Asia take my truck."

"OOOH, sum body's gonna get her freak on. About time," Macy said wit a big smile.

"Shut up, ain't nobody gettin' their freak on."

"Yeah a'ight, tell that to sum body that might and I say might believe you, cause I surely don't."

"What ever Bitch!"

"You'll tell us about it in tha mornin. If it's worth tellin'," Sinclair added.

"I guess she'll be telling y'all then," P.R. said in my defense.

"All y'all need to fall back, it's not that type of party."

"Truth be told, I would have thought y'all already handled that tha way y'all been swingin' these last 5 days."

"Let's get out of here Naz."

"I couldn't agree more."

We stopped at tha LQ to get a fifth of Bombay and sum wraps for tha weed I had. To my surprise, Feeza lived in a nice condo. Tha inside was laid out.

"Let me find out you a hustler."

"No, but I do defend them." Tha look on my face must've said what I was thinking.

"Yeah, I'm a lawyer. And a damn good one, if do say."

"Let me ask you a question, if I may."

"Sure, go head."

"How does a lawyer have time to party tha way you do?"

"I took my vacation this week for All-Star weekend. I don't usually go out like that. I don't even have a life outside of work."

"That's why ya girls said what they said?"

"Yeah, Naz I haven't been with a man in six months."

"I would have neva thought you would be into women."

"Pleeeease, I'm strictly dickly." I started laughing like that was a joke.

"Forgive me for not laughing."

"Is it OK for me to smoke in your house?"

"So now you being funny?"

"No, you might not smoke in ya house."

"I don't, cause I don't smoke at all."

"I didn't think you did." I lit my weed and took a long pull.

We talked about what made her want to become a lawyer. She explained to me that her dad was doing a life bid because his lawyer was working wit tha prosecutor to send him to jail. But she was working to get it overturned.

"I need to get comfortable, excuse me for a minute."

Damn, Asia might be right; I just might get myself sum tonight. Truth be told, he could have been got sum if he wasn't trying to be tha perfect gentleman. I decided to put on a pair of boy shorts and a wife beater.

When she walked back into tha room, I wanted to jump straight on her. Those boy shorts weren't doing her ass any justice and she knew it. I could tell by tha bulge in his pants that my plan was working.

"Would you like a refill?" she asked pointing to my almost empty glass.

"Yes please. May I use your bathroom?"

"Down tha hall, last door on tha right."

There was no doubt in my mind that tha dragon would be slayed tonight. And just to make sure, I popped my last E-pill. When I got back to tha living room, Feeza had Keyshia Cole playing on tha stereo.

"That's my Shit."

"Boy, you don't know nuffin bout Keyshia."

"I listen to R&B just as much as rap." I poured myself another glass of Bombay.

"You gonna be passed out drunk in a minute."

"I don't think so, but if I do, you'll wake me up when it's time for me to go."

"I might."

After another 15 minutes, my E's were in full affect. I took my shoes off.

"You comfortable enough?" she asked me.

"Almost," I said removing my blazer, "that's more like it."

"For a minute, I thought you were goin' to strip down to ya boxers."

"I was, but I thought that might have been too much."

"Boxers are just like wearing a pair of shorts."

"Well, in that case, I took my jeans and shirt off." I smiled to myself as I watched her eyes get big when she saw my mans through tha slit in my boxers.

"Oh Shit, my fault."

"Huh?"

"I said, my fault."

"Oh, don't worry about it," she said still looking at my mans.

"You a'ight?" I asked catching her off guard.

"Umm, Oh yeah I'm fine."

I was lying, just seeing tha size of his penis had my panties moist. I wonder if he knew what to do wit that Anaconda he had between his legs. Hopefully tonight I will find out. Before I knew what was goin' on, Naz reached over grabbed my face.

Then said, "We've played this game long enough, don't you think?"

Wit out answering, I put my lips up against his and explored his mouth wit my tongue. Next thing I knew, I had one hand on his well-toned chest and tha other on his penis which began to grow in my hand.

Damn, she had tha softest lips. I pulled her wife beater over her head exposing her bare breast.

When he took my shirt off and put one of my titties in his mouth. A soft moan escaped my mouth.

When Feeza moaned, I took that opportunity to pull down her shorts. Seeing that she didn't have on any panties only excited me more. I used my tongue to work my way down to her vagina. Once I got there, I made her go crazy. When it was all said and done, Feeza was more than satisfied. After a few more rounds of me turning her out. I knew that I would be back to tha M.I.A. to visit Feeza if nothing else.

Tha next morning, I woke up to smell of fried potatoes, waffles, beef scrapple, and cheese eggs.

Feeza walked into tha room, "I hope you're hungry; I made you sum breakfast. There's a new toothbrush and wash cloth on tha sink."

I went into tha bathroom to wash up and handle my hygiene. Once I was done, I walked down to tha dining room.

"Dig in, don't worry, I didn't poison you."

"I hope not for your sake."

When I got back to tha hotel you would have thought it was 4 o'clock instead of 9 in tha morning. As I was waiting for tha elevator Esco walked up.

I see I'm not tha only one who had a sleep over last night." (DING)

When tha elevator opened up I almost lost it. Before I realized it, I had pushed him back on tha elevator while punching him repeatedly in tha face. Esco pushed tha button to our floor. When we got there I was still beating tha shit out of Doe. There was no doubt in my mind that this would be his last day on earth.

"What tha Fuck is this about Naz!"

"Nigga you know exactly what this Shit is about Motha Fucka! We got him in my room. Call ery body, tell 'em to get over here right now!"

"We suppose to be peoples."

"That's what I thought until you framed me for murder!"

"I don't know what..." (SMACK)

"Nigga stop lying!"

By tha time everybody got there, this nigga looked like a mess.

"How much did you pay Eazy Hawk?"

"Who?" (SMACK)

"Nigga don't play wit me. I said Eazy Hawk!"

"I told you I don't know." (SMACK! SMACK! SMACK!)

"I can do this Shit all day Nigga. Eazy told me it was you who paid him to set me up for those murders."

P.R. kicked him in tha mouth causing one of his teeth to fall out instantly. Esco pulled out tha pistol that Juan had given him.

"I neva liked or trusted ya Bitch Ass anyway!"

"Not here, call Juan P.R., let him know we have a rat that needs to be taught a lesson."

"How much do you need? I run Virginia, I can get you what ever you want or need." HA! HA! HA!

"Motha Fucka! I don't need ya chump change! I have triple what ever you got. I want you to pay for what you put me through!"

"Nigga I ain't put you through a Motha Fucken thing." (SMACK)

"Who tha Fuck do you think you talk'n to?"

"I got a squad that will kill every Nigga in this room!"

"Damn! Where ya niggaz at when you need them da most?"

"We right here Naz," Chop said.

"You right."

5 minutes later, there was a knock on tha door.

"Who is it!" I yelled. When I heard Juan's voice I told Gunz to let him in.

"Damn, if it isn't Mr. Doe himself. Looks like you're in a lot of trouble."

"Fuck you Juan! I neva liked you anyway you Spic!"

"Tha feelin' mutual. It was only biz-ness and you wasn't gettin' enough."

"Do you think we can get him out of here unnoticed?"

"Who am I?" He pulled out his phone and made a call. 10 minutes later, there was another knock.

"That's tha cleaners, let them in."

When they came in pushing that cart wit tha caters jacket on all I could do was smile. After we had Doe taped and bounded we put him in tha cart. Juan let them know he would meet them at tha warehouse. They wheeled him out as if he wasn't even in their cart.

"What do you want done to him?"

"If possible, I want to kill him personally."

"Sure, only if I get to watch."

We pulled up to this big warehouse. When we got inside they had Doe hanging from these chains.

"Well, Well, Well, looky here."

"Fuck you Naz!"

"Nah Nigga, Fuck you! Because of you I didn't get to see my first son being born. I lost months of my life that I will neva get back!"

"Listen, like I said, I didn't set you up."

"Don't keep lying' to me!"

"I'm about to be a father too."

"We'll have sum thing in common then, neither of us will have gotton to see their child born. Tha only difference is, you'll neva get to see what your child looks like."

"Fuck you, I'll see you in Hell Naz!"

"And you just might my friend but not any time soon."

"You'll neva get away wit this. You do know that don't you?"

"Nigga I already did. Nobody knows that you're here and they definitely can't and won't connect me to you. They won't even know what happen to you."

Juan pulled down on this lever; next thing I knew, this tarp began to come off this pool. I took Esco's pistol and shot Doe in his knee cap. As soon as tha blood hit tha water tha alligators went crazy. Juan hit another lever and Doe started to come down close to that water. He stopped about an inch away; all tha gators were snapping like crazy.

"Let me shoot him in tha head," Esco said.

"Nah, that would be to easy. I want him to feel tha pain."

Juan lowered tha chains another inch. Within seconds, one of tha gators grabbed a hold of his legs and ripped them from tha limbs.

"AAAAAAAAAAH!AAAAAAAAH!" was all you heard from Doe's mouth.

I nodded to Juan who in return hit tha lever. Doe's body made a splash in tha water. Only sounds you heard were that of tha gators jaws chopping down on Doe's body. Juan looked at tha two men to make sure there's no traces of him left.

When we arrived back at tha hotel tha lobby was flooded wit stars. I heard this one guy asking his boy if he'd heard from Doe. I couldn't help smiling to myself at tha mention of Doe's name. Nobody would be seeing or hearing from him again.

CHAPTER 39

Missing

"Reep you still haven't heard from Doe?"

"Nah, he said he was coming down to tha lobby to grab sum thing to eat."

"Call Tooty to see if he's wit Marisol." No soon as he said that my phone was ringing.

"Hello."

"Hey papi. What you doin' today?"

"Hey is Doe wit Marisol?"

"No, she's upstairs putting on her clothes."

"And he hasn't been over there at all this mornin?"

"No why? Is ery thing a'ight?"

"Yeah, we jus ain't heard from him."

"He's probably shopping or tricking."

"Yeah, you probably right."

For tha next hour we sat in tha lobby sipping on Long Island Ice Tea's.

"Reep, try his phone again."

"You must have been reading my mind." After about 8 rings and tha answering machine picking up, I left a message.

"Doe this is Reep, when you get this hit me back ASAP!"

"I'm really starting to think sum thing happen. There's no way he wouldn't have answered his phone by now!"

"I know, but what can we do? Let's just give him a few more hours."

Before we knew it, 3 hours had passed by.

"Murder, do you think we should call tha police?"

"They gon' say he has to be missing for at least 24 hours."

"So we have to wait 24 Fucken hours!"

"Yeah."

"That's sum Bullshit. We might as well finish balling out."

"I don't want to jump tha gun on this Reep. He might just be out wit sum broad."

"Maybe, but we'll know by tonight. He's not goin' to just leave us hanging."

CHAPTER 40

Back to Da Block

Our plane had just landed back in Philly. We had a ball for tha week we were in Miami. I had finally caught up wit Doe. That would be a cold case that will neva be solved. I had met Nafeeza which would be my reason to travel to Miami.

By tha time we made it to tha block it was packed.

"Yo, what tha Fuck is goin' on around here?" Tha police and ambulance were out.

"Wendy, what tha Fuck is goin' on around here?"

"Ms. Smith had a heart attack. So how was tha trip?"

"Couldn't have been better."

"Do tell."

"I'll put you down after I come back from seeing my son."

"Him and Ashanti just left, they went to tha mall."

"Well, in that case, Wendy I met one of tha baddest chicks I've ever met in my life."

"What's her name, where is she from, and do you plan to see her again?"

"Nafeeza, Dade County, yes and to top it all off, she's a lawyer."

"WOW! Now I'm impressed."

"So was I."

"How did you meet her?"

"Juan paid her and her girls way into this club."

"A lawyer that likes to hang out?"

"Actually she only came out for All-Star weekend. Shit, Wendy her girls put her on blast. Saying it was about time she had fun and a man in her life."

"Sounds like a woman who throws herself into her work."

"Tha highlight of my week was running into Doe?"

"WHOOO?"

"You heard me right, Doe."

"So what did he have to say?"

"I didn't give him a chance to say shit at first. As soon as tha elevator opened and I saw him, I went straight on him."

"Did anybody see you?"

"Nah, except Esco." We both laughed at that.

"I know he enjoyed that since he can't stand him. Well, did you find out where he's staying at?"

"For what?"

"So you can ride on him."

"Wendy, Doe is no longer among tha living."

"You killed him in Miami?"

"Sure did, why put it off. Thanks to Juan, they'll neva and I mean neva find him."

"What about tha people he came wit?"

"What about 'em?"

"I know they got to be worried by now."

"Who cares."

"Yeah, I guess you're right."

"So, what's been happening around here besides Ms. Smith having a heart attack?" I could tell by tha look on her face that sum thing had went down while we were gone.

"Do you remember them boys from over 2nd & Girard?"

"Yeah, what about 'em?"

"They call themselves coming around here to open up shop."

"What?"

"Don't worry about it, they won't be tryin' that shit no more. You know I ain't even letting that go down," she said pulling her .380 out her pocketbook.

All I could say was, "I knew I could count on you to hold down tha fort."

"There was no way that I was goin' to let that Shit slide."

Whether she handled it or not, I take that as total disrespect and I will not be disrespect in anyway by any one! Me, P.R. and Esco down and of course and they were down.

Later that night, we suited up ready for tha mission ahead. P.R. had an AR-15 while me and Esco both had Tec's and .45s. I had gotton Tico to get his little cousins to steal us a car. We parked a block away from where they were.

"Let's take tha other way through tha ally." We went around tha block then slid in tha ally.

"It's about 15 people out there. I know at least 4 of them probably holding. So we have to make sure our shots are accurate."

When we got to tha ally, I put up my finger. They already knew once I reached 3 what to do. As soon as my third finger went up all you heard was TAT, TAT, TAT, TAT, TAT, TAT, TAT, TAT, TAT, TAT, TAT, TAT. They neva even stood a chance. Tha hail of bullets put them down wit out a second thought. And tha few that were fortunate to run didn't make it too far before our .45s found their targets. Once we were sure they were all dead we jumped in tha stolen car and peeled out.

"Yo, make sure you wipe this car completely down then torch it."

"I thought that we were just goin' to leave it?"

"Nah, change in plans." Better yet, I drove to tha bad lands.

"Let's wipe it down, then we'll leave it running, I'm sure sum body will eventually take it. If it doesn't run out of gas first. I need to get tha other car. I think 3 guys walking wit 2 Tec's, 2 .45s, and an AR-15 might look a little bit suspicious."

"You think?" Esco said joking, "so, have you talk to Janelle lately?"

"Yeah, we talk every day just about, why?"

"My aunt said she was suppose to be goin' to visit my grandmother in California."

"She did mention sum thing about that. I was even think'n about flying out wit her."

"You might as well, it will be fun."

"Are you goin'?"

"Yeah, I haven't seen my granny in a while."

"Yeah, I need to go visit my nana."

I went home took a shower then headed to nana's. My Uncle Charles was out front cutting tha lawn when I pulled up.

"Hey there Stranger, long time no see. I thought you moved out of town."

"Nah Uncle Charles, I just been really busy that's all. Is nana in tha house?"

"No, she's wit Ashanti and lil man."

"Where they go at?"

"I don't know, they alwayz hanging out. Shit, I see them more than I do you." Just as I was about to say sum thing Ashanti pulled up.

When Naz saw me he got all excited.

"Daa, Daa." I went to pick him up.

"Show Daddy you can walk," Ashanti said putting him down.

At first he was just standing there. Then he put one foot in front of tha other and started walking towards me. I couldn't believe it, Naz was walking. I looked at Ashanti.

"Don't even think about it."

"Ouch! Why you do that Nana?"

"Boy, don't even question me. You not to grown to get ya behind busted. And why haven't I seen you in weeks? Don't give me that nonsense about being busy. You can neva be too busy to come by and see ya Nana for a few minutes." I looked at Uncle Charles who in return shrugged his shoulders.

"I'm sorry Nana, you don't have to worry about that anymore." We went inside, Naz had toys everywhere.

"Looks like you running a daycare in here Nana."

"That's all my grand babies things." I talked to Nana for another hour before my phone started to ring.

"Nana, I'll be back to check on you in a few days. Oh Shit, I almost forgot."

"Boy you better watch ya mouth."

"Sorry Nana, this is for you." I handed her tha envelope that I had in my back pocket.

"Chile, you know I don't want none of that dirty money."

"This is money I won at tha casino a few days ago."

I was lying and I hated lying to nana but I knew it would be tha only way she would accept tha grand that was in tha envelope. Nana would have a fit if she knew that tha money Uncle Charles was giving her came from me.

"Are you coming home tonight?" Ashanti wanted to know.

"If I don't, I'll call you before it gets too late."

"Ok, I love you."

"And I you."

"Wuv you." I couldn't help but smile at my little man.

"It seems like he is growing up fast." I waited until after I got outside to answer my phone.

"What's up Janelle?"

"I thought you were screening calls."

"Nah, I was talk'n to my nana."

"Well, did you decide if you were gonna go wit me to Cali or not?"

"Yeah, make sure you get me a window seat. Oh yeah, First Class."

"What?"

"We flying First Class?"

"Excuse me, I don't got no First-Class money."

"But I do."

"Well, I'll give you my money and you can put tha rest to it."

"Janelle don't disrespect me."

"I wasn't, I asked you to come."

"I know, but you already know how I get down. So when are we leaving?"

"Next week."

"Make sure you reserve us a rental car."

"A'ight."

"Preferably a truck if they have any available. Did Esco tell you he was goin' too?"

"Yup, he called me to confirm that he was goin'. Are you goin' to be busy a little later?"

"I don't think so. Plus, I'm neva too busy for you."

"Sounds good."

"It's tha truth."

"Well, stop by."

"Give me about an hour and I'll be over."

"I'll be waiting."

I couldn't believe it; I had let myself fall in love wit a man that was already involved. But, you can't help who you fall in love wit. When tha doorbell rang, I thought it was Naz. I opened tha door.

"EEEEL, you must be expecting company wit that on."

"Bitch shut up and what do you want?"

"I need to crash here tonight."

"No you don't, you better take your ass home wit ya kids."

"They over their dads house and where's my nephew?"

"He's sleep and if tha kids ain't home, why do you need to stay here?"

"Damn, does it matter?"

"Yeah, I got company coming over in a little bit."

"Ain't nobody but Naz."

"Yup, sure is."

"If I didn't know any better I would think you were in love wit him."

"I might be."

"I'm happy for you cause Lord knows you deserve it."

"Me and Esco goin' to see granny next week."

"I know, Mommy told me. I don't have tha money to go."

"Esco said he'll give you tha money if you really want to go."

"In that case, count me in."

"A'ight, I'll call him and let him know. Mommy said she'll watch tha kids." There was a knock on tha door.

When Kina answered, I was surprised not to see Naz but to see him standing there wit a dozen white roses.

"Are you gonna let me in?"

"Oh I'm sorry, come in."

"What's up Kina?"

"I can't call it Naz. I need to find a man like you."

"As good as you look, I'm pretty sure niggaz are beating down your door."

"Don't tell her that Baby, it will go straight to her already big head."

"Too late, it already did," Kina said wit a big ass smile.

"Janelle, let me find out you a hater on tha low."

"I heard that brother," she said high fiving Naz.

"Don't you have sum where you need to be Kina?"

"Umm, not really but I'll take that as my cue to leave," then she looked at me and winked, "let me get ya keys."

"You better drive ya own car."

"My car is in tha shop."

"Again? You need a new car."

"I know, I'm so tired of that car."

"Hey, I got a car for sale."

"I seen tha cars you drive. I don't have that kind of money."

"Nah, it's my hoopty, I'm getting another one."

"I don't need to buy another problem car."

"Trust me, it's very, very reliable. I wouldn't sell my sis a lemon."

"Did I hear him right? Did he just call Kina sister."

"How much do you want for it?"

"What can you afford?"

"Truthfully, 2500."

"Well, since you my sis, you can give me a stack."

"Oh Hell No! I know it's a lemon now."

"Here," he said handing her tha keys, "if you like it, give me tha stack tomorrow."

"Where do I have to go to get it?"

"Out front." Kina opened tha door.

"I hope you didn't park around tha corner."

"Nah, it's tha red car out there."

"Daaamn, you joking, right?"

"Nah, it's yours if you like it." I had to come see what type of car it was.

"Shit!" I said, "you could've sold that to me for a stack."

"To late." It was a cherry red Crown Vic. wit a pair of 24s. Kina hit tha automatic start and tha car came alive.

"You on ya own wit getting a better system."

Kina ran to tha car and jumped in. She turned tha radio up, Keri Hilson's, *"Turning Me Off"* came blaring out. She waved at us then pulled off.

"You know I'm jealous, right?"

"For what?"

"Her car is better than mines. Why would you sell that car for a stack?"

"Because, I got it for free. Not to mention, I don't even drive it. Are you goin' to put those in sum water?"

"I guess." I could tell she was upset.

"Janelle, if you want I'll give tha car to you."

"That's Ok, you have already given it to Kina."

"Awe Boop-Boop, don't be mad, I'm sorry."

"You have no reason to be sorry. You didn't do anything wrong, it's my Shit."

"Hey, I got tha perfect solution."

"And that is?"

"Why don't you take off tomorrow and we can find you a better car."

"I just paid this car off, so I'm not tryin' to have another car note."

"You're not, trade ya car in and I'll pay tha difference."

"I couldn't ask you to do that Naz."

"You didn't, I offered. So call off! Tha next time you go to tha door like that I might be forced to thrash you." I looked down realizing that I didn't put my robe on.

"Shit, I meant to put my robe on when Kina came. But she kept rambling' on and before I knew it you were at tha door."

"Don't get it twisted, you look damn good in that teddy ma. It's just not for ery body to see."

"You know that you tha only one who is gettin' any of this. Naz truth be told, I'm in love wit you sum thing serious. For tha life of me, don't know how I let myself fall in love wit you when I know you'll neva be mines."

"Janelle you got me too." Wit that being said, we headed upstairs.

When I woke up Janelle was already in tha shower. I looked over at tha clock it read 7:45 a.m. I called Janelle's name, when she answered I let her know I was about to run home to get dressed.

"Do you need to use my car?"

"Shit, I forgot I sold that car to Kina. Nah, I'mma call Esco."

Once I did that, I went into tha bathroom to brush my gums. I could hear Esco honking tha horn out front. I let her know I would be back by 12 and to be ready. When I got outside, Esco was talking to Kina who had just pulled up.

"Here you go Naz, I can't thank you enough you're a life saver."

"Do I need to count this?" I asked jokingly.

"No, you can trust me." I counted out 300 and handed it to her.

"What's this for?"

"Get it painted."

"I like this color."

"Fine, give me my money back."

"On second thought, maybe a nice jet black will look good."

"Try midnight blue wit tha metallic sparkles."

"Nigga come on, I got to handle sum thing. You wouldn't even sell that car to me."

"She really needed a car. Nelle told me she goin' to Cali wit us. Of course, I got to pay her round trip ticket."

"You got it Nigga."

"I know."

When we pulled up to my crib, Ashanti was strapping Naz in his car seat.

"Make sure you're here when I get off; we need to talk."

"I'm not for that Bullshit Ashanti." Esco honked tha horn and pulled off.

"Naz all I want to know is who is she? And what is she doin that I'm not?"

"Go to work Ashanti."

"No! I want to Fuckin' know!"

"Call me when you get off." She got in and slammed her door shut.

"Damn, I couldn't believe my luck."

After I jumped in tha shower, I got dress then headed back to Janelle's. When I pulled up, Janelle and Kina were sitting on tha steps.

"You ready?"

"Yeah, let me grab my purse.

"I just dropped tha car off, it will done in 3 days."

"Did you get tha midnights blue?"

"No, I got a different color; you'll see it."

"Say no more then."

"I'm ready"

"Nelle, can I use ya car while you gone?"

"We taking my car."

"Oh a'ight, I'll get Esco to take me."

"Make sure you lock tha door when you leave."

"If you don't mind me in ya biz-ness. Where are you goin' that Ms. I neva take off' took off from work?"

"None of ya biz-ness."

"Excuse me."

"Sike, we goin' car shopping."

"Car shopping? Bitch you don't need no car."

"I know, but sum body won't take no for an answer."

"You just too good to be true. Do you have any brothers or friends like you?"

"No, and I wouldn't even turn you on to my friends."

"See y'all when y'all get back."

"Who driving?"

"You."

"So what kind of car do you want?"

"Sum thing like what you driving today."

"You know when I went home Ashanti asked me who I was dealing wit. I told her to call me when she gets off." Janelle had this funny look on her face.

"I am goin' to tell her tha truth."

"Why do you want to hurt her like that?"

"Janelle, I'm tha type of nigga that I don't volunteer information. But, if you ask me whether it hurts or not, I will tell you tha truth."

When it was all said, Janelle ended up wit a cream on cream 750. They actually gave her more than I expected for her car. I stopped by 'Rimz for

Rides' so that she could pick out a set of dub dueces. I didn't really like ones she picked but it was her choice.

"You don't like these, do you?"

"Nope but it's your car so as long as you like them that's all that counts."

"Which ones do you like?"

"If I was puttin' 'em on my car I'm goin' wit those."

"A'ight, give me those."

"Nah, get tha ones you want."

I had to admit her shit was nice. You couldn't tell her that she was not killing them in her new whip. We pulled up to her house, Esco and Kina were sitting on tha steps blowing sum Sour D.

"WOW!"

"Damn Nigga, let me find out my cuz got you sprung."

"Boy shut up ain't nobody sprung."

"You got tha 750 wit shoes. Her Shit looks better than yours Naz."

Even though they were tha same whips, Janelle's did look a little better. I think it was tha rims and color

"I talked to Sponge, I told him we'll be out there next week. He said they just opened this new club."

"Man, they be playing all that hyped Bullshit."

"I know, I don't be feelin' that Shit. This is suppose to be a hip-hop spot. You know I said sum thing about that trash they call music. Hey, why don't you come wit us to visit our granny." We all laughed.

"What's so funny? Let me in on tha joke."

"He's already goin' wit us."

"Look, I'll call you later, I need to go check up on tha block."

"Make sure you do that," she said planting a kiss on my lips.

"You working today?" I asked Esco.

"Yeah, I just had to give Kina a ride." On my way back to tha block Feeza called.

"Hey, how you doin'?"

"I'm cool as a fan."

"Was just think'n about you so I just figured I would give you a call."

"That's what's up."

"It's been a mess since you left."

"How's that?"

"This guy from Virginia went missing. His boys are running around snapping."

"How do they know he's missing?"

"Well, tha news said he was last seen leaving his room."

"Maybe he went back home."

"They said nobody has heard from him. You might know him."

"I doubt it, I don't know anybody from Virginia."

"He's originally from Philly, he just lives in Virginia."

"Did they say his name?"

"I think it was David Metch or Etch sum thing like that. But, his nickname was Doe."

"Oh Shit!" I said trying to sound shocked, "Yeah, I know dude. I didn't see him up there, that's probably why."

"I guess you right."

"But who would want to do sum thing to him in Miami?"

"Naz you neva know what people are in to. Then it was All-Star weekend so people from everywhere were there."

"Well anyway, how was your day been goin'?"

"So So, I'm working on this case of illegal search and seizure."

"Do you think you can win?"

"I don't think it will make it pass suppression."

"So you that good?"

"I'm one of tha best if not tha best in Miami."

"I know ya clients be tryin' to holla at you."

"Sum but I don't mix my biz-ness wit my personal first. When you coming back this way?"

"A few weeks, I'm flying out to Cali next week."

"Pleasure or biz-ness?"

"Neither, family." We talked for another 15 minutes before she had a client.

"Come in. I'll call you back later Ok."

"Sure, handle ya B.I."

When I hit tha block, Wendy and Lez were on her steps

"Hey Nephew."

"What up y'all?"

"You must've really pissed Ashanti off."

"Why you say that?"

"She called me on her lunch break. Told me that you had sum explaining to do when she got home. This mornin she asked me who this other girl is and what is she doing that she's not?"

"I gotta keep it funky not junky, sex wit her Wendy..."

"EEEEEEL that's sum nasty sex. So you gon' risk losing her to tell her tha truth?"

"Yup, I have to. Wendy it's nothing that she did wrong. It's just being a man; I don't think I can ever be faithful." Lez looked at me like I lost my mind.

"Boy you better really think about what you saying."

"I'm goin' to even tell her that I was Fucken you."

"You WHAT!"

"I'm just playing wit you, Damn."

When I heard my phone I knew it was Ashanti.

"Yo."

"I'm home." (CLICK)

I'll be back, that was her."

"Good luck."

When I walked in tha door Ashanti was sitting on tha couch smoking a Dutch.

"Where's Naz?"

"Wit Nana, so who is she Naz?"

"I'm goin' to be completely honest wit you. I love you to death, but I'm a man. I said that to say there's not just one broad."

"So you Fucking a whole bunch of Bitches?"

"Nah, like two. I understand if you want me to leave."

"Naz all I wanted was for us to be happy and to be a family. I love you and our son more than life itself. So I'm goin' to let you get this out of your system. When you do, you're more than welcome to come back."

"I don't know if I'll ever be able to be faithful."

"Like I said, I'll give you sum time. I'm not changing tha locks so you're more than welcome to come by and see your son."

"Ashanti I'm sorry and I do respect that. I'll make sure I call before I come by."

"Naz, I know you love me because if you didn't you would have lied to me." I hated seeing her in all that pain.

"I'm goin' to go upstairs to get sum of my things."

When I came back down she was balled up on tha couch crying. It hurt to know that I caused her this pain. I held her face in my hands.

"Baby know it's nuffin you did wrong."

I had to get out of there. I felt my own eyes starting to water. Instead of goin' to Wendy's, I took a long drive to clear my head. Before I realized I was sitting in Fairmount Park. My phone brought me back to reality.

"Hello," I said dryly.

"Is ery thing a'ight?" I didn't say anything.

"Naz, Naz!"

"Yeah."

"Where are you at?"

"Fairmont Park."

"I'm on my way."

"Nah, I'm leaving now."

"Where are you goin'?"

"I think I'mma shoot to Delaware to that Good Shot Bar to have a few drinks."

"Stop by here and get me."

"A'ight, I'll be there in 15 minutes."

"I'll be out front."

I decided I was gon' to get my own spot and not move in wit Janelle. I called Wendy to put her down; but Ashanti had already did that.

"Is there anything I can do to help?"

"Yeah, I need you to find me a nice two-bedroom apartment A.S.A.P."

"Will do, first thing in tha mornin."

"Thanks, Wendy."

"Boy, you don't have to thank me, we family. And just because you and Ashanti are on a little split she still family too."

"I know, I don't expect you to treat her any different. I'll holla at you in tha A.M. I'm bout to go to tha bar and take a few back."

"A'ight, be safe, love you."

"You too."

Janelle was out front wit Kina when I pulled up.

"I parked, you driving," I said as I headed toward her car. I could hear Kina asked if was a'ight.

"How do I get there?" I punched in tha address on tha Navi.

"You ever heard that song *'Socks in tha Air'* by tha boy Shizz?"

"Yeah, I like that cut."

"He supposes to be performing it tonight."

"Before you hit tha highway stop at tha LQ." Once we had tha Bombay and wraps we hit tha highway.

"Is it cool for me to blow this weed in here?"

"Yeah, but don't make it a habit," she said wit a smile. Which made me smile.

"There it is."

"There what is?" I asked.

"That smile that I love."

"Well, you know me and Ashanti broke up," I explained to Janelle what happened between us.

"I'm sorry to hear that Naz."

"No your not."

"Despite how I feel about you I would neva want to see you or anybody that you care about hurt. Judging by your actions you are hurt."

"I am, but only because I didn't like to see her crying because of me. Anyway, I decided to get my own place."

"Oh Ok."

"I didn't think it would be a good idea to move in wit you."

"You're more than welcome to come by any time you wish. Shit, you gon' have a key anyway." That brought a smile back to her face.

It was packed at tha Good Shot Bar. All eyes were on us. When we pulled up or should I say in Janelle's car.

"Do I look Ok?"

"You gon' be tha best lookin' in tha building."

"Now you making me blush."

She was lookin' good wit her black apple bottom jeans and white shirt wit a pair of black Christian Dior shoes.

"You made sure to put on your tightest jeans, huh?"

"No, I just threw this on."

"It doesn't matter what you wear that ass is alwayz fat."

"Boy shut up."

As for me, I had on black ACG boots, denim jeans, and a black T that said *'Born to Hustle'* in white. While we were in line there was sum commotion at tha front of tha line. Sum dudes tried to jump in front of everybody. They said they were there wit Shizz. Tha bouncers weren't goin' for it though. By tha time we got in tha club, I needed a drink.

After 15 minutes tha bartender finally took our order. She told me that they didn't serve bottles so I just ordered two of my drinks and a Long Island Ice Tea for Janelle. I hit tha bartender wit an extra dub so that when she saw me come back I wouldn't have to wait so long.

We walked up to where tha dance floor was it was j-peed. All tha dudes were eyeballing, Janelle. I wasn't worried about that Shit. I would be doing tha same shit if I saw a female that looked as good as her.

"Baby let's take a couple of pictures," she said pointing towards tha picture booth.

"How much are your pictures?"

"$10 apiece."

"Can I get 3 for 25?"

"All Day."

After we took our pictures, Janelle put them in her purse. Tha boy Shizz did his thing. I wanted him to perform at tha party I was having for P.R. next month.

"Come on Janelle, let me holla at Shizz for a second."

"Shizz."

"What's up?"

"I know you don't know me but I was wondering if you would mind performing at my people's party next month in Philly. I'm willing to pay you 5 stacks."

"Say no more."

"A'ight, let me get ya number." After we exchanged numbers he asked me what side of town I was from because he had neva seen me before.

"That's because I'm from Philly, 8th and Indiana."

"That explains ya piece."

"Can I buy you a drink?"

"Sure."

"What you drinking?"

"Remy straight."

"Babe, you want another drink?"

"Yes."

"Oh she wit you?"

"Yeah, this my girl." I knew that would make her smile.

I got tha bartender's attention from earlier who came right over. I ordered everybody's drinks.

"If you don't mind me asking, how did you hear about this spot?"

"A friend of mines brought me here before. That song you performed is a big hit in Philly. Well, I got ya info, I'll call you next week when I get back in town. Matter fact let's take a picture so when I make tha flyer, I can put ya picture on there. I'll also give you sum so you can have ya peeps come support you. Bet they'll definitely come thru. Well, we bout to be out but I'm definitely gon' get at you when I get back in town. Just in case you want to start telling ya peeps; tha party will be at Solo on Delaware Ave. Do you know where that is?"

"Yeah, what day?"

"Tha 14th of next month. I'm waiting on Jeezy to get back wit me, so hopefully, by tha time I get back, I'll know sum thing." Tha lights came on.

"This Shit over anyway." I looked at my watch it was only 1:30.

We walked outside to find people still partying in tha parking lot. There were two females sitting on Janelle's car.

"Excuse me, but could you please get off my car!" I could tell they were half-ass drunk. I just hope this wouldn't evolve into anything.

"Come on Shelly, let's get off her car before she has a fit." When they did Janelle said thank you.

"What Bitch!"

"Naw, Bitch is tha one that had ya Ghetto Ass!"

"I'm bout to Fuck this Bitch up!" I opened tha door and grabbed my pistol.

"Check this out Shorty, we don't want no problems."

"Well, tell ya Bitch to watch her mouth for it be one! First and foremost, y'all was sittin' on my car. I asked nicely for y'all to get off. You disrespected me."

"Yup, sure did." By now a few more broads had come over.

"Shelly y'all cool?"

"Nah, we bout to stomp a mudhole in this Bitch!"

"Y'all got me Fucked up fo' real!" Janelle said.

When they acted like they were about to jump on her is when I exposed my gun.

"Ain't gon' be none of that Shit!"

One broad screamed, "Oh My God! He got a gun!" Tha rest of them ran.

I saw Shizz walking over.

"Yo, you a'ight?"

"Yeah, we cool."

"There he is right there," tha one that screamed said to tha cops.

"Put your hands where I can see them!" I did as I was told. My gun was in my shoulder holster visible for him to see.

"Get on the ground! Get on the ground now!" I did what I was told.

As soon as I got on tha ground, he jumped on my back. Once he had me cuffed they stood me up.

"Listen, in my back pocket is my license to carry and permit for my gun." He retrieved my wallet and got tha paperwork.

They put me in tha cop car while they went over tha paperwork. 10 minutes later, they were taking me out and uncuffing me.

"Damn Baby Boy, I thought you were done."

"Nah, I'm legit peeps."

"You got a license to kill a Motha Fucka."

"Basically. Damn, that's how they do it down here. I guess that's why they call this Tellaware, huh?"

"What was that all about anyway?"

"They were sittin' on my car," Janelle said proudly.

"Shelly and her crew alwayz get drunk and don't know how to act."

"Yeah, well, they got tha right Bitch. Don't let this Pretty Ass face fool you."

"I heard that ma."

"We bout to hit tha highway."

"Be safe."

"Alwayz."

"Reep you still haven't heard from Doe?"

CHAPTER 41

Still Not Found

"Who tha Fuck would want to harm Doe in Miami? I'm starting to think it was those niggaz we had words wit in tha club that night. Tha ones that said they can get us touched."

Tha last two months has been Hell on everybody. Angie had tha baby who looks just like Doe. We all told her that she needs to go back to Philly. But she says she ain't goin' nowhere wit out Doe. Sticky and Cannon have been shaking everything and one down since Doe's disappearance. Me and Murder have been running tha biz-ness for tha past few months. We let Angie know that Lil Doe would be set for life. Doe had already set up a trust fund for him. Sticky and Cannon let us know that his family was having a memorial for Doe in Philly.

"No disrespect, but I don't think I'll be attending that one."

We also let them know they needed to fall back wit tha shake downs; they were starting to Fuck up tha biz-ness. I had assured everybody that they would not be shook down anymore.

We called Miami once a week to stay updated. They let us know that Doe's disappearance wasn't a priority. In other words, tha case was closed. It was different not having him around. It was definitely goin' to take sum getting use to. Me and Murder had decided to get tattoos wit Doe's face. So now, not only were me and Murder feared but we now ran Virginia.

CHAPTER 42

Preparing for tha Big Party at Solo

We had a ball in Cali. At first, I thought we were gonna have to deal wit all that gang bangin' you hear about in Cali. It was tha total opposite. Jeezy's peoples had called me to say that he would do tha party for 10 grand. I also let him know that for another 5 grand, I would pay him if he took a picture wit P.R. and Shizz for tha flyer. He was more than glad to make 5 grand for a picture. So we stopped in Delaware to scoop up Shizz. We turned an 11-hour drive into 9. We took a few pictures and hung out wit Jeezy for tha rest of tha day and night. Tha next morning, we headed home only to stop in Delaware to drop Shizz off.

"I'll hit ya phone later when tha flyers are done."

By tha time tha flyers were done I was tired as shit. I let Shizz know I would bring him sum down later when I got up. I had to admit they were nice as shit.

When I woke up it was after 6. I called Shizz to let him know I was on my way and to meet me at tha Tri State Mall.

"Yo Naz, I'm feeling tha Fuck out of these flyers."

"I brought you a hundred, that should be more than enough."

"Fo' Sho. That's good lookin' out."

"It ain't bout nuffin, real recognize real. So you got 3 weeks to prepare."

"That's plenty of time."

"Do you have another song you could do?" My phone started ringing.

"Hold on for a sec Shizz."

"Yo. Oh Shit, what up Jeezy? Nah. Fo' Real? Yeah, he right here. Hold up, let me ask him. Better yet, let me put him on." I passed Shizz tha phone.

"Damn right I'll get on a song wit you. What's tha name of it and what does it sound like?" I watched as Shizz started shaking his head. I figured Jeezy was playing tha track for him.

"Ok, I'll write two sixteens, you want me to come to Atlanta next week to record? No problem. A'ight."

When he handed me tha phone back Jeezy wanted me to bring him down next week. Who was I to tell Jeezy no?

"Can you believe my luck? Jeezy asked me to get on a song wit him. He even said he was feelin' my song."

"What's tha name of tha track?"

"Flippin' Birdz."

"Can you handle it?"

"Can I handle it?"

Tha next few days flew by. I had went by Ashanti's to see my son who was more than happy to see me. Ashanti let me know that she wasn't goin' to put her life on hold forever. As painful as it was to say, I told her to move on. I even took her keys off my keychain.

"I'll alwayz call before I come by." She didn't say anything, she just looked at me.

Then she asked, "Are you sure this is what you want to do?"

"No, but what else can I do?"

"Be tha man I fell in love wit."

"I'm still that man."

"Are you Naz?"

"Yes."

"Then why can't you just be wit me?"

"I honestly don't know."

"Truth be told, Naz I don't want to be wit anybody else but you. But how can I be wit you if you're wit me and ery body else?"

"Ashanti like I told you, I neva wanted to hurt you, but I refused to lie to you. I could have easily said that I was not doin anything."

"I know you could have and I would have accepted it wit no further questions."

"I know you would have, but I just couldn't do that. Babe, it was bad enough that I was cheating in tha first place."

"What is it gonna take for you to stop doin' what you're doin' Naz?"

"Ashanti, I honestly don't know."

After I finished wit Naz, I gave him a bath then he fell right to sleep.

"Just in case you want to come," I said then handed her a flyer.

"Shauna told me about that."

"Are you coming?"

"I might."

"You got money for sum thing to wear?"

"No." I went in my pocket and gave her tha 2 grand that Tico had just gave me from that bet he lost.

"You didn't have to give me this."

"Regardless of what we go through, I'm goin' to alwayz make sure you and Naz don't want for nuffin."

She didn't know but I raised my life insurance. This life I live, tomorrow is neva promised for me. I gave her a hug then left. I could tell by tha way she hugged me that she didn't want me to go, but I left anyway. There was no doubt I was feelin' sum thing for Janelle. But my heart belonged to Ashanti and probably alwayz would. No matter who she was wit.

P.R. had called me to ask if I wanted to go to this club in Delaware called tha Zoo Lounge. Peedi and Freeway were suppose to be performing there. He said tha dress code was casual; no Timbs or sneaks. When I got to my crib I went to my closet to find me sum thing to throw on. I grabbed tha first outfit I came across. White linen Capris, white and orange linen shirt wit a pair of orange Prada slip ons. I had picked this Prada outfit and shoes up at King of Prussia. Just as I was putting on my frames, P.R. was hitting my phone.

"What up Nigga?"

"You ain't dressed yet?"

"Yeah, I'm on my way out tha door. You know Janelle and her sister are headed down there."

"How you know?"

"They came through to get a couple of dollars from Esco."

"Hold on, that's her on my other line."

"Nah, just come on and pull tha Lambo out, Peedi said all tha players are coming out tonight."

"Nah, I'm saving that for ya Shit."

"It's old school tonight."

"A'ight, just come on."

"Make sure you grab a nice piece of Sour D and sum E-pills."

"Already took care of that." (CLICK)

"Hello."

"Damn, you must be really busy."

"Nah, I was on tha phone. What you doin' tonight?"

"I don't know, why?"

"Me, Kina, Ronya, and Jade are goin' to Delaware to see Peedi and Freeway perform. You want to go?"

"I'll see you there, probably."

"Ok, I'll see you if you come."

I could hear Kina in tha background saying, "Hey Brother."

"How do you know this is Naz."

"Who else is it goin' to be? Boy bye."

I pulled up to Wendy's, Esco, P.R, and Gunz were standing outside ready to roll.

"Y'all ready?"

"Yeah, I'mma follow y'all."

"Ery body strapped?"

"You better know it," they all said showing their pistols.

I took one of tha E-pills while P.R. lit up tha weed.

"You know how to get there? Peedi said get off at tha 4th Street Exit. Then go down to 2nd, make a right, take that all tha way up to we get to Union Street. At Union make a left, at tha first light make a right then it's a straight shot. He said we'll see it on our right."

"Gotcha, hold on," I said as I stepped on tha gas.

"We ain't got to rush, it's only 10 o'clock."

45 minutes later, we were pulling up at tha Zoo Lounge.

"I guess Janelle ain't here yet. I can see what's in here."

"They here, there go Kina car right there."

"Shit, I was lookin' for Janelle's whip." This was my first time seeing it since she got it painted.

"Nice paint job."

"That's what I told her." We all left our pistols in tha car.

When we got to tha line a few of tha females said, "That's tha guy who's having tha party at Solo."

"Can we get V.I.P.?" one of tha other girls asked. If Janelle wasn't in there I would be all over her.

"How you know Shizz?"

"I don't, my peeps do," he said pointing to me.

Gunz paid all of our way including tha broads. When we got inside, we all went our separate ways. Tha broads anyway. My pill had kicked in and I needed a drink. We made our way to tha bar to order drinks.

"There go Naz and them."

"Where?"

"Headed to tha bar."

"Let's go over there."

"No, I don't want him to think I'm stalking him."

"You can stay over here, I'm goin' to get Esco to buy me a drink."

"Do you then."

"I am, come on y'all."

"Y'all go head, I'm goin' to chill here wit Janelle," Jade said.

"Bitch, it's a lot of Niggaz in here tonight."

"I know, but mines is over there lookin' good as Shit in that Prada."

"I got my eyes on ya peeps."

"Who Esco?"

"Umm huh."

"Well, why you ain't neva step to him?"

"I don't know."

"He must be feelin' you too."

"Why you say that?"

"Cause, he's undressing you wit his eyes." She turned around to see.

She blew him a kiss which he caught out of tha air and put it on his face.

"He been around Naz too long."

"Bitch stop hatin'."

"Neva was I hatin'. That's my little cuz."

"Looks like you not tha only one that thinks Naz looks good tonight."

I turned around to see what she was talk'n about. There were four chicks in his face.

"I ain't worried about that. They don't have a shot."

"Bitch you real cocky and confident."

"Look at me and look at them, need I say any more?"

"True, true."

hen Peedi and Freeway came in they went to tha V.I.P. A few minutes later, Peedi got on tha mic.

"Where is cousin? P.R. Naz, Esco, and Gunz come to V.I.P.

When I heard Peedi say that, I got up. When we got there he told tha bouncers to let us thru.

"Ery body come out to Solo next Friday for my cousins birthday party. Wit performances by Jeezy and Delaware's own Shizz." Everybody went

crazy.

I spotted Shizz, Peedi handed me tha mic.

"Shout out to my peeps Shizz. Come on up to V.I.P." Free and Peedi did their thing; they had tha crowd hype.

I seen this dude keep trying to go at Janelle. It was funny to me because he wouldn't take no for an answer. I guess if I was trying to holla at tha baddest chick in tha club, I wouldn't take no for an answer either. No soon as he stopped, another nigga came up to her. She didn't seem to mind his conversation tha way he had her smiling and blushing. Since I had my frames on, she had no idea I was looking at her. When they played that song, *"She Got Her Own"* by Jamie Foxx, Neyo, and Fab, he pulled her to tha dance floor. Esco tapped me and pointed to where Janelle and dude were now dancing off *"Stanky Legg"*. It's a party, that's what you suppose to do. She was snapping. She had dude looking like he didn't know what he was doing. She looked up at me then motioned for me to come down.

"I'm goin' down on tha floor to holla at Jade."

"Bout time, y'all been playing that eye game since we got here."

"Looks like you might need to go down there ya self." I looked at Janelle who was doin' tha damn thing.

"I was goin' down anyway."

"I bet you was, I saw her tell you to come here."

By tha time we got down there they had my shit on.

"Ain't I Packin' Chrome, Ain't I Got it Goin' On. Ain't I. . ." I started doin' my Philly swag.

Janelle wasted no time coming over. We tore that song up; everybody was watching us. P.R. came down wit a bottle of Bombay for me which was right on time. We went to take sum flicks wit Peedi and Free.

At tha end of tha night, I was past feelin' it. Janelle told P.R. to ride back wit Esco and Gunz. Esco said that him and Gunz were gonna have to ride wit Kina and Ronya because he was taking' Jade wit him. Kina didn't protest since she had been all over Gunz all night anyway.

"Sis, don't turn my little cuz out."

She smiled then said, "I'll try not to."

"What you should have said was don't get turned out."

"I'm driving," Janelle said.

"Fine by me," I said handing her tha keys.

When she started tha car I said, "Pleasure P. Track 6, Volume 15." When *"Did You Wrong"* came on it sounded like a concert coming out my whip.

Two hours and a full stomach later, we were pulling up to my spot. Before we got out, what Janelle said caught me off guard.

"You miss Ashanti, don't you?"

"Yeah, I can't lie."

"I know you do. Why don't you go home?"

"Because I won't be able to leave you alone."

"Naz, even though I would love to have you to myself. I neva wanted to break up ya home."

"It wasn't you; it was me."

"So, is she coming to tha party next week?"

"Yeah, more than likely."

"I just wanted to know so I wouldn't be all over you."

"I'm still goin' to dance and take flicks wit you." We finally went into tha house where we took care of biz-ness until tha sun came up.

CHAPTER 43

Take Him Back?

"What you doin' Shauna?"

"Nuffin, just finished gettin' dressed. You still goin' tonight, right?"

"Yeah, I'm bout to put my clothes on. Oh, cause I was goin' to say. Tha reason I called is cause I need to know sum thing."

"What?"

"Do you think I would be dumb to make Naz back? Even though I know he told me he can't be faithful."

"Truthfully, look at me and P.R., I took him back knowing he's tha biggest dog. Like I told him, he better strap up and make sure home is alwayz straight."

"So you saying take him back?"

"What I'm saying is, follow ya heart. If it says leave then do that. If it says stay then stay. But if you do stay wit him, make sure you give him sum rules."

"Thanks Girl, let me get dressed and I'll be there."

"Ok."

I started to call Naz but I decided to wait until I saw him tonight to tell him face-to-face.

CHAPTER 44

Tha Big Party

"Tonight is goin' to be tha Shit," Esco said.

"I know, Jeezy said he's flying in."

"Oh word?"

"Yeah, his flight is scheduled to land at 4 o'clock. I told him I would be there to pick them up so I'm goin' to need you and P.R. to drive to tha airport wit me."

"It's 3 o'clock now."

"I know."

"How many people he bringing wit him?"

"I think he said six, I'm not sure."

By tha time P.R. pulled up, it was time to head to tha airport. When we got there, they were just coming out. I hit tha horn to let them know we were here.

"Yo what up peeps?"

"I can't call it."

"Love tha whips. I see you got nice taste."

"So, do you have anything special you want to do?"

"Nah, I just want sum good smoke."

"That ain't no problem, we got tha best weed on my block."

"You talk to Shizz?"

"Yeah, he should be on his way; if he not already here."

By tha time we got back to tha block, Shizz and his peoples were already there.

"Damn my Nigga, what y'all having a block party?"

"Naw, this my dope block."

"Look like y'all doin' numbers."

"Plenty, this is a one stop shop. Dope, coke, weed, and E-pills."

"Naz that was good lookin', here go that 10 I owe you."

"Bet Young'n, you cool?"

"For right now." I handed that money he just gave me to Jeezy.

"This that 10 I owe you."

"What da biz-ness is Shizz? Ready to get it poppin' tonight?"

"I'm wit you on that."

"Here you go Shizz," I said handing him his pay for tonight.

"I'm bout to shoot to King of Prussia to grab me sum thing to wear."

"Nigga you should have been handled that."

"I know, I had sum thing, but my shorty told me they had these Louis Vuitton sneaks I wanted."

"Well, we plan to leave at 11 o'clock for tha club."

"I'll be ready."

After I dropped Jeezy off at his hotel, I headed home to prepare myself for tha night ahead. I didn't realize I had dozed off until my phone started ringing.

"Hello. What up Janelle? Hold on, let me check. Yeah, it's here. A'ight."

Shit, it was 9 o'clock. I jumped in tha shower. I got out to find Janelle standing there lookin' good in her Ralph Pewter peach dress wit tha shoes to match.

"Damn, you lookin' good in that dress. Do we have time?"

Before I could finish she said, "Damn, I knew I should have drove myself."

I was looking good wit my Gucci jeans and shirt and Gucci shades and boots. I called Jeezy and Shizz to see if they were ready. Tonight we were bringing out our exotic whips. Shizz let me know he would meet us out front of tha club.

When I picked Jeezy up in my Lambo, all he could say was, "You tha man in Philly fo' real."

"I don't know about that but I do Ok."

"Nigga you do more than Ok."

We rode thru tha city getting high before we went to tha club. We pulled up out front in tha spots that were reserved for us.

"Damn, you brought 'em out my Nigga."

"Nah, I think they came to see you and Shizz." When we got out, tha chicks went crazy.

I looked at Jeezy and said, "What I tell you."

Shizz walked up, we all dapped him then went to tha front of tha V.I.P. line. When we got in, it was packed. I couldn't believe it. And tha line was still around tha corner. I knew that everybody wasn't goin' to get in. We made our way to V.I.P. where they had plenty bottles waiting on us. P.R. spotted Shauna and Ashanti.

"Damn, Ashanti was looking fine ass shit in her black Gucci dress, frames, and shoes. She even had on her diamond Ashanti necklace and bracelet that I had gotten her for her birthday last year. P.R. went and got both Shauna and Ashanti and brought them to V.I.P. Tha music was bumping.

"Hey Ashanti, you look good as Shit."

"Thank you, you're lookin' fine ya self. If possible, there is sum thing I want and need to talk to you about."

"Can it wait until tomorrow? I'm just tryin' to have a good time tonight."

"No. It can't wait!" I took her hand and led her to a table on tha far side.

"So what's so important that you couldn't wait until tomorrow?"

"After a lot of thought, I've decided to accept you back under a few conditions."

"Well."

"Shush, just listen. You will make it home every night. So if she can't understand that, to Fucken bad! You will wear protection when you Fuck one of those Bitches! Because I'm not excepting another baby! And last but not least, you will not disrespect me in any way. So you might as well tell them to fall back tonight." Tha look on my face most of said it all.

"I don't know why you lookin' like that. Did you actually think I was goin' to let you get away like that?"

"I didn't know what to think, honestly. I knew that I would alwayz love you no matter what."

"I know you would."

"What made you decide on this?"

"My heart!" I grabbed her face and kissed her as if it was my first time ever.

We walked back to where everybody else was. Wendy and Lez were now in V.I.P.

"I'm ready," Shizz said.

He grabbed tha mic and did his socks in tha air, tha club went crazy.

When he was done that, he did one more song.

Jeezy said, "It's a recession and ery body broke." Man they went bananas.

When he finished his songs he said, "Philly, Delaware this next track is for all my money gettin' niggaz. *I Know You Niggaz Heard We be Flippin dem Birds. I Know You Niggaz Heard We be Flippin dem Birds.*" Jeezy and Shizz went 16 for 16. It was my first time hearing it but there was no doubt it was goin' to be a hit. When they were done, I had to let them both know that they did their thing. And thanks to them, P.R. party was a total success.

We continued to party; we even took a lot of pictures. Shit, we took so many pictures, it didn't make sense. I even took pictures wit Janelle like I said I would. She said she saw me kissing sum girl. I let her know that it was Ashanti.

"WOW, she's beautiful Naz."

That made me smile to know Janelle thought Ashanti was beautiful. I explained ery thing that Ashanti had told me. While we were talking, Jeezy came up to me.

"Naz, you know how to throw a party. And you got tha two baddest chicks in tha club."

"I heard that."

"Yo, I'm bout to be out. You got my number, call me and keep in touch," then he said, "oh yeah, I want you to meet tha newest member of C.T.E." Shizz was all smiles.

Next, Jeezy took tha mic, "Philly, Delaware thanks for having ya boy. And look forward to an album from C.T.E.'s newest member Shizz."

Man you talk about losing it. Tha crowd totally lost it, especially

Delaware. I guess they were happy that one of their own finally made it out of tha hood.

I had even saw Heaven. She looked like she was pregnant but tha funny thing is, she had started messing wit Champ. He found out that I use to mess wit her and went at her for sum. Gettin' back for me messing wit Janelle. I didn't care, Heaven was history. When she Fucked a nigga in my house.

I let Janelle know I would be by in tha morning. She said that she understood, but I could tell by tha expression on her face that she was disappointed.

"Listen Naz, I'm not mad that you decided to go back home. I know my role and I will neva come between you and ya family but I love you too."

"I know you do." I kissed her on her forehead and walked away.

"Damn, how did I get to this point?"

Well, they say, "Da Game Ain't Fair!"

ABOUT THE AUTHOR

My name is Jerz Toston, I reside in Wilmington, Delaware. First, thanks to my fans for your continued support. This is my 6th book titled Da Game Ain't Fair. My other five books titled Trust is Ery Thing, Compromised, Street Dreamz: Ery Thing Ain't What It Seems, Who Can U Trust?, and Betrayal & Deceit are available now on all on-line bookstores. Also, you can call my publisher directly at 877.782.5550 x100 and them shipped to ya door.

Writing books is my passion and I'll continue to give you page turners. Just call me ya Fav Authors Fav Author.

Trust is Ery Thing

Compromised

Street Dreamz

Who Can U Trust?

Betrayal & Deceit